Last Assignment

LAST ASSIGNMENT

BRUCE AITCHISON

ARPress
45 Dan Road Suite 5
Canton MA 02021
Hotline: 1(888) 821-0229
Fax: 1(508) 545-7580

Ordering Information:
Quantity sales. Special discounts are available on quantity purchases by corporations, associations, and others. For details, contact the publisher at the address above.

Printed in the United States of America.

ISBN-13:   Softcover   979-8-89330-362-9
              eBook   979-8-89330-363-6

Library of Congress Control Number: 2024900544

DISCLAIMER

This is a work of fiction. All the names, characters, places, events and incidents in this story are a product of the author's imagination. Any resemblance to actual persons, living or dead, or actual events is purely coincidental.

READER REVIEWS: "LAST ASSIGNMENT"

Sharon Dom, Marietta, NY: *I couldn't put the book down. The author should write a sequel, perfect for a movie!*

Bruce Ross, Auburn, NY: *I became enamored with the story and human emotions. As the characters come to life, you sensed death, wondering how it will end for the main character.*

Doug Morris, Columbus, NC: *The author paints vivid word pictures. The novel has all the classic ingredients, love, danger, intrigue. The dialogue is exceptional, the best I've ever read.*

Jim Dye, Skaneateles, NY: *I read the book three times. The author should write a sequel. Each chapter leads to another. The reader feels like they're there.*

David Olcott, Rose Hill, NY: *When and if the author writes another book, I'm going to buy it. What an ending!!! I purchased two books.*

Dan Ho, Syracuse, NY: *I became hooked on the first chapter. If the average reader isn't interested in a western, they will be after they read, "Last Assignment."*

Jean Beale, Marcellus, NY: *The story provides the author with the perfect opportunity to write a sequel. I've encouraged my friends to read the book. They won't be disappointed.*

Pat VanHeusen, Saugerties, NY: *Once I started reading, I didn't stop until I finished. I loved the suspense. The novel should be made into a movie.*

Peter Jordan, Syracuse, NY: *After my business trip. I contacted the author, thanking him for writing the book.*

Lou Loidice, Marcellus, NY: *Great book. The author has a tremendous imagination. I became totally captivated.*

Norm Hinkle, Syracuse, NY: *Finally a novel with a moral message! A tremendous story, reads like real life.*

Kathy Luke, Marietta, NY: *The author writes so descriptively. He is to be congratulated.*

Charles Wakefield, Utica, NY: *What a book! As I neared the end I was sure how it was going to end but still couldn't lay the book down!*

David Henderson, Marietta, NY: *I liked it so much I bought four books as gifts for family members. My brother told me he couldn't stop reading the novel.*

John Stevens, Jamesville, NY: *As a music artist you want to leave your listeners with a desire to hear more. "Last Assignment" left me with a desire for more. Hopefully, the author will write a sequel. Even better, with the movie industry constantly redoing old classics, here is a story with the potential for a new classic to capture a starved movie audience.*

Jay Carbonaro, Auburn, NY: *When I reached the halfway point in the novel, I couldn't help but think, I didn't want the story to end.*

TABLE OF CONTENTS

CHAPTER 1

Reporting to Headquarters

William McKiever was instantly awake, gray morning light filtering through the hotel window, growing in strength. Despite the lack of sleep and last night's whiskey, McKiever knew exactly where he was. Sliding his six-foot frame from the warmth of the covers, he paused, thinking about the previous night. Despite feeling lousy, he smiled, remembering the Mexican girl and the evening of fun.

McKiever pulled on his pants, followed by his socks. Retrieving his boots, he straightened, shuffling over to the washbasin. Staring into the mirror, he noted the dark circles under his steel-gray eyes. McKiever wasn't a handsome man, but his angular face showed character, which always drew a second look. His face was deeply tanned with a small mustache slanting to the corners of his mouth. His body was lean, not a hint of fat showing.

Filling the washbasin, McKiever sloshed water over his face. Cringing as the water ran down his chest, he grabbed the lone towel, sopping up the water. Using his fingers, he raked his brown hair straight back. Considering last night, he congratulated himself for still looking human. Turning from the mirror, McKiever spoke softly, his voice a hoarse whisper, "Brain, we need some coffee."

Moving to the bed, McKiever slipped into his blue denim shirt, followed by a brown leather vest. Pinned to the vest was his Texas Ranger badge. Whenever he wore the vest, the badge hung directly over his heart. He always considered the badge's location as kind of a shield against death. McKiever lifted his gun belt from the bedpost. Buckling on his holster, he felt the comfort of the Colt .45 against his hip. The gun belt hung low, like most men wear who make a living with a gun. McKiever eased open the desk drawer. Lifting a black book, he retrieved his billfold from under the book. Pushing the book into the far corner of the drawer, he stared at it. Written on the cover in gold colored letters were the words, "Holy Bible."

Whenever McKiever saw a Bible, he thought of two people. One of those persons was a woman named Sara. She was very pretty, full of life, and very religious. Sara was the type of woman with whom a man could be content with for the rest his life. For a moment McKiever felt sadness for he had fallen in love with Sara, but he hadn't been ready for marriage. Now any hope was gone, for she had married Jeffrey Kincaid, his former Ranger partner. After the marriage, Jeff had left the Rangers. Although the three remained close friends, McKiever knew he would always have regrets. The other person was his boss, Captain Frank O'Rourke. The Captain always kept a large Bible on his desk. Often, the Captain would quote from what he called 'The Good Book.' McKiever thought about last night. He could almost hear Captain Frank saying how the lust of the flesh never satisfies the needs of the soul.

Moving back to the bed, McKiever wiggled into his boots. Pushing his hat on, he shrugged into his jacket. Scanning the room making sure nothing was left behind, he tossed a coin onto the dresser, his eyes captivated as the coin spun around and around before flopping on its side. Amused, he stared at the coin, knowing he couldn't do that again if he tried. Picking up the room key, he paused at the door, listening. Years of dangerous work had taught him patience. It never hurt to pause, look, and listen. No foreboding sounds came from the outer hall. Satisfied, he stepped into the hallway, quietly closing the door. Moving to the end of the hall, he descended the stairs. Crossing the lobby, McKiever approached the main desk.

A swarthy Mexican man with jet black hair showing streaks of gray grinned a toothy smile as McKiever approached.

The Mexican greeted him. "Good morning, Mr. Mac." Reaching out, he handed McKiever a steaming cup of hot coffee.

"Thank you, Pedro." McKiever handed Pedro the room key along with lodging money. Reaching into his vest, he pulled out another coin. "Here, buy yourself lunch, and remember, I was never here."

Pedro laughed softly, his voice quiet, confidential, "Yes, Mr. Mac."

McKiever smiled, tipping his hat as he walked over to the large window facing the street. Sipping the coffee, he stared at the deserted street.

Years ago, Captain Frank had told a young McKiever to always take care of the so-called unimportant people. The captain explained that if you did, they would take care of you. McKiever had taken that sage advice to heart and it had served him well. It was the little people who are the eyes and ears in any town. They always seem to know what was going on, and who was behind it, especially the service people, who always seemed to have a wealth of information. Mac always made sure he treated those people as important, and for him they were. Prominent individuals who viewed themselves as important were the people McKiever liked to avoid. Even local sheriffs were often manipulated politically. In his mind, important people know how to use people, and he had no intention of being used.

Fully awake now, McKiever considered another cup of coffee. The coffee tasted strong, almost bitter, but it hit the spot. He erased the thought from his mind. An early start on the trail would be smart. Once the late August sun peeked over the top of the hills, the morning would become instantly hot.

McKiever loved the early morning hours. The world was still, no demands from anyone on his time. It was a good time to think and to plan. Soon McKiever would be a changed man. He was returning to headquarters to turn in his badge and begin a new life. Over the years he had made payments on a small rundown ranch located in the foothills of northwest Colorado. Last year the ranch was finally paid off, and now it was time for a career change. For a moment Mac felt a touch of anxiety about his coming change in life. All he had ever known was law enforcement work, but he knew it was time to move on. By tomorrow this time he would be signing his papers at Ranger Headquarters. Setting the cup down, he shrugged off his anxiety, surveying the street. The only sign that any life existed in the street was a black dog stretched out next to the hardware store. Border towns like this one didn't bustle with activity, but he liked this town because it was a halfway point for many of his assignments, a place for relaxation without responsibility. Besides, in this town, people minded their own business.

McKiever moved to the door, stepping outside. The cool air felt good. Crossing the street, he headed for the livery stable. Nearing the barn he heard voices; one of those voices was arguing. McKiever paused to listen. The one voice he recognized as belonging to the stable owner, Luke Brumley. The second man's voice was getting louder, insisting on something.

Entering the barn, McKiever crossed the wooden floor near the small office. Stepping down hard on the wood, he announced his presence through sound. Moving off the wood onto the dirt, his eyes adjusted to the gloomy interior. Two men stood at the far end, both looking his way. The one man was the stable owner. The other man was dressed in black, all black. Mac eyed the man in black, focusing on how high he wore his gun holster. Too high for speed, he thought. The man's ornate holster shined like a beacon in the dim light. McKiever closed the distance, his jacket open, his hand brushing against his gun.

Stopping, McKiever kept his eyes on the man in black, speaking to the stable owner, his voice reflecting caution meant for the stranger, "Everything okay, Luke?"

The stranger eyed his badge, his face breaking into a bold smile, flashing a row of perfect white teeth. "No problem, we were just discussing horse lodging."

McKiever flashed his smile, matching the strangers. "Rates here are fair, but then some people are always looking for a steal at someone else's expense. You know, even if they have the money, just as long as they can get the best of someone." Again, McKiever flashed a smile. Dismissing the man, he shifted his eyes toward Luke. "I'll wait at your office. After you settle with him, we can clear the books."

The stranger's smile remained fixed. McKiever detected arrogance in the man's manner. He suspected the stranger was used to getting his way. The way he spoke indicated he was a professional man. Maybe a businessman, perhaps a lawyer? Turning, McKiever walked back toward the tack room.

Moments later the man in black passed McKiever, tipping his hat while flashing his perfect smile.

McKiever nodded, turning as Luke approached. Luke always had a contagious smile, a sincere smile. "Well Mr. Mac, I got your message. Looks guess you're ready to hit the trail."

"I'm ready Luke. How have you been!"

"Good, I've been surprisingly busy. Lots of strangers. How about yourself?"

"Luke, when I'm busy it's never good business." Looking in the direction of the departing stranger, McKiever asked, "What's the story on the man dressed in black?"

Luke responded, "Never saw him before. Said he was in town for several days of business, if you can believe that. He didn't like it when I asked him where he was from. He told me it was none of my business, especially since he was paying me in advance. I told him that it was just a precaution. I explained that this is an open town where things have been known to happen, and if something did, I could notify his next of kin."

McKiever nodded, curious. "Did he say where he was from?"

Luke pointed to the book in his hand. "He said Fredonia. The ranch he named was the Bar High."

Surprise registered in McKiever's face. Fredonia was where Jeff and Sara Kincaid had their ranch. Three years ago, while he was on assignment there, he remembered the ranch, but not the man in black.

Luke saw his surprise. "He did say that it was none of my business without anger, you know, kind of matter of fact like." Luke rolled his eyes, "And with a smile."

McKiever reached into his vest, handing Luke the money he owed, along with a little extra. "Here, and don't count it. Yes, there's a little extra, but you earned it." Knowing Luke would try to give back the tip, McKiever changed the conversation. "That fancy pants fellow, I'd guess he's a legal man. That's why he can smile and be rude at the same time." McKiever's eyebrow's arched, humor showing in his voice. "Lawyers practice that." Before Luke could answer McKiever asked, "Luke, where's my horse?"

"Your horse is saddled out back."

McKiever smiled; Luke knew how he liked to operate. "Come on, Luke, walk me to my horse. It may be a long time before you see me again. By this time tomorrow I won't be a Texas Ranger anymore."

Luke stopped, eyeballing McKiever. "Are you serious?"

"Just as sure as you're standing there."

Pointing at McKiever's badge, Luke asked, "You think you won't miss wearing that anymore?"

McKiever started walking, thoughtful before answering, "I hope not. I've been paying off a small ranch in northern Colorado territory and sending some money to a handyman to keep it from falling apart. If you ever get near Silver Springs, look me up."

Luke whistled. "I'll be darned."

Turning the corner, they approached McKiever's horse. Mac glanced at the stable boss. "Luke, he looks ready to run."

Luke laughed, agreeing, "You can bet on it, especially a big horse like him. Plus, it's nice and cool. Yes, sir, I think you better hang on."

McKiever stared at his horse. The stallion was roan colored, mostly tawny, with a few streaks of gray. When he first saw him as a colt, the young foal was blessed with a broad chest and long spindly legs. Seeing the potential, McKiever purchased him. The money was well spent. The colt developed into a powerful horse with tremendous endurance. Over the years on the trail, he often found himself talking to his horse, like a best friend. Because of that constant habit, he named him Friend. A lawman needed a horse that could cover ground with ease, and Friend could do that. He was not a sprint horse, but the big stallion could covet miles effortlessly.

McKiever reached for Luke's hand. Feeling Luke's strong grip, he almost winced. Years of blacksmithing had made Luke a very strong man.

Turning toward Friend, McKiever was greeted by the big male tossing his head. A Sharps rifle butt protruded from the saddle scabbard. Long ago McKiever had traded in his carbine for that long-range rifle. On more than one occasion that rifle had forced a fugitive to surrender from a distance.

Gathering the reins, McKiever slipped his boot into the stirrup. Grasping the saddle horn, he rose into the saddle. With a nod toward Luke, he swung Friend around. Skirting the buildings, they entered the town's lone road leading out of town. Turning north, they left the buildings behind them. McKiever loosened the reins, prodding Friend with his heels. The big roan bolted.

For a mile horse and rider were one, the landscape floating by. Another mile passed. Leaning over, Mac touched Friend's neck. Feeling the sweat, he eased back on the reins, slowing Friend into a cooling down trot. In another half mile they would reach a game trail that would take them to the top of the ridge. Up there they could parallel the road for miles without being seen. The ridge would be much cooler once the August sun crested the hills, and a lot safer. Most problems from highway robbers occur during the late afternoon hours, and rarely during the early morning. The first hours of daylight was a safe time to travel.

Approaching the game trail, McKiever turned Friend. Climbing upward they reached the top, swinging north. The sun was just clearing the hills, the sudden warmth feeling good. Opening his sheepskin jacket, McKiever enjoyed the peace, the only sounds coming from the muffled hoof beats on the soft soil.

By noon McKiever and Friend would be near a mining town for lunch, and by nightfall they would arrive at Ranger Headquarters for a meal along with a good night's sleep. The following morning, he would see Captain Frank and sign his mustering out papers in preparation for a new life. McKiever frowned, then smiled. Hadn't the captain always told him that life was a series of changes, and sooner or later everyone had to make a decision for change. He knew the captain was right, the question was, could he adjust to a life without the badge and the authority that went with it?

CHAPTER 2

Last Assignment

Captain Frank O'Rourke started up the wooden steps leading into Ranger Headquarters. The third step squeaked, the captain smiling. The maintenance man constantly suggested fixing that annoying noise, but he always said no. Frank liked sounds that indicated human presence. Years of dealing with dangerous people had made him cautious. The captain preached caution to his men, and he applied that same practice to himself. That noisy step might annoy some, but not him. Pushing open the door, he entered the building.

Frank O'Rourke was a big man, barrel chested, slightly bowlegged from his years in the saddle. He stood six feet, three inches, with long arms and huge hands. The captain's physical size alone commanded a strong presence, and his deep voice fit his body. Whenever he spoke, people stopped to listen. Frank's brown hair was cut short, military style. Even his eyebrows were trimmed. Frank did not slouch. He stood tall, walked with his shoulders back, and when he sat, he was as straight as an arrow.

The building was cottage size. The outer room was planked, built out of wide boards. The floor was the same. A row of wooden pegs ran the length of the wall for hats and winter coats. Two wooden benches graced the other two walls. Windows on three of the walls allowed for plenty of light.

Frank opened the office door, leaving it that way. Whenever the captain was in his office, he had an open-door policy for his men. If the door was closed that meant he wasn't present, or an important meeting was in progress. The office was spacious, very plain. A long oak desk faced the door. Behind the desk was a high-backed oak chair. The chair was well upholstered, the plush filling covered with black leather to accommodate the captain's heavy frame. From where Frank sat, he could observe anyone entering through the front door. A circular clothing rack stood upright on the right side of the door. Over by the west wall, a gun rack ran the length of the wall. Except for a single carbine, the rack was empty. The east wall had a large stone fireplace. Mesquite logs were neatly stacked on both sides of the large hearth. None of the medium-sized windows lined up with the desk. The reason was for safety against a possible bushwhacker with a grudge. A narrow rug ran from the door, between two chairs, ending at the desk. There was just enough room for someone to pass between the two chairs. A single lamp hung over the desk. The desktop was long and spacious. On the left corner sat a large table clock. An oversized Bible graced the right corner. Behind the Bible was a picture of the captain's wife, Emily, and their two daughters, Rachel and Kimberly. In the middle of the desk was a large muster roll containing Ranger names and their upcoming assignments. Behind the desk were three wall pegs.

Coffee aroma filled the office, the smell filtering into the outer room. Sitting on top of a small table to the left of the desk was a ceramic coffeepot with two mugs, compliments of whoever had clerk duty. Every man at the post knew the captain never placed coffee on the desk. As far as Frank was concerned, to spill anything on a desk was sacrilegious.

Removing his hat, Frank hung it on one of the pegs. Next, he removed his jacket, placing it on the outer peg. Opening the right desk drawer, he placed his Walker Colt .44 within easy reach. Turning to the wall behind his desk, he hung the empty holster on the middle peg. He was almost ready for his coffee.

Captain Frank sat down at his desk. He pulled open the left drawer, placing an ink bottle with a writing pen far enough out of reach to avoid any possibility of an accident. Reaching into the middle drawer, he pulled out several forms with William McKiever's name printed on them. Satisfied everything was in order, he reached for the coffeepot.

Frank smiled; the coffee tasted just right, slightly strong but not like roof tar. Perfect, he thought. Whoever the assigned Ranger was, he knew exactly how he liked his coffee brewed. If he was a betting man, he would bet the man was Sam Whitman, the second in command. Sipping the coffee, Frank glanced at the clock. The time was nine-fifteen. In another forty minutes, William McKiever would walk into Frank's office to report on his last field assignment before turning in his badge. The captain knew McKiever would be right on time; he always was.

No one who had an appointment with the captain would ever experience that he wasn't ready for them. A person might walk into his office unannounced, but if someone had a meeting scheduled with him, the captain was always ready. The forms containing McKiever's name were filled out; all that was needed were signatures and dates. Thinking about McKiever, Frank reflected on his own past. Sipping his coffee, he recalled his younger days, those times when he rode in pursuit of marauding Comanches and Mexican bandits.

Glancing at the lone carbine in the gun rack, O'Rourke thought about his skill with a revolver, which was more than adequate. But with the carbine he was a magician. He could shoot a rifle from his hip with uncanny accuracy. During his years in the field Frank avoided street shootouts. If a frontal confrontation happened, those he was pursuing were forced to face him from a distance. Few lawless men were as proficient with a rifle as he was. Even if a bad hombre was good with a rifle, few were comfortable using such a gun around town buildings. For the captain the solution in any dangerous condition was simple, take away the gunman's edge by forcing him into an uncomfortable situation. Over the years Frank's reputation with the rifle had become legendary, especially during the Indian campaigns.

Frank focused on the family picture on his desk. Eleven years ago, Emily had died. He still missed her. Her beauty and personality had been contagious. As far as he was concerned, there would never be another Emily. Long ago the social scene had lost any interest for him. Both their daughters were educated, and both had married successful businessmen back East. Often the captain went back to visit his girls, but be much preferred the uncluttered West. Over the years the men at the post had become his family.

There had been one thing that Emily and Frank wanted, and that was a son. McKiever had filled that void. As a young boy McKiever had been a troublesome youngster being raised by foster parents. Always in trouble, McKiever's foster parents approached the captain seeking advice. The captain had suggested giving the lad a job at the Ranger post. At first the boy had been rebellious, but over time he became fascinated with the men and their work.

McKiever's foster parents wanted him educated and the captain agreed. The boy was tutored, but one day a teenage McKiever walked into the captain's office with a gun strapped to his hip, declaring his intention to be a Ranger! Trying to discourage McKiever was fruitless. If the captain didn't accept him into the post, he would find another detachment and join up. Over time Frank relented. It soon became apparent that McKiever was uncanny with a six-shooter. Not even the oldest and most experienced men at the Ranger Post could match the young man's speed. Much of the captain's philosophy rubbed off on McKiever, and as he matured his tactics and arrest record became exceptional.

At first McKiever's foster parents had objected to their son becoming a Texas Ranger. Frank explained that in life certain gifts manifest themselves in individuals over time, pointing out that the young man's natural gift with the gun needed to be harnessed for the good and not the bad. If their son didn't become a Ranger, such obvious talent might go in the wrong direction. The older couple saw the wisdom in the captain's reasoning and relented. Their one request was for the captain to watch out for their boy. Captain Frank assured them that he would.

Eventually McKiever's parents returned East because of their declining health. Both the captain and McKiever stayed in touch. When one forgot, the other became the reminder. Within three years both foster parents died. First one, then two years later, the other. Each time the captain and McKiever journeyed back East for the funeral. Although it was a sad time for both, it was especially hard on McKiever. The solace for the captain was his knowledge that both foster parents believed in God and walked in faith.

The captain's mind returned to the present. He glanced at the clock, then at the forms on his desk. He frowned, knowing that in a few minutes McKiever would be walking through the office door with the belief that his career with the Rangers was about to end. But Frank was going to offer him one more assignment, an assignment that he knew William McKiever wouldn't refuse. The captain really didn't want a young man he had raised like a son to take this job, but he knew he would. It was bad enough that McKiever was reporting in to retire, but this assignment was dangerous, perhaps the most dangerous law enforcement job he had ever dispatched any of his men on. Frank was worried, and he had good reason to be.

McKiever left the bunkhouse, heading for his meeting. He was disappointed that all the men were in the field, disrupting his plans to have some fun, a kind of rub-it-in retirement fun. Crossing the yard, Mac reached headquarters. Climbing the stairs, he smiled as he heard the third step squeak. Entering the building, he hung his hat on a wall peg. Out of the corner of his eyes he could see a large figure looming behind the desk.

Before McKiever could start for the office, a voice boomed out, "Come on in, door's open!"

The captain was standing, a large smile spread across his face, his hand outstretched. "Mac, good to see you."

McKiever watched his hand disappear in Captain Frank's huge grasp.

Frank asked, "How about some coffee? The pot's still hot and I've only had one."

"No thanks, I've already had two, and more than two makes me jumpy."

"It's fresh."

"Nope, thanks anyway. Captain, you look good."

McKiever handed Captain Frank a large envelope. "Here's my written report."

Frank took the report. Starting to open it he stopped, asking, "Anything that you need to add to this report?"

"No, sir. I was disappointed that two hard cases got away, but at the very worst they were just two low-grade, hired guns."

Frank nodded. "I'm sure they'll pop up again. No telling where, but someplace."

"But," McKiever smiled, making a point, "now it's up to someone else because I'll be raising beef while managing a ranch."

O'Rourke's response was strange, no sign of humor, just silence.

McKiever had expected the captain to at least smile. Knowing him as well as he did, he waited, watching Frank's face.

Captain Frank pointed to the papers on his desk. "See those forms?"

"I see them."

"Those are your mustering out forms. All you have to do is sign them, hand them back to me, I'll date them and sign them. After that, you're no longer a Texas Ranger."

"Pass them over." McKiever extended his hand.

Frank held up a hand. "Not yet. I've got another assignment for you to consider."

McKiever slowly pulled back his hand, his voice adamant, "Captain, it took me a whole year to convince myself that a new and promising world was waiting for me, and I finally managed to do it." Mac leaned forward. "A whole year mind you. It was hard, but I managed to do it. Captain, I'm not going to mess up my mind now, not after a whole year. Thanks, but no thanks."

Frank didn't move, his eyes on McKiever. "I understand, but I'm still going to tell you what the problem is, because if I don't I would be derelict in my duty. Fair enough?"

McKiever shrugged. "Go ahead."

O'Rourke slowed his speech, "I hope you turn it down, I really do. I'm dead serious!" Frank's deep voice lowered slightly, "What's more, I want you to know that you don't have to prove yourself to me, or to any man at this post. Mac, I mean that. Let me repeat myself, you should refuse this assignment. You're set to retire, and you should. What's really bothering me is despite what you told me and what I just said, I know you'll take this job."

A quiet descended in the office, the captain watching McKiever.

This was strange, McKiever thought, not the usual way the captain gave an assignment. He waited several seconds before asking, "Captain, what's the problem, and where's the problem?"

"Fredonia."

McKiever went on alert. Alarmed, his thoughts jumped to Sara Kincaid, and then to his former partner, Jeff Kincaid, his voice surprised, "Fredonia!"

"Yes, Fredonia. I received a communication from Sheriff Olcott three weeks ago. It appears a certain ranch has suddenly been growing quite large at the expense of neighboring ranches. Do you remember Sam Cotton?"

"Sure, he acted as a scout for us while we were chasing a Comanche raiding party. Three years to be exact. He was a man you could really count on."

"Well, he's dead. Apparently, he got in the way of that ranch. They found him shot dead on his own land."

Anger welled up in McKiever. He had really liked Cotton. "What's the name of this ranch causing all the trouble?"

"The Bar High."

Hardly believing what he's just heard, McKiever's voice reflected surprise, "Well I'll be!"

Frank looked into Mac's face, seeing the surprise. "What's that mean?"

"I ran into a man all dressed in black at the livery stable at Grand Junction. The man was arguing with the livery owner about money. The fellow seemed quite educated. I got the impression he's well paid, you know, the kind that costs money, maybe a legal person. The stable owner told me the man was from the Bar High Ranch in Fredonia."

"Interesting, anything else?"

"I didn't like him."

The captain paused, pondering McKiever's dislike. If Mac didn't like someone, there was always a good reason. "Any reason in particular besides him arguing with the stable owner?"

"Yes, the man has money and he's haggling over horse lodging. I told him the rates at the stable are more than fair. Another thing, he has this sickening smile that never goes away. On top of that, he's wearing these fancy pinstriped pants jacked all the way up to his bellybutton just to show off his shiny black boots. I'd be surprised if he doesn't carry his own personal résumé in his black leather vest. The more I think about him, the more I don't like him. If you give me more time, I'm sure I'll come up with a few more reasons."

"I see." Humor showed in the captain's face. "Can I ask you another question?"

"Sure, go ahead."

"Why didn't you just shoot him?"

McKiever half smiled. "I thought about it, but I do represent the law, at least for the time being."

Frank chuckled before getting serious. "Well, let's forget fancy pants for a moment. There's more to the situation than what I've told you.

Apparently, this Bar High has hired three gunmen listed on our wanted posters. But even worse, do you remember a man named Sam Peckenpath?"

McKiever's eyes narrowed, his eyebrows arched. "I sure do, go on."

"One of Sheriff Olcott's deputies uncovered a wire message sent to Peckenpath retaining his services to the Bar High."

McKiever whistled.

The captain's face became very serious. "I don't have to tell you what that Peckenpath did to our Wendell Johnson. Next to you, no one was faster with a six-shooter than Wendell. But Wendell never cleared leather before Peckenpath killed him. I guess you could say that Sam Peckenpath's on our most wanted list!"

Frank rose, walking over to the window. He stared out over the street, still remembering Wendell. Looking back at Mac, he spoke, "For some reason we haven't figured out this Peckenpath. He's like a ghost. After he kills, he just disappears; it's like he really doesn't exist."

McKiever nodded, agreeing, "I know, we have no description, no face, no hair color, no nothing. Just a ghost, but a ghost that kills."

"And fast," Frank added. "Anyway, it appears this Bar High has acquired most of the ranches up near the northern foothills. First, they make an offer, but if it's refused, problems crop up."

McKiever interrupted, "That's where Jeff and Sara have their ranch. What type of offers?"

"From what I understand, very generous offers."

McKiever hesitated, surprised that the offers were generous. "What happens if the offer is refused?"

The captain spread his hands. "Usually bank foreclosure follows. You know, business goes bad with all sorts of problems developing. Rustlers steal cattle, investments go sour, mortgages get behind, eventually what happens is foreclosure. The ranches that don't fall into those problems can't keep hired help because of their fear from the hired guns of the Bar High."

"How long before the roof falls in?"

"About a year. At least that's what Sheriff Olcott told me. Things seem to go bad fast." Moving away from the window, Frank slipped back into his chair. "I understand that Jeff recently received an offer."

McKiever stood, curiosity reflecting in his face. "And of course, he refused?"

"No, he stalled. He told them he would consider their generous offer. In other words, he's buying time."

McKiever nodded. "That's smart. Well, Captain, you were right about one thing, I guess I do have one last assignment. But I'll tell you this, when I'm done, I'm not coming back to Ranger Headquarters. Winter isn't far away, and I've got to get things done at my ranch before the snow flies."

"Understood, you sign your papers now, I'll get my signature on them, and as soon as you finish up, I'll date them. Any money owed you will be forwarded to your ranch along with copies of your forms." Frank pushed the papers to McKiever. "How's that arrangement?"

McKiever sat down. "Obviously you were ready for me. How about help?" Dipping and withdrawing the pen, he scrawled his signature on the forms.

Frank watched Mac before answering, "I've already dispatched Josh Maclarin and Rick Marten. They're dressed up in business suits posing as investors. You'll find them staying at the hotel. Mac, I don't want people to know that Texas Rangers are in town until it's unavoidable. I want those scoundrels in a court of law to receive legal justice." A serious expression knit the captain's brow. "I don't want shootouts, especially concerning this Peckenpath! I gave you Josh and Rick because they're level headed and have always worked well with you."

McKiever nodded. "You couldn't have given me two better men. They think like I do, and you're right, we work well together."

Captain Frank rose. Leaning forward, he stared into McKiever's eyes. "I've given a lot of thought about this Peckenpath, and my instincts are telling me that his type loves the challenge of death; it's his trade. Don't get drawn into a shootout with this man, you hear me, Mac."

"Stop worrying Captain, I have no desire to get in a shootout with anyone, much less that killer."

Straightening, Frank kept his stare on McKiever."I don't like to repeat myself, but I'm feeling guilty about giving you this assignment. I'm not kidding when I tell you no hard feelings if you walk away from this job. Fact is, you ought to, and if you change your mind, we never had this conversation."

"Captain, a few minutes ago you told me you'd be derelict if you didn't inform me. You're right. As for me, I couldn't live with myself if I passed off this assignment to someone else. Jeff and Sara are personal friends, so that's that. Is there anything else I should know?"

"No, except I'm sure I'm wasting my breath to tell you to be careful. Come on, I'll see you to the door." Both moved into the outer room. "Mac, keep me posted. If things get worse, I'll dispatch help. Right now, every man is in the field. The way I got it figured, Jeff's a former Ranger, you have Olcott and his two deputies. Add Josh, Rick, and yourself, that's seven experienced law officers. That should be enough. Only one thing keeps bothering me."

Mac answered, watching the captain's face. "Let me take a guess, Sam Peckenpath?"

Leaving headquarters, they stepped into the sunshine. A soft breeze brushed across their faces. McKiever looked at the man who had raised him like his own son. "Stop worrying. Tomorrow's the first day of September. Hopefully, we'll get the problem solved before it cools down. Besides, I'm planning on a quick solution before heading for my ranch."

The captain touched McKiever's shoulder. "One thing you can be sure of is that I'll give you plenty of prayer cover."

"Now you know, Captain, there isn't anyone I respect more than you, but I must admit there is something that puzzles me about you."

"Go on, what is it?"

"How can you believe in something you've never seen before?"

Captain O'Rourke smiled. "William, are you telling me that you only believe in what you see?"

"Kind of. After all, when we make arrests we need evidence, don't we?"

"William, didn't I and your foster parents get you some education?"

"Yes, you did do that."

"Do you remember Isaac Newton's teachings about gravity?"

McKiever conceded, "It does appear to exist."

"Good answer, now show me some."

Mac didn't answer.

Frank continued, "Remember, we're on a round earth turning upside down. That's pretty miraculous, don't you think?"

Again, McKiever kept silent, not answering.

The captain paused, before going on, "The Bible says that faith is the substance of things hoped for and the evidence of things not seen. We can't see gravity, but it does have substance, which is a powerful force keeping us in an upright position. Mac, think about God that way."

"I have to admit, Captain, you and Sara Kincaid always seem to have some sort of an answer."

Captain O'Rourke looked up. "Do me a favor, Mac. The next time you're outside on a clear night, look up at the stars and ask yourself where does the order come from? You should also ask where does the universe begin and where does it end? Remember, what chance creates, by the same law it will eliminate. Now, how's that for some evidence to ponder!"

McKiever rolled his eyes. "Okay, okay, you win, at least for now. Speaking about evidence, I'm on my way to Fredonia to get some. I will stay in touch."

The captain watched McKiever leave. He felt a sense of foreboding, hoping his instincts were wrong. Through the years Frank's sixth sense had rarely failed him, but this time he hoped his feelings were out of whack.

Talking to himself, O'Rourke spoke out loud, "Lack of faith, Frank, if anyone can clean up the mess in Fredonia, Mac can." The captain sighed, muttering under his breath, "Too bad I'm not active in the field anymore. At least then I could actually do something."

Turning, Frank headed for his office. Now all he could do was worry while dispatching his best man, a man he had raised like his own son, and he didn't like it!

CHAPTER 3

Return to Fredonia

Jeffrey Kincaid pushed his plate back. Looking at Sara, he marveled at her beauty. He was a lucky man and he knew it. Not only was Sara extremely attractive, she always made sure his needs were taken care of; this morning was no exception. She always insisted that her husband had a breakfast that she made.

Sara had long black hair. This morning it was tied back into a single ponytail. Her waist was small, accented by a slender body with a nice flare to her hips. Sara's face was creamy white, with long black eyelashes, her full lips complementing a beautiful smile.

Sara looked at Jeff. "Well, Mr. Kincaid, what's on your agenda today?"

"Good question, I'm taking Ben and Sam into town to pick up some supplies. They can come back while I stop in to see Sheriff Olcott. Hopefully, by now Olcott's heard from Ranger Headquarters."

"Jeff, be careful." Sara frowned. "The Bar High is dangerous and now they're after us. If something happens to you, I don't know what I'd do."

"Well, just so nothing does happen, and since you're a woman of faith, give me some prayer cover. Speaking of agendas, what's yours?"

Sara sighed, "Nothing until tomorrow evening, then I have a Bible study at Wendy Philip's house."

Jeff rose from the table. He stood slightly taller than six feet, his muscular body v-shaped from the waist up. Jeff Kincaid was a handsome man, his face square and well proportioned. Whenever he walked into a social gathering, women noticed, and their attention remained until he left.

Jeff liked to tease Sara; this morning was no exception. "Sara, it's good I didn't hesitate when I first saw you, especially with McKiever around."

Sara turned, her hands on her hips. "Just remember, if you ever developed the roving eye, there's always Mac."

Walking over to Sara, Jeff placed his hands around her waist. "You sure know how to keep a man honest."

"Jeff, seriously, do you think Mac will come?"

Jeff was thoughtful before answering, "The last time I spoke with Mac, he told me this was the year he was retiring. If Mac's still a Ranger, I expect he'll show up. If not, we won't see him. Another thing, he could still be out in the field on another assignment, so who knows?"

Sara nodded.

"You know, honey, it might be some time before any Rangers can get here. Sheriff Olcott only sent that message ten days ago. Captain Frank might have to wait until he has some men available. Well, let me get going." Jeff kissed Sara. Stepping back, he lifted his gun holster, buckling it on. Grabbing his hat, he headed for the door. "I've got lots of things to do here at the ranch. I should be back early."

Sara watched the door close, her thoughts returning to the past. When she first met Jeff, it had been love at first sight. He was part of a Ranger detachment using their ranch as an intercept post while another group of Rangers were pursuing marauding Comanches through the northern pass, not far from her father's ranch.

Jeff was a master at flirting. His charm and good looks had smitten Sara. But a complication had developed. The problem was William McKiever. Mac wasn't dashing like Jeff, but he had a way about him. Although he was more reserved, his manner was intriguing. Of the two, the men always seemed to seek McKiever's approval. As time went on, Sara found herself excited when either man came into her presence.

Over time Sara realized she had fallen in love with both men. Because of her Christian convictions, Sara became prayerful, believing that only God could solve her dilemma. A week after her constant prayers, Jeff had asked Sara to marry him. Sara was relieved, believing God had supernaturally answered her prayers. Her answer was yes, finally feeling peace. The following day, in Sara's presence, Jeff informed McKiever of their marriage plans. Sara could see the disappointment in Mac's face. After complimenting them, McKiever had left. As she watched him leave, Sara's peace had deserted her, her emotional burdens returning.

Several days later, Sara and Mac were alone. Touching his sleeve, she explained how she had fallen in love with both of them. As she talked, tears had started down her cheeks. Holding his hand, she told him about her prayers, how Jeff's proposal was an answer to her confusion. Placing her head on Mac's chest, she told him that if he had asked first, she would have said yes to him. Openly crying, she finished by telling him she would always have a special place in her heart for him.

Sara glanced toward the foyer, remembering Mac's response. He had thanked her, telling her how her words would always be cherished. He told her he would take them everywhere he went. She could still feel him brushing away her tears, drawing her into a gentle hug. After that embrace, he departed. In the days that followed, Sara recalled how McKiever avoided her. The only time she saw him was in Jeff's presence.

The ringing chimes from the grandfather clock brought Sara back into the present. She shook her head, her eyes red. It seemed like McKiever was still standing there, still brushing away her tears. Touching her cheeks, she wiped them. How unfair life could be, she thought. She had this wonderful marriage with Jeff, a beautiful ranch, and now they were hoping Mac would come and rescue them from a dangerous situation at a risk to his own life. All because of a gunfighter by the name of Samuel Peckenpath. Jeff had openly admitted that only a man with Mac's skill with a gun stood any chance against such a dangerous gunman.

Sara's mind wouldn't stop swirling around. She so much wanted to see McKiever, to know that things had gone well for him. The more she thought, the more her conscience wouldn't leave her alone. As her frustration grew, she decided to turn to the only place where she would experience peace. Turning, she headed for the stairs leading to the bedroom. She would ask for God's help.

Sheriff Olcott's eyes burned. He was getting bleary catching up on his paperwork. Hearing the office door open, he felt relief. The timing was perfect; now he had a good excuse to stop. Looking up, he watched Jeffrey Kincaid walk in.

Jeff smiled. "Sheriff, you look like a man needing relief from your desk."

Olcott pushed his chair. "Why, are my eyes red?"

"And then some."

Rubbing his eyes, Olcott rose, displaying a somewhat obscured waistline thanks to his wife's home cooking. He had a full head of gray hair with just a slight thinning along his forehead. Leaning back, he stretched his arms. "Jeff, I heard from Ranger Headquarters. We are getting help, but don't ask me when because I don't know."

"Do you know who?"

Olcott thought about Jeff's question, asking, "You mean, is McKiever coming?"

"I was thinking about McKiever. He is the best, and maybe we need the best, especially with this Peckenpath, don't you think?"

"I have no idea who's being sent. Besides, I wouldn't want to match up anyone against a gunfighter like Peckenpath. I'll tell you what I do know: I'm getting too old for this job. It's time for a younger man to take over." Olcott sighed, "I'll ride out this storm and then let someone else become the new sheriff. Speaking about retiring, you wouldn't be interested, would you, Jeff?"

Jeff stared for a long minute. "You know, Olcott, I can just see myself telling Sara that I'm going to be the new sheriff, so you already know the answer to that question. As for this Peckenpath, I guess we'll just have to be cautious and use our heads."

Olcott laughed. "I guess so, although it sure would be interesting to watch you try to explain to Sara how you're going to be the new sheriff. I do hope the Rangers show up soon, but until they do, we'll just have to hold the fort. Anyway, at least help is on the way. Now, young man, I've got to make the rounds. You know, let the town see my face. As soon as I know more, you'll be the first to know." Olcott's face became serious. "I want you to know that I'm thankful that this town has a citizen like yourself. I sure do appreciate you. Oh, one last thing. If your friend McKiever shows up, do you have a message for him?"

"Tell him that he's expected to stay at my ranch."

"I'll pass that invitation along. In another hour it will be time for lunch. You want to meet me?"

"Thanks, but I've got some business at the bank and lots of neglected jobs. I'll stay in touch; you do the same."

Jeff opened the door, both men stepping outside. Olcott watched Jeff cross the street, angling toward the bank. Fredonia was sure fortunate having a man like Jeff Kincaid, he thought. A man with his law enforcement experience was invaluable. He just hoped if McKiever did come, there wouldn't be any strain between them because of Sara. It had been common knowledge that only one man had been the fortunate one. Strange, Olcott thought, the situation in Fredonia might trigger old hurts. He hoped not. Digging into his vest, Olcott pulled out fixings for a smoke. Rolling the paper and tobacco, he scratched a match, lighting the cigarette. Puffing, he started up the boardwalk.

The late afternoon sun cast shadows over Fredonia's buildings. McKiever reined in Friend, eyeing the busy street below. He thought of Sara, a nervous feeling seeping into his bones. Funny, he thought, being nervous rarely disturbed him, but thinking about her always made him anxious.

Horse and rider were still for several minutes. Leaning over, McKiever talked to his horse, as if Friend would relieve his anxious feelings. "Remember this town, old boy? Looks peaceful, doesn't it? Well, maybe it is, but then looks are deceiving. What do you think?"

Friend shook his head.

Straightening up, McKiever unpinned his badge, slipping it into his shirt pocket. It would be better if no one knew he was a Ranger until the time was right. "Come on, Friend, let's go down and check things out." Descending, they entered the town. McKiever marveled how the town looked exactly the same as the day he rode away. It was as if time had stood still. The street bustled with activity, the people ignoring them.

Passing the general store, McKiever's eyes focused on a wagon overloaded with supplies. He couldn't help but think if those supplies were heavy, and the trail rough, he could envision the owners of the wagon fixing a broken axle. Burned into the back seat was the name Upper Forks Ranch. Surprised, he twisted in the saddle. The wagon belonged to Jeff and

Sara Kincaid. Stopping Friend, he eyeballed the store. Whoever was with the wagon must still be inside, probably paying the bill, he thought. Mac's thoughts turned to Sara, that nervous feeling creeping back. He spoke to his nerves, his voice a silent whisper, "Nerves, leave me alone."

Almost three years had passed since he'd last seen Sara. He could still picture her, as if he ever forgot! McKiever warned himself to forget Sara and remember Jeff. He and Jeff had faced many dangerous situations together. Jeff was a person you could depend on, a man you could trust with your life. Mac scolded himself to remember that.

Turning Friend, they headed for the saloon. McKiever couldn't think of a better place to leave his horse with the intention of not being noticed. There were always more horses waiting for their owners at the town watering hole than any other place. Pulling up to the hitch rack, Mac smiled. Only one space remained. Dismounting, he tied Friend next to a chocolate-colored mare.

"I tell you, my friend, I sure do take care of you." Patting Friend's flank, McKiever glanced across the street, eyeing the wagon. Wrestling with his curiosity, he considered heading for the store.

Voices, threatening voices, pulled his attention away from the wagon. Two young cowhands were backing into the street, their eyes focused toward the saloon. Staring down at the cowpunchers from the boardwalk was a black bearded man wearing a gun, butt out, on his left hip. Standing next to the bearded man was a fellow companion, with long brown hair hanging down to his shoulders. A cigarette tangled from his mouth, his gun on his right hip. Both looked eager for violence.

McKiever shifted his eyes back to the cowhands, frowning at what he saw. Their arms hung stiff, their faces tense. They needed a way out and there wasn't any. Mac grimaced, not wanting to get involved. If he didn't interfere, he would remain unknown, something he wanted. He felt frustration. What were those young men doing in a saloon at this hour? Maybe, he thought, they deserved their predicament. McKiever cast his eyes back to the bearded man and his companion, not liking them. He'd seen their type before, the kind that loved trouble. Both had stepped off the boardwalk into the street. Both were separating. It was obvious they were experienced. Mac's eyes jumped back to the cowboys. They stood too close, their shoulders almost touching. If he was going to act, it had to be now. Stepping away from the horses, McKiever squared, his voice a command, "Hold it!"

All heads jerked around, staring at the stranger in the street. For a second there was silence. The bearded one's voice broke the quiet, "Mister, you should mind your own business."

McKiever didn't want to sound like a lawman. It would be good if he could keep them guessing without blowing his cover. "Well, here's my problem, I've been sent by investors who believe this is a quiet town to do business in, and the first thing I'd have to report is what I see." McKiever smiled. "Now, if this problem can be resolved peacefully, no bad report."

Black beard snarled, "Like I said, you should mind your own business!"

"But you don't understand, that's what I'm talking about. This is about business. Besides, if it wasn't for the whiskey this wouldn't be happening, right?"

Black beard's eyes narrowed. "Looks like you don't understand. Like I keep saying, you should mind your own business." He smirked, moving away from his partner.

Not much time left, McKiever thought. His shoulder twitched, the Colt .45 appearing in his hand, the gun pointing at black beard's chest, his voice menacing, "Go ahead, big mouth, let that whiskey get you killed."

Startled, black beard stammered, "Easy, mister, no need to get trigger happy. We were just having a little fun."

"There's nothing funny about a bullet in your chest. Like I told you, my investors want a quiet town and I'm going to get your cooperation." McKiever thumbed back the gun's hammer, the ominous sound making the bearded one stiffen. "Both of you reach across with your opposite hands and dump those six-shooters in the street." McKiever's eyes narrowed, his voice deadly, "You can start now, or I'll shoot your legs out from under you. You got two seconds."

The bearded one moved first. Reaching across his body he dragged his gun out, letting it fall. His long-haired partner followed, both revolvers lying in the dirt.

McKiever nodded. "Both of you saved yourself some serious pain. Now step forward, away from those guns."

Again, the bearded one moved first. It was obvious who the leader was. When black beard moved, his long-haired friend followed. Watching both step forward, McKiever stopped them. "That's far enough." He shifted his stare at the cowpunchers. "You two move around behind and pick up those guns."

Both cowhands stared at McKiever, not moving, their eyes had a vacant look.

McKiever's voice snapped, "Wake up, get behind those two and pick up their hardware!" Reacting suddenly, both men bolted. Circling, they reached down retrieving the six-shooters. Straightening, they looked at McKiever.

"Good, now empty those guns and dump those bullets in the pockets under their holsters. After you do that, stick those guns back in their gun belt. Go ahead, do it!"

Waiting until the cowhands finished, McKiever fixed his stare at the bearded one and his partner. Maybe he could play with their minds, keep them from guessing who he was. "You two are lucky, real lucky! I cost a lot and there's a reason why. Now, where are your horses?"

Black beard pointed to the hitch rack.

McKiever waved his gun. "Climb aboard and vamoose."

Black beard started, then stopped, glaring at McKiever, his voice reflecting curiosity, "You're awful fast with a gun. Your name wouldn't be Sam Peckenpath, would it?"

Caught by surprise, McKiever hesitated, recovering. "Never heard of him, who is he?"

Black beard shrugged. Turning, he headed for the hitch rack, his companion following. McKiever shifted farther into the street, keeping his line of fire clear. Seeing the rifle stocks protruding from their saddles, his voice stopping them. "Let me give you some advice, try to use those rifles and I'll pick you off with my Sharps. Do yourselves a big favor, get on those horses and don't look back, just ride."

Black beard had stopped, head bowed, listening.

McKiever prodded, "Go on, mount up and get out of here."

Rising into his saddle, the bearded one backed his horse into the street. Swinging his mount, he eyed McKiever. "I don't know what business you got in this town, but you might think about not staying longer than necessary. Better yet, tell your investors this ain't a peaceful place."

McKiever looked into the man's eyes, not answering.

Black beard kept his eyes on McKiever, speaking to his friend, "Come on, Clem, let's go."

Clem moved alongside. Keeping their horses in a slow walk, they rode down the main street, their slow ride making a statement.

McKiever kept his eyes on the departing gunmen, his voice questioning the cowpunchers, "What's your names?"

The taller of the two spoke. "My name's Sam Ellis; this here's Ben Thompson."

"Where do you fellows work?"

"At the Upper Forks Ranch."

Surprised, McKiever looked at Sam, gesturing with his head. "That your wagon by the general store?"

Sam's face showed surprise, his eyes narrowing, the man seemed to notice everything. "Yes, sir, we were getting supplies."

"Tell me, what supplies were you picking up in the saloon?"

Sam's face was sheepish. He looked at Ben before answering, "We got done early, I guess too early."

"Good answer, hopefully you learned something. You two finished loading up?"

"Yes, sir."

"Well, here's some advice. Head back to your ranch. Those gunmen still have plenty of whiskey in them, and whiskey causes men to take chances. Do you get my drift?"

"We sure do, mister, and much obliged."

Ben spoke for the first time. "Mister, are you a lawman?"

McKiever dodged the question. "Like I said, I'm here because of business. Now, both of you get going so I don't have to watch your backs along with me."

Waiting until the wagon disappeared from sight, McKiever crossed the street, his destination the jail. A lone horse was tied in front of the building, indicating someone was there. Opening the door, he entered.

Olcott looked up, a look of pleasure flooding his face. "I'll be darned, the best of the best. William McKiever, how have you been?"

"Sheriff, it's just you and me, how's that sound?"

"Tell me you're kidding," Olcott grunted.

Unable to contain himself, McKiever laughed. "Yes, I'm kidding. Actually, there's already two other Rangers in town. Matter of fact, I think they've been here for a week."

Olcott was surprised. "I had no idea, a week you said. Well, I'm liking the odds a lot better now. How about some coffee?"

"Thanks, but no thanks. I could sure use some water though, I've been on the trail most of the day and my throat feels like cotton."

"You're in luck." Olcott rose, walking over to a large pitcher. Pouring water into a tin cup, he handed it to McKiever. "Water always tastes better in a tin cup."

McKiever drank. Sheriff Olcott was right, water always tasted special in a tin cup. Just seeing the condensation on the side of the cup seemed to improve the taste. "Sheriff, how about another?"

"Please, help yourself."

The gurgling sound of water flowing into the cup was a pleasant sound. He looked at Olcott, taking another swallow before speaking, "Captain O'Rourke figures that between you and your deputies, the two undercover Rangers at the hotel, myself and Jeff Kincaid, that adds up to seven lawmen. He thinks that should be enough to solve the town's problem." McKiever tilted his head back, draining the cup, listening.

Olcott perched on his desk. "Normally I would say that's more than enough. Normally, that is. Were you informed about this Peckenpath fellow?"

Mac set his cup down. "I have, anyone see him yet?"

Olcott sighed, "I wouldn't know him if I saw him." Stepping behind the desk, he crossed his arms, rolling his eyes. "How would I? Fact is you fellows don't even have a poster out on him, and he killed one of your men."

Shrugging his shoulders, Mac agreed, "You won't either. No one's identified him. The man seems like a ghost. He comes, he kills, then disappears. His reputation is legendary. Seems like everyone's scared of him. No one has witnessed against him, much less given us a description."

Olcott shook his head. "Tough to get a drop on a man without knowing what he looks like, especially a man that dangerous. It's like you just said, people must refuse to witness out of fear. Makes a person wonder, don't it?"

"I think you might be right, Sheriff Olcott, this Peckenpath must scare the hell out of people. The problem seems to be that he only shows up when it's time to kill." McKiever scratched his chin. "One thing's for sure, because of what he does he must be well paid. The good news is that this is the first solid lead concerning him that we've had in years. Maybe it will pan out."

"Tell me, Mac, how much you know about the situation here?"

"I'll tell you what I do know, after that you can fill in the blanks. The Bar High has suddenly become very prosperous while acquiring several ranches. The owner has hired professional guns, including three men wanted by us, not forgetting Peckenpath. Last, but not least, I've been told by Captain Frank that you suspect the Bar High was involved in Sam Cotton's death." McKiever looked at Olcott. "How'd I do?"

Pouring water for himself, Olcott was impressed. "Seems like you know most of it, except for one thing."

"I'm listening."

"Somehow the Bar High gets lots of cooperation from the bank. The old president retired, and the new president seems very helpful to the Bar High's expansion plans."

"Who is the owner of the Bar High?"

"A man by the name of Mike McCormick."

"Tell me about him?"

"He came here seven years ago, kind of kept to himself for a time. But all of a sudden, he's acquiring defaulting ranches. The suspicious thing is that those owners were always doing well until McCormick became civic minded."

"What's that mean, are you saying politically motivated?"

"Yep, he's become a political hound. He shows up at all the town meetings offering solutions to local problems."

"Go on, nothing terrible about that."

"It's the way he talks and his presence. McCormick's a powerful man physically who's not afraid to express himself. He's built like a block of granite, and his presence is very intimidating to others. When he talks, he's very abrasive and everyone tends to shut up."

McKiever considered the Sheriff's words before responding, "I guess it's reasonable to say that McCormick's passing himself off as a concerned citizen with ulterior motives. In other words, a snake in the grass."

"I like that description."

"No offense meant, Sheriff, has he intimidated you?"

Olcott smiled. "No offense taken. Not yet he hasn't. I'm too old, and I've seen it all, except maybe for this Peckenpath. But he's not the first scoundrel I've had to deal with. I'll tell you this, if McCormick ever got elected as mayor in this town, I won't be sheriff anymore."

"Why's that?"

"It would be impossible for me to work with that man. Fact is, politicians aren't my favorite people anyway. I guess I'm a lot like you, I'd have a tough time letting McCormick use me to get ahead. I can just hear him now, how he brought peace to Fredonia. That answer your question?"

McKiever chuckled, liking this Olcott. "You know, Sheriff, Captain Frank was right about you. Your attitude about politicians confirms what he said. He told me you're an honest man who could be counted on." McKiever paused. "He also told me something else."

"What's that?"

"He told me politicians are necessary evils, and we get caught in the middle."

Olcott rolled his eyes. "Isn't that the truth. Most politicians are former lawyers who make a bundle of money, get elected to public office, write more laws, retire, go back to being lawyers, making more money from the laws they wrote while in office. Some racket, huh?"

Grinning from ear to ear, McKiever eyed Olcott. "That's the best explanation of a politician I've ever heard."

Olcott appreciated this McKiever, adding, "Then, of course, you get some ranchers who get too big for their own britches, like we have now. Anyway, thanks for the compliment. I heard a lot about Captain Frank, all good. As for me, I've been pushing my luck for too many years. For a long time, I'm getting by on savvy while surrounding myself with young deputies. So far, the formula has worked, but I think it's time for this town to get a younger man."

When Olcott mentioned retirement, McKiever thought about his delayed change of life, a frown crossing his face.

Olcott saw the frown. "Speaking about retirement, weren't you supposed to be at your ranch in Colorado territory by now?"

Nodding, McKiever shrugged. "As we speak. If it wasn't for Jeff and Sara, I doubt I would have taken this assignment. Fact is, I was returning to headquarters to turn in my badge when the captain told me about this problem. So here I am."

Olcott was tactful. "You three remained friends despite how things worked out?"

McKiever was slow to answer, wanting to put any concerns to rest. "Jeff and I had a strong friendship long before we came to Fredonia." He paused, looking at Olcott, adding, "We've kept it that way."

"Sorry I asked, but I make it my business to consider everything. Having seven lawmen is better than six and a half. My turn to say, I hope no offense taken?"

"None taken. Knowing about people in a dangerous situation is smart thinking. I would have done the same."

Olcott sipped some water. "I know you just got here, but have you given any thought to a plan of action?"

"Not yet. Whatever plan we come up with will be through joint thinking. I'm always open to suggestions. After all, you know this town better than I do. You have any ideas?"

"Can't say that I do, but I'm sure your old partner Jeff might have some ideas. By the way, he was here this morning. He wanted me to tell you you're invited to stay at his ranch."

McKiever felt that anxious feeling again. "Thanks for telling me. Before I head out, I better catch up with my undercover men at the hotel. The captain has them all dressed up as businessmen. Be interesting to see if anything's happened with them. Tell me, Olcott, is there anyone at the bank we can trust?"

Olcott's interest showed. "You know, McKiever, you always were a quick thinker. It sounds to me like you're coming up with a plan. The answer to your question is yes. The man is Jonathan Barker; he's a loan officer at the bank."

"What makes you think he's our man?"

"I've known him since he was a young boy. Jonathan grew up in this town and cares about people. Fact is, his daddy was a rancher. Jonathan's helped a lot of people in this town, until recently that is."

"Why's that? What changed?"

"The new president moved Jonathan away from ranch financing. Gave him other responsibilities. It seems once McCormick got hooked up with the new president, Jonathan was out."

"Interesting, he does sound like a good possibility. Anything else about him?"

"Well, he attends church on a regular basis, always has. The way I see it, going to church shows something about a man's character. Unless of course," Olcott widened his eyes, "someone's doing it for political reasons!"

McKiever liked Olcott's reasoning. "I think this Jonathan Barker may work out. The best way to catch a crook like McCormick is to follow his money trail. The best way to do that is to see if he has a paper trail, and the local bank may be the place to find that incriminating evidence. Yep, I think our two businessmen at the hotel will make an appointment with this Jonathan."

Olcott noticed something for the first time, pointing toward McKiever's shirt. "I notice you're not wearing your badge?"

"Seemed like a smart idea. Right now, no one knows Texas Rangers are in town. I figured, why arouse suspicions while gathering evidence. Unfortunately, I might have blown my cover."

"How so?"

"After I tied up at the saloon, I broke up a potential gunfight."

Olcott leaned forward. "You don't say. How about some details?"

"Not much to tell. Two professional looking gunmen were bracing two young cowpunchers. It was going to be a mismatch and I knew it. I really thought about slipping away, but my conscience wouldn't let me, so I broke it up. A black bearded fellow forced me to draw my gun."

"And?"

"No contest, no shots fired."

"Thanks for saving me the trouble. Who were the cowpunchers?"

"Two young men from Jeff's ranch. They were picking up supplies. Unfortunately, they stopped over at the saloon before leaving."

"How about the other two? You mentioned one had a black beard."

"He did, and his partner has long brown hair hanging down to his shoulders. I heard the bearded man call the other fellow Clem as they rode off."

"Congratulations, Mac, you didn't know it, but you just met the two characters on your wanted posters. The long-haired fellow is Clem Johnson, the other man is Raymond Floyd. Floyd's real trigger happy, always looking to start something. Matter of fact, I think he's the one who killed Sam Cotton. Can't prove it, but I'd bet on it!"

A hint of anger reflected in McKiever's voice. "It's good I didn't know that; you might be digging some holes for those two. I liked Sam, I really did. He was a big help when we were here the last time."

"Now that would have really blown your cover, don't you think?"

McKiever agreed, "I reckon, but it would have been worth it."

Olcott showed a hint of frustration. "You're right about Cotton. I liked him a lot. It would be real justice if we could string tip his killer, or killers, and maybe we will!"

McKiever stared at the floor for a minute, remembering something. "You're not going to believe this, so hang on to your desk. That black bearded fellow asked me if I was the gunman, Sam Peckenpath."

Olcott leaned forward, surprise showing in his face, staring for several seconds before speaking, "Did I hear you correct? He asked you if you were Peckenpath?"

McKiever nodded, not answering.

Olcott became silent, thoughtful. Apparently McKiever was fast, awful fast. There was no other reason for being mistaken for Peckenpath, he thought. Sitting down, Olcott considered what McKiever had just told him. Looking up, he voiced his thoughts, "What you just said means several things. We now have confirmation from another source that the killer is definitely going to be used by the Bar High. I'm also thinking that the man's not here yet. The next question becomes, when will we see him?" Olcott looked at Mac. "But the most important thing is, whoever sees him better be ready."

Silence descended on the room, each man lost in his own thoughts. McKiever rose, moving to the window. The far side of the street was in shadows, the day slipping away. Feeling hunger pangs, McKiever broke the silence, "I've got to get my horse watered and fed. After that, comes me. Once that's out of the way, I'm going to check in with my men at the hotel."

"Tell you what, Mac, use the stalls behind the jail. There's plenty of feed and water for your horse. While you're taking care of him, I'll order food from the eatery. How does that sound?"

"Perfect, order me whatever you're having. When a man's hungry, he's not picky." Grabbing his hat, he followed Olcott. Crossing the street, he felt the cooling air. Friend greeted him with a nod. "Come on, big boy, this is compliments of Sheriff Olcott."

Watching McKiever lead his horse across the street, Olcott felt a measure of comfort he hadn't felt before. With McKiever's arrival, they had someone to match the gunfighter. It was time to order the food while doing some hobnobbing.

CHAPTER 4

Reunion at Upper Forks

anger Josh McClarin pointed toward a table in the far corner of the dining room. His partner, Rick Marten, nodding his approval. Both knew it was always smart to sit where everyone could be observed, especially in a strange town with serious problems. Reaching the table, both positioned their chairs against the wall. Surveying the room, they relaxed, waiting for a waitress.

The eatery's large windows allowed for plenty of daylight. The once white flowery wallpaper showed a tinge of yellow from the constant cooking. The tables were well spaced, leaving ample room for comfort and a measure of privacy. For eavesdroppers the spaced-out tables might be frustrating, but not for those wanting a private conversation.

A large clock on the far wall showed it would be another hour before the room would become crowded with hungry people. The tantalizing smell of food permeated the room, wafting out into the street. A few street people paused, tempted by the smell, finally moving on.

Rick and Josh watched the red-haired waitress approach, her voice sounding bored, "Afternoon gents, my name is Clare. May I get you something to drink?"

Josh answered, "Two beers sounds about right."

Clare smiled, handing them menus. "I'll be right back."

Rick wasn't looking at his menu, instead he rolled his eyes, his voice hushed, "Wow, she's a knockout?"

Josh, too, was watching the redhead's departing walk, the roll of her hips. "Easy, hoss, remember why we're here?"

"Yeah, I know, but in case you didn't think of it, a local waitress knows everything." Rick smiled, thinking how clever he was. "Therefore, I can't think of a better way to find out what's going on in this town than to ask a pretty waitress. Don't you think?"

Josh eyed his partner. "Let me get this straight, your interest is strictly professional?"

Shaking his head, Rick remained clever. "Can't a man have more than one reason while staying focused on a common objective?"

"Normally yes, but knowing you, I doubt you can keep one separate from the other. Matter of fact, I'd be willing to bet that the common objective gets forgotten in about five seconds. Care for a wager?"

Rick didn't answer, watching Clare return with the drinks.

"Are you gentlemen ready to order?"

Rick decided to have some fun. "Clare, I noticed a poster about a square dance on the bulletin board when we came in. If I remember correctly, the dance is this Saturday." Rick rolled his eyes. "And you look like the dancing type. I'd he honored to escort you. How about it?"

Clare peered over her notepad, her eyes twinkling, her pencil poised. "Actually, I'll be working the refreshment table—with my husband!"

Laughing, Rick persisted. "Is he the jealous type?"

Clare's voice purred, "Why do you think he's working the table with me!" Clare smiled. "I feel very safe with my husband, especially since he's a deputy sheriff in this town!"

"You know, Clare, one of these days I'm going to get lucky with a pretty girl like you. I hoped this was the day."

Placing one hand on her hip, Clare stared at Rick, then Josh, before turning back to Rick, her voice mocking, "Sure, sure, you businessmen all have your wives back home, and while you're on the trail what they don't know won't hurt them. Isn't that right?"

"Actually, Clare, I'm not married." Rick spread his hands. "It's too bad you were in such a rush to get hitched. If you had waited for me, you would have seen the city lights with all the glamour and not be stuck in a town like this."

"Really?" Clare laughed, her voice still mocking, "Is that why no one's found you yet?"

Josh had heard enough. "Can we stop this conversation that's going nowhere?" He winked at Clare. "My partner's right about one thing, Clare, you sure are pretty, but what he doesn't realize is you're also smart. The truth is it's not by accident that a man his age hasn't found a spouse yet, and your intelligence protected you. Now, I'm getting hungry, and the steak and potatoes smothered with gravy looks good to me."

Rick feigned disappointment. "You two have no zest for life, but I don't give up easy. Clare, maybe sometime in the future we can continue this conversation without him. Until then, that steak and potatoes also look good to me."

Both men laughed. Clare enjoyed the banter, her voice reflecting it, "I'll get your orders in."

Watching Clare depart, Rick complained, "You know that happens to me all the time."

"That's because your approach is all wrong. You should have watched Jeff Kincaid when he was with us. He never got a no."

"Why's that?"

"We could start with good looks."

"So you say, what else?"

"How about charm and personality?"

"Hey, I've got that!"

"Don't you wish. Did you ever think it helps to have all three?"

Rick changed the subject. "Josh, don't look now, but a man all dressed in black is heading our way. Wait till you see this guy!"

Causally, Rick shifted his gaze, observing the man approaching their table. As the man neared, he couldn't help but think why would a man dress in such a way except to attract attention? The man's boots were so polished that they could be used as a mirror. His pinstriped pants actually could be seen reflected in the boots. His shiny silver six-shooter appeared like an ornament, his holster like a decoration. Rick whispered a soft sarcasm to Josh, "He's a real showpiece all right."

The man arrived at their table. "Good afternoon, gentlemen, my name is Randell Wynncliff. On behalf of the Bar High Ranch, I would like to welcome you to Fredonia."

Pushing back their chairs, Josh and Rick rose. Wynncliff, flashing a smile, extended his hand. First Josh, then Rick shook his hand, Rick speaking first, "Pleased to meet you. I'm Rick Marten. This is my associate, Josh McClaren. How may we be of help to you?"

Wynncliff removed his hat with a sweeping motion. "My employer, a Mr. Michael McCormick, is aspiring for political office in Fredonia. And I, as his legal counsel, have been instructed to look for future investors. If you will excuse my presumption, both of you gentlemen look like businessmen. And, as you know, business and politics is a formula for opportunity, leading to success. Wouldn't you agree?"

Josh was amazed how the man in black believed he and Rick were businessmen. It was time to jump in and be part of the deception, his voice drawing Wynncliff's attention. "You are an observant man, Mr. Wynncliff. Yes, we are here on business." He paused, eyeing Rick, before adding, "That is, potential business."

Wynncliff's smile radiated, his voice reflecting intense interest. "I see. Is there something I could do to promote that potential business, whatever that might be?"

Curiosity tugged at Josh's brain. It was obvious Rick was enjoying himself. The question was, what was his partner going to say next? He waited.

Rick continued, "Your offer will be given serious consideration. We actually represent several investors, but any investment in Fredonia depends upon the railroad coming here. Perhaps you may have heard?"

Wynncliff's face registered surprise. "No, I have not heard. Is there a date?"

"No, at this time Fredonia is one of several towns in consideration to link the southern part of the state with the northern, and beyond. But as of yet, no final decision has been finalized. Once we know, we will make it a point to contact you."

Digesting Rick's words, Wynncliff spoke slowly, "I must admit your information is news to us. Good news, I might add! Perhaps we could schedule a time together with my employer. I know he will be extremely interested in this potential development."

Rick felt himself relaxing too much, cautioning himself to be careful. One slip of his tongue might make Wynncliff suspicious. It would be better to consult with his partner before continuing. The best way to direct Wyncliff's focus away from them would be to ask questions. He got started, keeping his manner professional. "Where is McCormick's office, Mr. Wynncliff?"

"Our office is next to the General Store." Wynncliff flashed his smile. "You can see the sign hanging over the door, it reads, McCormick Enterprises. The office isn't open every day, but if you try the door and it's open, walk in. May I ask you where you're staying?"

Josh was getting tired of Wynncliff and his smile, a smile that was nauseating him. Seeing their food approaching was a relief, providing him with a perfect opportunity to get rid of the man wearing black. "If you contact the desk clerk here in the hotel, we will get back to you."

Wynncliff also saw the food, gesturing with a nod. "I can see your meal is arriving. Well, this has been a productive conversation. Please keep us posted on any developments." Extending his hand, he excused himself. "Let's hope the railroad chooses Fredonia. Good day, gentlemen."

Josh shook Wynncliff's hand. "Yes, let's hope so."

Rick reached over, his voice business like, "Again, if we receive any positive information, I can assure you, that you will be the first to know. Good day, sir."

Watching Wynncliff depart, Josh whispered, "Can you believe what just happened?" He stopped talking as Clare arrived.

Rick remained the charmer. "Clare, if you want, you could join us for conversation."

Clare smiled. Ignoring Rick, she addressed Josh, "I'll check back for dessert?"

The food was good, the steak exceptional, both men eating in silence. The dinner completed, Josh generously left a dollar on the table. "I might as well leave the tip. After all, Clare pretty much cut you off. I think if anyone has a chance for a dance with her, most likely it will be me."

Rick's face showed a sly look, his answer quick, "Maybe that was my plan all along. You know, you pick up the tip, and when her jealous husband arrives, I move in."

"You wish. Come on, let's pay the bill and discuss our recent invitation upstairs, or should I say, my two opportunities. You know, one business, the other fun!"

Josh chuckled, following Rick. The bill paid, they climbed the stairs. Entering their room, Josh waited until the door closed. "I can't believe what happened. Just think, we have an appointment with the people we' re investigating, and even better, at their invitation!"

"Yeah, I guess dressing like businessmen opens up doors." Rick stared into the mirror. "Maybe we should become businessmen and make big money."

"You mean, get corrupted?"

Rick turned from the mirror. "Something like that. You know, Captain O'Rourke might be the smartest man I ever worked for in the Texas Rangers. Having us pose as businessmen was pure genius."

Josh nodded. "We better handle this opportunity smart. I was glad when the food arrived."

"Why's that?"

"Two reasons. First, we didn't have a chance to compare notes and make sure that whatever we say doesn't arouse suspicion. I figure our story needs to be well thought out. Also, I was sick of that nauseating smile, weren't you?"

A knock on the door stopped Rick's reply. Josh backed toward the far wall, his hand dropping on his gun. Slowly, Rick circled behind the bed, his voice loud, "Who's there?"

"William McKiever!"

"Door's open, come on in!"

McKiever entered the room, the door closing behind him. Smiles broke out, Rick's wit making McKiever chuckle. "Well, look who's here, a Ranger on assignment. You know, Josh, the last I knew a certain person was supposed to be heading for a ranch in Colorado territory."

"I remember the same thing. I guess seeing is believing, 'cause you just can't believe what someone tells you, can you, partner?"

"Listen," McKiever interrupted, "the captain pleaded with me about two men being in over their heads, so how could I refuse?"

Laughter breaking out, Rick and Josh plopped onto the bed. McKiever pulled over a chair, surveying the room. "How are the accommodations here? You two going easy on the captain's budget?"

Josh answered, "Yeah, like it's all his money, but what the heck, linen's clean and the food's good, so what's to complain about? Besides, the boredom ended about an hour ago."

"What does that mean?"

"Tell him, Rick."

"You won't believe this, a man all dressed in black comes over to our table and wants us to meet his boss. Guess who his boss is?"

McKiever pursed his lips, thinking. Obviously, it had to be somebody he knew. He shrugged his shoulders, taking a guess, "Don't tell me it's the man we're investigating, that would be too good to be true."

"Almost, but you're close. This man works for the Bar High owner."

"You mean, he works for Mike McCormick?"

"Yep, he's McCormick's lawyer."

McKiever rolled his eyes. "Talk about opportunity! Tell me, was this man dressed in black, wearing pinstriped pants, fancy black boots, and carrying a silver-plated forty-five?"

Josh was surprised. "You know him?"

Smirking, Mac answered, "Yeah, I met him. I ran into him in my favorite border town. He was giving the stable owner a hard time. I tried to shame him, but he didn't even blink. I figured him for a lawyer. The last thing I couldn't forget was that smile of his."

"That's him." Josh shook his head. "He told us he's McCormick's legal counsel for the Bar High."

"Why did he come to your table?"

Josh looked at Rick, both laughing, Rick answering, "I was flirting with this waitress and he shows up thinking we're businessmen. I gave him a phoney story about how the railroad is considering Fredonia. I told him if the railroad decides to come, we represented investors who would be interested in the town. He bought it hook line and sinker, didn't he, Josh?"

"He sure did. Even better, he invited us to stop at McCormick's office in town and meet with them."

McKiever looked at both men, pleased. "Seems too good to be true, doesn't it? Well, a visit to McCormick's office will have to wait. I have another appointment for you two. I want you to go to the bank and see a Jonathan Barker. He's a loan officer, who Olcott thinks can be trusted. If possible, I want a trace on McCormick's money trail. From what I've been told, the Bar High isn't making that much money from raising beef, so the question is, where is all the money coming from? A word of caution here, stay away from the bank president, apparently he's a puppet for McCormick's interests." McKiever hesitated, not wanting to forget anything, before continuing, "Everyone has a paper trail. This McCormick didn't arrive out of nowhere, so let's find out where he came from. If we can uncover his past history, we might get enough evidence to arrest the scoundrel."

Josh liked it. "What you say makes sense."

Rick spoke up, "Yeah, good idea. If we can catch the snake, we cut off the money. No money, no payroll, which means no crooks. You have any other plans, Mac?"

"Not yet. After you uncover what you can at the bank, we'll develop a plan for your meeting with McCormick and his fancy pants lawyer. Right now, I want to avoid being seen by that lawyer fellow. He knows I'm a Texas Ranger. I'm pretty sure he's the only one. By the way, what's the lawyer's name?"

Josh answered, "Randell Wynncliff."

"That's an easy name to remember. Before I forget, I won't be staying in town. I'll be using Jeff's ranch as my headquarters. You can get word to me through Olcott, or when Jeff's in town. Also, check the stalls in back of the jail. If I'm in town, my horse will be there. Other than that, you know where I'm staying, and I know where you're staying. Any questions?"

Rick looked at Josh. "I can't think of any."

McKiever rose. "Good, both of you have the ideal cover to snoop around while posing as investors. Which means you can nose around without attracting suspicion. Just be careful not to sound like lawmen. Make sure you ask money questions, remember, you represent investors."

Josh spoke up, "Character references are important in the business community, so wouldn't it be natural to want to know about McCormick? The same's true about his lawyer, right?"

"I like the way you're thinking, Josh. You're right, I'm also thinking you should also visit with the local merchants who keep money accounts. Don't forget the little folks, strike up some conversations with them. You'd be surprised how much they know, and how they like to talk. Tell them you represent businessmen. I guess that's about it for now."

McKiever started for the door, stopping. "Keep Sheriff Olcott informed whenever possible since I'll be checking with him on a regular basis. Good luck, and keep me posted."

Jeff Kincaid stood still, watching the sun send shafts of gold stretching across the flats. The late afternoon sun was dropping rapidly, bathing the hills in different shades of yellow. Jeff often reminded himself to stop being so busy and enjoy the beauty surrounding his ranch. Today he remembered, watching the tapestry of unfolding colors. Relaxing, he leaned against a fence post, letting time slip by. Finally, Jeff checked his timepiece. In another hour it would be dark; it was time for him to finish up before he got caught by the night.

Swinging his gaze toward the south, he saw a dust cloud rising from the road leading toward the ranch. It was then that he remembered the overdue supplies. He had completely forgotten Sam and Ben. He frowned, wondering why they were so late.

Watching the wagon piled high with supplies rolling into the yard, Jeff marveled. Maybe that's why they were so tardy, he thought. It was easy to imagine the supplies constantly falling off the wagon as they traveled along the road. He approached the rig, his voice curious, "I plum forgot about you fellows. Why so late?"

Sam fidgeted, Ben seemed uncomfortable, neither speaking.

"All right," Jeff's voice a command, "let me hear about it."

Sam spoke, looking toward Ben as if wanting help. "I reckon we made a mistake. We got the wagon loaded early. After that we went over to the watering hole."

"You mean saloon?"

"Yes, sir, saloon."

"So, you soaked up some whiskey?"

Both nodded, Ben speaking up, "We're mighty sorry, Mr. Kincaid."

Jeff scolded them. "Both of you know the rules, no drinking while on the job. When you're off payroll you can do anything you want, that's your business. But today you were hauling ranch supplies with my wagon, while doing ranch business. That translates into ranch money, my money. If you had an accident, I would have skinned you two alive!"

Ben answered for both, "We won't do that again, we promise."

Jeff eyed his men. "I'm surprised you stayed in the bar all day. That's not like you two."

Sam shook his head. "No, Mr. Kincaid, we didn't plan on staying long, but two Bar High men started up on us. We were trying to look like we wasn't afraid, so we had another round."

Ben interrupted, supporting Sam, "That's true, Mr. Kincaid. We stayed longer 'cause we didn't want those men to think they could run us out the saloon."

"You know, Ben, bad as your reasoning was, I believe you. So what happened next?"

"Well," Ben continued, "we stayed a little longer, hoping they would leave. But we could see they wasn't going to let up, so we left. As we walked out the door, they followed us. When we got into the street, they got real personal, trying to goad us into a gunfight. Right, Sam?"

Jeff shifted his stare at Sam.

Sam suddenly looked eager to talk, blurting out, "We got saved by a stranger!"

"Saved by a stranger, go on."

"We surely did. He came out of nowhere. Seems like he was between the horses. We didn't see him till we heard him. When we saw him, he was standing in the street."

Jeff waited, this story was getting interesting. "I'm listening."

"He told them bad guys he's looking for a quiet town for some investors. That black-bearded gun slinger tells him to mind his own business. The next thing I see, the stranger draws his gun." Sam rolled his eyes. "Mr. Kincaid, I never seen such a fast draw. He's the fastest gun I ever saw."

Sam hesitated, his eyes wide, his voice excited, "Tell you the truth, Mr. Kincaid, he handled them two like a man of the law, didn't he, Ben?"

Jeff eyed Sam. "Why do you say that Sam?"

Sam thought a minute. "For one thing, it's the way he used Ben and myself. He told us to get behind those two gunfighters, pick up their guns, empty them, then stick those bullets in their pockets. He said to put them bullets in their holster side. That part really got me. After that, the man told us to put the six-shooters back in their holsters. He was very professional."

Ben interrupted, "Mr. Kincaid, the man saw everything. I mean, he don't miss nothing. When them two is climbing on their horses, he warned them not to use their rifles. If they did, he had a Sharps, and would shoot them off their horses."

Jeff recoiled, hearing the word Sharps. His eyes sparkled, his voice excited, "Hold it! Did I hear you say the word Sharps, as in rifle?"

Sam, startled at Jeff's reaction, nodded yes.

Holding up his hand, Jeff looked at each man. "You didn't think to ask for the man's name, did you?"

Sam felt stupid. He looked at his partner. "We were in a bad situation and just glad to be out of it. At times like that you don't think to ask the questions you should."

"How about a description, what did he look like?"

"About six feet tall, kind of lean with brown hair and a small mustache. His face was a little weather beaten, like he spent time out on the range. Ben, did I miss anything?"

"Not really. I kind of remembered his eyes, they kind of bore a hole right through you. That's about it."

Jeff's question was quick, "You didn't happen to notice the color of his eyes, did you?"

Ben remembered, his response as quick. "Steel gray."

Feeling excitement, Jeff needed more confirmation. "How about his horse, you didn't happen to see a big roan-colored horse, did you?"

Sam's eyes widened. "Say, now that you mentioned it, there was a big roan tied up to the hitch rack. Do you know this fellow, Mr. Kincaid?"

Jeff pushed his hat back. "Maybe. If he's who I think he is, we have some serious help on the way." He shifted his eyes to the wagon. It was time to get the supplies unloaded. "How do you two have the wagon loaded?"

Sam was still curious about the stranger. "Mr. Kincaid, who is that man?"

"Sam, he may be a man I used to work with. We should know pretty soon. If it's him, I'll introduce you. Now, back to the wagon."

Sam gestured toward the rear. "We remembered what you told us; we loaded the barn stuff first, then the kitchen supplies."

"Good, you two did something right today. Both of you know the drill. What goes on last, comes off first. Take the wagon around back to the kitchen door. I'll meet you there." Spinning away, Jeff crossed the yard. Climbing steps two at a time, he pushed open the front door. Sara was in the alcove, a dust rag in her hand. She turned, smiling.

"Sara, I think you better set an extra plate at the dinner table tonight. I'm not sure, but I think we might have company."

Sara's face showed pleasure; she always enjoyed visitors. "Okay, Jeff, but you did say might, didn't you?"

"I did say might. It's a hunch I have, and my instincts are usually pretty good. Besides, it's better to be prepared than not."

Laughing, Sara teased him, "Jeffrey, you always confuse me. Would you please tell me who might be coming?"

"The person who might be coming is William McKiever."

Sara's heart jumped, her voice eager, "How do you know? Is Mac in town?"

"Ben and Sam ran into trouble while picking up supplies. A stranger bailed them out. Sam said the man was lightning quick with a gun. I asked for a description, and based on what they told me, if it's not Mac, then he has a double. What makes me think it's him, is that Sam saw a roan tied up to the hitch rack. Sara, I don't have to tell you what type of horse Mac rides."

Sara felt excited, her voice hopeful, "Jeff, if it's Mac, what makes you think he'll come tonight?"

"Because I left word with Olcott. I told him if McKiever shows up, send him here." Jeff could see Sara's eagerness. "Honey, I hope I'm right, but we'll just have to wait and see. In the meantime, tell Louchow to make extra food." Turning, Jeff started for the kitchen. "If you need me, I'll be out back helping the boys unload kitchen supplies."

McKiever turned Friend onto the main road leading away from the darkening streets. The moon was already halfway into the evening sky. Mac marveled at the soft glow illuminating the road. Thanks to the night sky, the ride was going to be easy. Friend kept tugging at the bit, wanting to run. Relaxing the reins, McKiever gave permission. Friend broke into his mile-eating trot, the trail unwinding, the ride almost surreal. The road steepened, curving west. Pulling back on the reins, McKiever slowed Friend into a walk. Topping the rise, horse and rider stopped. Mac stared into the valley below.

The lights from the Upper Forks Ranch twinkled below, mixing with the moon's soft glow. It was a breathtaking sight. Looking at the distant ranch, McKiever thought about Sara, that anxious feeling returning. Shifting in his saddle, he tried to shake it. The feeling remained, refusing to go away. Again, he reminded himself of those dangerous years when he and Jeff had faced death, each depending on the other. He scolded himself to remember those times and that friendship.

Forcing his mind away from his feelings, McKiever swung his gaze away from the ranch. Staring at the dark hills, he stiffened in the saddle. A light had flickered high on the hill. Alert, he watched, waiting. Again, he saw it. Someone was up on the mesa. Shifting in his saddle, McKiever reached into his saddlebag, pulling out his brass telescope. Bringing up the scope, he flipped the reins over Friend's head. Squeezing with his legs, a signal for Friend to be still, he scanned the mesa. A cigarette, barely distinguishable, glowed in the darkness. To the right of the glowing cigarette, a match flared briefly, highlighting a face. Two cigarettes now glowed in the darkness.

McKiever brought the scope down. At least two men were up there, the question was why? Turning, he slipped the scope back into the saddlebag. Stretching over Friend's neck, he recovered the reins. It was time to find out how many men were up there. Swinging Friend, they started back down the road. Keeping his horse at a slow walk, McKiever searched for fresh tracks. Three hundred yards down the road he found them. Two sets of hoof prints could be seen leaving the road, following a game trail leading toward the mesa.

McKiever considered his options. He could sneak up on whoever was there, but what good would that do? Not much, he reckoned. Another option was to continue down the road heading for the ranch. If he did, he would be seen, which might arouse suspicion, something he didn't want. His third option was to follow the game trail down the hill, and ride in from the south. He would be seen, but most likely mistaken for a hired hand coining in from a late chore. Mac liked his last choice. Turning Friend, they started down the hill.

The mule deer path was easy to follow, eventually swinging west. A half hour later McKiever pointed Friend up the hill toward the ranch. Cresting the hill, they entered the yard. Better to ride in slow, he thought. He would tie up at the bunkhouse. The yard was big, almost five minutes passed before they neared the bunkhouse. Pulling up, he dismounted. He could hear loud cursing and laughter coming through the walls. It sounded like the men were having fun, perhaps a card game was in progress. Wrapping Friend's reins, he started for the ranch house. Pausing at the steps, Mac wrestled with his emotions. He was about to see old friends, yet he was jumpy, almost scared. He chided himself. What type of Ranger was he anyway? Almost angry, he climbed the steps, grabbing the brass knocker, slamming the knocker against the stout door. Listening, he heard footsteps. The door swung open, bright light flooding the porch.

Jeff Kincaid stood in the doorway, a large grin spreading across his face. Damned if he didn't look as handsome as ever, McKiever thought. Jeff's hand reached out wrapping around Mac's arm, pulling him inside, his voice enthusiastic, "Sara, look who's here!"

"William McKiever," Sara's soft voice bridged the distance, "we're so glad you're here. Come over and give me a hug."

Still smiling, Jeff pushed him.

Sara snuggled into him, her hands digging into his arms. Suddenly McKiever relaxed, a special feeling overcoming him, his anxiety gone. It felt good to be wanted, maybe loved. Sara let go, stepping back. "Jeff told me to set a place for you. Are you hungry?"

Surprised, McKiever looked from Sara to Jeff. "Wait a minute, how did you know I was in town?"

"Because," Jeff touched his arm lightly, "you saved my men in town, that's how I knew."

Puzzled, McKiever eyed Jeff. "But how did you know it was me?"

"When my men got in late, I gave them the third degree. Of course, neither of them had the good sense to ask for your name, but I kept prodding them. Eventually they got to telling me how you threatened them two no-accounts with that Sharps rifle you own. I got to thinking it was you, so I asked them if they happened to see a big roan-colored horse tied up near the saloon. Sam remembered seeing such an animal, the rest is history."

McKiever shook his head, chuckling, "You still haven't lost your Ranger skills, have you?"

"You know, Mac, once a Texas Ranger, always a Ranger. After all those years a man doesn't lose that." Jeff pointed to the dining room. "Mac, we have hot food. Are you hungry?"

McKiever looked at Sara. "Sara, I did eat, but now I'm feeling guilty. I just might have room for more, especially since it's home cooking."

Sara felt elated; just seeing Mac gave her such happiness. Reaching out, she held his hand. "Only if you're hungry, but we did hold off from having dessert. We planned on having fresh apple pie with you after dinner." Sara laughed, knowing his favorite pie was apple. "We saved ourselves."

"Sara, bring on that pie."

Sara jumped up, disappearing into the kitchen. Gesturing toward a chair, Jeff escorted McKiever to the table. "Mac, get comfortable. I'll get the coffee." Starting for the kitchen, he stopped. "I almost forgot, you don't drink coffee after the morning hours."

McKiever waved his hand. "Tonight, I make an exception. Get the coffee."

Sara was back, her voice radiant. "Don't either of you dare eat until I say grace."

Jeff nodded, placing the coffeepot on the table. He wagged his finger at McKiever. "Around here, Mac, some things don't change."

McKiever smiled, looking at Sara. "Yes, I remember."

Sara scolded them. "Hush, you two, both of you please bow your heads." Waiting until their heads were bowed, she began, "Dear Lord, we're so thankful for you bringing us back together again. We missed William; he is part of our family. Most of all, protect us in our dangerous circumstances. We trust in you, and are thankful for this day and all that it has brought. In your precious blood, amen."

Mac took the first bite, stopping, he complimented Sara, "Delicious! Sara, what a treat! Jeff, you sure got lucky, I might add, in more ways than one. You know what, Sara, I bet if we ask him, he'll admit it!"

Jeff stopped eating. "Don't worry, Mac, she reminds me all the time. Don't you, honey?"

Looking at the table, and at the men she cared for the most, Sara felt her world was complete, laughing, "Not every day, but most of the time. Whenever Jeffrey gives me a hard time, I remind him about you."

"Does it work?"

"Yes, and you can ask him."

The small talk ceased, the pie rapidly disappearing. Reaching for his coffee cup, Mac figured it was time to talk business. He usually avoided talking about danger with womenfolk present, but Sara needed to know. Pushing his plate back, he spoke, "Well, that was some surprise. Sara, thanks, you remembered apple pie is my favorite, so that was special." Taking a sip of coffee, he became serious. "I met with Sheriff Olcott before I came here, so I'm going to bring you up to date. After I finish, if there's anything you can tell me, please do so."

Jeff set down his cup. "You go ahead. If you miss anything, I'll let you know."

McKiever took his last sip, placing the cup out of reach. "Two of our undercover men have been at the hotel for over a week." Mac saw Jeff's surprise. "They're posing as businessmen. Jeff, you know them, one is Rick Marten, the other is Josh Maclaren. By tomorrow they will have met with Jonathan Barker, a loan officer at the bank. The idea is to trace McCormick's money trail, and whatever else. Hopefully, that investigation will lead to something we can use. We do know McCormick's cattle aren't making money for the Bar High, so that brings up the question, where is McCormick's money coming from? There's another recent development. A lawyer representing the Bar High approached Josh and Rick, extending an invitation to meet with McCormick. The lawyer mistook them for businessmen, so that's in the works. This brings up your ranch. I understand you received an offer from McCormick?"

"Yes, we did."

"How much time before you give him your answer?"

"This coming Wednesday."

McKiever stared at Jeff. "All right, I'd like our plan of action to be built around this coming Wednesday. That doesn't give us much time, but it should be enough. Hopefully we'll have more information by then. From what I understand, this McCormick doesn't waste time. If and when he moves, we can make arrests. There is something else. Jeff, I'm going to ask Olcott to deputize you. Is that okay with you?"

"Why not a Ranger? Why a deputy?"

"Sorry, but you're a local citizen, so you're going to become a town deputy."

Jeff wasn't happy. "Fair enough, but just so you know, there wasn't any way you could come here to help us without me becoming involved. I want you to know that."

"Jeff, I never doubted that. There's something else both of you need to know."

Sara spoke for the first time, "You look concerned, why?"

"Do I? I guess because I'm always cautious until I swing into action. But you need to know that as we talk, your ranch is under surveillance."

Jeff's body tightened, "By who?"

Sara, her eyes wide, glanced at Jeff as he spoke.

Mac rolled his shoulders. "I have no idea. As I was riding in I stopped to enjoy the view. Looking around I saw a match flare up on the mesa.

Using my scope, and studying some horse tracks, I determined two men are up there. Based on your reactions, you didn't know?"

Jeff leaned forward. "I had no idea. Where up on the mesa?"

"Right at the base, where the steepest part starts up. It appears your ranch is important to someone. Tell me, is it possible to get a man up there without him being seen?"

"I'm not sure, but I'm going to find out! I do have one man who knows that ridge."

"As soon as you can, get a rifle up there. If we can keep those spies under observation without them knowing it, it should work to our advantage. If we can get a description, we can make some isolated arrests. It's always easier grabbing one polecat at a time. In this case, two would be even better. At any rate, we want every arrest to be permanent."

Looking at Sara, Jeff folded his arms, making a decision. "Tell you what, Mac, I'll send two men up there. That way we can have a rifle on them at all times while the other man can give us regular updates." Jeff spoke to Sara. "I'm going to post Clay Johnson at the house. He'll be here every day. Sara, please do not leave the ranch without Clay or myself, okay?"

"Yes, Jeff, I understand." Sara turned her attention back to McKiever. "Mac, how dangerous is our situation?"

"Hard to say, right now I like the way everything's falling into place. We do have the element of surprise, and that's good. However, we are dealing with dishonest people, which means we have to use our heads and take precautions. As of right now, they don't know we're on to them, so we have the edge. Even better, uncovering something from McCormick's past would allow us to initiate the law. Instead of us waiting to catch them in the act of breaking the law, we can start making arrests because they're already criminals." Mac saw a look in Jeff's face. "Looks like you were about to say something, Jeff, go ahead."

"We could arrest those spies if they're on wanted posters. That way McCormick would have three less guns when we make our move."

"Right, but I'd rather wait until we have some evidence on the others. If we do this right, we can get that whole crowd. As of now, McCormick has no idea three Texas Rangers are in town." Liking his logic, Mac shrugged. "That gives us time to sort out who's who. Now, before I take care of my horse, I notice at least three slices of pie remain, and since Sara made that special for me, I'm thinking I should have another piece."

Jeff eyed the pie, laughing, "Tell you what, I'll take care of Friend. Besides, Sara wants some of your time. Of course, when she gets done with you, I'll know everything without asking." Rising, Jeff headed for the door. The door swung shut, Jeff's footsteps fading.

Sara had her eyes on McKiever, her voice throaty, "William McKiever, I've been dying to know how you've been since you left us three years ago, wondering if you met someone. Have you?"

"You mean someone like you?" Mac teased.

Sara teased back. "That would mean you're going to church. Well, are you?"

"Sara, are you telling me the only way I'll find someone like you is in a church?"

"Yes, Mr. William McKiever, that's exactly what I'm telling you."

McKiever looked at Sara fondly. "Suppose I find a woman like you, but not in church. What would you say then?"

"First of all, you're not going to, but if you did, I would say you better take her to church. That is, if you're as smart as you think you are." Sara's hand reached out, resting on his. "Mac, I think about you all the time. Jeff and I talk about you. He knows exactly how I feel about you. We both love you. He in his way, me in my way, but regardless, you're part of our family."

Emotions stirring, Mac put the fork down. Staring at the floor, he fought for words, his voice hushed, "Sara, give me a moment."

Sara brushed away a tear, watching him.

Looking up, he smiled. "I can still remember the last time I saw you. I never forgot what you said back then, so I guess this is another moment to remember. You know, Sara, you always have a way of making a person feel special, thank you."

"No, Mac, thank you. You are special. We thought you'd be retired now. I was hoping you weren't, that you would be the one they sent. Now that you're here, I'm feeling guilty. It isn't fair of me to expect you to save us, but I still wanted it to be you. Mac, please forgive me?"

Patting Sara's hand, McKiever felt back in control of his emotions. "Sara, the only way I wouldn't have come was if I didn't know. You have to understand something, we Texas Rangers are a clannish bunch. Retired or not, we come to each other's aid."

The main door groaned open, Jeff entering, carrying McKiever's rifle and saddle bags. "I'll stick these in your room. One of the men is bedding down your horse for the night. You'll find Friend in the last stall at the far end. Did I give you two enough time?"

"Jeff, your timing was perfect. I was running out of words."

"Mac, you look kind of bushed. Either you're trail weary, or Sara's got you all stirred up."

"How about both. Truth is, I feel like I've been on the trail forever. I just got back to Ranger Headquarters, and then I'm on my way here."

"I recall those days. Come on, let me show you to your room."

McKiever rose. "Sara, thanks for my favorite dessert, and for making me feel welcome."

Smiling, Sara stood up. "We'll see you in the morning, Mac."

CHAPTER 5

The Bar High

Mike McCormick shoved open the office door, stomping toward his desk. He was a short man, built like a boulder. Thick slab-shouldered muscles seemed cemented to his stump-like neck. McCormick's face was round, his nose small. A furrowed brow gave his face a pig-like appearance. The man's wrists were thick like the trunk of a young juniper tree, a tree just beginning its journey toward maturity. Everything about his physical appearance suggested a man built for work requiring great strength.

McCormick ran his chubby fingers through his thick graying hair. His eyes darted from the door to his desktop. "Charlie!" he yelled.

The scraping sound of a chair came from the hallway. Seconds later a middle-aged man scurried into the doorway. "Yes, Mr. McCormick."

"Where's my morning schedule?"

"It's in the center drawer, Mr. McCormick."

"You're right, Charlie, I forgot I locked it up last night."

Charlie knew that was the closest type of an apology he would ever get from his boss. He spoke slowly, "You've got two appointments this morning, Mr. McCormick. One is with your lawyer, Randall Wynncliff, that's in another hour. The other appointment is with a Mr. Samuel Peckenpath. I do not have the exact time for his arrival."

Looking at Charlie, McCormick waved his hand. "You know why I keep you, Charlie?" Before Charlie could answer, McCormick answered his own question, "Because you are efficient at what you do." Sarcasm slipped into McCormick's voice, "If it wasn't for that, I'd fire you. You sure aren't handy with a gun, are you?"

"No, Mr. McCormick, I guess I'm not. Is there anything else you need?"

"Get me a fresh pot of coffee and three cups."

"Coming right up, Mr. McCormick."

McCormick chuckled. He liked to abuse Charlie, and the more he did, the harder Charlie tried to please him. Mike McCormick thrived on intimidation. He loved to watch people squirm; it gave him an immense feeling of satisfaction. Seeing Charlie looking for an opportunity to flee before scurrying away was intoxicating. McCormick had big plans, and so far, his abusive personality had produced results. As far as he was concerned, results were what mattered! Sitting down at his desk, McCormick congratulated himself. So far, his bold approach was opening up opportunities. Leaning back in his chair, McCormick thought about his political aspirations. Texas was a large state, large enough to cover his past. The town of Fredonia would be his springboard toward political success. This morning's appointment with Wynncliff was a first step toward providing a connection with people in high places at the state capital in Austin.

Charlie entered the room carrying a pot of steaming coffee along with three white porcelain cups. "Anything else, Mr. McCormick?"

"No, but when Wynncliff shows up, just send him in. As for Peckenpath, as soon as you see him coming, I want to know. And that includes interrupting me at any time, do you understand, Charlie?"

"Yes, sir, I'll keep a sharp eye out for him."

"You do that." McCormick dismissed Charlie with a wave of his hand. "Now get out of here."

Engrossed in catching up with his paperwork, McCormick lost track of time. The sounds of footsteps caught his attention. Looking up, he watched Wynncliff walk through the door with his ever-present smile. Sweeping the Stetson from his head, the lawyer bowed, his voice gushing with enthusiasm, "Good morning, Mr. McCormick, I trust I'm right on time."

McCormick eyed the clock, wishing the lawyer was late. How nice it would be to correct Wynncliff for being tardy. The man, always prompt, had a nauseating, do-good personality. Pushing back his chair, he greeted the attorney, "You're right on time. How about a cup of coffee?"

"Thank you, that would hit the spot."

"Help yourself." McCormick would be damned if he'd serve a man working for him!

Wynncliff poured his own coffee. Holding the cup in both hands, he took a sip before speaking, "Whoever made this coffee should be complimented." Flashing that smile, he noticed a white envelope with his name on it. Keeping his eye on the envelope, he settled into a chair, his voice pleasant, "The person who brewed this coffee is someone you should keep."

McCormick didn't try to restrain his sarcasm, "Charlie made the coffee, when you leave, tell him he's good for something." Wrapping his chubby fingers around the large white envelope, he passed it to Wynncliff. "Here's the paperwork you wanted; everything should be in order."

Wynncliff opened the envelope, scanning the paper quickly. "Good, before I head for Austin, I will go over everything. If all the T's are crossed and the I's dotted, you will not see me until I return." Looking up, he flashed his smile.

Seeing that smile, McCormick almost snapped, refraining himself. "How long will that be?"

"Hard to say, but at the most, three weeks. Oh, I almost forgot, I ran into two businessmen in town. They informed me that they represent several investors back East."

For a second McCormick's face showed alarm. "Where back East?"

"They didn't elaborate, but they did inform me that Fredonia was being considered as a possible railroad town connecting the south with the north."

Regaining his composure, McCormick relaxed, his voice reflecting curiosity, "Now that could affect property values, wouldn't you say?"

Wynncliff agreed, "Yes, very much. I took the liberty to invite those businessmen to your office in town. I explained that you are looking for investors." Wynncliff paused, his voice sounding self-congratulatory. "I pointed out that business and politics go hand in hand, which eventually promotes success for all those involved. I informed them that you are a rising political influence in Fredonia."

"What did they say?"

"They showed interest but expressed that any decision by the investors they represent depended on the railroad coming to Fredonia. Here, I wrote down their names." Reaching into his briefcase, Wynncliff handed a slip of paper to McCormick. "You may want to run a check on them." Rising from his chair, he offered his hand.

McCormick couldn't contain himself any longer, his personality gushing out, "How many times do I have to shake your hand?"

"Well," Wynncliff kept his hand out, "it's a common practice when a businessman and his attorney discuss matters of mutual concern, a handshake is proper protocol for departure."

McCormick growled, "What does protocol mean?"

"The word protocol means a business agreement on paper in proper order, and in this case, a conclusion of this meeting between two mutually interested gentlemen relating to that agreement."

"Is that so? Well, where I come from you shake hands when a deal is completed, and as of right now I'm looking at lots of loose ends." McCormick was feeling superior now; it was he and not the fancy pants attorney who was in control. "When you get back with this deal drawn up, and signed, that's when we'll do this handshake thing."

Wynncliff laughed, pulling back his hand. "As you wish. Good day, Sir."

Watching Wynncliff leave, McCormick shifted his stare to the paper containing the names of the businessmen. Was this good news, or bad news, he wondered? Whatever it was, tomorrow he would ride into town and open up the office. Perhaps those two businessmen would show up giving him an opportunity to size them, determining whether they were legit or not. The quicker he could confirm this railroad thing, the better he could take advantage of rising property values.

McCormick walked out of his office, crossed the room, stepping outside. Reaching into his vest, he extracted a cigar. Watching the lawyer ride off, he struck a match, lighting the cigar. McCormick wished he didn't need a man like Wynncliff, but he did. He needed the man's legal knowledge, but even more important, the man had connections with people in high places. Another advantage was how the bank president trusted the lawyer's legal expertise. That was important.

Puffing on his cigar, McCormick observed his foreman, Russ Wagle, crossing the yard. McCormick liked Wagle. The man was a quick thinker and as ruthless as himself. The only difference between them was that he had the money, and the foreman didn't. He smirked, whoever had the money, had control.

Russ stopped. Leaning against the porch he looked up at McCormick, his voice containing a strong Texas drawl, "Two of your men had a problem in town."

"Go on, what type of problem?"

"Clem and Ray were having a little fun with two Upper Forks cowhands when a stranger interfered. One thing led to another and the stranger pulled his gun. Clem said it was the fastest draw he's ever seen." Russ wiped his forehead before continuing, "Fact is the stranger was so fast that Ray thought he might be the man you hired, that Sam Peckenpath fellow. So, he asked him."

"Was he?"

"Nope. The stranger said he represented some money people back East who were looking to invest in a quiet town."

"A quiet town! Now, that's the third stranger who's suddenly interested in doing business in Fredonia." Flicking his cigar ashes over the railing, McCormick rubbed his chin.

Wagle's drawl slowed even more, "You don't say!"

McCormick nodded. "Wynncliff ran into two businessmen in town at the hotel who said they were interested in this town because the railroad might come here. You know, Russ, that means we might have to move faster than I wanted."

Russ shrugged his shoulders. "Funny, I ain't heard nothing about no railroad. I usually get wind of things like that."

McCormick looked at his foreman. Russ had a point, he thought. For several seconds both fell silent, each thoughtful. A gust of wind blew red dust across the yard. McCormick squinted at his foreman. "You said this stranger was fast, real fast?"

"Yep, and I'm thinking the man's a hired gun for someone. Maybe he's a railroad man?"

"Tell you what, Russ, get Clem and Ray over here, 'cause I want to hear more about this stranger."

"Sure enough, boss, be right back." Wheeling around, Russ crossed the yard, his destination the bunkhouse.

McCormick looked down at his cigar, the damn thing had gone out. Reaching into his vest he found a toothpick. Shoving the pick into the end of the cigar, he found another match. Tossing the toothpick, he scratched the match across the rail, watching it flare. Sticking the cigar back in his mouth, he brought the match up. Puffing furiously, the cigar came to life. Satisfied, he watched Clem and Ray approaching, followed by Russ.

McCormick was a man who liked to anticipate, his reasoning was simple, anticipation gives a man an edge. As the trio neared, McCormick guessed Ray would speak first. He was right.

"You want to know about this stranger, Mr. McCormick?" McCormick stared at Raymond's black beard, not answering. He was going to make Floyd feel uncomfortable before speaking.

Puffing on the cigar, he stared at the man, finally speaking, "First I want to know why you pushed them two cowhands? I told you we weren't starting anything until I said so! Go on, I'm listening."

"Yes, sir, I guess you did."

McCormick let Ray squirm, staring, before lashing out, his voice reflecting anger, "The next time you don't follow orders you'll be spreading wire at the north end of the range with the rest of the hired hands. You two understand?"

Both men nodded.

"Now, tell me about this stranger."

"We were in the street and he got behind us. I told him to mind his own business, then we swung around. As we were spacing ourselves, he pulled his gun."

McCormick's voice dripped with sarcasm, "Why didn't you pull yours?"

"We never had a chance; the gun just jumped into his hand."

Wagle asked the next question, "What did he look like?"

"About six feet, lean. But it was his eyes, and how he wore his gun that I noticed."

"Go on."

"He wore his gun low, tied down, kind of flared out. I knew he was trouble, but I never thought he would be that good."

McCormick's face broke out into a mocking smile. "You mean you were actually thinking?"

He looked at his foreman. "Russ, did you hear that? Raymond was actually thinking."

"I heard him, kind of tough to believe."

"Tell me," McCormick's stare intensifying, "why did his eye's spook you? They did spook you, didn't they?"

Ray glanced at Clem before responding, "Those eyes kind of froze you. It was like they kind of bore a hole right through you. Yeah, I guess you could say we were kind of spooked."

Clem nodded in agreement. McCormick saw that movement, his question directed at Clem, "What about you, Clem, you got something to add besides silence?"

"No, sir, not much more. The only thing was how relaxed he seemed, and when he pulled his gun, I could see why. Fact is, he could have killed us easy."

McCormick prodded, "Anything else?"

Ray answered, "He handled us like a lawman, that's what."

"Why do you say that?"

"He made us reach across with our opposite gun hands. Told us to drop our guns in the street. Then he tells them cowhands to get our guns and empty those bullets into the pockets next to our holsters."

"Why's that so strange?"

Ray shrugged, looking toward his partner, who remained silent.

Wagle answered McCormick's question. "I'll tell you why, boss, both of them are right-handed shooters. It's pretty tough to get them bullets out of the same pockets while using your gun hand, and still be ready to shoot."

McCormick understood. "By what I'm hearing this stranger's got experience at disarming people, which is something lawmen are good at. Is that what you're saying?"

"Maybe, or former lawmen. But whatever, that's professional work by someone used to handling a dangerous situation. Kind of makes a man suspicious, don't it, boss?"

Nodding, McCormick agreed, "Yes, it does. You two got anything else I should know?"

Clem spoke up, "I think Ray's right 'cause that stranger don't miss nothing. He saw our rifles and told us if we don't keep riding, he'd pick us off with his Sharps. Told us our carbines were toys."

McCormick crossed his arms. "You also said this gunman was representing investors, is that right?"

"Yes, sir," Clem's voice was eager, hoping to impress. "He told them investors wanted a quiet town, and he wanted our cooperation."

McCormick smirked. "Well now, he sure got that, didn't he! You two stick around the ranch for the rest of the day, I just might think of more questions to ask you. I'll let you know what I want done tomorrow." Sneering, McCormick looked sideways at both men. "Maybe you two should practice drawing your guns so the next time a fast gun shows up, you won't have to stick your hands up in the air!"

Russ couldn't help himself, doubling over in a gasp. McCormick enjoyed his foreman's outburst, the sneer remaining in his face, his voice chastising, "You two get out of my sight."

Waiting for Russ to stop chuckling, McCormick watched his hired guns depart. He turned his attention to his foreman. "What do you think, Russ?"

"I'm thinking that maybe this hombre is tied in with the railroad, and railroads hire detectives with law enforcement backgrounds." Russ looked at his boss. "That might explain some things. On the other hand—"

McCormick liked his foreman's possible explanation. "Tell you what, tomorrow you and I are going into town, open up the office, and see if the two business fellows walk in. I'd sure like to check them out, so I know what's going on."

"What time, boss?"

McCormick cursed, throwing his cigar into the dirt. "Damn thing's gone out again!" He looked at his foreman. "Russ, I'll see you at nine in the morning." Turning, he crossed the porch. Entering the hallway, he saw Charlie standing near the large front window.

"Charlie, don't forget, the moment you see this Peckenpath, let me know."

"Yes, Mr. McCormick."

McCormick entered his office, snuggling into his spacious leather chair, his mind mulling over the sudden arrival of so many strangers. Lost in his thoughts, at first, he didn't see Charlie standing in the doorway. "What is it, Charlie?"

"A rider's coming in. He's riding a black horse. He should be here in a minute or two."

"You know what I want; just do it."

Opening his desk drawer, McCormick pulled out an envelope with a blank piece of paper. Spinning around, he reached over, touching the coffee pot. Good, it was still hot. Hearing a whisper of sound, he swung his chair around. He froze, a chill shooting through his body. The man standing in the doorway looked like death. Two black eyes stared at him. It seemed as if the eyes had no pupils, only dark recesses. The man's face was a ghostly white, stringy black hair accentuating the eyes. Except for the face and shirt, everything else was black. Two mahogany-handled revolvers hung on each hip.

Regaining his composure, McCormick avoided the man's eyes. Instead, he looked at the man's mouth. Not staring at those black eyes gave him some relief. "You must be Samuel Peckenpath. I've been expecting you."

Peckenpath's voice froze McCormick. The man's words were deliberate, spaced out, "Who do you want me to kill?"

An ominous feeling rippled through McCormick. The man's voice didn't sound human, the sound coming from everywhere at once, almost like an echo from some distant location. A small bead of sweat broke out over his lip. Trying to maintain his composure, the Bar High owner cleared his throat, "I'm not sure yet. Right now, I need you as an insurance policy. There's a retired Texas Ranger in town who's snooping around, and just the other day a stranger appeared in town who's awfully fast with a gun." McCormick leaned back, suddenly feeling back in control. "I may need you for more than one person."

"It will cost you. You won't get two for the price of one. I don't come cheap, and that's not negotiable!"

It took a second for McCormick to answer; the man's eerie voice kept spooking him. Again, he cleared his throat. "That's no problem. You can stay here until I need you."

"Sorry, I never stay where I work." Peckenpath's voice hissed, "I come, I kill, then I leave."

McCormick felt like he was in a box-canyon. It was as if this killer wasn't in the room with him. Even worse, it was the killer who was in control, not him. He managed to keep the fear out of his voice. "I see, how will I contact you when I do know?"

"The same way you first did. You send a telegraph message. When you do, I'll be here in seven to twelve hours."

Licking the perspiration from around his mouth, McCormick protested, "That's kind of lengthy. Can't you move faster than that?"

"That's your fault. When you know who you want killed, I work. I won't hang around for maybes. Another thing, I want half the money up front in cash. The other half can be sent to the address I gave you. If the money's not there in thirty-six hours, I'll kill you next."

For McCormick, time seemed to be standing still. It was like he was suspended in an eerie void, the killer's echoing voice freezing him into a state of immobility!

The killer's voice continued, "The minute you tell me who, or how many, I'll come. I work fast, so have the balance of money ready."

Never in his life had McCormick been so intimidated. He was scared with no alternatives. The gunfighter had gained complete control and he knew it. McCormick needed this killer, but it was like dealing with the devil. If, he thought, there was such a thing. Trying to look relaxed, he glanced at the fixture hanging from the ceiling. "Alright, but I still don't know who. How should we do this?"

"I suggest you make it easy on yourself. Give me a total payment for one person, and if it becomes two, you've met the retainer requirements for two. If I just kill one, you're all paid up."

"Charlie!" McCormick bellowed, "get in here!"

Charlie materialized in the doorway. "Yes, Mr. McCormick."

Writing a money amount on paper, McCormick stepped forward, handing it to Charlie. "Get this amount from the safe. Hurry up, Mr. Peckenpath has other commitments."

Standing next to Peckenpath was unsettling, McCormick feeling queasy. Handing Charlie the paper brought him close to the gunfighter, much closer than he wanted. There was an ominous aura surrounding the man. Turning, McCormick retreated behind his desk. Seeing the coffeepot, he stole a glance at Peckenpath. "Can I offer you some coffee?"

The man didn't answer. He just stood there, as if not hearing.

"Perhaps," McCormick tried again, "we could wait out on the porch till my man gets back? The morning is quite pleasant."

The gunfighter smiled, McCormick wishing he hadn't seen it. He was more unnerved now than before. The smile was eerie, Peckenpath's narrow lips curling upward, displaying a thin smile, but his cheeks never moved. The corners of his mouth showed no visible wrinkles, the smile almost looking like a snarl. McCormick felt sweat gathering on his forehead. He hoped the man didn't see his fear. Dammit, he thought, what was taking Charlie so long? For the moment, time seemed to have stopped.

McCormick almost jumped. Peckenpath was pushing the door closed, that awful voice reaching his ears, "We'll wait here; it's better not being seen."

McCormick regained his composure, looking down at his desk. "As you wish. How about a cigar?" There was no answer. McCormick felt like killing Charlie for being so slow. Feeling trapped behind his desk, McCormick breathed a sigh of relief seeing the door swing open. Charlie walked in, clutching a bulging white envelope.

Relieved, McCormick gestured toward the gunfighter. "Charlie, give Mr. Peckenpath the money."

Charlie hesitated, surprise registering on his face. McCormick always counted any cash transaction. Puzzled, he passed the envelope to Peckenpath. The gunfighter slipped the money into his vest.

It was McCormick's turn to be surprised. "Aren't you going to count the money?"

"Why? If the money's not right, I know where you are."

Out of the corner of his eye, McCormick saw Charlie recoil. For the first time Charlie was hearing that voice. McCormick felt some solace; it wasn't just him getting spooked.

Peckenpath's voice changed, even more sinister. "One more thing, my identity is sacred to me. If I find out that either of you is responsible for disclosing it, it will be four deaths for the price of one."

Charlie's eyes grew round, staring at his boss. McCormick returned that stare, both shuddering. McCormick looked back, gasping. The killer, without making a sound, was gone. McCormick, seeing the front door ajar, headed for the porch. Hustling through the door, he searched for Peckenpath. Horse and rider were gone. A shiver swept through him. Stepping back, he eyed Charlie coming through the door. Charlie had a vacant look, his face ghostly white. McCormick broke the spell. "What do you think, Charlie? Did you see what I saw?"

Charlie was slow in answering, his voice a whisper, "Death, we just saw walking death!"

Grimacing, McCormick couldn't believe he'd asked Charlie! He never asked for Charlie's opinion on anything before! It was time to go back into his office and collect his wits. Leaving Charlie standing on the porch, he slowly crossed the hall, walking toward his office, his mind racing. Moving behind his desk, he considered what had just transpired. The man was a ghost, but that was good because the killer couldn't be traced back to him. After the job was done, the killer would disappear into thin air.

Reaching into his cigar box, McCormick grabbed for a cigar, his hand shaking. Unable to stop it, he growled at himself, his voice shattering the quiet, "Stop shaking, damn you!"

Charlie Walters hustled across the yard, heading for the sloping hillside. He needed to find a refuge where he could relax. He paused, hearing McCormick's yell. Starting again, he picked his way past a scattering of rocks and bushes, angling up the slope. Climbing high above the ranch, he found where the slope leveled off onto a wide ledge. Leaning against a large table rock, Charlie relaxed. Feeling the gentle breeze wash across his face, he listened to the sound of a meadow lark serenading the hillside. Up here, surrounded by sagebrush, he felt at peace.

A chirping sound attracted Charlie's attention. Two white-footed mice darted back and forth from beneath a clump of rocks. Studying their antics, he soaked up the sun's warmth. Distracted by the mice, Charlie forgot about the killer, the Bar High, the ranch owner Mike McCormick, and Russ Wagle. Almost an hour slipped past before his thoughts returned to the present. With a sigh, Charlie reflected on his situation. He needed this job at the Bar High and McCormick paid good wages. Everyone needs money, he thought, but he hated himself for staying there. The only thing saving him was that McCormick thought he was incompetent with a gun. For the first time today, Charlie half smiled. He had fooled all of them. None of the men knew he was skilled with a gun. As long as they thought his only value was that of a clerk, he wouldn't be dragged into their shenanigans. Unfortunately for Charlie, during the last year he'd seen too much. He was convinced that if he tried to leave now, he'd be killed. He had hoped to wait it out, but after seeing Peckenpath, he knew it was time to find another job. He had never seen such a man. Even McCormick himself was unnerved! Somehow, he had to figure a way to leave the Bar High, but how?

CHAPTER 6

Plan of Action

McKiever stepped into the hallway, the tantalizing smell of coffee and bacon pulling at him like a magnet. Entering the kitchen, he watched Sara turn, her smile radiant, her voice affectionate, "Good morning, Mac."

Returning her smile, he checked the kitchen clock, his eyes straying back to the stove. "Morning, Sara, looks like I slept in kind of late."

"You're not late; you're rested." Sara moved closer, looking into his face. "I can tell by your eyes you had a good night's sleep. I think you needed that." Touching his arm, her voice soft, she pointed toward the dining room. "Mac, please sit down. I'm going to wait on you. How many eggs, how much bacon, and how do you want your eggs cooked?"

McKiever sat, smiling. "Scrambled would be fine. As for the bacon, fill up the plate."

The coffee was hot. McKiever sipped, his mind jumping around. So much to do, and not much time. He was hoping for a completed plan by Wednesday. Strange, he thought, it was McCormick's upcoming meeting with Jeff which had given them their strategic time for initiating action. What type of action depended on last-minute evidence gathering.

Hopefully, the bank might provide some evidence. At least for now they had several advantages. Mac ran them through his mind. One advantage was that McCormick didn't know Texas Rangers were in town. Also, knowing McCormick had political aspirations, Mac was betting that the Bar High owner didn't know he had wanted men on his payroll. Another advantage was that he doubted the ranch owner had any idea he was under investigation. Other than those possibilities, it would be catch them in the act of breaking the law. Watching Sara enter with his plate piled high, he forgot about work.

Placing the plate before him, Sara saw McKiever was occupied with his thoughts. "Mac, I'm going to let you eat in peace, but after you're done, I have some questions. If you want anything, just yell."

"Sara, I'm getting spoiled and I like it. You can ask me questions whenever you want, including while I'm eating."

Sara turned, heading for the kitchen. "I'll be back when you're finished eating. I'm going to catch up in the kitchen, don't forget, call if you want more eggs or bacon."

Watching Sara disappear, Mac dug in. The food tasted good, so good that he was gulping it down. Scolding himself, he stopped. Taking a sip of coffee, he congratulated himself for gaining control. Savoring the food, he finished. Looking up, he observed Sara peeking through the doorway. "Sara, that was great. I'm full, no more room."

"Are you sure?"

"Positive." He poured himself another cup of coffee. "Come in and ask those questions."

Drying her hands, Sara sat down. "Mac, tell me about your ranch."

McKiever was surprised; he was anticipating more serious concerns. He adjusted his thinking. "Not much to tell, the barn's bigger than the house, the property has good grazing land with plenty of water. Besides that, there's a picturesque mountain behind my ranch."

"It sounds very pretty, is it?"

McKiever smiled. "Real pretty. You know, Sara, Colorado is God's country."

Sara's voice was wistful, "I would love to see your ranch and the land. Are you anxious to get there?"

"As soon as we fix up this town, I'll be on my way."

Sara's worries returned, her face showing concern. "Mac, how dangerous is our situation?"

McKiever measured his words, not wanting Sara to become overly frightened. Knowing she trusted him made him honest, but tactful. "Nothing I haven't seen before. Only one thing is bothering me."

"It's that gunfighter, isn't it?"

McKiever didn't answer her question. "One thing I don't want you worrying about is Jeff. I will make every effort to see that he doesn't get into a shootout with Peckenpath. I can't guarantee anything, but any assignment I give him should keep him away from that gunfighter."

Anger flooded Sara's face. "I hope you don't think I take any solace that it will be you who goes up against that killer! How do you think I would feel if something happened to you?" Her face tightened, eyes sparkling. "I would never forgive myself if anything ever happened to either of you!" Sara jumped out of her chair. Spinning around, she crossed her arms, staring at the ceiling. Shifting her stare at McKiever, her voice becoming a whisper, "Mac, I'm scared."

"Sara, sit down."

Sara sat, waiting.

McKiever's voice reflected authority. "I was placed by Captain O'Rourke as senior Texas Ranger in charge here in Fredonia. That's my job. I would never place one of my men in greater danger than myself. I never have and I'm not going to start now."

"I understand," Sara interrupted, "but I don't want anyone hurt because of us."

"It's not because of you or Jeff. This is a situation that you didn't cause, and I'm in the business of law enforcement. Can I make it anymore plain than that?"

"I guess not, but you would have been retired by now if it wasn't for us."

"You don't know that. The truth is I'm not retired, which means I'm still a Texas Ranger. You know what that means, Sara? That means I still have a job to do. As for your concern about me being here because of my concern for you, if I knew there was trouble in Fredonia, I would come anyway. It's an understanding we lawmen have; we protect each other."

Sara felt less guilty. Leaning back, she felt some of the tension leaving her body.

Mac continued, "You also need to know something else: Jeff did retire. In other words, he's not a Ranger anymore. Jeff will be deputized by Sheriff Olcott as a deputy sheriff. He won't be a Ranger, which also means he's not under my command. Now, I can't guarantee anyone will be safe, but I'm not placing a deputized ranch owner in the same responsibility as an active Ranger. Jeff's theater of responsibility will be here at the Upper Forks Ranch, and Sara, that would be his responsibility anyway, even if I wasn't here because of this problem."

Taking another sip of coffee, he let Sara digest his reasoning. Shrugging, he smiled. "Besides, where's your faith? You know, the faith you're always telling me about. Didn't you always tell me how God's in control?"

A little sparkle returned to Sara's eyes. "Yes, God's in control, and his control is sovereign concerning personal decisions. Do you understand what that means, William McKiever?"

"No, but I'm sure you're about to tell me!"

"You are given the opportunity to say yes or no. If you say yes to God, I wouldn't have to worry about your soul. That translates into why this Sunday you should go to church with us."

"I have to admit one thing, Sara, you and Captain O'Rourke have no quit in you. I'll think about your offer, and while I'm thinking, you pray about what's happening here. When and if God answers your prayers about our situation, you tell me about it. Look, Sara, I like the idea of God being real, but I need some evidence before I say yes. Isn't that reasonable?"

"William McKiever, you are a doubting Thomas! It's not good to test God, because God can bring a man very close to death to make him believe."

"Who is Thomas?"

"He was a disciple who didn't believe Christ rose from the dead until he pressed his fingers into the Lord's wounds. Then he believed."

"Now, I could go along with that Thomas fellow, because he saw evidence. Sara, I'm a lawman, and in my profession, we need evidence. You show me when God acts in this problem, and I'll go to church with you to check things out. You know, like that Thomas fellow did!"

With a sigh, Sara gave up, at least for the moment. The outer door swung open, Jeff entering, dropping a bundle of mail on the table. "Mac, you look rested. Has Sara been talking your ears off?"

"With my permission, but she's also been feeding me like a king. Jeff, you must be the most spoiled man in Texas!"

"I won't deny it. Life is good and whenever you get to that ranch of yours, you'll know what I'm talking about. That's if—" Jeff winked at Sara, "you find a gal like I did."

"Sure, sure, rub it in. Since you want to stick a little salt on the wound, let's change the subject. Since it has been awhile, I thought we should mount up and you can show me the range. At the same time, I can pick your brains. After that, if it's okay with you, we can ride into town. I want to formulate a plan with Olcott. How's that sound?"

"Like a plan. Sara, you stay inside, if you do go outside, don't go alone. I told Clay to stay handy; he's your escort until I get back." Jeff eased himself over to the window, gazing at the mesa. "I sent two sharpshooters up on the mesa early this morning. If those two spies are still up there, we've got them covered. I told my men to take turns coming down after dark. That way we can keep them in gunsight, and at the same time, know what they're up to."

McKiever stood up. "Smart move. Sara, thanks for the breakfast; it was great. Jeff, I'm going to slip out the back door and get saddled up. Give me a few minutes. I'll meet you behind the barn. I was real careful when I rode in last night so those spies wouldn't suspect anything. No sense advertising my presence until it becomes unavoidable."

Josh and Rick left the bank. Crossing the street, they approached the jail. The early afternoon sun's rays were pleasantly warm, the day almost hot. Both stopped as they neared the jail, Rick speaking, "I'm going to go around back to see if McKiever's horse is in the barn. Give me a second; this won't take long."

Josh watched him disappear around the corner. Shifting his attention across the street, he eyed McCormick's office. Two horses were tied up in front of the building. Rick appeared from around the corner, his voice eager, "Mac's horse is there. Let's check in with Olcott."

Josh held up his hand, stopping Rick. "Guess what, partner, two horses are tied up in front of McCormick's office. Take a look."

Staring across the street, Rick grinned. "Darned if you're not right. First, let's see if Mac's at the jail. If not, we'll go over to McCormick's office."

Stepping up on the boardwalk, Rick pushed open the jail door, slipping inside. Josh followed, pulling the door shut behind him. The jailhouse was full, Josh exclaiming, "Can you beat this, Rick? This town is full of Texas Rangers, even an ex-Ranger. Hello, Jeff, long time no see."

Jeff Kincaid, his smile a mile wide, extended his hand, joking, "Hey, McKiever, I thought Ranger Headquarters was going to send us some help, not these two womanizers."

Josh rolled his eyes. Grabbing Jeff's hand, he defended his partner and himself. "I was wondering about that myself. Except for Sheriff Olcott and his men, where's the help?"

The room filled with laughter, Olcott speaking out, "Thank God for me and my deputies, right, Mac?"

McKiever enjoyed watching the men have fun with each other, his voice adding to the banter. "You know, Olcott, I wouldn't have taken this assignment without you and your men. I did tell the captain I needed the best, but you know yourself there are times when we're forced to work with what's available." Waiting for the laughter to stop, McKiever asked a question, directing it at the two Rangers, "You two get to the bank yet?"

Rick spoke with enthusiasm. "Did we ever. Sheriff, you were right about Jonathan Barker; he's a straight shooter. We got a real good lead. It appears McCormick's money trail goes all the way back East."

Olcott was surprised with their success. "Where back East?"

"The Boston area. It looks like this McCormick has some connections to a seafaring business. Apparently, he started out as a deckhand on a freighter, became a first mate, and later a bookkeeper at the shipping end. After that, he seemed to disappear until he showed up here."

"Well," McKiever spoke, eyeing Olcott, "that's a solid lead to pursue. I'll contact Captain O'Rourke for a trace. You two did a nice job."

Eyeing his partner, Rick held up a hand for silence. "Josh, tell Mac what we just saw."

"We saw two horses tied up by McCormick's office. It looks like his place is open for business. We were thinking about going over and making contact with this McCormick. To tell the truth, I'm dying to size him up!"

"I'll tell you what, Josh," McKiever encouraged, "no time like the present. You two have an invitation, so take advantage. Just make sure both of you are on the same page. I'll catch up with you later at the hotel."

"Sounds good to me. Come on, Rick, let's pretend we're businessmen again."

Watching the two leave, McKiever had a thought, turning his thought into a question, "Tell me, Olcott, is there anyone at the Bar High who we might use? You know, an inside man?"

Olcott's face showed surprise. He was impressed, this McKiever was always thinking. "You mean, someone who works for McCormick?"

"Yes, that's exactly what I mean."

Jeff started to smile; he also liked Mac's thinking. "I know someone. His name is Charlie Walters."

Olcott frowned. "What makes you think Charlie's okay?"

"I'm not sure he's okay, but I see him every Sunday at church. Whenever I talk with him, he's very pleasant. What's more, he really gets into the worship service."

McKiever was hopeful. "If I'm hearing correctly, this Charlie's a strong candidate."

Jeff didn't hesitate. "I think he's a very good possibility. At least he's worth a try."

"Do you think you could catch up with Charlie at church and set up a meeting?"

"I think so," Jeff's face showed a hint of mischief, "but I've got a better idea."

"Go on."

"Why don't all of us go to church this Sunday? That way we have the perfect meeting place without arousing suspicion. Besides, none of that Bar High crowd ever attends church. You know, the more I think about it, it's the perfect location," Jeff looked slyly at McKiever, "especially since we're pressed for time."

Out of the corner of his eyes, McKiever could see Olcott was enjoying Jeff's suggestion, as well as his discomfort. Suspicious, he challenged Jeff, "The perfect place you say?"

Jeff nodded. "Absolutely. Who would suspect anything?"

Olcott wanted to agree, but knowing why politicians go to church made him cautious. "Now, Jeff, we know McCormick's interested in politics, but you say he never goes to church?"

McKiever picked up on Olcott's point, hoping for a way out. "Jeff, that's unusual. I mean, is that possible? McCormick's interested in politics, but he never goes to church?"

"Mac, normally I'd agree with you, and I'm sure if McCormick ever got elected to anything, he'd start playing the game. But as of right now, the man doesn't go to church. You know, Mac, it wouldn't hurt you to spend an hour in church; it might do you some good. Besides, Sara would be thrilled."

Olcott almost doubled over, regaining his composure. "Mac, look at it this way: since Charlie's a regular attendee, that provides the perfect meeting place as well as the time."

"All right, all right, I guess I can be bored for an hour."

Both Jeff and Olcott suppressed smirks, wrestling against laughter. Mac looked at one, then the other, his voice accusing, "Obviously, both of you are enjoying this."

"Onward Christian soldiers," Jeff laughed.

Walking over to the window, McKiever studied the street. "Well, both our deputies are in McCormick's office. I'm going to ride over to Fort Stockton and get a telegraph message off to headquarters. The sooner we get someone to contact that Boston shipping company, the quicker we'll find out about McCormick."

Moving to the door, he paused, searching out Jeff. "If I leave now, I should be back in time for dinner. How's that sound?"

Jeff grinned. "Sounds like you've been spoiled by Sara's cooking."

"I sure have." Mac looked at Olcott, asking, "Sheriff, I did tell Rick and Josh I'd see how their meeting went. Could you check for me and see how it turned out?"

Olcott nodded.

"Good, because if possible, I'd like a plan in place before Wednesday."

"Wednesday!" Olcott's face registered curiosity. "That's moving pretty quick!"

"Yes, but Jeff's supposed to let McCormick know if he's going to sell his ranch by Wednesday. The way I figure it, the minute he tells him no, McCormick will move. Once the Bar High starts causing problems, we need to be ready. I don't know of a better way to catch crooks than in the act." Grabbing the door handle, McKiever started to leave. Stopping, he stepped back inside the room. "I almost forgot, Sheriff Olcott, would you deputize Jeff after I leave?"

"Will do."

"Much obliged. Jeff, your area of responsibility will be your ranch. You already have two hard cases up in the hills spying on your place, not to mention whatever else McCormick's planning for your herd. Also, correct me if I'm wrong, but didn't you tell me that McCormick will be in town waiting for your decision?"

Jeff pointed across the street. "Yes, right over there, at his town office. McCormick told me once we reach an agreement, we'll finalize the deal right at the bank. In other words, the papers will be signed and I'll be paid in full."

"That's what I thought. Sheriff, when McCormick's in town, who's usually with him?"

"Hard to say. Most often he has two hired guns with him."

"Which means all of us will start right here in town. Let's hope that the black-bearded fellow and his buddy are with him. If we get good news from headquarters, maybe we can arrest all three and wipe out at least two of McCormick's gun hands before grabbing him. Since McCormick's the source of money, when we get him, the money supply is cut off!"

"Suppose," Olcott added, "we don't get the evidence we need from headquarters, then what?"

"Good question. Let's hope this Charlie Walters has some information we can use. Having an insider might give us the break we need. At least we're not putting all our eggs in one basket."

Olcott agreed, "I got to hand it to you, McKiever, you think of most everything."

"Not really, I'm just making educated guesses. I start with a plan and then adapt. I'm betting the minute Jeff gives him the bad news, McCormick will send his men into action. If we don't have any evidence on McCormick by then, we'll be forced into a defensive response, which is not my favorite way of operating. The good news is we still have some time, so let's be positive. In the meantime, I better get going if I'm going to get back in time for a home-cooked meal." Pulling open the door, McKiever walked into the street.

Walking up Main Street, McKiever stopped. Standing in the street staring at him was the man in black, Randell Wynncliff. "Well, Ranger, what brings you to Fredonia?"

Act natural, Mac told himself. "Just passing through, stopped to see a few friends. How about you?"

"This is one of several towns where my services are needed. I notice you're not wearing your badge."

Shrugging, McKiever's response was quick. "Even Rangers retire. Tell me, what type of services do you supply?"

"Legal service of the highest quality. I make sure all business transactions are legally correct. Compliance with the law is always given the strictest priority. I'm sure a man like yourself can appreciate such thoroughness?"

"So," Mac pretended ignorance, "you're a lawyer. I don't believe I know your name?"

"My name is Randell Wynncliff. I don't believe we have been formally introduced?"

"I guess we haven't. My name's William McKiever. Tell me, Mr. Wynncliff, are you expensive?"

Wynncliff smiled, pleasure showing in his face. "I'm very expensive. May I inquire why you ask, Mr. McKiever?"

"My new career is to become a rancher, which means I need to purchase some land. I was thinking you might be of service to me, but being expensive wasn't what I had in mind," Mac smiled, "especially, very expensive!"

"I see. Well, for a man representing the law I would make an exception. Men like yourself are a credit to this growing frontier. Here, let me give you my card. Tell me, Mr. McKiever, how might I contact you for any future transactions?"

McKiever took Wynncliff's card, studying it before answering, "I prefer not to give out my address. As you must realize, years of law enforcement work makes for lots of enemies. The way we avoid someone with a grudge is to keep my place of residence a secret. I'm sure you can understand that. Since I have your card, if I need legal services, I'll contact you."

"Certainly, I do understand. Of course, all client business is strictly confidential. You can rest assured of that."

"I'm sure, and again, thank you for being understanding." McKiever tipped his hat. "Now, I've got to move along, good day, Mr. Wynncliff."

Wynncliff remained still, watching McKiever depart. Interesting, he thought. The man's answers were evasive. Obviously, the years of law enforcement work served him well. The Ranger, or ex-Ranger, knew how to find out more than he told. Although the man was no longer wearing a badge, the obvious can be deceiving. Reaching into his vest, he pulled out a pad. He would send a note to McCormick before leaving. His messenger would be the stable boy, a good tip assuring delivery.

Turning the corner McKiever frowned, wishing he hadn't encountered Wynncliff. He didn't doubt his cover was blown. Shrugging, he continued on. Long ago he'd accepted the fact that life didn't always go the way one wanted. Nearing the stable, he heard Friend whinny. Entering his stall, he rubbed the big stallion's neck. Holding out a carrot, his horse gently removed the morsel from his hand. Reaching over, McKiever grabbed his saddle and blanket, flipping it over Friend's back. He waited until Friend finished eating before tightening the cinch. Slipping the reins over Friend's ears, Mac slipped the bit into his mouth. Rising into the saddle, he backed Friend out of his stall. Swinging south, they stayed behind the buildings. Reaching the last house, they turned, passing through a narrow alley. Turning at the end of Main Street, the road narrowed, becoming a trail leaving town.

"Come on, Friend, let's cover some ground. I'm planning on home cooking tonight."

CHAPTER 7

Sunday Morning

The church was typical for a small town. The outside was painted white with a tall steeple rising over the town. A white picket fence surrounded the building. Inside the fence, a few red roses contrasted against the white fence. Two long wooden benches faced the sparse flower beds. A well-raked dirt path passed between the benches leading up to the front door. The double entrance doors were made out of planked oak. Inside a single aisle separated two rows of wooden pews. Stained glass windows ran the length of the walls. Today the pews were full, the ladies dressed in flowery dresses, the men wore dark suits, blues and blacks dominating.

Pastor Harmon Olgilvie asked the congregation to rise for the singing of the doxology, to be followed by "How Great Thou Art" in preparation for dismissal. As the singing filled the church, McKiever couldn't help but enjoy the harmony rising toward the rafters. The singing ended, a hush settling over the congregation, giving Pastor Olgilvie a captive audience. He thanked the people, wishing them well, urging the congregation to walk in faith. If they did, Pastor Olgilvie assured them that they would experience God's remarkable influence in their daily lives. With that statement, he dismissed the people.

Sara turned, her face beaming. "Mac, wasn't it interesting how Pastor tied God's laws into what's wrong today?"

"I guess," McKiever conceded. "He did catch my attention on some points."

Sara looked at Jeff, her face still glowing, her voice enthusiastic, "What a perfect message for both of you. Mac, would you like to meet Pastor Olgilvie? I know he could answer any questions you might have."

"Maybe another time. Remember, Sara, we have an understanding that when God answers your prayers for our situation, you'll tell me. And when that happens, I'll visit with the pastor."

Sara looked at Jeff. "Jeffrey Kincaid, can't you speak any sense to him?"

Jeff leaned over. "Sara, if you can't influence him, how do you expect me to?" Watching Sara stare at him, Jeff laughed, "I'll tell you what I'll do. Give us some time and I will introduce Mac to some people, the type that might interest him. Okay?"

Sara agreed, "All right, how long?"

"Tell you what. Why don't you meet up with some of your lady friends. I see Wendy Phillips looking over here. Why don't you start with her? I'm going to take Mac over to meet Charlie Walters who's talking with Sheriff Olcott. Give us at least a half hour." Kissing Sara's cheek, Jeff assured her, "We won't be long."

As Sara departed, Jeff saw Olcott and Walters disappear into the church library. "Mac, Olcott and Charlie went into the library. Let's get over there." Leaving their seats, they worked their way across the room, stopping as church folks introduced themselves. McKiever was gracious, very polite. It seemed like it took fifteen minutes before they finally entered the library. Olcott and Walters were in the rear reading room.

Olcott spoke as they approached. "Charlie, I'm sure you know Jeffrey Kincaid."

Charlie smiled. "Jeff, good to see you again, especially in church."

"Hello, Charlie. Yes, it is good to be in church. Charlie, I'd like to introduce you to my good friend, William McKiever. Mac, this is Charlie Walters."

McKiever reached out gripping Charlie's hand. "Charlie, my pleasure."

Olcott shifted the conversation away from pleasantries. "Charlie, how's everything going at the Bar High?"

Charlie's beaming smile faded. At first, he didn't answer, trying to think of something positive to say. Finally, he spoke with a shrug, "I stay busy and that's good. To tell the truth, if the pay wasn't so good, I'd try to find another job."

Jeff was pleasantly surprised; Olcott's opening question had opened up an early opportunity. He took advantage. "Why do you say that, Charlie?"

"Well," Charlie looked around before completing his answer, "let me put it this way: McCormick and his hired men aren't my type of people."

"I see. Charlie, if you were offered another job, would you take it?" Charlie grimaced, not answering.

Olcott saw Charlie's reaction, drawing his attention. "Charlie, if we found you a ranch job paying the same money, would you leave the Bar High?"

For the first time Charlie suspected these questions had a purpose besides idle conversation. Alert, he looked at each face. "I'm afraid if I tried to leave the Bar High my life would be in danger." Charlie shifted his focus to Jeff. "Why are you curious about my work? I don't mean to be rude, but this meeting seems unusual to say the least. As a matter of fact, this is the first time I've ever met Mr. McKiever, so why is he here, and why all the questions?"

"That's a fair question. Sheriff, why don't you tell Charlie why we're having this meeting, and who McKiever is?"

"Sure" Olcott agreed. "Charlie, William McKiever is a Texas Ranger who's been sent here to investigate your boss. We figure you can help us, and that's why we're having this meeting."

Astonished, Charlie stared at McKiever. Seeing Charlie's reaction, McKiever's voice reassuring, "I asked Jeff and Sheriff Olcott if there was someone working at the Bar High we could trust. Charlie, both thought of you. I think that's quite a compliment, which tells me something about your character."

Jeff interrupted, "That's true, Charlie. I don't know what that skunk McCormick pays you at the Bar High, but anytime you're ready, I'll give you a job at my ranch with the same wages."

Charlie couldn't believe he was hearing this proposition. He studied Jeff's face, shifting his look at McKiever, returning his stare at Jeff.

Seeing Charlie's hesitation, Jeff prompted, "Charlie, what's sticking in your craw?"

Charlie became silent, focusing on the floor.

Jeff persisted. "I know that you believe in God. I told them I see you in church all the time, and how you get moved in the spirit. Now, Charlie, you know that God's about truth and standing up against evil. This is a chance for you. God's opened up a doorway of opportunity, which might not come again."

Charlie spoke slowly, concern written in his voice, "McCormick won't let me go. I know too much. If I try to ride out now, he'll kill me."

McKiever had an answer for Charlie's fear. "Who said you have to leave. We want you to stay at the Bar High. The only thing we need to know is—can you be trusted?"

Charlie stared at McKiever, slightly aggravated. "Yes, I can be trusted."

Satisfied, McKiever responded, "Good. We understand that McCormick won't let you go, but neither can we. Since you know what we're up to, you are now caught between a rock and a hard place, aren't you, Charlie?"

"I reckon."

"You reckoned right. The good news is that you have a way out. You work with us, and when McCormick gets taken down, you will not only have a good job, but also a clear conscience." McKiever paused, hoping to nail Charlie down, his voice encouraging, "A very good situation for a godly man."

Charlie paused before speaking, "In other words, you're looking for an inside man?"

Impressed, McKiever answered, "Yes."

"Tell me, Ranger McKiever, where's the rest of your help? The Bar High has lots of guns."

McKiever was beginning to respect this Charlie, the man's mind was quick, his concerns deserving an answer. "I'm not the only Texas Ranger in town, but I'm thinking it would be better if you didn't know about the others. Let me put it this way, what you don't know can't be pried out of you by McCormick. I can assure you of one thing: we have enough men to do the job."

"Charlie," Olcott spoke up, "I've also got two deputies, including Jeff who's been sworn in. Trust me, what Ranger McKiever said is true, we have enough lawmen."

"That's good because you're going to need them. McCormick's hired a killer, and I ain't never been more scared in my life!" Charlie paused, a shudder running through him, fear creeping into his words, "The man's name is Sam Peckenpath."

McKiever leaned forward, his eyes intent. "You've actually seen this Peckenpath?"

"I've seen him."

"Go on, Charlie."

"The man's walking death. Honest to God, this Peckenpath looks like the devil himself! I've never seen such a man in my whole life." Charlie frowned, clenching his fists. "Even McCormick looked like he'd seen a ghost!"

For a second McKiever couldn't think of a response. He glanced at Jeff, then Olcott. Both were frowning, staring at Charlie. McKiever realized they were about to be told what this killer looked like, curiosity in his voice, "Charlie, give us a description?"

"For one thing, he's got no eyes."

Olcott started to laugh, "Come on, Charlie, no eyes?"

Charlie didn't like anyone laughing at him, his face showing anger. "I said no eyes, and I mean no eyes! You can laugh if you want, but if you ever see him, you won't be laughing."

McKiever was quick, "I believe you, Charlie, but why did you say no eyes?"

"Because they look like two black coals without pupils. He has black eyebrows, and his face is pale, so pale it looks like a whitewashed picket fence." Charlie shook his head. "When he looks at you, it's like you're looking into your own grave."

The room was dead still, everyone staring at Charlie, thinking about his unbelievable description of the gunman.

Charlie's voice became a whisper, barely audible. "I'm telling you, Peckenpath looks like death. He don't make no noise when he walks. He's there, and then he's gone, almost like he was never there in the first place."

This time Olcott was more tactful. "Was he wearing boots?"

"Yeah, he was wearing boots, black ones. Fact is, everything he wears is black except for his shirt, that's white."

McKiever spoke, "Is he right handed or left handed?"

"Can't tell, the man's packing six-shooters on each hip. But there's something else that gives a man the shivers. It's how he sounds when he talks."

"How does he sound?" McKiever asked.

"Like an echo out of hell, that's how!"

"Echo out of hell, what type of sound is that?"

"Kind of like the sound of wind sweeping through a canyon, producing a voice from everywhere at once. You can see the sound's coming from him because his lips are moving, but his voice is all around you." Charlie looked at each man. "He's a killer from hell alright, and I wish I'd never seen him."

McKiever could almost feel Charlie's fear. "Why do you say that, Charlie?"

"'Cause he told McCormick and myself that if he ever finds out that we gave out his identity, he'll kill us. I guess since I just told you, I'm as good as dead. Anyway, I've never seen anything so evil!"

Jeff interrupted. "Charlie, do you know where he's staying?"

"Tell the truth, Jeff, that Peckenpath left the office and goes outside. After we got over our shock, we followed after him. We were only a couple seconds behind him, but when we got outside, he's gone. We don't see no horse, no nothing!"

Jeff felt spooked. "Charlie, please don't tell me there were no tracks?"

Charlie cocked his head, shrugging his shoulders. "Yeah, there was tracks. This Peckenpath's real alright, but he's a mystery man. I'm telling you, he's a bad one for sure."

McKiever could see a concerned look in each face. Not liking what he saw, he changed the subject. "Charlie, can you tell us what went on in McCormick's office?"

"I didn't hear everything. I only got called in to go get the money from the hidden safe to give to Peckenpath. After I gave him the money, that's when he threatened us. But I could see McCormick was all shook up because he didn't even count the money. That's all I know."

"I see, do you know if McCormick keeps records in his safe?"

"Yep, he does. Every transaction has two records, and he keeps receipts for every dollar removed, or added to that safe. McCormick also keeps records in his desk drawer until the end of the day."

"Do you know the combination to the safe?"

"No sir. He was expecting Peckenpath, so he left it open."

"So, Charlie, he kind of trusts you, isn't that right?"

"Yes, up to a point. He reckons I don't have much backbone, but because I'm good at keeping records that makes me valuable as his clerk."

"Where is the safe?"

"It's in a linen closet behind the wall. But I got to tell you this, I'm sure he has another safe somewhere. I know he moves the money around because he don't trust anyone. I think it's in his bedroom, but I don't know for sure."

"Interesting. Charlie, does he also move the written records to another place?"

"I don't think so, but he might."

McKiever looked at Olcott and Jeff. "You two have any questions, something I might have missed?"

Olcott spoke up, "I have a couple. Charlie, you still haven't told us if you'll work with us. How about it, are you with us?"

"Yes, I'll do it. Like Ranger McKiever said, I'm between a rock and a hard place, might as well."

"That's a good decision, Charlie. You might say this opportunity is an answer from prayer. Oh, another thing, are you still staying at Salley Milford's boarding house just outside of town?"

"Yes, I'm on the ground floor. I have a private entrance in the back. I do some chores for her, so I get a reduced rate."

"Charlie, what's the best way we can stay in touch with you? I don't want anyone becoming suspicious."

"Let me give that some thought." Charlie paused for a moment, before speaking, "How about I give you my schedule and we can plan around that?"

Olcott nodded. "Perfect."

"I check in at the Bar High at nine in the morning and leave by five. McCormick doesn't worry about me; he just uses me. After the morning, he doesn't keep track of what I do."

"Charlie, you're a lot smarter than McCormick realizes. You're going to end up being a first-class lawman. Fact is, I'm going to deputize you. That's all the questions I got. Jeff, you think of anything else?"

Jeff looked at McKiever. "Can't say I do, maybe in a minute."

McKiever thought of something. "Charlie, could you make a list of every man on the Bar High's payroll? If you could, I'd be obliged. Also, any suspicious routines you notice around the ranch, especially any activity involving his hired guns. How about his foreman, what's he like?"

"The man's name is Russ Wagle. He's like McCormick, real nasty and intimidating. That's about all I know about him. I'll work on that list tonight; you should have it by tomorrow."

"Good. Jeff, back to you, have you thought of anything yet?"

"Yes, I did. Charlie, are you handy with a gun?"

"Matter of fact I am, but I don't ever wear one. That way McCormick never bothers me for any of his dirty work."

McKiever was impressed, his voice reflecting it, "Fellows, we got the right man. Charlie, you're smart, real smart, I mean that. You keep on with your normal routine, and if you can get any additional information to us by Tuesday, it will be a big help. I may not be in town, but you know where to find Sheriff Olcott, so take advantage. I've got one last question. Have you ever heard McCormick or Wagle ever giving orders to anyone about breaking the law?"

"No, not really. Like I said, I've pretty much avoided being involved. But I'll tell you this: McCormick's got himself surrounded by some real tough gun hands."

"Charlie," McKiever apologized, "I almost forgot something. What do you know about a man named Randell Wynncliff? He's always dressed in black, real fancy like."

"Sure, I know him. He gives McCormick legal advice. Any ranch that gets bought is examined by him to make sure everything's legally correct. Wynncliff always writes up the new deeds. Matter of fact, the bank president likes his work."

"Tell me, Charlie, where did McCormick find this guy?"

"I don't know, but Wynncliff has political connections at the governor's office. Besides that, he's well paid, very well paid."

"The governor's office you say. Any chance he's in on anything corrupt?"

"If he is, it's legally covered, you can bet on that. I know one thing: McCormick doesn't like him because the man's expensive, so it figures he needs him. Otherwise, he would have dumped him. That's about all I know."

McKiever reached over, touching Charlie's arm. "Thanks, Charlie. Now, things will get interesting in a few days, but the good news is that McCormick's days are numbered. You work with us and soon this will be over. Another thing, and make no mistake about this, you're very important in this investigation, which means we're counting on you. You can go now, but don't forget, we'll be waiting for any new information you provide."

Charlie started to move. Jeff stepped forward, blocking his path. "Charlie, after this is over, you'll be working for me. I guarantee you're going to like working at the Upper Forks Ranch."

"Thanks, Mr. Kincaid." Moving to the door, he looked back. "I reckon it's better being on the law's side even if it is dangerous. At least a man is right with God." Turning, Charlie left.

Several minutes ticked by, McKiever finally breaking the silence, "Well, based on Charlie's description of Peckenpath, we should have no trouble recognizing him."

Jeff agreed, looking at Olcott. "I guess not."

Olcott rolled his eyes. "What a description. I never heard of such a man. Kind of gives a man the jitters, doesn't it?"

"Amen," Jeff muttered.

Olcott kept thinking about the killer's description. "Mac, you want me to ask Charlie to draw up a wanted poster of Peckenpath? That is, if we can get him to do it?"

McKiever liked Olcott's idea. "Good thinking, have him draw up several. But be careful, we don't want to spook Charlie. He's already rattled. Why don't you tell him that we're not planning on using them unless Peckenpath gets away. Tell him his drawings will stay with him unless we have no other options. That way Charlie will feel in control, which should give him peace of mind."

Olcott nodded. "I'll tell him."

McKiever looked through the door at the now-empty church. "I think we had a real productive meeting with Charlie. I like him, and I think he's going to work out. I do have something to tell the both of you. I ran into Wynncliff in the street after our meeting the other day. He was going by the jail when we met. Talk about bad timing, that was it."

"It looks like," Jeff rolled his eyes, "you've been made."

"I guess you could say that. He sure remembered me. He also noticed I wasn't wearing my badge."

"So," Olcott asked, "you obviously made a big impression on him the first time you two met. What did you tell him?"

"I told him that even Texas Rangers retire. I covered my tracks by telling him I was seeing old friends in Fredonia."

"That was quick thinking," Jeff chuckled. "Did he buy it?"

"Maybe, but the type of questions he asked gave me the impression he was suspicious, but I did get his business card."

"That's interesting. How did that come about?"

"I told him I was buying a ranch. I asked him if he was expensive. He told me he was. He did say he would make an exception for a man of the law. Something to do with taming the West, you know, making it a safe place to do business."

Jeff made a face, his voice sarcastic, "That would be right up his alley. You think he was talking to you like you're a retired Ranger, or he's a suspicious lawyer checking you out?"

"I didn't volunteer, and he didn't ask. But if you want my opinion, I suspect he smells trouble. I reckon the man didn't get where he is by being gullible."

"So," Olcott pointed at Mac's vest, "when are you pinning your badge back on?"

McKiever thought a minute before answering, "Not yet, the lawyer was leaving town, so I figure we have a few more days, but I'm not counting on it." McKiever reached into his vest. "Anyway, Sheriff, here's Wynncliff's business card. Maybe you could run a local check on him? I'll have headquarters do the same. Based on what Charlie told us, I doubt we'll be able to tie him in with McCormick, but who knows, under the pressure of questioning he might provide some incriminating evidence against McCormick, especially if he gets worried about being disbarred. Now, I'm going to hit the trail back to Fort Stockton to see if headquarters uncovered anything. Jeff, I'll be back Monday night for some home cooking. I do have one more request, if possible, could someone check in with Josh and Rick to see if anything has developed that we might use?"

Jeff stuck his hat on. "I'll take care of that, as well as tell Sara to leave a dinner plate out for you. I think it might be smart if we drift out of here separate. Since Sara's waiting for me, I'll go first. Mac let's hope the captain has something we can use, that sure would be nice! Adios, see you back at the ranch."

Olcott watched Jeff go, speaking to McKiever, "Mac, I think we got a working plan. I'm going to have a brief talk with Pastor Olgilvie so it won't look like we've been together. Give me a minute, and Mac, watch your back trail." Patting Mac's arm, Olcott left.

Staring at the numerous books surrounding the table, McKiever thought about Charlie's description of the gunman. What was most unnerving was Charlie's fear. If what Charlie said was true, they all had a reason to be concerned, very concerned! Lost in his thoughts, McKiever looked up, seeing Pastor Olgilvie approaching.

"I don't believe I've had the pleasure of meeting you." Olgilvie smiled, extending his hand.

McKiever grasped the outstretched hand. "My pleasure, name's William McKiever."

"Welcome, Mr. McKiever. I understand you're visiting with the Kincaid's. Is this the first time you've been to our church?"

"Yes, it is. The truth is, Pastor, I'm not much of a church-going man. I guess you could say, I kind of struggle about a belief in God."

"I see, but I did notice you were in church today. Are there any questions I might be able to answer?" Olgilvie smiled, continuing, "You know, I'm used to people who are a doubting Thomas. I guess you could say, it comes with the territory."

McKiever liked Pastor Olgilvie. The man had an easy way about him, a way of making a person feel comfortable. "You just used the name Thomas, which reminds me of a conversation I had with Sara Kincaid. Can I ask you some tough questions, Pastor?"

"Please do."

"Tell me, Pastor, why so much evil in the world?"

"The answer is choice. Choice with responsibility followed by a curse. You see, if man wasn't given that choice, then God would have just created another animal. Man was given choice to do what is right, or the opposite, which promotes evil. Do you understand what I'm saying?"

"Sure, but why do bad things happen to innocent people?"

Pastor smiled. "They don't. The truth is that all men are sinners. People who you might think are innocent, are indirect accomplices with evil because of a failure to walk with God, which is how most people choose to live. The truth is, Mr. McKiever, the greatest sin that leads to the other life-threatening sins, is a people tolerance for a godless lifestyle. Believing in God is more than going to church on Sunday morning."

McKiever nodded, agreeing, "I've seen plenty of that."

"So, have I, Mr. McKiever, so have I."

"Tell me, Pastor, why death?"

"Good question, obviously you've given some thought to tough questions. First of all, it was man who chose death through rebellion. We see that even today. Isn't a man who breaks the law with a gun only a bullet away from death himself? Logic then tells us that the lawbreaker is flirting with death through choice, which brings us to the conclusion that nothing has changed since the beginning of time." Olgilvie smiled. "Now, just for a moment, let's think about death the way God might. In other words, is it possible that death has a Godly purpose as a deterrent to be used by God? The answer is yes. Death ultimately forces man to make a final decision for or against God. And because of that, death becomes a tool for God, doesn't it?"

"I guess. How about children dying, as well as people being killed from diseases?"

"It's a curse that man brought on himself through choice. Without the curse, no death. Scripture says that all creation groaneth and travaileth since the beginning of time. As for the children, their souls are preserved until such time as they reach adult maturity, accepting or rejecting God. Just think about this, a mother loses her child through a disease, but because she walks in faith, she will be reunited with her baby one day. Now you tell me, where else can someone have so much assurance for the future, but in God? And that includes after a tragedy!"

McKiever was impressed; the Pastor wasn't stumped for answers. "I hear you, Pastor. I must admit, you give reasonable explanations, but it does bother me when I see decent people killed by bad folks. It just doesn't seem right to me that God allows that to happen!"

"Tell me, Mr. McKiever, how many town citizens stand up against bad people?"

"Very few."

"You have your answer. I agree with you, it's terrible, and that's why God desires man to glorify Him. Because if we did, then there would be peace on earth and good will towards men. I think you will agree, that type of life would be far better than what you see now."

"Just one more question, Pastor. If God is real, why doesn't he show himself?"

"He did, but even then, men rebelled, so why would that change things now? When Christ was producing miracles, he had a crowd following him, but when he stopped—" Olgilvie paused for emphasis, "no more people followed him. You see, Mr. McKiever, it's faith that produces results. Someday I would love to tell you about the power of faith. You see, through faith we can have a personal relationship, and because of that relationship people change for the good."

McKiever pushed his hat back. "Maybe another time, Pastor, but right now I'm behind my schedule, and I've really got to hit the trail."

"Certainly. While you're on the trail, think about this. If God is God, and God can do anything, then God would have power over death. When Christ rose from the grave, that showed he was God. Now, here's another question for you to ponder. How would it be possible for man to have a relationship with God outside of this dimension, which is where God exists?"

"I'm not sure I follow you."

"When God set aside his deity and walked on earth as a God man, that allowed men to have a personal relationship, just the same as you would with a friend. In other words, since man is created in the image of God, then a relationship is possible because God's not just a mystery that man can't relate to. If that's true, and it is, then men are without excuse."

McKiever sighed, "If you say so, Pastor. I have to admit, this has been an interesting conversation, but it's time for me to get going. Again, much obliged."

"It was my privilege. Are you leaving town, or will you be returning?"

"I'll be in town, at least for a while. Then I have plans to get to my ranch in Colorado."

"Well, hopefully I'll see you again. If I can answer any questions, please, don't hesitate."

"Thank you for your hospitality. Good day, Pastor." McKiever left the room, crossed the vestibule, stepping out into the bright sunshine. The sun was directly in his eyes. Squinting, he pulled his hat down low, observing the deserted grounds. It seemed strange. Just an hour ago people were everywhere, but not now. One thing that often bothered him about church people was how they were holy in church, but after church they seemed like everybody else. It seemed like they were quick to go home and leave that holy stuff behind. Of course, there were exceptions, and Sara and the captain were exceptions. They surely did follow their beliefs. Pastor Olgilvie also impressed him. He was very knowledgeable and communicated in a godly way. He certainly was a man with answers, the type someone could respect.

Looking past the picket fence, he saw Friend, his head turned toward him, his ears perked. McKiever smiled, his constant companion was always eager to see him. It was time to ride, time to get things done. Approaching Friend, he swung into the saddle. "Okay, big boy, you're going to like this trip."

Starting up the street, McKiever reminded himself to remain alert. It was easy to become relaxed, not to see things, especially signs of danger. Long ago he had learned that lawbreakers don't always run, and when they don't, that's when they become dangerous. His eyes shifted to the rooftops, then the alleys. The last building slipped by, the road opening up. Giving Friend a gentle nudge, the roan broke into his mile-eating stride. Staying on the shady side of the road, McKiever glanced back. The road was empty, the town rooftops no longer visible. Thinking about the mystery killer, his hand brushed up against his forty-five. His skill with the handgun always gave him a measure of confidence. He also remembered how Captain O'Rourke constantly cautioned his men, telling them that there was always somebody better than you. He sternly insisted that his men take every precaution. Thinking about Peckenpath, Mac wondered if that killer was the one man who was better than him. He grimaced, the disturbing premonition tugging at him. Hopefully, he'd never find out, but for now, the man lurked in his thoughts.

Lost in his thoughts, McKiever almost missed the game trail. Reining Friend around, Mac stared down the empty road. There was no sign of life, just him and his horse. Why so jumpy, he wondered. For several seconds, horse and rider didn't move. Maybe Charlie's description of the killer's ability to move silently had spooked him. Finally, sure that he was alone, he turned Friend from the road, following the game trail upward. As they climbed, McKiever scanned the ground for fresh horse tracks. The ground remained bare, showing no recent signs of men or horses.

Reaching the top, McKiever turned southeast. During his years of protecting border towns from marauding Indians, McKiever had uncovered every game trail for miles in any direction. Knowing the back country allowed him to travel undetected. Always cautious, McKiever would rather lose time than be exposed to an ambush by highwaymen lying in wait for some unsuspecting traveler.

Fluffy white clouds hung suspended against the blue sky. Clouds so soft, it seemed like a man could climb into them and lie down. The brightness of the day seemed softer up here, the green shrubs breaking the harsh glare from the overhead sun.

McKiever thought about Sara. She was as beautiful as he remembered, maybe more so! Jeff was a lucky man, and Mac knew his old sidekick knew it. Jeff hadn't hesitated, and he sure couldn't fault the man. For a moment McKiever felt a twinge of jealousy. The moment passed. Smiling, he reminded himself that he also had his chance. Too dumb, he thought. Jeff was smart and deserved what he had. Mac chuckled, knowing he wouldn't have beaten out Jeff with his good looks anyway.

McKiever talked to his horse, speaking out loud, "I just got to keep reminding myself, that's all. How's that, Friend, am I making sense?" Friend was quiet. "Well, it might not make horse sense to you, but it does to me. Besides, we got a new life waiting for us in Colorado, and maybe there's another Sara out there for me."

Topping a small rise, two brown bodies exploded from the underbrush. Startled, Friend jumped sideways. McKiever's heart pounding, his .45 pointing at the deer. Watching the two-mule deer pogo jumping through the brush, he relaxed, his heart still racing.

The two deer topped a rise, stopping, they watched him. Now, McKiever thought, this was the moment if a man had his rifle up and needed meat, this was the time to shoot. Mule deer always stop to look back, providing a good opportunity for the hunter.

McKiever talked to Friend, "I should have seen those fresh tracks, old boy. I was caught daydreaming, dreaming about something I can't touch anyway." Suddenly he laughed, patting Friend's shoulder. Despite being surprised by those critters, his speed with the gun was still there. Uncocking his Colt, he slipped it back into his holster.

The two deer melted into the scrub bushes. McKiever always marveled how deer appear, and then disappear, as if they were never there in the first place. An Indian scout had once told him that the freshest tracks a hunter would ever see was when the animal was making them. McKiever stared at the ground. The tossed dirt from the running tracks was still there, but the deer were gone.

Looking at the sun, McKiever realized the day was sliding by. "Let's go, Friend, we've got a few miles to cover."

CHAPTER 8

Sunday Afternoon

The road was dry, the land showing effects from the lack of rain. The hoof beats from the horses pulling Kincaid's wagon kicked up dust, the breeze blowing the dust into little red puffs. Jeff kept the wagon centered in the road. Sara leaned against him, each quiet. Sara knew something was bothering Jeff. She would wait until he was ready to talk. A mile passed before Jeff glanced at her, his voice breaking the silence, "Sorry for my lack of conversation."

Sara snuggled closer, her voice soft, "What happened with Charlie?"

"McKiever thinks it would help if we have an inside man working at the Bar High. Since Charlie works for McCormick, he became a likely candidate."

"What was Charlie's response?"

"He accepted, but he's scared."

"Why?"

"Sara, I've got to tell you something but give me a minute to figure out how to say it." Pausing for a second, Jeff continued, "You know I don't like to worry you, but I've always been honest with you, right?"

"Yes, you have." Sara looked into Jeff's face, seeing his concern. "Go on, Jeff."

"I guess the best way to tell you is for me to keep it simple. Charlie's seen the gunfighter. Honey, the description of that killer is frightening." Jeff felt Sara stiffen, her body tense.

"Why, what does he look like?"

"He looks like death. That what Charlie said. He also said that when the man talks, he sounds like death."

"Sounds like death! How does a man look and sound like death?"

"Charlie told us that looking into the man's face was like looking into your own grave. When the man talks, Charlie said it's like his voice is coming from some distant place."

Sara felt fear seeping into thoughts. "Jeff, is that possible?"

"According to Charlie it is. We know the man's real, but we don't know where he's staying. He's got to be someplace, but where, we just don't know."

A frown etched Sara's face. She squeezed his arm. "Everything you're telling me seems so strange."

"You should have heard Charlie. We do know that Peckenpath's under contract and he's been paid."

"Why wouldn't he be staying at McCormick's ranch?"

"I don't know. You would think so, but Charlie said he rode off."

"Jeff, what does Mac think?"

"He thinks Peckenpath is dangerous, real dangerous! Mac thinks he doesn't stay locally, just shows up to do the job, then disappears. That would explain why the man's such a mystery."

"So," Sara whispered, "Mac thinks the gunfighter shows up when the time is right and not before?"

"Yep, that about sums it up. I guess the good news is that at least we have a description of what the killer looks like. The bad news is McCormick doesn't pay a man like that to drive cattle. The question then becomes, who has Peckenpath been paid to kill?"

Both stopped talking, the sound of turning wheels replaced their voices. Topping the hill, the ranch loomed in the distance.

Sara broke the silence. "Where's Mac?"

"He's headed for Fort Stockton to send a message to headquarters. He'll be back Monday night. Hopefully, Mac will have some information we can use on McCormick."

Entering the yard, Jeff's mind thought about the two spies up on the mesa. It would surely be a relief when they finally swing into action. Not taking action bothered him, especially knowing his ranch was being watched.

Pulling up in front, Jeff watched his foreman, Tom Sullivan, approaching. Tom's deep voice bridged the distance. "Afternoon, folks, I'll take care of the wagon and them horses."

"Thanks, Tom." Jeff jumped to the ground, offering Sara his hand.

"Say, Mr. Kincaid, one of your men from the mesa is here. He's waiting for you inside the study room."

"Good, I'm anxious to hear what's going on." Jeff escorted Sara into the parlor. Leaving her, he headed for the study.

Billy Clifford sat at the table, staring into a book. Jeff smiled, knowing Billy couldn't read. Pulling up a chair, he asked, "What are you reading, Billy?"

"Nothing, Mr. Kincaid, just thought I'd look. Can't read, but I sure would like to be able to read."

"I'll tell you what, Billy, once we get past our immediate situation, I'm going to start a reading and writing school right here at the ranch. You're not the only one who can't read. How's that sound?"

"I'd like that, Mr. Kincaid, I surely would."

Jeff reached out, touching Billy's arm. "One thing's for sure, Billy, you might not be able to read a book, but I never saw a man who could read trail signs better than you. You may not realize it, but that's a gift. Tell me, what's going on up there on the mesa?"

Closing the book he couldn't read, Billy looked at his boss. "Two men are using a telescope. They seem to pay special attention to who comes and goes. The spot they picked gives them a good look at the road leading into the ranch, and most of the range. A man can see a long way from up there. They got carbines, but they're a mite too far away to shoot into the yard. Besides that, they take turns who goes for fresh supplies."

Jeff was impressed. Billy was always thorough. Jeff complimented himself; he had chosen the right man. "Nice job, a very complete report. How about you two, are you in rifle range of their camp?"

His face lighting up, Billy grinned. "Them two is like sitting ducks."

Jeff stood. "Billy, I want you to look at several posters." Walking over to a gray, somewhat battered, file cabinet, he slid open the top draw, removing three posters. Bringing the posters to the table, he placed them in front of Billy. "Billy, do any of those men up there look like these characters?"

Placing his stubby finger at the middle poster, Billy looked up. "This here fella looks like one. Now remember, Mr. Kincaid, we're looking from quite a distance, so I can't say for sure."

"I understand, but let's believe it is him, because that gives us a good reason to arrest them, not to mention the fact that they're trespassing anyway. Now, Billy, if they ever look like they're about to bushwhack anyone, you have my permission to stop them."

Billy looked up. "You mean, shoot them?"

"That's exactly what I mean. Those two spies are making me nervous. McKiever will be back tomorrow. I'm going to ask him if we can grab them. Since at least one is wanted, we do have proper cause to arrest them, and not just run them off. As soon as I know, I'll let you know."

"Have you thought of a plan, Mr. Kincaid?"

"Yes, I do have a plan. You two will keep them covered with your rifles while myself and a few others will sneak up on them. But I need you to figure out the best way to approach them, so when the time is right, we can move on them without being seen."

Billy felt relief; his skill was with the rifle, not the handgun. "No problem, Mr. Kincaid. No problem. Fact is, I've already got it figured out."

Standing, Jeff walked over to the large window facing the east slope, his eyes finding the mesa. For several moments he was still. Turning, he gestured toward the kitchen. "Billy, go have a good meal. Better yet, tell the cook I want you to have a hot meal. Also, raid the food pantry for anything you two needs. Tomorrow, you send Clancy down for a hot meal."

"Sure thing, Mr. Kincaid." Wheeling around, Billy headed for the kitchen.

As Billy left, Jeff thought about his own skill with the six-shooter. He was good, not nearly as fast as Mac, but quick and accurate. He tried to remember how long had it been since he had drawn his gun, guessing almost two years. A skill becomes rusty without use. Tomorrow he would practice out in the barn where no one would see him. Just the thought of

Peckenpath sent a chill through him. Someone was going to have to face that killer before this was over, and he hoped it wasn't him.

Monday morning dawned cooler with a touch of crispness in the air. The afternoon arrived, the day uneventful. Olcott paused, his voice addressing his young deputies. "The information I've just given you should make you both aware of how dangerous this situation is. We're not dealing with some young cowboys misbehaving, but with men skilled with the gun, men with no conscience." Olcott paused, letting his words sink in, before concluding, "That about sums it up, any questions?"

Wayne Johnson spoke, his voice measured, "I reckon not. You spelled it out pretty good."

"Best as I can," Olcott responded. "How about you, Mike? What's on your thoughts? Anything sticking in your craw about what's ahead of us?"

Mike stared at the floor, before looking up. "Any chance for more help?"

"Maybe, but don't count on it. No sense in deputizing more people; they'd only get in the way. No need for a posse yet, nobody to chase. Like I said, we got three Texas Rangers, one of them is the best, also an ex-Ranger. No, I think we have enough."

Both deputies waited, anticipating Olcott had more to say. They were right.

Olcott eyed each man. "One other thing, after this mess is cleaned up, I'll be retiring."

"Hell," Wayne chuckled, "looks like you should have retired a year ago." Thinking about what he said, Wayne jerked his hands up, excusing his outburst, "Now, don't get me wrong, boss, nothing personal, 'cause you paid your dues. I'm just saying your timing is bad,"

"I got no argument with what you just said, Wayne. If I was smart, I would have retired last year, but I didn't. Even if I knew about this Bar High problem ahead of time, I couldn't ride out until the problem was solved. But after this town is back to normal, I will be turning in my badge. I want you to know that I consider both of you qualified for this job, so think about it."

Wayne looked at Mike, both smiling, both rolling their eyes upward, Mike asked, "Don't a man have to be elected before becoming sheriff?"

"Yes, unless he's appointed by the mayor, or the town board. Anyway, I'm going to recommend that both of you be considered. One thing both of you should know, to stay on this job you need to understand politics."

Mike was surprised. "Politics, what are you saying?"

"I'm saying you have to be a babysitter for every merchant in town, and your boss is the mayor, which means you can be on the hot seat at any time. Once you get elected, then the only way you can get ousted is if the people get disgruntled. Regardless, if you get the job, you better understand politics."

"You know," Wayne grunted, "I never seen anyone boss you around!"

Olcott smiled. "Longevity, that's why. The local merchants saw the town get cleaned up, so I had their support. Our mayor wasn't in office then, and the old one endorsed me. The biggest problem is to find ways to get cattle ranchers and town folk to get along. If a man can do that, he's done a good job, and that will keep a person in office."

Wayne cleared his throat. "Shoot, Sheriff, it's almost like you're telling us why we might not want to be sheriff."

Olcott shook his head yes. "That's exactly what I'm saying. You got to understand that politics has the final say in any town. Once you understand that, then you know how to play the game. By now I'm sure you know this job can get dangerous, but you should also know if things get scary in any town, you might lose the town's support. On the other hand, if you get a good reputation, another town will always hire you because of your past record. Also, a good reputation helps keep the peace. Anyway, I'm going to submit both your names to the town for consideration. End of speech. You two have anything more to say?"

Mike looked at his partner. "We appreciate that. Any other options for men like us?"

"I can think of several relating to the law. You can wait till the town elects a new sheriff and become his deputies. I can't see why a newly elected sheriff wouldn't want two experienced lawmen. Good deputies are hard to come by. Another option to consider is joining the Texas Rangers. Also, railroads hire men with law enforcement backgrounds." Olcott rose. "That about sums up what I had to say. Wayne, tonight you have the late rounds. As for me, I'm going home for a hot meal." Closing the door behind him, Olcott walked into the late afternoon sun. Crossing the street he tipped his hat to several ladies, heading for the little house at the edge of town.

He knew his wife, Norma, was already preparing dinner, and he was hungry. Approaching the house, he cautioned himself to put on his happy face. Thank goodness, he thought, that two more Rangers were in town. Otherwise, he might not be able to hide his worry from his wife.

Wayne scratched his chin, looking at his partner. "Mike, you think McKiever can beat Peckenpath in a gun draw?"

"Maybe, maybe not. I know one thing, I sure wouldn't want to match up against that killer." Leaning back, Mike placed both hands on the back of his neck, his voice reflective, "You know, working for Olcott all these years has been a pleasure. The man's taught us a lot, but maybe it's time for a change. I'm not sure I want to be sheriff, but I kind of like the idea of becoming a Texas Ranger. How about you?"

"Well, you're footloose and fancy free, but I'm married, and Clare likes it here. I guess I'll have to discuss those options with her. At any rate, when Olcott leaves I suspect we'll be in charge until the town makes a decision. Either way, that gives us a little grace time. Tell you the truth, Wayne, right now that gunfighter keeps popping up in my brain. The rest of that Bar High crowd doesn't bother me, but that man does. Once we get past him, then we can think about our future."

"Yeah, I hear you," Wayne growled. "If we don't get by him, we may not have a future."

Mike eased over to the window, staring at the street. "You think if McCormick got arrested, Peckenpath would go away? You know, leave because there's no money."

"Good question. If there's no money, why stay? I sure wouldn't, would you?"

"Hell no, but if he's already been paid, what then? When I get a chance, I'm going to ask McKiever. In the meantime, you're the late man tonight. How about some chow?"

"You know what I like about you, Wayne? You got that practical side that makes sense. Good thinking, let's go eat." Reaching for their hats they stopped as the door swung open, McKiever entering.

Wayne couldn't believe it, his voice sounding pleased, "Just the man we've been hoping to see."

McKiever chided, "Nothing like walking into a question. Go ahead, what is it?"

"Well, we were thinking that if McCormick got arrested, wouldn't that gunfighter vamoose? We figured he'd have no reason to stay."

McKiever shrugged. "Don't get your hopes up. I think a man like that always gets paid in advance, and if he does, I would anticipate him fulfilling his contract obligations. I don't know that for sure, but that's what usually happens when someone hires an out-of-town killer."

Wayne cleared his throat, "What you're saying is that we're going to have to deal with him one way or the other!"

McKiever dusted his hat off before answering. "I really don't know. What I do know is that he's dangerous. What's more, he's already killed one lawman, no telling how many more he could kill. Which means, Peckenpath needs to be stopped." Mac inspected his hat, returning it to his head, making a point. "We are men of the law with a job to do. If either of you are afraid, let me know so I'll know how to use you."

Wayne broke in, his voice slightly agitated, "It's not about being afraid! My nerves always go on edge in a dangerous situation, but that's never stopped me from doing my job. The way I see it, this Peckenpath is the most dangerous gunfighter I've ever heard about. Tell me, McKiever, aren't you concerned about him?"

McKiever liked Wayne's agitated response. The man could be riled up, showing character. "Like you just said, being nervous never stopped you from doing your job."

"So," Mike interrupted, "we all feel the same way, don't we?"

"Fair enough, Mike. I like to repeat something Captain O'Rourke always told me. He said a smart lawman always stacks the odds in his favor. He also said that a man needs two things in life, and one of those things is luck."

Both deputies harmonized in unison, "What's the other?"

"The other one is to know where your soul is going when you run out of luck."

Wayne eyed his partner, sounding grim, "You mean death?"

McKiever didn't answer.

Wayne's question leaped out, "How about you, Ranger McKiever? You seem to have had lots of luck. Do you know where your soul is going?"

"No, can't say that I do."

Mike leaned forward, his question bringing a temporary silence. "Tell me, McKiever, you think you can beat Peckenpath in a gun draw?"

McKiever's eyes locked onto Mike, several seconds passing before he spoke. "I don't know. What's more, I don't want to find out. Fact is, I believe in luck, but I don't believe in pushing it. I also believe in keeping the odds in my favor, and when they are, take advantage."

Mike laughed, "How are we doing with your formula?"

"Good. The last time I looked I'm still alive. My only worry is, where is Peckenpath?"

"So," Wayne sighed, "the real problem remains Peckenpath?"

"Not really, the solution to any problem is in the implementation of a plan. Once a plan's in place, then you deal with each situation as it develops, including Peckenpath. That's why I stopped at the office, I thought I might get lucky and catch up with Olcott."

Wayne answered, "You just missed him. Since I'm the late man tonight, I'll tell Olcott."

"Thanks, Wayne. Tell Sheriff Olcott I've got good news that we can use. Tell him I'd like a meeting Tuesday night with everyone."

"Consider it done. Mike and I are going to eat. You want to join us?"

"Thanks, another time. I promised Jeff I'd be back in time for supper, so I better get going. If you would contact Josh and Rick about the meeting, I'd be much obliged."

"Sure thing. One way or the other, they'll be there."

McKiever started for the door, stopping. "Oh, one more thing, ask Olcott to make sure Charlie's there."

"I'll see to it. You go ahead and hit the trail. Come on, partner, let's go eat."

"I'm right behind you. Hey, maybe this will be our last supper, just like the Bible says."

Wayne chuckled, "Then maybe we better make peace with the man!"

All three laughed, closing the door behind them.

CHAPTER 9

Contract to Kill

McCormick crossed the yard. Approaching the bunk house, he poked his head through the open door. Cigarette smoke obscured the long room, the bunks barely visible in the smoky haze. Three cowhands lounged against the far wall, McCormick's gravelly voice disrupting their conversation. "Anyone see Wagle?"

The nearest man spoke. "No, Mr. McCormick, he's out on the range."

"When he gets in, send him over."

"Yes, sir, we'll send him right over."

Slamming the door shut, McCormick headed for the main house. Nearing the building he observed Charlie Walters exiting the house. McCormick looked at his watch, his voice sarcastic, "It must be five o'clock. I see you're leaving right on time."

Charlie answered meekly, "Everything's in order, Mr. McCormick. I left the papers you wanted on your desk. I'll be in your office promptly at nine in the morning."

"You better be. I want everything in order for the acquisition of the Upper Forks Ranch." With a wave of his hand, he dismissed Charlie. Watching Charlie scurry away prompted Mike to chuckle. The sound of horses shifted his attention to the yard. Russ Wagle, along with several hired guns, were riding up to the bunkhouse. McCormick leaned against the porch rail, waiting.

Minutes later Russ left the bunkhouse. Stopping at the bottom of the steps, Russ looked up at the owner. "What's up, boss?"

"Come into the office; I want to run a few things by you." Stepping inside, Russ watched the Bar High owner unlock the office door, both entering. "Grab a chair, Russ." Walking behind his desk, McCormick seated himself. Pulling out a piece of paper, he handed it to his foreman. "Here, read this. I received it from a stable boy while in town."

Opening the note, Wagle read slowly. The note was from that slick lawyer, Wynncliff. The note read:

Saw a man by the name of William McKiever as I was leaving for Austin. He came out of the Sheriff's office. Three weeks ago the man was wearing a Texas Ranger badge. He told me he was retired, and visiting some old friends. He wasn't wearing a badge. Just thought I'd let you know.

Yours truly,
Randell Wynncliff

Russ handed the note back. "Interesting, but seems fishy to me. What do you think, boss?"

"I'm thinking we got three strangers in town, all claiming to represent investors, but none of them will tell us who the investors are. What's more, one of them pulls a gun on my men, and they told me they never seen a man faster with a gun. This note says that McKiever was visiting friends, so I'm thinking one of them is Sheriff Olcott. Another thing, Jeff Kincaid is a retired Texas Ranger, who's probably another old friend. You know what I think, Russ, I think we got three Texas Rangers snooping around, that's what I think!"

Russ thought for a moment before speaking, "You met with those two fellars in town. How'd you size them up?"

"Both sounded okay, but I did some checking. I couldn't get any information about the railroad coming here, and I checked around pretty good."

Russ nodded.

"That ain't all! Both those men talked like businessmen, but I'm an observant man. They talked evasively. And another thing, they wore their guns like professionals."

"I hear you, boss, you suspect they act more like lawmen than business people."

"Exactly."

Russ scratched his chin, "What are you going to do?"

"I'll tell you what I'm going to do, I'm going to use Peckenpath. Right now's the perfect time. I'm going to tell him to kill McKiever and then Kincaid. No one will suspect me because I'm negotiating with Kincaid in good faith, so why would I kill him! As for McKiever, lawmen make lots of enemies. Even if the law suspects us, there ain't a thing they can do because everything's legal on paper. But even better, Russ, this Peckenpath fellow is like a ghost. Once he kills, he'll disappear into thin air."

"I'd say you got it figured out, boss, at least as best as a man can."

McCormick leaned back. "Only one thing worries me: it's that McKiever fellow. According to Raymond Floyd, he never saw anyone so fast with a gun. If he kills Peckenpath, we could have real trouble on our hands."

"Yeah, but like you said, everything's legal. Besides, if Peckenpath got killed, dead men don't talk."

McCormick nodded. "Tell you what, Russ, I don't think anyone can kill a gunman like Peckenpath, and after he finishes, they'll be chasing a ghost. No sir, this is the right time. If we wait longer, those Rangers snooping around might uncover more than we want."

"You know what, boss? I'm thinking you want them dead before Wednesday."

McCormick looked at his foreman. "Why?"

"Cause the signing is on Wednesday. Right now, you got the perfect alibi, but if Kincaid says no to your offer, then the law could establish a motive."

"You think like I do, Russ. I'm going to dispatch a telegraph message to Peckenpath to get rid of McKiever and Kincaid, hopefully before Wednesday." Reaching into his desk drawer, McCormick pulled out a notepad. Writing quickly, he paused, asking, "Where do you think McKiever's staying?"

"I'd guess he's at the Kincaid ranch."

"Makes sense." McCormick finished writing. "Here, get this on its way. Use the telegraph station at Indian Wells."

"I'm on my way. Say, boss, I sure wouldn't mind a chance at them lawmen."

"Russ, you just might get your wish, but for now we got to lay low. We don't want anyone connecting us to anything, you understand?" McCormick's eyes squinted. "Who knows, a year from now I could be mayor and you'll be running the Bar High. You might even end up as the local sheriff, or whatever you want. I need a man like you, Russ, a man who thinks like me. Now, get that message on its way."

Watching Russ leave, McCormick thought about the latest developments. Regardless of what happened in the next two days, the circumstances were in his favor. The gunfighter was well known, but a mystery, a man who left no trail. If they tried to blame the Bar High, he could tell the law that Peckenpath was wanted dead or alive. He would point out that most likely McKiever had run into him, trying to apprehend him. As for Jeff Kincaid, right now he had the perfect alibi.

One thing still gnawed at McCormick. There was something about that McKiever that worried him, especially if the lawman got lucky and killed Peckenpath. For several seconds he mulled over that possibility. Remembering his meeting with the gunfighter, he ceased worrying. No one was going to kill that man, or whatever he was. McCormick shuddered, a chill creeping back into his bones. He had never seen such a person. The man had killer written all over him. Just looking at the man was frightening. Nope, McCormick was sure the gunfighter had no equal. As far as he was concerned, Kincaid and McKiever were as good as dead. He congratulated himself for hiring Peckenpath. His contracting the gunfighter had been a stroke of genius.

Relaxing, McCormick started for the kitchen. A subtle noise at the window stopped him, his pig-like eyes focusing on the glass. The noise was alien, like someone sliding along the outer wall. Easing himself toward the window, McCormick craned his neck, his eyes searching. He saw nothing. A scrub pine moved slightly in the breeze. Suddenly McCormick detected movement. A pine squirrel jumped from one branch to another, before dropping to the ground, disappearing around the corner.

McCormick relaxed, his suspicion satisfied. The squirrel must have caused a branch to brush against the house. McCormick's hunger reminded him to head for the kitchen.

McKiever pushed open the door, letting Jeff enter first. He was pleased: everyone was there, including Charlie Walters. What surprised him the most was seeing Charlie with a six-gun strapped to his waist. He acknowledged Charlie. "Charlie, glad you're here. Well, I see everyone's here, so let's get started. I've got good news. We won't have to wait for the Bar High to start trouble. I received information from Ranger Headquarters that Mike McCormick is wanted back in Boston for embezzling money from a seafaring company. I understand the man's been wanted for some time. It appears that McCormick has a ruthless reputation and disappeared with lots of money by manipulating the books. He started out as a deckhand, became first mate, and eventually the company's bookkeeper in the shipping department. Apparently, he's good with the figures." McKiever grinned. "Which means, tomorrow we're going to send him back to Boston." Mac leaned forward. "Jeff, not only are you going to tell him you're not selling, but also have the pleasure of knowing he will be arrested the minute you leave. How's that sound?"

Jeff answered, "Like music to my ears."

McKiever nodded. "Before I go on, you men have been doing some information gathering, so bring me up to date." He focused on Josh and Rick. "What did you two find out at the bank?"

Josh spoke up. "Not as much as we wanted. It seems the old president was a community-type person. Kind of like a father figure for all the ranchers. But the new president is strictly business with no conscience. His motto is, make as much money as possible, no matter what. The loan officer, Johnathan Barker, he's a straight shooter. He knows where all the records are kept. He said he'll connect us to any transactions that were questionable, but he did inform us that after McCormick hired Wynncliff, everything became legally correct." Josh looked at Rick. "What did I forget?"

"Just that Jonathan thinks there's circumstantial evidence on paper that can be used. He also thinks the money records at the bank should line up with any money obtained illegally from wherever it was stolen. And based on what you just said, that Boston shipping company."

McKiever was pleased. "Good, what happened with your meeting in McCormick's office?"

Rick shrugged. "He's politically motivated, that's for sure. I'll tell you what, though, he was very suspicious. He must have asked at least a dozen times who our investors were. We figured if nothing else, maybe we could have nailed him because of the company he keeps. You know, guilt through association. Heck, three men working for him are on our wanted posters."

McKiever looked at Olcott. "Anything you or your deputies want to add?"

Olcott shrugged. "I've kept accurate records since all the trouble started. Most of the problems for the ranch owners started after they refused McCormick's offer. That's been true for every ranch. Also, all shooting problems began after McCormick hired those wanted men. Prior to that, no shootings. I do have some hard evidence, like the rifle casing we found not far from Wendell Cotton's body. I must admit, most of the evidence is circumstantial, but once we get into McCormick's records, things could get interesting!"

McKiever's eyes shifted to Charlie Walters. "So far I like everything I'm hearing. How about you, Charlie?"

Charlie's face was grim. "I just overhead something, but you're not going to like it."

McKiever's curiosity was aroused. "Okay, spill it."

"I was leaving the ranch yesterday when McCormick got back from town. He had a meeting with his foreman, Russ Wagle. I snuck over to the window and eavesdropped. I couldn't hear everything, kind of breezy, but I heard enough. McCormick told Wagle to send a telegraph message to Peckenpath." Charlie paused.

"Go on, Charlie."

"I heard McCormick say your name, then Jeff's name."

"Meaning?"

"The contract is to kill you and Jeff."

Olcott broke the temporary silence, "I'll be damned! How did McCormick find out about you, Mac?"

Charlie answered, "I heard him say he got a note from a stable boy while in town."

All eyes turned toward McKiever, who was looking at Jeff. Shrugging, McKiever grimaced. "That note had to come from Wynncliff. I was hoping he bought my line about retirement. I guess not. Anything else, Charlie?"

"Yes sir, he mentioned Indian Wells."

"Indian Wells, maybe that's where Wagle sent the telegraph."

Charlie picked up a handful of papers, handing them to McKiever. "Here, I drew these up. No sense in wasting time."

Looking at the top paper, McKiever's face tightened. He took a moment before speaking, "Thanks, Charlie." Mac's eyes circled the room, looking at each man. "Men, I'm going to pass these around. Take a good look. It's a chilling sight. You're about to see a drawing of Sam Peckenpath."

The rustle of paper was followed by silence. McKiever watched each man's face as they stared at the drawing. Every man's expression showed surprise, followed by a look of disbelief.

Jeff broke the spell. "I guess we won't have any trouble identifying this Peckenpath. Man alive, what a sight!"

McKiever looked at Charlie. "Now I understand why you said the man looks like death; he surely does!"

Charlie was staring at the poster in his hand. "Tell you what, this picture is close, but he looks worse in real life." Charlie's voice dropped to a whisper, "I tried, but it's tough to give someone life who looks like death."

McKiever knew it was time to change the subject before everyone became too spooked. "How about you, Jeff? What about those spies up on the mesa?"

Jeff pulled his attention away from the poster. "One of them is wanted. Right now, both of those spies are within rifle range by my men. As soon as you give me the word, I want to grab them. As far as my cattle is concerned, my foreman informed me that the herd's been scouted by strange riders. The good news is, that they're not hanging around the herd."

McKiever tossed his poster on the table, as if dismissing it. "Good, here's the plan of action, subject to revision by mutual consent. Remember, this isn't my plan; it's our plan. Jeff, we already talked about your zone of responsibility, which is your ranch. Sheriff Olcott, you and your deputies will start making arrests in town. I'll be with you when that happens. Jeff, as soon you give McCormick your answer, you leave and go get those two men up on the mesa. Josh, you and Rick meet up with Jeff as he rides out of town. I want to make sure Jeff has enough help. Is that okay with you two?"

Rick answered, "Fine with us. We feel like we've been stuck in one place forever."

Josh sounded eager. "Sounds good. I can't wait to get going."

McKiever liked their eagerness. "Sheriff, the minute Jeff walks out, you'll lead Mike and Wayne into McCormick's office. I'll be right behind you. He won't be expecting us, so we should have the advantage of surprise. Once we're in, we arrest anyone with McCormick. How does the plan sound, or should I say, our plan?"

Olcott nodded. "I like it."

"Good. Jeff, by then you should have a good head start. It would be good if you have those spies rounded up by the time we meet at your ranch. If not, wait and we'll get them together. After we meet at your place, we head for McCormick's ranch. Charlie, that's where you come in. When we get there, we're going to need you."

"I'll be there; you can count on it."

"Perfect. Once we make our initial arrests, I want to move fast. Right after we grab McCormick, we can shake down his office in town. After that, I want to catch those men on our wanted list. The quicker we move on them, the less chance they get away. When we arrive at McCormick's ranch, we'll tear his office apart. I especially want to get into his two hidden safes. Now, I've left one thing out of our plan of action."

"Let me guess," Jeff uttered in a grating voice, "his name is Sam Peckenpath."

"Yes, and that's why we need to move fast. I want everything out of the way before we tangle with him. Whatever happens, avoid him. When we go after him, I want to move in force. Anybody disagree? Anyone have a better plan?"

McKiever waited, finally taking advantage of the silence. "I'm not hearing anyone." Again he paused, before going on. "Okay, once we get into the Bar High's records, they might lead us to Peckenpath. I miss anything?"

"Yep, you did," Olcott chided. "Where do we meet, and at what time?"

McKiever rolled his eyes. "Yeah, basic fundamentals. Thanks, Sheriff. Nine o'clock, right here at the jail. Eight-thirty wouldn't hurt either. Just make sure no one's late. Charlie, you get to the Bar High, so when we show up, you're there."

Wayne spoke up, "I got one question. Suppose Peckenpath unexpectedly shows up?"

"Don't engage him. If he pops up, he gets priority over McCormick. I can't stress this enough: get all the help you can. Hopefully, we'll be together when we see Peckenpath. But no matter what, if possible, use rifles, which will give us the advantage. The man's deadly, and I don't want anyone committing suicide." McKiever stared at each man. "I've got a hunch we won't see him." Looking over at Jeff, Mac rolled his eyes for emphasis, his meaning clear. "If I got this killer figured out right, and based on what Charlie told us, Jeff and I will run into him in an isolated situation. The man's a loner who picks his spots, and we're the one's he's been contracted to kill. That's the problem about killers like him: they show up when you least expect them. So I doubt we'll see him while we're making arrests." McKiever picked up his drawing of the killer, dismissing everyone. "You men get a good night's sleep, have a nice breakfast, and be confident in your skills. We have the advantage of surprise, and we're about to rid this town of a had problem. I'll see all of you in the morning."

CHAPTER 10

Wednesday Morning

Watching Jeff and Mac strapping on their gun belts, Sara felt her body becoming taut, her voice worried. "Jeff, when do you think you'll be back?"

Jeff could see the concern in Sara's face. He made sure he sounded reassuring. "This won't take long, honey. I'm going to be back before noon. Mac will follow."

"Is that right, Mac?" Sara crossed her arms, her eyes intent. "Is it?"

McKiever spun the cylinder of his gun, his voice calm. "Yes, Jeff's going to be the messenger in town before heading here. I should be along in about an hour. Sara, we're initiating the action, which means we will be in control, not them." McKiever dropped his walnut-handled Colt into his holster. "Our plan is to meet back here before heading for the Bar High, so you're going to be the first to know how things went in town." He smiled, giving her a wink.

Sara couldn't shake the tension from her body. She nestled in Jeff's arms. "Jeff, be careful, please be careful. I don't know what I'd do if anything happens to either of you!"

Jeff kissed Sara's brow, his hug gentle. "You can do one thing when we leave, and you know what that is, don't you?"

"Yes, I know, and I will." Stepping back, Sara reached out, grasping McKiever's hand. Squeezing gently, she looked into his face. "Mac, please come back safely."

McKiever squeezed back. "Sara, this is going to be quick." Removing his hand, he pushed open the door. "Jeff, time to go."

Sara followed, watching the two men mount their horses. Seconds later they were gone, only the fading sounds from the hoof beats could be heard. Her heart hammering, Sara crossed her arms, her fingers digging into her flesh. It was time to head for the bedroom, a time to pray. Sara spun around, heading for the stairs. Pushing open the bedroom door, she recalled verses from scripture, verses that gave her peace over anxiety. Kneeling down she prayed, a quiet peace overcoming her.

Dropping down on the game trail, Jeff suddenly reined around his horse. He looked at McKiever, asking, "Do you feel it?"

Mac was puzzled. "Feel what?"

Jeff answered, "Sara's prayers, I can feel them. It's like being lifted up onto higher ground. You can't feel them?"

Peering into Jeff's face, McKiever saw his friend was serious. "Jeff, I can't say that I do. Maybe you were thinking about Sara. Were you?"

Jeff shook his head. "Nope, can't say that I was." Wheeling his horse around, Jeff started down the ridge. Finding the horse trail, he turned. Soon the trail turned, angling upward toward the ranch road.

McKiever thought about Jeff. He was a man you stake your life on, a man of courage. Certainly, Jeff was not given to imagination, but instead, commonsense. If he didn't respect Jeff as much as he did, he might have laughed, maybe even question his friend's sanity. But Jeff could be counted on; his courage had been tested through time. Then there was Sara. Not only was she beautiful, but a woman who wouldn't compromise trust. Both Sara and Jeff had a strong faith in God, both believed in prayer. McKiever's thoughts shifted to his deceased foster parents, then to his mentor, Captain O'Rourke. They also were people of prayer. McKiever shrugged, realizing he had never asked the captain how he came to a belief in God. Perhaps some day he would.

Breaking out onto the road, McKiever eyed Jeff. "You still have that feeling?"

"Yeah, it's quite a feeling. A tremendous peace comes upon you. A man completely loses any fear. It's like a trust thing." Jeff stared at his friend. "You ever have such a feeling, Mac?"

McKiever made a face before answering, "What relaxes me most is when I take action against something that's bothering me. Once I'm solving the problem, then my instincts take over and everything's okay." Mac laughed, "Like right now! Come on, let's let the horses run."

The rhythm of the horses was relaxing. In the distance the town grew larger, the road sloping downward.

Charlie Walters slipped his gun and holster into the saddlebag. Mounting his horse, he left the yard, heading for the Bar High. Charlie checked his pocket watch. McCormick had told him to be on time, and this morning Charlie would be early. Today was the day he would get his manhood back. For too long he had been burdened, but now his constant compromising was ending. Didn't they have God on their side, he thought. That thought was very comforting to Charlie Walters.

Sheriff Olcott had been watching McCormick's office for some time. As of yet, there was no sign of anyone arriving. Pulling out his watch, Olcott checked the hour. It was only eight-thirty. Relax, he told himself. Turning back, he looked at his deputies and the two Rangers. Everyone was looking at him, Olcott's voice was calm, "No one is at McCormick's office yet."

The sound of horses drew Olcott's attention back to the window. McKiever and Kincaid were at the hitch rack. Minutes later the door swung open. Jeff entered, followed by McKiever. Mac's eyes swept the room, his voice relaxed. "Everybody have their coffee?"

All heads nodded.

"Good, let's check our guns, no empty chambers today."

The sound of spinning cylinders filled the room. McKiever looked at Olcott. "Anybody over at the office yet, Sheriff?"

"Not yet, but McCormick could be in town. He might be having breakfast at the hotel."

McKiever leaned against the desk, rubbing his hands. He looked at Josh and Rick. "I didn't think you two were here yet. Where are your horses?"

Rick answered, "Behind the jail. We reckoned it wouldn't be smart for anyone seeing the hitch rack full of horses, might arouse some suspicions!"

Mac agreed, eyeing Jeff. "That's smart. Jeff, how about taking our horses around back?"

Jeff slipped outside, the door creaking shut.

Mike asked a question, "Ranger McKiever, you got this all figured out?"

"Let's give Jeff time to get back and then we'll review everything." Several minutes passed, the door swinging open. Jeff entered, pulling the door shut.

McKiever's voice captured everyone's attention. "The plan's simple enough. As soon as Jeff heads for McCormick's office, Josh, you and Rick get your horses and wait for Jeff to ride out of town. Your assignment is to arrest those spies up on the mesa. Myself, Olcott, and you two deputies, we'll go in right after Jeff comes out. Once we're in, we arrest everybody."

Olcott checked Mac with a question. "Even if whoever's in there isn't on our wanted list?"

"Yes, we're in a danger situation. We can sort it out later."

Josh spoke. "You sure we shouldn't stick around in case something goes wrong?"

"I'm positive. I want to get to the Bar High as quick as possible. The longer we take at Jeff's ranch, the more likely some of the people we're after at the Bar High may slip away because of some advanced warning. Since one of those men spying up on the mesa is on our wanted list, as soon as they're rounded up we can head for McCormick's. Now, if you hear lots of shooting before you're out of town, swing back. Other than that, ride."

Josh repeated himself, "just as long as you're sure."

"I'm sure. Again, you know the exception, lots of shooting."

Wayne held up his hand.

McKiever acknowledged him. "Go ahead, Wayne."

"You comfortable with Charlie?"

"Yes, but I'm not depending on him because I depend on lawmen. But I'm convinced Charlie's going to be very valuable. Fact is, he's already given us valuable information. Anything else?" Reaching into his vest, Mac held up his badge. "Time to pin these back on."

Rick chuckled, "Good bye business world. You know, I never felt comfortable not wearing the badge."

"Isn't that the truth," Josh cracked. "It was like I was out of balance or something."

McKiever glanced at his watch. "We've still got a few minutes. Remember, we have the element of surprise, so let's use it. Anyone of those characters tries to react, don't hesitate; nail them anyway you can."

Olcott's voice drifted back from the window. "As of right now, McCormick's entering the building with two men. Even better, one of those men is on our wanted list. I don't know about the second fellow."

McKiever's eyes intensified. "Right on schedule. Jeff, get your horse, swing around and come down the main street. Once we see you, we'll cross the street and move into position. When you come out, we go in."

Jeff eased himself out the door. Circling behind the jail, he mounted his horse. Riding slowly, he entered the street. Angling across to the far side, Jeff kept his horse in the shadows, making sure the sun's rays didn't blind his vision. Approaching McCormick's office, he pulled up. Sliding from his horse, he wrapped the reins. Stepping onto the boardwalk, he saw McKiever crossing the street, followed by Olcott and his two deputies. Jeff pushed open the door, entering.

McCormick looked up. The clock showed 10:00 o'clock. Leaning back, he was pleased. "Right on time, Kincaid, right on time. Have a chair."

Jeff eyed the two men on either side of McCormick. The man wearing the gun on his right hip was to the right of McCormick. The other gunfighter was a lefty, standing at McCormick's left side. Both were well spaced, leaving themselves plenty of room for gun clearance. Professional, Jeff thought, very professional.

McCormick saw Jeff hesitate. "Sit down, the papers are ready. Have a cup of coffee."

"Thanks, but no thanks. My answer to your offer is no."

McCormick's face tightened. "This offer's very generous; you won't get a better one."

Jeff waited before answering, stalling for time. Every second helped those moving into position. "I reckon it is, but I talked it over with everyone affected, and the answer is no."

McCormick growled, "What changed your mind? You trying to jack me up for more money?"

"I wouldn't even have considered your offer, but it was generous, which made me think about it. But all things considered, the answer is still no."

"I see."

Jeff turned, starting for the door.

McCormick pushed his chair back, his voice lashing out, "Kincaid, you got twenty-four hours to reconsider. You would be smart to take this offer."

Jeff eyed the two gunmen, answering McCormick. "Like I said, no thanks." Jeff walked out into the sunlight. Turning, he brushed past Olcott.

McCormick fumed, staring at the unsigned papers on his desk. Starting to speak, he stopped as the door swung open. Sheriff Olcott entered followed by his two deputies. The fourth man startled him, the man was wearing a Texas Ranger badge. McCormick reached for the desk drawer.

"Don't," McKiever's voice shot across the room, a gun appearing in his hand. "No one move."

The man on McCormick's right reached down, his hand touching his gun. Wayne Johnson rolled, his right fist shooting out, crunching the man's jaw. The gunfighter slammed against the wall, slumping to the floor.

The left-handed gunman froze, keeping his hand away from his revolver.

McCormick snarled, "What's this about, Olcott?"

"You're under arrest. We have a warrant for you from Boston. It seems you're a thief, McCormick. Turn around so we can cuff you."

Sneering, McCormick rose, his voice sarcastic. "Boston, what the hell are you talking about? I'm going to have your badge, Olcott!"

Deputy Pickett reached out, spinning McCormick around. With a push he pinned him against the wall. "You heard the Sheriff, get your hands behind your back. Your days of scaring people are over."

McKiever walked behind the desk, opening the drawer, eyeing the small derringer. Pulling out the gun, he eyed the Bar High owner. "Say now, McCormick, you weren't going to use this against four officers of the law, were you?"

Jerking his head around, McCormick stared at McKiever. "Who the hell are you?"

"I'm your worst nightmare. I've been sent by the Texas Rangers to investigate the death of Samuel Cotton and all the rustling that's been going on, not to mention some other shootings."

"You can't pin that on me."

"That so? It just so happens that all the evidence points to the Bar High. You do own that ranch, don't you?"

"So what!" McCormick snarled, his face contorting. "You're arresting a law-abiding citizen, and after I get your badge, I'll get Olcott's next!"

McKiever smiled. "If I were you, I'd forget about our badges. You're going to be an old man before you get out of prison, that's if they don't hang you first. I understand you were a pretty ruthless first mate while on the high seas. I heard something about men missing at sea."

Wayne eased behind the lefty gunfighter, lifting his gun. "What's your name?"

"Cliff Mayberry."

"Where are you wanted, Cliff?"

"I'm not. You got no cause to arrest me."

"Well, Cliff, we're going to lock you up until we run a check on your past. After all, you are hanging out with some pretty bad company."

Mike reached down, snapping handcuffs on the fallen man. "I better throw some water on this one; he's out like a dead steer."

McCormick glowered at McKiever. "You still haven't told me your name."

Shrugging, McKiever responded, "Knowing my name won't help you. Your lawyer can check the arresting report."

"A man has a right to know his accuser's name, don't he! Your name wouldn't be McKiever, would it?"

"Hmm, that's interesting. How come you know my name?"

"I make it my business to know names."

"Makes sense, except for one thing, before today you never saw me."

McKiever cocked his head, asking, "So how come you know my name?"

McCormick leaned forward, his chin jutting out, not answering the question. Instead, he growled, "I have friends in high places, political people."

Spacing out his words, McKiever gave McCormick a mocking look. "You mean, you had friends in high places. Those people are going to drop you like a bad rumor, which is what you've become." Looking away from McCormick, he eyed Olcott. "Let's get these characters over to the jail so we can finish our roundup." He cast a glance back at McCormick. "Most likely the men on our wanted list will be at the Bar High, don't you think, Sheriff?"

Olcott was enjoying the moment. "All but one who's up on the mesa spying on Jeff's ranch. But he should be in custody by now. Come on, you jailbirds, start moving. Mike, toss water on that hired gun and get him up."

Pushing McCormick from around the desk, Olcott waited for McKiever to open the door before nudging McCormick forward. Nearing the door, McCormick stopped, his voice nasty. "I've got news for you, Ranger, I'm going to be released for lack of evidence, and when that happens, you'll wish you never tangled with me."

McKiever's eyes bore into McCormick. "Killing Samuel Cotton doomed you. A noose is waiting for you, McCormick. Later today we'll be dispatching someone to Indian Wells to talk to the local telegraph dispatcher about a message your foreman sent. Your days are numbered with a rope waiting for you, which means good bye and good riddance."

McCormick's neck swelled. "Like I said, McKiever, when I get back it's all over for you."

McKiever taunted McCormick, "I'm wasting time talking with you, but one last thing: we won't auction your ranch until your guilty verdict comes in. After it does, we're going to give the ranchers back all the money you stole from them. Sheriff, get this riffraff over to the jail."

Rage racked McCormick's body, his voice lashing out. "McKiever, you will never see my trial because you're a walking dead man!"

Olcott rammed his gun barrel into McCormick's back. "Move, jailbird, time to turn you over to a couple of federal marshals from Boston."

McCormick staggered onto the walk, screaming, "I got more news for you, McKiever, your friend Kincaid is just like you, a dead man! The both of you are on borrowed time! You hear me, McKiever, borrowed time!"

Olcott's voice was harsh. "We like it when you keep talking in front of all these witnesses. In the meantime, move."

Waiting for Mike to lead the disheveled, semiconscious, hired gun past him, McKiever closed the door. It was time to shake down the office.

Rummaging through the desk he found nothing but the unsigned contract. At best, only circumstantial evidence, certainly nothing to hang a hat on. Opening the lone file cabinet, it too was empty, containing nothing but a few empty folders with blank contracts. The man was careful, McKiever thought. Picking up the unsigned contract with Jeff's name on it, he headed for the street, slamming the door shut.

Olcott was already returning, Mike Pickett following him. Olcott's voice bridged the distance. "I left Wayne at the jail. Told him to check with the bank while keeping an eye on the prisoners. He's not happy, but somebody's got to stay behind. Find anything?"

"Not really, just the unsigned deal. It can be used as circumstantial, showing their methods of dealing with the different ranches, but better than nothing. I guess any hard evidence will be at the Bar High. Here, Sheriff, you take it and file it."

Olcott took the contract, his voice sounding serious. "Take Mike with you. I'll file this and start the ball rolling at the bank. I'm going to enjoy spending a few minutes with the new bank president. Letting him know I expect his cooperation will be a real pleasure. As soon as I'm finished at the bank, and satisfied everything's secure at the jail, I'll ride out and meet you at Jeff's ranch. Mac, don't go to McCormick's without me. There's no telling what you'll run into at the Bar High."

McKiever agreed. "Don't worry, I won't. Mike, let's get our horses and head out."

Jeff pulled back on the reins. Turning in the saddle, he spoke in a subdued voice. "We'll climb up to the mesa from here. The path's steep, but we won't be seen. I don't want our horses making noise, so we're going up on foot." Dismounting, he led his horse into a jumble of rocks. Finding a small clearing, he tied up his mount. Waiting, he watched each man do the same. Grabbing his canteen, he made a suggestion, "Take a slug of water; the day's hot and the climb's steep. Also, make sure the horses get watered."

Rick filled his hat, waiting until his horse finished drinking. Placing his hat back on his head, he enjoyed the cool water running down his neck. Taking a long drink for himself, he wiped his mouth. Strapping the canteen back on the saddle horn, he reached into his saddlebag, dragging out a linen bag. Dumping the contents, he ordered, "Don't just stare. Grab a pair that fits."

Jeff grinned, remembering his days on the trail with McKiever. "It's those moccasins again. I've gone from being a rancher, back to a lawman, and now an Indian."

Josh's eyes reflected humor, replying, "Being a Texas Ranger was always a learning experience. This was a McKiever tactic, isn't that right, Rick?"

"Sure was. Actually, an Indian scout gave Mac his first moccasins, and ever since then he got us to using moccasins when sneaking up on some fugitive in hiding. The darn things are real quiet and you can feel everything underfoot. They work great. I like 'em."

Jeff changed the conversation, "I guess everything went good in town. I didn't hear any shots."

Rick, placing his boots on a flat boulder, answered, "Yeah, and now it's our turn. Lead out, Jeff Kincaid, it's time to enforce the law."

Following Jeff single file, they climbed, grabbing at anything. The sun was hot, sweat bathing their faces. In minutes Jeff's shirt was soaked. Holding on to a gnarled root, he paused, glancing up. He could see Billy and Clancy staring at them. Keeping his voice low, he hissed, "You two going to extend a helping hand or just sit there with those funny grins?"

Billy Clifford's smile melted away, his voice soft. "Sure will, Mr. Kincaid, but my arms don't reach that far. I got a rope if you want."

"No, we don't need a rope. Just get ready to give a hand because here we come."

Billy grabbed each hand, pulling them up. One by one they stood. Wiping his forehead, Jeff waited until he stopped gulping for air before speaking, "A man thinks he's in shape until he acts like a mountain goat."

Josh, panting heavily, rolled his eyes. "That's for sure. Thank God for horses. May we never do this again."

Rick wanted to agree, but instead sucked air back into his lungs.

Jeff scanned the surroundings. "Billy, where are the spies? Are they above us, or below us?"

"We're above them. You picked a good time 'cause they're getting ready to eat. I can't think of a better time to sneak up on someone than at chow time."

"Can they see us?"

"They could if we get careless. We got to move slow and stay hunkered down. Come on, I'll show you where they are." Lying down, Billy slithered next to a scrub bush. Jeff followed, crawling close to the edge. Peering over the rim, Billy's voice was a whisper. "If you look to the right of that outcropping just within the shadows, you can see them. Here, take the scope, just be careful the sun doesn't reflect off the lens."

Jeff shaded the lens with his hand. Getting comfortable, he focused the scope. "I see them, but not their horses. Where are their horses?"

"On the other side of that outcropping by the north slope."

"What's the best way to sneak up on them?"

"There's a goat trail just below the rim. That trail will take you just to the right of their camp. Their horses shouldn't scent you because the wind is blowing in our direction."

"Perfect, show me where that goat trail is."

Slithering backward, Billy rolled onto his knees before standing, pointing a stubby finger toward two boulders. "You pick up that trail ten feet below that gap between them two rocks. You'll be out of sight until you climb up on the mesa where them spies are camped. As soon as you hit the shadow line, you will be slightly below and to the right of them. I expect if you listen carefully, you should hear them. Regardless, you'll be real close."

Jeff nodded, eyeing Billy and Clancy. "Sounds good. Now, let me bring you two up to date. McCormick, along with two of his men have been arrested in town. McKiever, Olcott, and his deputies are planning to meet up with us at Jeff's ranch. After we get those spies, we'll meet with them, and we're all going to the Bar High. I want both of you to come because of your shooting skills with those rifles. You two okay with that?"

Billy answered, "Whatever you say, boss. I reckon you know me, and Clancy aren't very good with them handguns."

"Don't worry about that, we'll take care of the close range stuff. This brings us back to now. I want you two to cover us until we get the jump on those spies."

Clancy's brogue voice caught everyone's attention, "Don't worry, Mr. Kincaid. If them two twitch, they're dead!"

Jeff liked the way Clancy said that. He looked at Rick and Josh, returning his stare to Billy, keeping his voice low. "Billy, how long will it take us to reach them?"

Billy thought for a second. "Can't be sure, but I'd say no more than twenty minutes."

Jeff looked at his time piece. "Well, time to become mountain goats again." Urgency crept his voice. "Come on, herd, let's do it." Moving to the two large boulders, Jeff started down. Sliding onto the narrow goat path, he was pleased how well the moccasins clung to the narrow trail. What a difference compared to those cumbersome boots, he thought. Moving quickly, he deliberately opened up some distance between himself and Josh. It was better they were spaced out in case one of them stumbled. One thing was sure, skirting the ridge was a lot easier than the climb up.

Billy picked up his rifle. Half opening the breech, he stared into the chamber. The brass bullet shined in the sun's rays. Closing the action, he looked at Clancy, his eyes sparkling, his soft brogue muffled. "Locked and loaded."

Dropping down, both men squirmed to the edge of the rim. Pushing his arms forward, Billy brought up the scope, cautioning Clancy. "First, let's make sure no one's looking this way." He studied the camp. "It looks good; both of them are watching the fire. Go ahead, get set up."

Rolling up his jacket, Clancy placed it under his rifle barrel. Working his elbows into the soil, he peered through the rifle sights. "Target in sight. Your turn."

Billy handed Clancy the scope. Working quickly, he removed a small rock. Staring down the barrel, he lined up the sights on the figures below. Removing another rock, he made sure his arms were comfortable. He eyed the nearest bush. Studying the leaf movement, he peered at Clancy, asking, "What about this breeze, how many clicks should we allow?"

Clancy eyed the bush. "Hang loose, let me do a check." Grabbing a fistful of dirt, he rubbed his hands together until it became powdery. With a flick of his wrist, he tossed the dirt over the rim. Watching, he spoke softly. "I'd say no more than a click and a half at the most."

Billy always marveled at Clancy's ability to gauge trajectory. "A click and a half it is. As soon as we see our men, we'll get serious. Them crooks still eating?"

"They are."

A slight breeze eddied upward, then died. A hawk rose from the canyon, spiraling upward on the rising thermal currents. The bird's shrill whistle broke the silence. Billy and Clancy pulled their hats down, shielding their eyes from the sun's rays. Waiting, they watched, both seeing the distant men at the same time, Billy's voice a command. "Our guys are there. Time to get serious. Your man's to the left, mine on the right."

Jeff stopped, staying within the shadows. According to Billy they should be just to the right of the camp. The goat trail no longer circled the rim, now it angled toward the top. If Billy was right, they should be close, real close. Holding up his hand, he watched Rick and Josh move up. Easing closer, they circled him. Jeff kept his voice hushed. "Let's get our wind back before we rush the camp." Leaning against a boulder, Jeff forced himself to relax. Looking toward the mesa, he reckoned it would only take a few seconds to climb up and close in on the camp. He returned his attention to Josh and Rick. "You two ready?" Both nodded, a look of anticipation showing in their faces. The sound of voices drifted over the rim, followed by a clink of metal. The sound came from above, slightly to their left. Billy was right they were close. Pulling his gun, Jeff leaned over. "Nice and easy, let's get on top and fan out. Move quick and try to get as close as possible before I say anything. Ready?"

Nodding, both men pulled their forty-fives.

Jeff bent over. Using his one hand for balance, he pushed off, scrambling up over the rim. Rick followed, swinging toward his left, Josh was next, fanning out to the right. Moving quickly, they closed the distance toward the two men squatting over the fire.

Clancy's voice was excited, his voice a whisper. "They're up." Snuggling against the rifle stock, he took a deep breath, letting half out. Keeping his finger away from the trigger, his sights settled on the man hunched over the fire. Billy let out a gush of air, then inhaled slightly. Holding the gun sight to the right of the man bent over the fire, his finger slowly wrapped around the trigger, the barrel becoming still.

Reed Barton stuck his knife into the mangled end of the cigar. Twisting the knife, he growled, "I should have told you to bring back some fresh smokes. Why didn't you?"

Russ Cooper stirred the hot ashes of the fire. "What good would that do? You smoke one cigarette after the other, then all the cigars. You want smokes, give me more money."

Reed didn't answer.

Russ looked at Reed, also wanting something to complain about, and he did. "I'm getting sick and tired of watching Kincaid's ranch. How much longer you think we have to stay up here?"

Reed shrugged. "Hell if I know. I've been told today's the big day."

"What's that mean?"

"McCormick's meeting with Kincaid, if all goes well and he buys the ranch, we're out of here. If not, we've been given a target to kill."

"You mean Kincaid?"

Disgusted, Reed threw the cigar in the hot coals. "No, the ranch foreman. With him gone, the boss figures a woman can't run the ranch. That way she'll be forced to sell."

"What makes McCormick think she'll sell to him? The way I hear it, she can't stand him."

"Who knows, I sure don't."

Reed glanced toward Cooper's saddlebags. "You sure you got no more cigars?"

Cooper didn't answer.

Reed's eyes bore a hole into Cooper. "I think you're holding out on me. Russ, I got to have a smoke. Without a smoke I ain't fit to be around."

Russ stared at Reed, knowing the man wouldn't let up. "Alright, but you better nurse this one because I only got three left, and I plan on smoking the last two." Rising, he started for his bedroll. Looking forward, he froze. Three men with guns drawn were almost on top of them. He exhaled sharply, "What the hell!"

Startled, Reed looked up.

A voice followed Cooper's gasp. "Touch those guns and you're dead!"

Reed didn't move, his eyes squinting at his partner. Slowly, his head turning, he started to rise. Out of the corner of his eyes he could see men, men with badges.

"Reed Barton, keep your back turned and don't touch that sidearm."

Recognizing the voice, Reed acted dumb. "Why the drawn guns, Kincaid?"

Josh stepped forward. "The real question is what are you doing here? But since you asked, the reason we're here is to arrest you. Barton, in the name of the Texas Rangers, you're under arrest. Place your hands behind you nice and slow. If you reach for that gun, I'll bring you in dead. Either way, it don't make no difference to me."

Cooper's mind calculated his chances, none of them good. Instinctively, his hand edged toward his gun. Rick Marten's voice stopped him. "You better think real careful. We got two rifles covering you from the mesa. They have you in their sights with instructions to shoot."

Cooper pulled his hand back. "What's this all about? We ain't done nothing."

Jeff's voice showed anger. "How about you being squatters along with spying. We've had you under surveillance for days."

Rick broke in. "Not only are you two trespassing, but all three of us heard what you said." Moving forward, he snapped the handcuffs on Barton. "And I'm not talking about you wanting cigars!"

Reed felt trapped. "Talk don't mean nothing."

"It does when bad things are happening. In law enforcement work, we call that circumstantial evidence."

Sara was troubled. Something must have gone wrong. Jeff should have been back an hour ago. Gripping the porch railing, she scanned the road for distant riders. Squeezing the railing, she tried relaxing. It didn't work. She was sure McKiever had told her that Jeff was only a messenger, so where was he? Imagining the worst, she remembered the gunfighter. Fear started pulling at her thoughts. Letting go of the rail, Sara paced, her nails pressing into her palms.

Foreman Tom Sullivan saw Sara pacing. Leaving the corral, he walked over, his voice reassuring. "I wouldn't fret, Mrs. Kincaid. They'll be along shortly."

Sara crossed her arms. "Tom, I'm worried. Mac told me Jeff would be right back."

Tom removed his hat, his soft drawl always comforting. "Nothing ever goes like clockwork. We want it to, but it don't. Besides, I never saw worry solve anything. Best anyone can do is stay busy. Staying busy always helps 'cause that's when the mind works best. Standing around worrying just makes things worse," Tom reassured Sara. "Even worse, in the end a person finds out they got all worked up over nothing."

Sara tore her eyes away from the road. "You're right, Tom. I guess until Jeff shows up, I better find something to do."

Torn nodded. "You do that, Mrs. Kincaid. I'll keep an eye out, and the minute I catch sight of them I'll let you know."

Sara was thankful. The foreman always had a relaxed way of dealing with problems. Never in a rush, he just solved one problem at a time, until there were none. She smiled. In his quiet way Tom was a gifted person, a man respected by everyone who worked under him. For a moment Sara forgot her fears. Turning, she started for the kitchen, her voice grateful. "Thank you, Tom. I'll be in the kitchen."

Tom's voice stopped her. "Hold on, Mrs. Kincaid, I see dust rising from the road. Looks like riders coming in."

Climbing up the steps, Tom Sullivan stared down the road. The shimmering heat made seeing difficult. Slowly, the distant specks loomed larger, still undistinguishable. Squinting, Sara began counting, "I see one, two—" she stopped. "Tom, there are two riders. I wonder who's with Jeff."

The riders separated from the heat waves, drawing closer. Sara gasped, fear shooting through her body. Mac was there, but not Jeff. Sagging, Sara leaned against the post, her voice barely a whisper. "Tom, it's Mac with another man." Sara feared the worst, her breathing becoming labored. "Dear God, please help me!"

McKiever's eyes scanned the yard looking for horses. He didn't see any, a question crossing his mind. Pulling up in front of the porch, he looked at Sara. Anguish was written all over her face. Turning Friend sideways, he leaned over, focusing on Tom. "Where's Jeff?"

Hearing McKiever's question, Sara almost fell.

Sliding from the saddle, McKiever vaulted two steps at a time. Touching Sara's shoulder, he looked at Tom.

The foreman spoke before he could ask again. "We thought you was Jeff."

McKievers lips tightened, his mind quick. "Tom, you hear any shooting from the mesa?"

"Can't say that I did, and I've been outside most of the morning."

Mac felt relief, stealing a look at Sara. "That means nothing bad has happened. You hear me, Sara? If things went wrong you would have heard shooting. Tom, which way would Jeff go to get up on the mesa?"

"That would be off the ranch road, about three hundred yards after you cross the top. Look to your left, there should be plenty of tracks."

McKiever looked over at Mike. "Mike, let's go back and find out where they went up. Once we get to the mesa, we can help out." Squeezing Sara's shoulder, he tried to comfort her. "Sara, trust me. Everything's okay. No shooting, no problems!"

Sara straightened herself, her face white. "Mac, something has gone wrong!"

"I understand, but neither of you heard shots, which means they're probably on the way here as we talk." Starting for the steps, he spoke to Tom. "Olcott should be arriving soon. When he gets here, update him. I would appreciate you staying with Sara until we get back."

Tom, his eyes still on the road, stopped McKiever. "Yes, sir, but I think you better wait. Right now, I'm seeing more riders in the distance."

Sara steadied herself, rising on her toes, she stared. Counting softly, her voice grew in strength. "One, two, three, four, five, six, seven—there are seven riders coining in."

McKiever pulled out his scope.

Sara's voice was eager. "Mac, who do you see?"

"I see Jeffrey Kincaid and two prisoners, along with the rest of the men. That's what I see." He looked at Sara, winking.

Relief flooded Sara's body, her voice a sigh. "Thank you, my Lord, oh thank you."

McKiever stared at Sara, seeing both her love and her relief, admiring her more than ever. He reminded himself to take care of business. "Sara, any chance for some grub before we head for the Bar High?"

Smiling, Sara tore her eyes away from the approaching riders, answering him, "Mac, I have a pile of food on the table, enough for everyone."

"Good girl, I don't know why I asked."

Sara laughed, watching the riders sweep into the yard.

Jeff was out of the saddle, his face beaming. Speaking to McKiever, he eyed Sara. "Mission accomplished."

Crossing the porch steps, Sara met Jeff, falling into his arms. "Jeffrey Kincaid, I was so worried. What happened? What took you so long?"

"I guess that climb up to the mesa took some time. Then we moved real careful, sneaking along the ridge to get a jump on those polecats. That, and getting back down took more time than I figured." Squeezing Sara tight, he stepped back. Looking at Mac, he gestured toward the men in handcuffs. "Thanks to your old moccasin trick, them two were so busy complaining they never heard us."

McKiever looked at the captured men. "Which one of them is on our wanted poster?"

Rick answered, "That scruffy one wearing the blue bandana. His name is Reed Barton."

McKiever eyed the man. "Get those two men handcuffed to the porch posts. The rest of you head for the kitchen; there's food on the table. Don't waste time, because as soon as Olcott arrives, we're heading to the Bar High to get Charlie off the hook. Jeff, why don't you assign two men to keep an eye on our prisoners?"

Jeff pointed to his foreman. "Tom, you decide who guards the spies."

Tom was pleased; responsibility was something he thrived on. "Consider it done. You just go about your business, Mr. Kincaid."

Jeff, with Sara at his side, walked inside. Tom looked at McKiever. "I'd appreciate if you'd keep an eye on them until I get some help from the bunkhouse. I'll only be a minute."

"Go ahead, Tom, I'll wait."

Watching Tom's bowlegged gait, McKiever became aware of Rick easing alongside him, the Ranger's voice a whisper. "If a man had a woman like Sara, life would sure take on some extra meaning. Now I know what you went through."

McKiever looked at the ground before raising his head. "Are you saying you'd leave the Texas Rangers for a woman like that?"

Rick tried to be careful with his answer, but failed. "I reckon I would. Being around a woman like that would sure shorten a man's day with some excitement."

McKiever had to smile, thinking about what Rick was saying. "I guess you're right. A flower like that only comes along once in a man's life. If a man had a chance and hesitated, I guess the next fellow wouldn't. Anyway, not to get you off the subject, but why don't you go inside and get some grub. I'll be in as soon as Sullivan gets back."

Pushing his hat back, Rick gave McKiever's arm a squeeze of sympathy. Half smiling, head down, he sauntered inside.

McKiever pried his thoughts away from Rick's words, focusing on what needed to be done. The arrests had gone easily, maybe too easily. He would feel better when they got things wrapped up at the Bar High. One thought kept bothering him: where was the gunfighter hired by McCormick?

CHAPTER 11

No Choice

The road steepened, the Bar High looming in the distance. Leveling off, the posse spread out. For a moment McKiever was distracted by the surroundings. The distant pass was touched with autumn yellows, the mountain peaks tinged with white. Sheriff Olcott was also captivated by the beauty. Both shifted their attention away from the scenery as they neared the ranch. A solitary man was crossing the yard. Stopping, he looked in their direction.

Moving toward the bunkhouse, Russ Wagle heard the horses. Turning, he stared at the riders. He knew McCormick was due back, but there were too many riders. Frowning, his hand dropped to his gun.

Raymond Floyd tightened the cinch, his horse ready for the morning ride. Placing his left foot into the stirrup, he lifted himself into the saddle. Pulling on the reins, he started toward the yard. Stopping, he listened. He could hear horses, lots of horses. Backing the stallion up, he dismounted. Slipping into the barn, he stayed in the gloom. Tiptoeing where he could see the yard, he squinted in dismay. The place was full of lawmen. Three of the men were wearing Texas Ranger badges. One thing Floyd knew, if those Rangers saw him, he was headed for the rope. Crouching low, he slipped from view, breaking into a trot. Reaching his horse, he mounted. Keeping the barn between himself and the yard, he kept the stallion at a slow walk. The last thing Floyd wanted was to attract attention, and a running horse could be heard. His plan was simple: he would slip away and get to those mountains. Once in the mountains, they would never catch him.

Charlie Walters had the perfect vantage point from the upper veranda. He saw the riders long before the foreman did. Buckling on his gun belt, he kept his eyes on Wagle. Bending over, he tied the leather thong to his leg. Straightening, he headed for the stairs. Using the side door, he slipped outside. Circling, he came up behind the foreman. Charlie pulled his gun, thumbing back the hammer. His voice mingled with the deadly sound from the forty-four. "Hold it, Russ. Don't even think about reaching for your gun."

Russ stiffened, his head swinging around, astonishment flooding his face. "Charlie, what the hell are you doing?"

"I'm working for Sheriff Olcott, along with some Texas Rangers who are arriving, so keep that gun in its holster."

Disbelief giving way to anger, Wagle snarled, "Put that gun down or I'll blow your head off."

For a second Charlie felt anxiety, but his nerves steadied. "Russ, don't try it. I'll shoot you if I have to!"

Russ couldn't believe it. Charlie was nothing more than a two-bit bookworm who was now threatening him with a gun. If the men ever heard about this, he would never live it down. He decided to kill Charlie. Starting to turn, Russ changed his mind as the riders swept into the yard. Charlie would have to wait, his hand drifting away from his gun.

McKiever's voice snapped, "Everything okay, Charlie?"

Charlie nodded, keeping his eyes on Wagle. "It's safe. This man here is the Bar High foreman by the name of Russ Wagle."

Wagle's eyes shifted from McKiever to Olcott. "What's going on, Olcott?"

"As of right now, you're unemployed."

"I'm what? What are you saying?"

"That means," McKiever interrupted, "your boss is under arrest, which means no more pay checks." McKiever slipped out of the saddle, his eyes searching the yard. "Charlie, lift Wagle's gun."

Moving behind Wagle, Charlie's voice was bold. "My pleasure." Pulling the foreman's gun was a great feeling, a liberating feeling. He officially had his manhood back.

Wagle seethed. The idea of Charlie taking his gun was unthinkable, but it was happening. Glaring at Charlie, his question went to Olcott. "Sheriff, am I under arrest?"

"Let's just say that's up to you. Right now, we're looking for Raymond Floyd. Where is he?"

"So, if I'm not under arrest, why have you pulled my gun?"

McKiever stepped toward Wagle, his voice a command. "Answer the Sheriff's question."

Russ shrugged. "I don't know."

"You're the foreman, aren't you? If you don't want to be an accomplice, let's try that question again. Where's Floyd?"

"Around somewhere, it's his day off."

Charlie's voice broke up the questions, his arm pointing toward the distant flats. "I think that's him?"

McKiever's eyes followed the pointing arm. Spinning around, he dug into the saddlebag, pulling out his scope. "What type of horse does he ride, Charlie?"

"A big gray with a dark mane."

McKiever nodded. "That's him. Now I remember him. He's the man with the black beard. Jeff, where do those flats lead to?"

"Into the foothills and then the mountains. If he gets into those mountains, you'll never catch him. Come on, I'll show you."

"No, you won't. You stay with Sheriff Olcott."

"Mac, I'm coming. I know that territory all the way up to the pass."

"Sorry, Jeff, this is Ranger work and you're a deputy who's needed here."

"Now wait a minute, Mac. Don't try to protect me."

McKiever vaulted into his saddle. "Jeff, you retired, remember?" Wheeling Friend around, he felt the roan's muscles bunch. Hauling back on the reins, he held his horse back. "Charlie, you know where everything is. Show them McCormick's office and where those two safes are."

Charlie's chin jutted out. "Sure thing, Mr. McKiever. I won't disappoint you."

"I know you won't, Charlie." Turning Friend, a hint of urgency crept into his voice. "Come on, you two, we've got work to do." Friend, his neck arched, started sidestepping, wanting to run. Josh and Rick moved alongside. Mac kept his eyes on the distant figure. "Let's not be obvious until Floyd drops over that ridge. Once he's out of sight, we'll push."

Dropping below the ridge, Floyd was pleased. So far, so good. He had taken his time to avoid looking suspicious. Anyone seeing him would just think he's a cowboy riding out to do his job. Once he reached those hills, they would never catch him. It was not by accident he'd paid more money than he wanted for the horse he rode. His horse was a big stallion who could run. Floyd felt very confident. Reaching the bottom of the gully, they started up. Cresting the top, Floyd stole a look toward the ranch, his body jerking taut. Three riders were coming hard towards him. Booting the big male, he leaned forward, as if his weight shift would help his horse. The stallion lunged forward, his hooves kicking up puffs of dirt from the dry ground.

Rick shouted. "There he goes!" Josh was quiet, riding easily. Reaching the narrow gully, McKiever slowed Friend. No sense in wearing him out until the time was right. Trotting down to the bottom, they rose upward, Friend surging over the top. Mac could see Floyd had gained back some distance. Josh and Rick moved alongside.

McKiever's voice rose over the noise from the bounding hooves. "We'll take it easy until we hit the shade from those hills. Then I'm going to turn Friend loose and get him. You two catch up when you can."

Josh, followed by Rick, veered away. Spacing their mounts to avoid each other's dust, they flared out even further. McKiever admired their knowledge and tactics. They understood how to chase, and were avoiding being a bunched-up target.

Floyd felt better. He had gained lost ground and his horse was running easily. It wouldn't do him any good to push his horse harder unless he had to. It was a long ride through the pass, and a crippled horse would only get him captured. Up ahead he could see shadows stretching over the flats. Once he escaped from the heat of the sun's rays, he would use the cooler air to his advantage. Entering the shadows, he thumped the big gray, urging him on.

McKiever watched Floyd enter the shade, his horse running harder. Rick swung toward him, his voice showing concern. "Mac, he's making his run."

"Let him. He wants to sucker us into overheating our horses in the sun."

Rick half yelled. "He knows the game."

"Yeah, and he knows if we catch him there's a rope waiting. He won't surrender without a fight, making him dangerous, real dangerous, so watch yourselves."

Floyd looked back. His pursuers hadn't taken the bait, they were maintaining their pace. Floyd thought about the man on the roan horse. The real danger would come from him. He remembered the stranger's speed with the gun, and now he knew why: the man was a Texas Ranger.

Entering the shade McKiever felt the temperature drop. Half rising in the stirrups, his voice a shout, "When you two catch up, flank me!" Leaning forward, he spoke into Friend's ear. "Come on, big boy, get him." Friend exploded, the landscape becoming a blur, the grays and browns melting together. Already Floyd appeared larger, the distance closing.

Floyd looked back, his eyes bulging. The man in the middle was closer, a lot closer. Digging his spurs into the gray, he felt him accelerate. Running harder, his horse started up the gradual incline. Leveling off they approached another slope, slightly steeper. Thundering upward, Floyd turned in his saddle. Grimacing, he swore. The Ranger was already at the base of the slopes. For the first time he realized he might not get to the mountain before his pursuers caught him. Refusing to look back, he scanned the terrain looking for an ambush site, the barren ground offering nothing, not a rock or a hush could be seen. It was obvious his only hope was those mountains. Floyd talked to his horse. "Come on, he's got to climb these slopes just like you."

McKiever was surprised. Friend was closing the distance, but not as quickly as he had hoped. The man's horse was a big stallion, and fast. If Floyd got to the jagged base of the mountain, things could get uncomfortable. McKiever thought about his Sharps, thinking he could shoot Floyd's horse out from under him. He knew the captain would say to not be a softy, always warning his men to do what is necessary. Shaking his head, he spoke to Friend. "I can't shoot that horse. It's up to you, old boy." McKiever felt Friend's strides lengthen.

Floyd looked back. The lawman had closed within rifle range. He raked his horse with his spurs. The big gray's breathing was getting labored, his body covered with sweat. For the first time Floyd saw the jumble of boulders scattered over the ground. Behind the rocks loomed the mountain. Floyd knew the race was going to be close, his mind becoming deadly. He would shoot the Ranger's horse as soon as he reached the rocks. No need to kill the man, just his horse. By the time the other two lawmen arrived, he would be gone.

Josh glanced at Rick. "Let's slow down so when we catch up our horses will be fresh."

Rick pulled back on the reins. "Josh, look at those two go. Man alive, they're covering some ground."

"Yeah, a race to the death. Let's hope we get there in time to make a difference."

McKiever leaned over, listening to his horse, pleased that Friend's breathing wasn't labored. Satisfied, he straightened, looking ahead. For the first time he saw the distant boulders. Floyd was going to reach the rocks first, and once he did things were going to get dangerous.

Floyd eyed the boulders. The jumble to his left looked good. He would have just enough time to dismount, get behind a rock, and shoot. The mammoth stones were coming up fast. Floyd shifted his weight, grabbing for his carbine. The sudden shift of weight threw the big gray's strides off, his right hoof dragged, the leg buckling. Swerving, they went over, the ground rushing to meet them. Floyd kicked his feet free. Rolling, he narrowly avoided the crushing weight. Dust swirled around him. Spitting, Floyd rose, brushing his eyes clear. The gray was trotting away, the rifle still in the scabbard. Any chance to shoot from rifle distance was gone, the pursuing rider closing in on him. Drawing his gun, he snapped a shot at the Ranger's horse. Diving toward the rocks, Floyd saw horse and rider disappearing off to his right.

McKiever heard the hiss, the bullet passing dangerously close. Swinging Friend toward an opening in the boulders, they slid to a stop. Leaping off, he slapped Friend's flank. Pulling his six-shooter, he waited, watching his horse trot out of sight. Sliding toward an opening, McKiever stopped, letting his mind work. The advantage had shifted to him. Floyd had no rifle, no horse, and no water. The question was, what would the outlaw do? The answer came to him. Floyd's only hope was getting to a horse, anyone's horse! That was it, he thought, the man needed a horse, and that was how he'd find him. He'd hunt Floyd by locating the outlaw's horse.

McKiever moved, letting his instincts take over. Hearing horses, he stopped. Seconds later a shout broke the quiet. "Mac, we got his horse!" The voice belonged to Josh. Again, Josh yelled. "Mac, we got Floyd's horse!"

Mac heard horses moving away. Smart, he thought. His men had given him the advantage in a deadly game. Without a horse there was little chance Floyd could escape. It was time to think like a fugitive. The next question was, would the gunman rather face one man, or two? Logic said one man, which meant him. If his reasoning was correct, Mac needed to set a trap before Floyd could figure a way to put a bullet into him.

Sliding along the boulder, McKiever stared down a narrow pathway between the rocks. If he stalked Floyd, the advantage was with the gunman. He needed an edge, but how could he get it? Occasional gaps in the boulders gave him an idea. If he ran through the boulders, and Floyd saw him, the gunman might think he was being flanked. Maybe Floyd would break for the flats, looking for a horse. If Floyd took the bait, he just might surprise him by doubling back. Hesitating, Mac gave the plan more thought. At the very least, when he ran, Floyd might shoot at him, giving away his position. It was better to try something that might fail, than to do nothing. It was time to see what might happen. Gathering himself, he bolted from behind the boulder. Running through the narrow rock-strewn path, he darted past the gaps. Expecting gunfire, none came. Nearing a cut in the rocks, he dropped down. Sucking air back into his lungs, Mac's mind calculated quickly. Better give the fugitive a few seconds. No sense in Floyd seeing his blue shirt going back the other way.

Ray lay prone atop the boulder, propped up on his elbows. He had two Rangers to the right of him, and one to his left. Up here he could see, but the sun was sucking his body dry. Floyd licked his lips. If he stayed on the rock he would be cooked like a t-bone steak. He needed to make a move. The longer he waited, the worse it would get. The way he saw it, going up against one gun was better than two. The more he thought, the more Floyd liked the idea of the hunted becoming the hunter. He would double back, find the Ranger's horse, and if the man got in the way, shoot him.

Sudden movement caught Floyd's attention. Alert, he stared. A blue shirt flashed through a gap in the rocks. Shifting his stare ahead, he watched. The blue shirt darted through the next gap. Perfect, he thought, the lawman was flanking him. This was his chance. It was time to vamoose and find the man's horse. Sliding off the boulder, Floyd raced for the flats. Breaking into the open, he found horse tracks skirting along the edge of the rocks. Floyd scrambled, knowing those hoof prints would lead to the maker. Breathing hard, Floyd rounded a slight bend. Eyes darting, he jerked to a halt. Pivoting, he brought his gun up, pointing it at a man in a blue shirt.

The slug bunched into Floyd's chest, pushing him backward. A second bullet spun him around. Floyd's gun bucked, the bullet plowing harmlessly into the ground. Slumping backward, Floyd crumbled to the ground, his eyes becoming a vacant stare.

Staring at the dead man, McKiever felt a tinge of remorse. For the longest time he didn't move, his gun tangling at his side. Everything had happened fast, too fast. He could still see Floyd's gun swinging toward him, the man's body jerking from the bullets, then the blank look in his eyes. McKiever wanted to curse the man, but he couldn't. Floyd had taken away his choice. His plan had produced death, but he was alive. Feeling the slight breeze wash across his face felt good. Slowly approaching the lifeless body, he stared at Floyd's face. Grimacing, he pushed his hat back. A body without life was a disturbing sight. Mac shook his head. Out of necessity he had killed before. Yes, it was part of the job; the part he didn't like. The captain had always said let the courts do it. That way a man who broke the law did it to himself through the law.

A sharp whistle broke McKiever's musings. Whistling back, he shouted, "Over here!" Stepping away from the boulders, he saw two men and three horses moving towards him.

Josh and Rick dismounted. No words were spoken. Grabbing the dead body, they slung him over the gray. Lashing legs to arms, they stepped back, Rick speaking, "You said he was dangerous, and you were right. Glad you're alive, Mac."

Looking at the gray stallion, Mac sighed, "Beautiful animal. He'll make a great horse for someone." He looked at his two Ranger partners, his voice a suggestion. "Be an outstanding Ranger horse, don't you think?" Shrugging, McKiever half smiled, his voice wistful— "Don't fight over him." Opening his Colt, he punched out the empty cases. Reaching into the gun belt, he slipped two bullets into the empty chambers. Snapping the cylinder shut, he looked at his friends, his face serious, his voice soft. "Thanks, Rick. Yes, he was dangerous. The man gave me no choice."

CHAPTER 12

Appointment with Death

Pushing past the front door, McKiever eyed the open door leading to the jail cells. Smiling, he looked at the loose circle of men. "It looks like all rooms are full, no vacancies."

Everybody laughed, Olcott answering, "Actually, we do have more room in the third cell. A man by the name of McCormick has departed with an armed escort for the Boston area, leaving us with one more vacancy."

More laughter filled the room.

Olcott continued, "With all the evidence we gathered at the Bar High, along with bank records, we could have hung him here, and maybe we should have. I told the two U. S. Marshals, if he beats the rap in Boston, ship him back here and we'll string him up."

Jeff spoke up. "Hey, Sheriff, tell Mac what those jailbirds told you."

McKiever shifted his eyes to Olcott.

"Sure, you're going to like this. We separated them for questioning. They couldn't stop squealing on each other, but they all agreed on one thing. They told us that Raymond Floyd murdered Sam Cotton. They said he lay in wait, bushwhacking him."

"You think," McKiever questioned, "you think they weren't just covering for themselves? You know, trying to save their own skins."

Olcott's response was quick. "No, like I told you before, I always figured he did it."

Mike Pickett jumped in. "That Floyd was a mean one all right, with a temper to match. The man was always looking for a chance to shoot somebody."

McKiever nodded. "Well then, I guess I shot the right man." Turning his head, he spoke to Charlie Walters. "Charlie, how do you like working for Jeff at the Upper Forks Ranch?"

Charlie chuckled, "Like manna from heaven."

McKiever's smile faded. "Charlie, we have one loose end and I think you know what that is. His name is Peckenpath. We promised you we wouldn't use those posters without your permission. How about it?"

Charlie took a second. "Tell you what, the Lord said don't be afraid of the one who can kill the body, but be afraid of the one who can kill both the soul and the body. I got my soul back. You go ahead and stick them posters up."

"Thanks, Charlie." McKiever looked at Olcott. "What about that foreman, Russ Wagle?"

"We released him. Unfortunately, the telegraph operator at Indian Wells didn't remember who sent the message to Peckenpath. Mike told Wagle to stick around until we finished our investigation. He told him we were still uncovering new leads."

Wayne Johnson started laughing, spacing his words out. "That Wagle couldn't get on his horse fast enough. I doubt if he'll stop until he crosses the Mexican border."

Smiling, Mac's eyes shifted back to Charlie. "You let us know if Wagle shows up looking for revenge, that includes a retired Ranger like myself. I'm serious, Charlie."

Charlie heard the sincerity in McKiever's voice, nodding in appreciation.

Wrapping his hands around the back of a chair, McKiever leaned forward. "I sure would like someone to question that legal beagle, that Wynncliff fellow."

Wayne answered, "Mike and myself spent a lot of time with Jonathan Barker, and so far it seems that Wynncliff's nothing more than a paper advisor. We couldn't connect him to anything. We looked hard, but nothing came up."

"But," Olcott interrupted, "when and if he shows up, he will be questioned at great length."

"By the way," Wayne grinned, "you should have seen the fun we had with the boss banker. We had him all shook up."

McKiever liked what he was hearing, his voice reflecting it. "That would have been worth watching." Crossing his arms he stared at the floor before raising his head. "It seems this assignment is wrapped up. My only concern is Peckenpath. Truth is, I don't know where he is, or if he's going to show up. I wish I knew because, if I did, I'd stay in town. But it's time for me to move on. With winter coming on, I have to get to my ranch." Frowning, he rubbed his hands. "For all I know, Peckenpath may have left since we've made all those arrests. Anyway, it's been a pleasure working with all of you. Keep me posted on what's happening through Jeff. I will be at his ranch before I leave in case Peckenpath shows up. I guess that's about it. Good luck to everyone, you sure earned it."

Each man rose, moving toward him. Shaking each hand, he eyed Josh and Rick. "I have a special request for you two. As my last official act as a Texas Ranger, I'm going over to the telegraph office to send the captain a report. After that, I'm coming back to leave my badge with Olcott. I'd be obliged if you'd pick it up and return it to headquarters."

Rick looked at McKiever, answering for both, "Sure thing. Anything else?"

"No, but if I think of anything I'll send word before I leave. Like I said, since we're supposed to be Peckenpath's targets, I'll stay at Jeff's ranch for several days. After that, I will be heading for my own place. Jeff, whenever you and Sara are ready, I'll ride with you."

Jeff stood up. "Tell you what, Sara's at the store picking out some dress material. Give me about twenty minutes. By the time you get back from sending the telegraph, we should be ready." Walking toward the door, Jeff paused, rolling his eyes upward. "Mac, don't rush. Picking out material for a dress isn't like chasing crooks. A person has to be real cautious."

The room exploded with hoots and laughter.

Jeff stepped out, easing the door shut, the smile leaving his face. For several seconds he stood still, his thoughts on the gunfighter. Mac was their equalizer, but with him gone there was no one who matched the killer. Well, maybe Mac was right, maybe the killer had left.

Rick stopped laughing, looking at Josh. "I'm going across the street to get a cut and shave. How about meeting me at the hotel? The day's still early enough to check out from the hotel, grab some lunch, and then hit the trail for headquarters."

Josh agreed, facing McKiever. "Sounds good to me. Mac, expect visitors at your ranch. I could use some time off, you know, a little rest and relaxation."

A fondness crept into McKiever's face. "You bet. I'll look forward to seeing you. As for the rest of you, I sure would be pleased having some company. Josh, you and Rick don't forget, before you leave pick up my badge at Olcott's. Another thing, tell the captain I expect a visit."

Josh nodded, both slipping through the door.

Turning back to Olcott, Mac pulled up a chair. "Let's get the arrest forms finished and signed so I can get going."

Olcott sat, holding out a pen. He pushed over three forms. "Read them if you want, but they're all filled out. All you have to do is sign them. Like I said, read them if you want."

Not looking, McKiever signed them. Standing, he eyed Sheriff Olcott. "You still planning on retiring?"

"Sure am. At the beginning of the month, to be exact. You know, Mac, I'm kind of like you, except for one thing."

"What's that?"

"I'm really retiring. You're starting out in a new career."

"I guess you have a point there. Anyway, I want you to know that I never worked with a better lawman than you." McKiever looked at the two deputies. "Tell me, Sheriff, which of those two is going to be the new top lawman in town?"

"You'll have to ask the mayor, but I got to say this. If one of them isn't sworn in, I'm sending them over to the Texas Rangers."

Mac shifted his eyes to the deputies. "You do that and I'll make sure they get priority. You men have been trained by the best. I'm quite sure the captain will take you." With a salute, Mac moved to the door. "Olcott, make sure you check with Jeff and stay in touch." He looked at Wayne and Mike. "You two do the same." Touching his hat brim, Mac pushed open the door. "Adios."

Scanning the street, McKiever let his eyes adjust to the bright sunlight. Stepping on the hard-packed dirt, he paused, a sudden feeling of caution seeping into his body, his nerves tingling, his body becoming taut, his eye's searching. The street appeared normal, a few people hurrying toward their places of business. Standing still, he waited to see if the feeling would stop. His muscles remained taut, his instincts warning him to be careful. Moving deliberately, he started toward the telegraph office.

Clearing the jail, McKiever paused, looking into the alley. No one was there. Turning his head, he eyed the far alley. Thanks to the morning sun, he could see everything. The alley was empty. Ahead lay the general store. Reaching down, he lifted his gun, checking each chamber. Slipping the Colt back, he began a deliberate walk, careful to miss nothing. Reaching the General Store, Mac observed Kincaid's two wagon horses. Both animals seemed content, their tails swishing back and forth in the warm sun. For a second he relaxed, but that strange feeling seeping back, growing stronger. On edge, he glanced behind him. The street and boardwalk appeared void of human activity. Funny, he thought, where was everyone? The only sign of life was him and the two horses. McKiever's instincts wouldn't leave him alone. Somewhere danger was lurking; he could feel it. For several minutes he didn't move. Lips compressed, McKiever eased further into the street. Passing the general store, he eyed the narrow corridor between the buildings. The shaded alley revealed nothing. McKiever turned his head, examining the far boardwalk. Seeing nothing, he shifted his stare back to the street. Everything appeared normal, no one lurking in the shadows. Relax, he told himself. He was strung too tight. Starting to move, his head jerked around, fear shooting through him. A man was standing in the alley. He was dressed in black, with a face like a ghost.

A voice sounding like an echo reached McKiever. "You would be Texas Ranger McKiever, would you not?"

Not answering, Mac remembered Charlie's description. He was right, looking into the man's face was like looking at death. Unable to find his voice, he stared.

The man's lips moved, the sound everywhere at once. "We have an appointment with destiny, Ranger McKiever." The sound died, before returning, "Just you and me."

Willing his mind to respond, McKiever found his voice. "And you would be Sam Peckenpath. I'm surprised you're still here. Your employer is headed for the rope."

An eerie smile followed the voice. "That really doesn't matter. What is important is that I've been paid in full. Even more important, I always finish my obligations. You see, Ranger, my reputation means everything to me."

McKiever shuddered. The man's black eyes seemed without pupils. The killer was relaxed, enjoying the moment. Mac needed a way out. He spoke, hoping to buy time. "Being wanted by the Texas Rangers means your days are numbered, Peckenpath."

Peckenpath's soft laugh produced a foreboding hiss. "I live for death; it's my friend. Death is man's ultimate challenge. You and I are about to have that ultimate moment, life or death."

McKiever's life flashed through his mind. Captain Frank once told him that everything has an origin, and so did evil. Staring into those black, lifeless eyes, he couldn't help but think, if there was a devil, this was surely him.

The eerie voice washed over McKiever. "I respect a man of the gun, a worthy opponent. I have heard about you and your reputation. It's been a long time since I've faced a man who can give me the ultimate test."

McKiever was sure if he was going to have a chance he needed a distraction. If someone showed up, it might give him a slight advantage. Stalling, he talked. "I learned something long ago, Peckenpath, that there's always somebody faster with the gun than the last man you faced."

"Yes, I agree, but there's only one way to know, and I live for the knowing. Today you are my ultimate moment. After you, I will fulfill my contract by killing Jeffrey Kincaid, who's in that store. Once the shooting starts, he'll be the first to arrive. But for now, you are my real challenge, not him."

Feeling his senses numbing, McKiever felt fear grabbing at him, draining his strength.

Peckenpath's sinister voice stopped Mac's slide into desperation. "I always let my opponents draw first, and you're no exception. But the time is now. When I start counting, you must go for your gun before I reach ten. After that, I won't wait, and if I go first, you can't win."

McKiever tried to read the man's face. His eyes made it impossible. Don't watch those eyes that don't have pupils, he warned himself. They wouldn't give him any advanced indication.

"Remember," Peckenpath repeated, "you must go for your gun first, or you will have no chance." The killer's voice rose as he began counting. "One, two—"

McKiever felt his mind and senses returning. His only chance was to dive as he pulled his gun. He would lose a split second, but he was facing a man like he'd never seen before. Regardless, if he was going to die, he would die like a Texas Ranger. His voice leaped out with authority. "Sam Peckenpath, you're under arrest. Drop your gun belt and raise your hands."

The eerie voice continued, "Three, four, five—"

Lunging sideways, McKiever rolled, his .45 leaping up, the gun bucked. Three shots thundered as one. He felt the first bullet hit him. Driven backward, he felt the shock from the second bullet. Numbness enveloped him, his Colt spilling out of his hand. The ground met him, his world turning dark, then black.

Jeff chuckled, watching Sara's enthusiastic attempts to hurry up. She looked at him, her eyes sparkling. The thunderous explosions of gunshots seemed to come through the wall. Sara's smile froze. Jeff's face turned to stone, his voice lashing out, "Dammit, where's Mac!" Wheeling, he clawed at his gun, lunging for the door. Sara's hands flew to her face, fear gripping at her heart. Jeff bolted through the door.

Rick placed his hat on the peg, eyeing the barber. "A trim and a shave, how much?"

The black handle-bar-mustached barber stared at him. "Normally two bits, but because of what you fellows did for this town, this one's on me."

"I guess I can't refuse that price." The sounds of gunfire froze Rick. "What the—" Jumping to the door, he looked toward the General Store. He could see Jeff running toward someone on the ground. Rick started to run.

Jeff felt anger flooding his face. McKiever was down, not moving. Sliding to a halt, his gun pointed toward the alley. A man lay face up, unmoving. Dropping to one knee, he choked back anger. Reaching for McKiever's neck, he searched for a pulse. Blood completely covered McKiever's chest, seeping into the street. Jeff looked at Sara, seeing tears streaming down her face. She wailed, "Oh my God! Oh God no, please no!" She tore her eyes away, looking at Jeff.

Jeff forced himself to talk. "He's got a slight pulse, Sara, pray—pray like you've never prayed before!"

Sara sobbed, pleading unashamedly. "Please Jesus, save him—oh God, help us!"

Starting to rise, Jeff stopped, watching Rick run past him. Rick, his gun drawn, stared at the man in the alley, a shudder passing through him. Turning, Rick eyed Jeff, his face white, his voice hushed, "He's dead. How about Mac?"

"Barely alive. We've got to get him over to Doc's—and fast!"

A crowd began gathering, Olcott pushing through. He stared at Jeff, his face grim.

"Sheriff, we need to get him over to Doc's right now!"

Olcott nodded, his voice a shout. "You men, make a stretcher with your arms and get this Ranger over to Doc's. Dammit, I don't care if you have to run with him, but get him there!"

Jeff rose, moving over to Peckenpath, he recoiled, his gun rising, almost pulling the trigger. Halting his reaction, Jeff looked at Rick, who was still staring at the dead killer. Jeff couldn't keep the awe out of his voice. "My god, I've never seen such a face. How'd you ever touch him to make sure he's dead?"

Rick shrugged. "I didn't have too. Mac shot his heart out, dead center. You going over to see if Mac's going to make it?"

"Not yet, I guess I'm too afraid. You go ahead. I'll follow shortly. I got some curiosity about this. I want to check a few things out." Reminding himself to holster his gun, Jeff retrieved McKiever's revolver. Opening it, he felt numb. Only one bullet was fired. Positive he'd heard three shots, he stared at the gathering crowd, ordering the people to clear the area. "I need to do some checking here. You people back up!" Bending over, he picked up the killer's mahogany-handled revolver. Straightening, he swung the cylinder open, grimacing. Two bullets were spent. Despite McKiever's speed, the killer had shot twice. Jeff shook his head. It was tough to believe someone was that fast. Staring at the chambers, he felt guilt. If Mac hadn't shot the gunfighter, he would have been next. He was the first to arrive, and his speed with a six-shooter didn't compare with Mac's. He felt a numbness seeping into his bones. Jeff felt someone touch his arm. He looked into the face of Fred Kendall, the town undertaker. Kendall pointed at the dead man, his voice hushed. "What you want done with the body?"

"That's a question for Sheriff Olcott. I reckon for now you better stick him in a pine box and slap the lid on."

Kendall nodded. "I'll get right to it" Turning, he scurried away.

Watching the stooped undertaker hurry away, Jeff's eyes shifted across the street, staring at Doc Mason's office. Except for a few people milling around, no one had come out. Jeff felt a glimmer of hope. Not wanting to hear bad news, he stalled. Sooner or later he had to know. If McKiever died, he knew he would never get over it. Reluctantly, he started walking, his boots feeling like they were caked with mud, his steps slow. Jeff couldn't shake the dread of what he might learn. Crossing the street, he slowed down to a crawl. Reaching the boardwalk, he stopped to listen. Hearing nothing, he climbed the steps, pushing open the door. Stepping inside, he saw Rick, his hat pushed back, his face grim. Rick greeted him, his voice matching his face. "Doc's in there cursing. Sara's praying. That all I know."

Jeff felt temporary relief. "Good, he's still alive?"

Rick made a face. "So far. All I know is what I'm hearing from the room, and the sounds have been kind of disturbing. I'm thinking things aren't good."

"How about Mac's wounds? You know anything?"

"One bullet went through his chest; the other lodged in his shoulder. Doc's trying to stop the bleeding while removing the bullet from his shoulder."

Jeff squinted, shaking his head. "Why is Doc bothering with that second bullet now?"

Rick took a moment. "Doc said it was now or never. I guess he knows what he's doing."

Jeff was out of questions. Both became quiet, facing the closed door. Cringing, they heard Sara's cry. "Oh God help us, please help us!"

Jeff felt drained of energy. Easing into a chair, he closed his eyes, softly repeating Sara's plea.

Rick stared at the ceiling.

The minutes ticked by, all sounds ceasing. Jeff cast a wary eye at the door, straining to hear. Occasionally he heard voices, then silence.

The door creaked open, Doc stepping out, a frown on his face. Both jumped, tensing.

Rolling down his sleeves, Doc Mason eased the door shut. "Your Ranger friend is alive. For how long, I don't know. To be quite frank, if he makes it through this hour, he'll probably pass away by late afternoon." Doc looked at both men. "Anything past that will be a miracle. If a miracle does happen, it will be because of that woman in there. She's quite a gal." Finishing buttoning his sleeve, Doc stepped in front of Jeff. "Sara wants you to get Pastor Olgilvie."

Not answering, Jeff wheeled, heading for the door. It was a relief to be doing something, anything! The church was at the far end of town. Pushing through the crowd, he ignored the questions. Breaking into a trot, he reached the church. Racing through the hallway, he stepped into the pastor's office.

Pastor Olgilvie looked up.

Jeff leaned against the doorway, breathing hard. "Pastor, we need you!"

Rising, Olgilvie could see Jeff's anguish. "What's the problem, Jeff?"

"Ranger McKiever's been shot. Doc said only a miracle can save him, and you're in the miracle business!"

Olgilvie's voice remained calm. "Of course, I'll come. Just give me a second to activate the prayer chain. How about some details?"

"Mac's been shot twice. Right now, Sara's over there praying."

"Jeff, where is there?"

"Oh, forgive me, Pastor. He's at Doc's office!"

Olgilvie held Jeff's arm, pulling him into the sanctuary, his voice shouting across the pews. "Warren, are you there?"

A tall man emerged. "I'm here, Pastor."

"Warren, a Texas Ranger's been seriously wounded. We need to activate the prayer chain. When you get things started, you will find me at Doc Mason's office. Come on, Jeff, let's go ask the Lord for the miraculous."

Rick heard running footsteps, watching Josh burst into the room. His eyes wide, Josh stared at the closed door. "I heard. How's McKiever?"

"Barely alive, but hanging on."

"Is he going to make it?"

"Probably not."

"Dammit, anyone contact the captain?"

Rick growled. "Ain't I the dummy, never thought about Captain Frank."

Josh understood. "I'll go over to the telegraph office and send a message. Be right back."

Again, the door swung open. Jeff entered, followed by Pastor Olgilvie. Rick gestured at the door. Olgilvie's voice was calm. "Thank you." Opening the door, he slipped from sight.

Sara looked up, hope showing in her tear-stained face. Seeing her despair, Olgilvie kneeled, his voice comforting. "Sara, let's be people of faith. Let's really believe and wait on God's deliverance through prayer. Okay?"

Sara sensed the Pastor's spirit; it was strong. Olgilvie's voice began to fill the room.

Hearing Olgilvie's voice resonating from the room, Rick's attention was drawn towards the door. Feeling his skin prickle, he wondered if prayer would work. At least, it was better than nothing, he thought. Often, he'd noticed how Christians seem to have an inner peace despite desperate circumstances. Well, this was certainly a desperate time, and if prayer worked, this was the time to try it. Feeling uncomfortable, he headed for the door. Stepping onto the boardwalk, he reflected on the day. What a day, he thought. From happiness to catastrophe! A voice broke his concentration.

"Say, Ranger, how's the other fellow? He going to live?"

Focusing on the balding man, Rick answered, "Some things are only answered with time, death being one of them." Turning, he went back inside. Minutes later Josh entered, all three staring at the back room.

The door creaked opened, Doc walking out, his voice subdued. "He's hanging on. I'm going to the supply room for more bandages, be right back." Doc stopped, gesturing toward the door. "I'll tell you one thing: if prayer really works, we just might find out."

Moving away, Doc suddenly turned. "Oh, I almost forgot something." Reaching into his vest he pulled out a badge, handing it to Jeff. "You might want to look at this."

Surprise flooded Jeff's face. Josh and Rick moved up, staring at the mangled metal.

Doc's finger rested on the curled corner. "It appears the badge deflected the bullet that ended up in his shoulder." He looked at each man. "That bullet was headed for his heart."

Jeff gasped.

Doc tapped the badge. "If it wasn't for that hunk of metal, them two in there wouldn't have anyone to pray for." Doc left.

Rick spoke first. "I guess if McKiever lives it's because of that badge."

Josh began shaking his head.

Rick eyed him. "Why are you shaking your head?"

"I was thinking, if Mac had given us his badge before going to the telegraph office, Doc would be right."

Jeff's voice became a whisper, a shudder passing through him. "Yeah, he wanted to wear the badge on his last official act as a Ranger. If that don't beat all."

CHAPTER 13

Against the Odds

aptain O'Rourke ran his massive hand through his hair, his eyes focusing on the mantel clock. Despite the gusting wind buffeting the window pane, he could still hear the clock's steady ticking. The big hand pointed toward the roman-numeral twelve, the little hand on the number eleven. Putting down his pen, he capped the ink jar. Rubbing his bleary eyes, Frank pushed his chair back. Rising, he stared at the subdued light filtering through the window. Normally by this time the sun brightened the whole room, but not this morning. He walked over to the window. The day was dark, with gray patches of moisture laden clouds scudding across the sky. A cold front had arrived, bringing a soaking rain, followed by dropping temperatures.

Frank was captivated by the cloud movement. Except for an occasional shower, the heavy rain had ceased. In the far horizon he could see a break in the clouds. As the sky brightened, he saw a tinge of white on the distant hills. He shuddered, knowing winter was coming.

Turning from the window, Frank heard his stomach growl. It was time to put away the paperwork. Moving behind the desk, he lifted his holster from the wall peg. Buckling on the gun belt, he removed his gun from the desk. Starting to reach for his hat, he paused, hearing the muffled sounds from a horse. Someone was arriving, maybe someone to have lunch with? Waiting, Frank heard the third step creak. The door groaned open, a sandy-haired man entering. Frank was always pleased whenever he saw Slim Whitman. Slim's real name was Aaron. Clutched in his hand was a yellow slip of paper. Aaron was called Slim because of his honey frame. Slim was a popular Ranger, his humor contagious. His face was so weather-beaten that whenever he smiled his wrinkles appeared like cracks in a plaster wall in desperate need of fixing.

Frank's voice boomed. "Slim, good to see you."

Slim stepped into the office, the yellow paper dangling in his hand, his face grim.

O'Rourke went on alert. Slim always had something humorous to say, but the only sound Frank heard was the gusting wind. He gestured toward Whitman's hand. "You going to tell me what that message says, or do I have to read it?"

Whitman's eyes locked onto the captain, his words spaced out. "It ain't good news. The message is from Fredonia."

A chill shot through O'Rourke, his body tensing.

Slim's voice cut through him. "There was a street shootout in Fredonia."

Frank braced himself, his voice barely audible— "Who?"

Stepping forward, Slim placed the yellow paper on the desk. "Josh says you better come quick; McKiever's in bad shape."

A queasy feeling shook Frank, a strange buzzing filling his head. Willing his brain back to life, he stared at the message. "Was the shootout with a man named Peckenpath?"

"Yes, sir, it was."

"And?"

"Peckenpath's dead."

"Go on."

"Mac took two in the chest."

O'Rourke sagged, catching himself. It took him a second before speaking, "Slim, I'm going to need my horse and some trail provisions. I'm not planning on stopping until I get to Fredonia."

"Captain, that your horse outside. You got a bedroll, rain slicker, and trail food in the saddlebags. I also strapped on two canteens. All you got to do is mount up and ride."

Frank nodded, his voice thankful. "I should have known; you're always on top of things. You know the drill, you're in charge until I get back."

"Captain, don't you worry about nothing, just ride." Slim pointed to the gun rack. "Don't forget your long gun; you might need it."

Two long strides carried Frank to the rifle rack. Half opening the rifle's breech confirmed what he already knew, the carbine was loaded. Not looking at Slim, he left the office. Reaching the outer door, he waited until the wind let up. Pushing outside, a gust slammed the door shut behind him. Sliding the Winchester into the rifle scabbard, he hauled himself into the saddle, grimacing slightly. The years were catching up on him. Turning his horse, he looked up at Slim. "Tell them I'm on the way." Swinging around, his horse crossed the yard. Passing a small cluster of houses, he saw the men watching him. Each man tipped his hat, a look of angry concern on each face.

Urging his horse into a trot, Frank forgot his aching body, his mind calculating. He should reach Fredonia by noon tomorrow, at the latest, by late afternoon. He wished he was already there, but thanks to Slim, he was on the trail. A man had to be thankful for small favors. Frank's mind turned toward the only one who could give him peace. His thoughts becoming a prayer, a plea escaping his mouth. "Please, Lord, I only have one son, keep him alive so that he might know you." Tears started running down the big man's face.

A shaft of sunlight broke through the overcast. A pool of light illuminated the road as though an escort from above was leading the way. Frank felt his fear replaced with calm.

Doc Mason tucked his stethoscope under his vest. Standing, he eyed Sara and Pastor Olgilvie, his voice calm. "The man has a strong will to live. Somehow he's hanging on."

Pastor spoke while eyeing the patient. "Doc, what can we do?"

"You want my advice? Just keep on doing what you're doing. I'll take care of the practical part. There is one thing you can do, tell me if his face suddenly gets flushed. If that happens, get me. Other than that, you're doing what I can't do." Doc suddenly looked puzzled. "To tell you the truth, I can't for the life of me understand why his blood pressure hasn't dropped." Shaking his head, he admitted, "I've never seen anything like it. A loss of so much blood always causes a loss of blood pressure." Starting for the door, Doc stopped. "Pastor, you got some church people crowding the outer room. I'm going to have to chase some. What do you want me to tell them?"

"Tell them I'll be out in a few minutes."

Wiping his glasses, Doc looked at the patient, muttering out loud, "He's a tough one all right." Quietly he closed the door, facing the crowded room. "Pastor will be out shortly. In the meantime, I'm going to ask you church folk to go outside. One or two can remain. Sorry, but it's too crowded and people carry germs." Watching the group trickle out, Doc located Jeff. "Your friend's hanging on. I'm not sure how, but he is."

Jeff felt encouraged, fighting his emotions. "Thanks, Doc."

Doc shrugged. "Don't thank me. Something mysterious is going on."

"What do you mean, Doc?"

Not answering, Doc stared at his watch, finally looking up. "Your ex-Ranger friend has lost so much blood, I'm surprised he's still alive." Doc stuck his watch back into his vest. "If he makes it through the evening, I doubt he'll make it through the night. But if he does, maybe those prayers are working. I got to admit, something very unusual is happening."

Jeff interrupted. "Can you clarify that, Doc?"

Doc peered over his glasses. "Now listen, young fellow, I don't want you to get your hopes up. Fact is, be prepared for a funeral. However, if he makes it through tomorrow morning, I just might go to church." Doc started for his office.

Jeff cut him off, his voice insistent. "You still haven't told me exactly why, Doc. Is it because something supernatural is happening?"

"Listen, I'm a medical science guy, and medical procedure stopped that bleeding, not God." Doc held up his finger. "If he lives, I'll tell you why I'm puzzled, but not before. Like I told you, get ready for a funeral."

"Don't get me wrong, Doc, I sure appreciate what you're doing."

"I know you do, young man."

Jeff felt tired, slumping slightly. "Doc, I got to admit, I'm feeling kind of exhausted."

"Ah," Doc touched Jeff, peering into his eyes. "You're suffering from mental fatigue. That's understandable 'cause you've been running on adrenalin, but reality is bringing you back to earth."

Shifting his feet, Jeff stole a glance toward the door. "Doc, any suggestions?"

"Yes, go eat and get some rest. That way when we need you, you'll be rested." Moving closer, Doc peered into Jeff's eyes. "You hear me, young man?"

"I hear you, Doc. I guess you're right. I reckon I better get some food."

Pushing gently, Doc was encouraging. "You do that, and Jeff, if anything develops, I will personally get you. Just tell me where you're going. Now, go eat."

Pastor Olgilvie's prayers were powerful, his words soothing. Sara began to feel hope instead of desperation. Finishing, Olgilvie looked at her. "Sara, I've got to step outside for a few minutes to coordinate the prayer vigilance. As soon as I'm finished, I'll be back."

Sara's face showed alarm. "Pastor, please don't leave me."

Olgilvie patted her arm. "Sara, you're not alone, when two or more are gathered in His name, He's here. I'm just going to the outer room. I promise I'll be right back, okay?"

Sara wiped her tears, trying to smile. "I know, Pastor."

"Good, I want our church ladies to provide meals for however long the vigil takes. This is a spiritual battle, and we need to be prepared."

"Pastor, I know you're right, but right now my spirit is telling me we don't dare let up, not for a second."

Caught by Sara's warning, Olgilvie suddenly felt the danger. Sara was sensing death, and now he felt it. Urgency filled his voice. "Sara, we've got to pray, death is at hand!"

McKiever's world was dark, a black vortex pulling at him. He could feel himself moving, picking up speed. A white force engulfed him, all movement stopping. Distant sounds came from the darkness, the black hole tugging. The white intensified, pulling him away, the sounds fading.

A restless night of sleep had robbed the men, and it showed. Every man needed a shave, every eye was red. Sheriff Olcott appeared the most rested, Jeff Kincaid, the most haggard.

Clare poured the coffee, studying each face. Yesterday they were pleased, this morning unhappy, and she knew why. The coffee would help shake their cobwebs. She eyed Wayne, her voice soft, "I'll be back to take your orders."

Olcott looked at Jeff. "Well, what did Doc say?"

Jeff stared into his cup, watching the steam rise. "He's amazed Mac's still alive. Actually, he told me he's dumbfounded! Says he can't figure out why his blood pressure never dropped. Said it's a mystery!"

Josh felt confused. "Doc don't know why? You telling us he's got no idea?"

Jeff nodded. "Doc says when a man loses blood, the heart works faster trying to keep everything going." Jeff paused to take a sip from the coffee cup before continuing. "What's more, Mac never dehydrated. Go figure that one!"

Olcott looked at Jeff, his voice curious. "Explain?"

"Doc and Sara haven't been able to get any water into McKiever, yet there are no signs of body dehydration. Also, no developing infections."

Deputy Pickett sighed, "Wow, Mac might beat the odds."

"You know," Olcott leaned forward, sounding positive, "if a badly wounded man gets through the night without a fever, the odds get better, a lot better! Did Doc say anything else?"

"No. Tell you what though, all I wanted was good news, and I got that. So now I'm believing he can make it."

Olcott pushed his hat back. "Jeff, how's Sara holding up?"

Jeff shook his head. "She's unbelievable. She won't leave his side. Sara told me that only prayers are keeping Mac alive. She dozes off, wakes up, and starts praying. I guess both of us feel guilty, kind of responsible."

Olcott understood, trying to comfort Jeff. "Now hold on. Danger comes with being a lawman. We all knew that when we signed on."

"You're right, Sheriff, but the way Sara and I figured it, Mac would be retired now except for us."

"That might be so, but McKiever told me that you two go way back. Tell me if I'm wrong, but if it was the other way around, wouldn't you have done the same for him?"

Jeff just stared.

"Since you're not answering the question, I'll tell you. Yes, you would have."

Jeff's face had a vacant look, his voice soft. "I reckon."

The outer door swung open diverting everyone's attention. Charlie was headed for their table. Seeing Charlie, Jeff remembered something. "Sheriff, do you remember what Charlie said?"

"I don't know, refresh my memory."

Jeff paused to welcome Charlie. "Morning, Charlie." He refocused on Olcott. "Charlie told us that Peckenpath was hired to shoot myself and McKiever. I'm convinced that if Mac hadn't braced him, I'd be dead."

Deputy Wayne interrupted. "Maybe you would have been luckier."

"Not likely, I'm not close to Mac's speed with a gun. That killer got off two shots to Mac's one, and except for this badge," Jeff reached into his vest, pulling out the mangled star, holding it up, "except for this badge, Mac would be dead. What's more, I was the first one who arrived. Yes, sir, Peckenpath would have gunned me down next."

No one said anything as Clare approached. "You men ready for ordering?"

The noon sun bathed the street, drying the puddles from the night of rain. Captain O'Rourke saw Rick's and Josh's mounts tied up in front of the restaurant. Turning, he rode up. Dismounting, his body aching, he wrapped the reins. Climbing the steps, his huge body filled the doorway.

Josh and Rick saw the captain first, their chairs scraping across the floor as they rose. All heads swung toward the door, Rick's voice bridging the distance. "Captain, mighty glad to see you."

Frank crossed the room, stopping at their table. With a quick nod toward Olcott and his two deputies, he eyed his Rangers, his face a question. Seeing the look, Josh spoke. "Mac's still alive. He's in Doc Mason's back room."

Jeff stepped forward. "Come on, I'll take you."

Frank's deep voice froze the room. "Good, I'll follow you. As soon as possible, I'll get back to see you men. Jeff, lead the way."

The street was crowded, people milling around. The throng separated, staring at the big man with the badge.

Doc looked up at the giant of a man, his eyes widening. Seeing the badge, his mind was quick. "You must be the Captain."

"Pleasure to meet you, Doctor. How's my man?"

"Somehow, still alive. Sara Kincaid's in there right now, praying." Frank's booming voice resonated through the walls. "Thank God she's there. I'm going to join her."

Sara heard the voice. A huge man loomed in the doorway, a silver star pinned to his shirt. Gasping, Sara knew this man had to be the man she'd heard so much about. He had to be Captain Frank O'Rourke.

Hat in hand, Frank covered the distance, his voice gentle. "Hello, Sara, I've come to pray with you."

Tears started down Sara's face, her voice breaking. "I'm so glad you're here, Captain O'Rourke."

Melting down beside her, Frank's huge hands engulfed hers, his voice filling the room.

Jeff had never heard the captain pray before, but he did now. The deep voice rose like rolling thunder. Doc Mason stared at the closed door, not moving.

Never before had Sara so felt God's presence. It was as if an uplifting force was suspending time, angelic music filling the room. As the captain's voice subsided into a whisper, Sara felt drained, but secure. Moved by his presence, she looked at this huge man they called the captain. The floor below his bowed head was soaked from tears. Slowly, he opened his eyes, turning his face toward her. She felt a gentle squeeze from those huge hands. "Sara, now I know why he's alive; it's because of you. Scripture says the prayers of a righteous person availeth much. Sara, God heard your prayers."

Feeling her emotions overwhelming her, Sara began to let go. Collapsing into the giant of a man, sobs wracked her body. He held her like a huge blanket, waiting. It seemed forever before she subsided. Straightening, she looked into his eyes. Captain Frank touched her cheeks with a white-linen handkerchief, drying her face, his voice encouraging. "It's a privilege to know you, Sara. And now I know why Jeff left us."

"Captain, I feel so guilty."

"Sara, so do I."

A puzzled look captured Sara's face.

Frank placed both hands under Sara's arms. Standing, he lifted her up. Captivated by her beauty and sincerity, he spoke. "Sara, I knew McKiever would come because of you and Jeff. I also knew how dangerous this assignment was."

Sara crossed her arms, almost hugging herself "Captain, I wanted to see him again. I was selfish and now look what's happened."

"Sara, life's not always fair, just real. What you and I have to do is to trust that God has a plan and a purpose in all of this. So, let's be at peace and trust the Almighty."

Searching the captain's face, Sara tried smiling. "Thank you for saying that, Captain. I'll try."

"Good girl. Now, I've been on the trail since yesterday morning, which means I need some grub to keep this big body going. Truth is, Sara, I burn up lots of energy just thinking. As soon as I finish and talk to the men, I'll be back to stay with you. Will you be okay?"

Sara touched his arm. "Captain, I've heard so much about you, and now that I've met you, I'm so glad you're here. Yes, I'm okay."

As the captain left, Sara felt her body relaxing, a feeling of peace surrounding her. Easing into a chair, her eyes closed, sleep claiming her.

The white light grew stronger, shapes swirling around. McKiever's eyes opened. Things were spinning. Slowly the room came into focus, where was he? Who was he? Someone was by the far wall. With an effort, he turned his head. Then he remembered. The woman was Sara. Everything was coming back to him. He had seen and felt death, but he was alive. His eyes closed, sleep recapturing him.

Sara stirred, raising her head she looked at McKiever. He hadn't moved. Closing her eyes, she slept. An hour past. Uncomfortable, Sara shifted. Glancing toward the bed, her eyes starting to shut. She saw Mac's eyes were open, staring at her. Springing upright, she lunged across the room, her voice crying out, "Oh thank God, praise you, Lord!" Her hands held his face, tears streaming down her cheeks, soaking her blouse.

McKiever felt her hands; they were warm. His eyes closed, then reopened, his voice weak. "Sara, where am I?" Trying to move, he felt pain.

Sara's voice was a whisper, choking with emotion. She pressed her head next to his face. "William McKiever, you're at Doc Mason's. You were badly wounded. Oh, Mac, I'm so glad you're alive! I 've been, we've been, praying for four days and three nights."

Four days, Mac thought. He shifted, a searing pain shooting through his chest. Grimacing, he lay still.

Sara saw his pain. Stroking his face, she recalled Doc's instructions. Doc wanted liquids given to him if he came out of his coma. Reaching for the pitcher, she half-filled a cup. Moving gently, she pressed the cup to Mac's lips. "Mac, you have to drink, please drink."

Slowly he sipped, then ceasing.

Setting the cup down, she buried her face against his. McKiever's eyes closed, sleep returning. Sara started humming, her voice turning into a soft song of thanks. Again, she remembered Doc's instructions. He had told her to get hot chicken broth, which would provide strength. Kissing his forehead, she rose.

The news that the legendary Captain Frank O'Rourke was in town had brought the people out in force. Every head turned as the captain left Doc Mason's, entering the Red Spot Restaurant. A few people drifted over, peeking through the window. A few folks entered, milling around, before leaving. A scattering of town folk actually went in to eat and stare. It was easy to see the legend; he sat head and shoulders above everyone.

Frank was a good listener. One by one each lawman gave his account. Satisfied, the captain's voice stilled the room. "Much obliged, all of you were very thorough. As far as I'm concerned, none of you left anything to chance. Each of you did a very professional job. In the next two days I may want some additional information, so we might speak again. Sheriff, I reckon we can work on that together."

"Just as soon as you're ready."

Frank glanced toward the floor, slowly raising his head. "Right now, I'm going back to Doc Mason's to be with Sara. I'm sure all of you understand."

The sudden rustle of a skirt turned their heads. Sara was approaching the table. Her eyes were red from crying, her cheek's soaking wet. Jeff felt his heart leap. Captain O'Rourke gripped the table. Rick felt his muscles tensing, stealing a glance at Josh. Olcott braced himself, preparing for the bad news.

Stopping, Sara tried to speak, instead a sob escaped her. Jeff moved quickly, Sara collapsing into his arms. Tears began gushing down her face. Wrapping her arms around Jeff, she sought the captain's face. "Captain," she sobbed, "I just talked to Mac. He's alive!"

The huge man sagged, relief flooding his face. Jeff squeezed Sara, joy replacing anguish. Only Olcott spoke, "I'll be damned!"

Around the table frowns became smiles. Bystanders began to clap, cheers spreading into the street. Men and women stopped, looking toward the eatery.

Sara pushed away from Jeff, still holding his arm. "I have to get some broth, but I wanted all of you to know, especially you, Captain."

O'Rourke was moved. "God bless you, Sara."

Sara saw tears welling in Captain Frank's eyes. "Captain, I felt something right after you prayed."

Frank waited.

"Right after you prayed, I felt danger pass. It was like a force had chased death from the room." Sara fought back a sob. "Captain, your prayers were so alive, I felt evil flee."

Humbly, the captain's voice became a whisper. "Thank you, Sara."

"No, thank you." Squeezing Jeff, she lifted her face to him. "Honey, you have to tell Pastor Olgilvie; I want him to know."

"I'll go right over, but Sara, what did Mac say?"

"He was confused. He didn't know where he was. I did get him to sip some water. I was so happy, I started singing." Sara started to laugh, "The next thing I realized, he was sleeping."

Olcott chuckled, before asking, "Does Doc know?"

"Yes, he's with him now."

"Well," Jeff looked around, "I'm on my way to get the Pastor. I'll be right back."

Captain O'Rourke gestured. "Sara, why don't you get that broth. I'll escort you."

Watching Sara disappear in the kitchen, Frank thanked God. "Thank you, my Lord and master, praise you." He wiped a small tear as Sara appeared, carrying a cup, the steam spiraling upward. Moving over, he opened the door. The crowd parted, people smiling.

Doc stood in the outer room, nodding with approval at the steaming cup of broth in Sara's hands. "Good girl. Captain, I'd like a word with you before you go in. Go ahead, Sara, he'll be along shortly."

Sara smiled; looking at both amused her. What a contrast, she thought. Doc wasn't much taller than five-nine, dwarfed by the captain. With a smile at both, she spoke to the captain. "I can hardly wait to see Mac's expression when he sees you." With a twist of her head, she disappeared behind the door.

A slight smile lingered on Frank's lips. "What's on your mind, Doc?"

"Just thought I'd bring you up to date and caution you on what we don't want. Right now, I want lots of rest, and not a lot of talk. He needs nourishment, along with plenty of fluids. Besides, that girl is the best medicine I ever saw. She's totally dedicated to his recovery. I guess I'm asking for limited visits. Hope you're not offended."

"Not at all."

"You know," Doc's face took on a strange look, "that man in there by all accounts should be dead."

"Why's that, Doc?"

"Medical reasons, that's why. First of all, he never dehydrated. We tried, but never got water into him. But that's the least of it. His blood pressure never went down. Even more unbelievable, when you lose as much blood as he did, the heart races to keep up with what it needs, but his didn't." Doc shook his head in amazement. "I've never, and I mean never, seen such a thing before!"

"So then, how do you explain it, Doc?"

"I can't."

"Now, Doc, you've handled situations like this in the past. There must be something different about this than the others."

Doc hesitated before answering, "There was one thing."

"What's that?"

"I don't want you to misunderstand me, because I'm a man of practical medicine. I don't believe in the supernatural, just the practical." Doc hesitated before continuing, "But I've got to admit, I was impressed how that gal in there, the town pastor, and how all of them church folks never stopped praying for that fellow, especially Sara. She would never leave his side, not for a minute. So maybe I'm saying that was the difference. Fact is, I really don't know!"

Frank digested the doctor's words before responding, "I think you know I'm a God-fearing man, don't you, Doc?"

"Yes, I've heard that about you. But like I said, I practice medicine and that's scientific. Still, I got to admit, I've never seen this before."

"Thanks for telling me, Doc. I do appreciate your information."

"You're welcome. At any rate, you go in there and say hello. Just remember what I said about McKiever needing rest. He just came out of a coma, and his condition is still critical. Which means, it's possible for him to have a relapse at any moment. Since you're the boss man, I'm depending on you to help me keep things under control. That all I got to say. Go enjoy your visit." Doc turned, disappearing into his office. Frank's voice followed the Doc. "I'll see to it, Doc." That was something new, he thought. It wasn't often that someone told him what to do, but of course, that man was the doctor.

Doc's voice drifted back, "I'm going over to the Red Spot Café to grab a bite to eat. If anything develops, let me know."

Frank turned his attention to the door. Taking a deep breath, he entered. Sara looked up, her face beaming. McKiever stared at the man who had raised him like a father. Starting to speak, he grimaced.

Frank brought his finger up to his mouth. "I'll do the talking for now, that's an order. You just eat and get rest. The only time you talk is if you need something. Whatever you need, we get. It's that simple, at least for now."

The door swung open, Olgilvie entering. "Sara, I heard the miraculous news. God is faithful, isn't He?"

Sara closed her eyes for a second before opening them. "Pastor, I have to tell you something."

"Go ahead, Sara, what is it?"

"I was so desperate, but when you came, I sensed God's presence." Pausing, her voice becoming husky, "When you began praying, I felt something lifting me. It was like being on wings of an eagle. I've never felt that before. For the first time I actually felt the power of prayer."

"Sara," Olgilvie's eyes shifted toward McKiever, "God arrived in the street with you, and we were just reinforcements."

Silence captured the room. Captain Frank felt overwhelmed by what he was hearing. Sara turned her face, looking at him. "Captain, I actually felt evil flee after you prayed." Again, she hesitated, her mouth trembling. "Right after you left, I experienced peace, followed by sleep." Placing both hands on her cheeks, Sara couldn't help herself. She sobbed, finally gaining control. "When I awoke, I saw Mac looking at me."

Olgilvie reached out, touching Sara. He eyed the captain. "Let me introduce myself. I'm Pastor Olgilvie. You must be Captain Frank O'Rourke. I've heard much about you."

Frank's huge hand engulfed the Pastor's hand. "Pleased to meet you. God provides, doesn't he, Pastor? Just as He provided for Abraham, he made a provision for us."

Both smiled, each touching Sara. Olgilvie nodded. "Amen, Captain, amen."

CHAPTER 14

Maybe There Is a God

McKiever handed Sara his tray, forcing himself to look away. She was so beautiful, but even better, she was nursing him back to health. As he had done before, he reminded himself about Jeff and their friendship. Despite his attraction for Sara, he was not going to violate that friendship. Shifting his thoughts, Mac remembered that moment on the street with Peckenpath. Closing his eyes, he recalled the gunman's face, the numbing impact from the bullets, and how that black hole was always pulling at him. He remembered the force that saved him. First it came from his right side, and later from his left. He opened his eyes, aware that Sara was staring at him.

Sara wiped his forehead. "Why are you frowning, Mac?"

Not answering her at first, he looked up. "Sara, how many days since I woke up?"

Laying the soft cloth on the bed, Sara held up two fingers. "Why?"

Propping himself, Mac shook his head, his voice sounding thoughtful. "Something strange happened when I was lying in the street, and it happened often."

"What was strange? I don't understand."

How, he thought, was he going to explain this?

Sara repeated herself, "What was strange, Mac?"

"I felt myself moving toward a black hole." He stopped himself; what he was about to say had to come out right.

Sara was watching his eyes. They were squinting. She prompted him, "And—"

McKiever glanced toward the ceiling. "Sara, you said you were praying for me in the street?"

"Yes."

"What side?"

"I'm not sure why you're asking?"

"That doesn't matter. When I was lying in the street, what side of me were you praying from?"

Pausing to think, she answered, "Your right side, why?"

"And later, when I was in the room, where were you then?"

Sara looked at Mac. "Right where I'm sitting now, on your left side."

"And all that time you were praying?"

"Yes."

Mac rubbed his chin, a thoughtful look in his eyes. "Sara, I was heading toward a black hole, and a powerful force kept stopping me. I lost track of how often, but every time I was heading toward that hole, this glowing force surrounded me, pulling me back. At first that force came from my right side, and later, it kept coming from my left side. It was like I was in a giant tug of war. And Sara, that's where you were."

Sara's eyes were wide, chills racing through her. "Oh, Mac, don't you see? God is real! It was prayers that saved you." Tears started down Sara's cheeks. "William McKiever, do you remember asking me to prove that God is real, do you remember?"

Mac didn't answer, thinking back. "Go on."

"You asked me to pray about our situation, and when God answered my prayers to tell you about it."

"Yes, I recall saying that."

"Do you also remember how I warned you not to test God because it can be life threatening?"

Mac nodded. "Now that you mention it, I do remember you warning me."

The door swung open. Frank O'Rourke could see a serious conversation was in progress. Sara greeted him with a question. "Captain, will you tell Mac what the doctor told us about his medical condition."

"Sure, Doc told us something strange was at work. He said your pulse should have been racing because of a loss of so much blood. Another thing he couldn't understand is why your blood pressure never went down." A touch of awe seeped into the captain's voice. "Doc said by all accounts you should be dead." Frank stopped, watching Sara rise, seeing a look on her face, her glowing expression telling him to listen.

"Captain," Sara's voice struggled with emotion, "Mac told me that when he was lying in the street a powerful force came from his right side, pulling him away from a black hole. Later, when he was in Doc's room, that force came from his left side. Each time it pulled him away from that hole." Slowly, Sara's voice eased into a whisper. "Captain, when I was praying in the street, I was on his right side. Later, all my prayers came from right here, at the left side of the bed."

O'Rourke felt a tingling. McKiever felt a chill ripple across his arms, his memory vividly remembering something else, a gasp escaping him. He shuddered.

Frank saw Mac's reaction. "Mac, what just bothered you?"

"I just recalled something else, at least I thought I did."

Sara reached down, stroking his forehead. "What did you see? Tell us."

"I saw the man I killed go into that black hole."

The air seemed to be sucked out of the room. Frank steadied himself. Seeing Sara sway, he held her, both eyeing McKiever. Captain Frank broke the spell. "Mac, you once told me you needed evidence to believe in God. Well now, how's that for evidence?"

McKiever pondered the captain's question. "Maybe I was delirious."

"How about those two bullet holes in you, that a dream?"

Mac didn't answer, Sara scolding, "William McKiever, you are the most stubborn man I've ever known. The only reason you're alive is because of God's divine intervention because of prayer!"

O'Rourke agreed, supporting Sara's conclusion. "That's so. Even Doc admitted he doesn't know how you survived."

Sara could see Mac thinking, a strange look in his face.

The door swung open, Sheriff Olcott entering, followed by his two deputies, then Josh and Rick. Waiting for the door to close, Olcott spoke. "Well, young fellow, how's it feel to be amongst the living?"

Looking around, McKiever smiled. "Sara and the captain are telling me it's a miracle."

Josh agreed, everyone shifting their attention to him. "Mac, you know me, I'm not a religious person, but from everything I've heard, there's no other explanation. Even the Doc can't figure it out."

Again, the door opened, Jeff slipping in. He eyed McKiever, his voice almost an accusation. "You, my good friend, put the fear of God into us."

McKiever's face took on a look of humor, chuckling, "Another god man!"

Olcott spoke, curiosity etched in his voice. "I got to admit I'm dying to know what happened in the street. Tell us, Mac, tell us about Peckenpath?"

Every eye stared, silence capturing the room. Mac cleared his throat. "Sheriff, right after I left your office, I sensed danger. Everything looked normal, but I couldn't shake this foreboding feeling. I moved real cautious, checking everywhere, but everything seemed okay." McKiever's face became intense, his mind flashing back to the alley. "After I passed the General Store, I checked the alley next to me. No one was in it." A puzzled look creased Mac's brow, making a point, he looked up. "I mean, I gave that alley a real good look, checking every nook and cranny. It was like something was there, but I couldn't see it. I checked across the street. The boardwalk was empty. Not a soul could be seen anywhere. But all of a sudden, he's in the alley next to me."

Doc entered the room, asking, "Who was in the alley?"

Mac answered him, "That gunfighter, Peckenpath. Charlie was right, looking into that man's face is like looking at your own grave. I was sure I was about to die with no way out. At first, I lost all my strength, feeling numb all over." McKiever looked up, finding Jeff. "Jeff, he had it all planned out. First, he was going to kill me, then you."

Jeff felt his jaw tightening. His instincts had been right. "Just like I figured. Go on, Mac."

"He told me he was paid in full, and he always fulfills his obligations. He told me you'd be the first to arrive after he shot me."

Sara gasped, her face white.

McKiever lifted his head, eyeing the staring faces. "Peckenpath told me that death is the ultimate challenge, said he lived for that test. I never saw someone so confident, so eager. I was sure I was about to die." McKiever picked up a glass of water, sipping slowly, before setting it down. "I tried to buy time, but he told me the moment had come, said it was time for the ultimate test. He gave me till the count of ten to draw my gun, warning me, that if I waited for him to draw, I would have no chance. You know what, I believed him." Mac shrugged his shoulders, his face showing resignation. "When he started counting, I decided to die like a Texas Ranger."

Sara rubbed her arms, closing her eyes. It was as if she was there. How hopeless he must have felt, she thought.

"I told Peckenpath he was under arrest, told him to drop his gun belt. I knew I had to draw first. I figured to dodge when I pulled leather. It was my only hope."

Josh broke in. "How did you know that? Mac, how could you know that 'cause I never seen a man faster than you?"

Rick grunted in agreement. "Me either!"

Shrugging, McKiever looked around the room, studying each face. "It was because of his eyes; they spook a man. When I went for my gun, I felt that first bullet hit me, then another. After that the only thing I remember was how something kept surrounding me, keeping me from being sucked into a black hole, and that struggle seemed to go on forever. That's all I can remember until I came out of it and saw Sara. Since then, she's told that prayers saved me."

"You forgot one thing." O'Rourke eyed McKiever, nodding at the men. "Tell the men who you saw go into that black hole."

"All right. I'm pretty sure I saw Peckenpath go into it."

It seemed forever before anyone spoke, and it was McKiever. He shifted his gaze to Sara. "Maybe you're right, maybe there is a God."

Doc interrupted. "It's time for me to check this man's vital signs. Everybody out."

Waiting until everyone left, Doc sat down. Placing the stethoscope into his ears, he opened Mac's shirt. "That's quite a story, young man."

"What do you think, Doc?"

"I think I'll start going to church, that's what I think. Now, breathe deep."

The sun was setting earlier, the days growing shorter. Each morning was colder than the last. Thanks to the sun, the afternoons remained warm. Each day the pain in McKiever's chest lessened, his strength growing. Doc Mason checked him daily. The captain had left, taking Josh and Rick with him. Jeff and Sara were back at the ranch, often meeting him for lunch. Soon Olcott would be stepping down, the mayor still delaying naming the next sheriff. The captain had assured Olcott's deputies they had a job with the Texas Rangers if they wanted it. McKiever was becoming more and more anxious, but the good doctor wouldn't release him. Just eating, sleeping, and visiting Olcott at the jail was making Mac restless.

McKiever stepped into the street. Two ladies strolled by, one of them acknowledging him, her voice pleasant, "Good morning, Mr. McKiever." Mac touched his hat brim. She kept her eyes on him before turning away. Passing the corner of the jail, he headed for the horse barn. Friend greeted him with his usual whinny. The big male muzzled him, looking for a treat. A carrot appeared in McKiever's hand. Friend took it gently, Mac's voice conversational. "Well, old boy, you getting anxious like me?" McKiever stroked him, checking to see if his saddle was near. It would be a great feeling to ride again. Being able to climb aboard his horse would make him a free man. McKiever stared at the distant mountains. Each day they seemed a little whiter. Slowly, snow was being added to those distant peaks.

Mac chided himself. "Friend, I have to be patient."

A soft voice startled McKiever. He turned. Sara stood in the doorway, sunlight bathing her dark hair. She nodded at his horse. "He is your best friend, isn't he?"

"Sara, you got the drop on me. Not too many people can do that. Yes, he is, one I can always count on." He was glad to see her, his voice reflecting it. "Then comes you and Jeff." He wished he had said Jeff first, but he hadn't. Careful, he warned himself, don't get too personal.

Sara smiled, adding, "And the captain."

"Yes, the captain," he answered.

Sara moved close, her body brushing against him. She reached out stroking Friend's neck. "He's a beautiful horse. You're lucky to have such a friend."

McKiever didn't want to move away, but he did. Shifting slightly, he rubbed Friend's chest. Sara followed him, staying close, her voice soft. "I know you're getting anxious to leave, to go to your ranch. When you do, I'm going to miss you."

The distant peaks seemed a little closer, the sun brighter. Mac felt a lump in his throat. Sara crossed her arms, her voice husky. "I felt so guilty when you came, but I wanted to see you. When I saw you lying in the street, I became desperate, fearing that someone I loved was about to die." Sara wiped away the gathering moisture around her eyes. "I love Jeff, I really do. Often, I wished you had never been there, but you were. I wish I could change my feelings, but I can't. The good Lord knows how hard I've tried. Each of you is special in a different way, and in each way, I'm attracted. I guess I always will be."

McKiever's voice became hushed, worried that someone might overhear them. "Sara, you don't have to explain."

"Yes, I do. You were willing to pay with your life for Jeff and myself." Sara moved a little closer. "I only know of one other example like that."

"What example is that?"

"Imagine, someone willing to give his life despite knowing the person he loved wouldn't accept that love. What would you think of such a person?"

"I don't know, maybe a fool."

"Are you a fool, Mac?"

"Hard to say, maybe."

"Well, you're not a fool, and neither was Jesus!"

"Oh," Mac smiled, "him again. I guess I'm in some very good company."

"Yes, but he knew he was going to be brutalized before he died. But he did it anyway, so we could live. You did something like that. Please, Mac, think about what happened to you, and what saved you. Remember, even Doc can't explain it."

Feeling moved, but uncomfortable, Mac was at a loss for words. Sara inched closer, trapping him. "Do you know what I want?"

"What do you want, Sara?"

"I want you to meet someone who you fall in love with, someone who makes you forget about me, that's what I want."

McKiever gulped. "I don't know what to say. Part of me has been hoping for that. I spent a year trying to forget you, convincing myself that it was time to move on. Then the captain gave me this assignment. I knew I would see you again, and I was glad. But it's like you just said, I almost wished you had never been there, especially with Jeff and me being such good friends."

"Mac, I'm in love with Jeff, and we have this great marriage. My problem is I can't forget you. I know I can never have you, so where does that leave me? Let me tell you where that leaves me. I'm comforted knowing you're alive, and that the Lord can redeem any circumstance, including this one. If you meet someone you fall in love with, that will help me."

Seeing Sara's tears, Mac wiped them with his bandana. "Come on, Sara Kincaid, I have an appointment with the Doc. You can escort me. Maybe he'll tell me I'm ready for the saddle and I can go find this other woman you're talking about."

Sara laughed, relieved from her shaky emotions.

Mac kept the conversation light. "Where's Jeff? You didn't ride into town alone, did you?"

"No, he's at the bank."

"Does he know you came to see me?"

"Yes, Jeff knows everything."

Mac felt moved. "Jeff's quite a man." Looking at Sara, he patted her. "You married the right man. I'm not so sure I could be so trusting."

Doc was reading the paper. Looking over his glasses, he nodded. "Morning, Sara, you too, young fellow. You go right in, Mr. McKiever." Doc smiled at Sara. "Young lady, this shouldn't take long." Closing the door, Doc picked up his stethoscope. "How are you feeling?"

"To tell you the truth, Doc, except for an occasional twinge, I feel pretty good."

"That twinge in the chest area?"

"Yes."

"That's normal. You still have some healing scar tissue. Take off your shirt, and let's listen." Doc listened intently, before laying the stethoscope down. "Button up, young man, You've got good lungs and a strong heart. Except for them little twinges, you're almost back to normal. Fact is, I'm releasing you."

"Doc, can I ride?"

"You can ride, but only short rides. A bouncing horse can jog things loose and you don't want that."

"How long before I can hit the trail?"

"Depends on how you feel. Like I said, go easy at first. If you start to feel weak, get back to my office fast."

"What would weak mean?"

"That would mean something tore loose, causing a loss of blood. I don't think that will happen. As for your question about hitting the trail, I'd say in about a week, but we want to be cautious."

"So, this is my last visit with you?"

"Yep, unless of course it's a social visit."

"Doc, you've been great."

"So, have you, young fellow. This town is much obliged for what you did. Come on, I'm going to give Sara some last-minute instructions concerning you."

Jeff was standing next to Sara when they stepped into the outer room, his voice cheery. "How's the patient, Doc?"

"It appears I don't have a patient anymore. I cleared him for some riding. Notice, I used the word some! Jeff, do you know why I used that word?"

"I do. Does he?"

"I think so. I'm depending on the two of you to impress upon him the necessity to follow doctor's orders. Any questions?"

Jeff rolled his eyes. "I'll try."

Doc removed his glasses, peering at McKiever. "Young man, you have defied medical understanding." He eyed Jeff and Sara. "Because of people like you, I guess I'll never say never again." Doc's focus swung back to McKiever. "I'm going to repeat something I said earlier because some things are worth repeating." Doc studied each face, his words measured. "I still haven't figured out how our friend made it, other than a miracle. You know, I had a nice conversation with the captain. He said that a man needs two things in life, one is luck. The other thing he said is that when a person runs out of luck, he better know where his soul is going. Well, young man, I don't know about the soul thing, but I do know you are one lucky fellow. As for that miracle thing, you received that too." Doc shoved his glasses into his vest pocket. "One other thing," Doc leaned forward, his eyes on McKiever, "the captain loves you like a son. You stay in touch with him, you hear?"

"I will, Doc, and thanks."

"You're welcome." Turning, Doc retreated into his office.

Placing his arms around Sara and Jeff, McKiever guided them outside. Looking up, he stopped them. "See that hawk up there?" All eyes watched the bird of prey. "Look at him rise on those air currents. He's free, and that's how I feel. I've been set free; I can ride again."

Jeff squeezed his friend's shoulder. "I reckon riding a horse does give a man a feeling of freedom. Let's a man leave when he wants and go where he wants."

McKiever watched the hawk soar. "Just look at that bird go. You know, I always marveled how birds fly. I used to watch them flit through the trees, dodging everything, and then land on a branch at full speed." Shaking his head in wonder, he spoke with awe, "They must be built something special!"

Sara leaned against Mac, her hand holding Jeff's arm. She felt contentment.

McKiever broke their spell. "I'm going to get my stuff at the hotel, then go saddle Friend. If it's all right with you, I'd like to visit with Olcott and his boys. After that, I want to see Pastor Olgilvie. Once that's done, I'll catch up with you two. How's that for a plan?"

Sara spoke. "I'm glad you're seeing everybody before we go, but don't you think you should ride in the wagon?"

"Nope, I'm following doctor's orders. The ride to your ranch is short, and it's time for me to ride my horse."

Jeff figured it was time to come to the aid of his friend. "How long do you need?"

"Give me an hour, that should be enough."

"An hour it is. Meet us at the eatery for lunch."

Mac stepped into the street, angling for the alley, the alley where he almost died.

Sara squeezed Jeff. "Where is he going? Oh my God, Jeff, what's he doing?"

Jeff squeezed back. "Sara, he's settling some issues. He's conquering a place of fear. You know, getting it behind him."

Mac entered the alley. Walking through the shadows, he stopped, eyeing the ground where Peckenpath died. Despite the recent rain, the blood stains remained. Strange, he thought, he remembered pulling his gun, but not pulling the trigger, well, one thing was sure, he must have pulled the trigger. Clearing the alley, he headed for the stable. Friend greeted him with a toss of his head. McKiever smiled. Reaching up he grabbed Friend's bridle. Moving into the stall, he stretched out, feeling some discomfort. Not bad, he thought. Friend stood still, making it easy for him. Sliding the bridle on, he placed the bit in Friend's mouth. Now, he thought, would come the real test. Lifting the blanket and the saddle, he felt a twinge. Sliding next to Friend, he set himself. With one motion, he hoisted the saddle onto Friend. Grimacing, he waited for the sharp pain to subside. McKiever smiled, talking out loud, "Too late, pain, the saddle's on." He tightened the cinch. Holding the reins in his right hand, he gripped the saddle horn. "Let's see how this feels." Pushing up, he settled into the saddle. The twinge was slight. He sat still, enjoying being in the saddle, talking to Friend. "That wasn't so bad. One more test, old boy." Dismounting, he was pleased. The getting off was easy. Holding the reins with his right hand, he led Friend out of his stall.

Olcott looked up as McKiever entered. "You got a certain look about you, Mac. I've seen it before. Looks to me like you're ready to hit the trail."

McKiever was impressed. "You would be right. You say you've seen it before?"

"I have. It's a look of eagerness."

"I reckon you have, Sheriff, 'cause I'm sure enough eager. I just stopped by to say adios." Mac stuck out his hand. "I'd be pleased if you'd say good bye to Wayne and Mike for me."

Olcott rose, grabbing Mac's hand. "Be my pleasure." Swinging around the desk, Olcott lifted a cedar box. Opening it, he held it out. "Take one for the trail. Hell, take two if you want."

McKiever laughed, eyeing the cigars. "I haven't had a good cigar since I don't know when. You got to promise me one thing, Sheriff, you won't tell Doc!"

Olcott guffed, waving his hand. "He smokes them all the time. Sneaks out his back door, that's what Doc does."

"You don't say. I guess it doesn't matter anyway, since I'm no longer his patient. Tell you what, Sheriff, I'll be spending a week at Jeff's spread, but when I hit the trail, I'm going to enjoy a nice smoke at my first campfire."

"Good, you do that. Come on, I'll see you to your horse."

Walking outside, McKiever nodded toward his horse. "You can watch me climb into the saddle. I already climbed aboard him once in the stall, even though I wasn't sure I could do it." Lifting his boot into the stirrup, he rose. Grimacing slightly, his face breaking into a smile. "That was better than the first time. Sheriff, enjoy yourself, no more politics, no more danger, and say goodbye to Mrs. Olcott for me."

"I'll do that. Good luck, Mac, you sure earned it."

Watching McKiever ride away, Olcott felt immense pleasure. Thank God, he thought, that he had come back to Fredonia. Men like him were few and far between. The town was fortunate, very fortunate. Turning, he went back inside.

Approaching the white building with the tall steeple, Mac eased himself from the saddle. He owed Pastor Olgilvie a visit with a special thank you. Entering the church, he removed his hat. The light filtering through the stained-glass window reflected on a large wooden cross hanging high above the pulpit. Mac thought about what Sara had said. Staring thoughtfully, a voice broke him away from his thoughts.

Pastor Olgilvie was standing in the office doorway, gesturing. "Welcome, come on in."

McKiever eased through the doorway, eyeing the desk. It reminded him of the captain's desk. The only difference was where the Bible was. On Olgilvie's desk, the Bible was open and in the middle. On the captain's desk, the good book sat in the far right corner.

Olgilvie spoke. "It's good to see you up and about."

"Pastor, it feels good to be up and about. Even better to be back in the saddle. Today was the first time I rode my horse. It sure felt good."

Olgilvie nodded, smiling. "I'm sure it did. Did you feel any pain?"

"Some. You know, Pastor, you have some real nice people in your church."

"Thank you, Mr. McKiever."

"No, thank you. Over the years I've known some church folks who are real holy in church, but after church I couldn't see it anymore." Mac eyed the pastor. "But I did see it in your folks. They seem to have a spiritual presence. Pastor, that I can respect."

"I'm going to tell my congregation what you said. They will appreciate your kind words. Tell me, Mr. McKiever, are you getting ready to leave?"

"Yes."

"Would you do me a favor?"

"You bet. What is it?"

Olgilvie reached into the bookcase, holding a Bible. "Please take this with you."

"Sure, that's the least I can do."

"I have one other request."

"Go on, I'm listening."

"When you hit the trail, the first night you stop, please open the Bible to a place I'm going to mark. I would like you to read a verse."

"If that's what you want, that's what I'll do."

"Thank you." Opening the Bible, Olgilvie marked a passage. Placing a marker between the pages, he handed the Bible to McKiever. "You said you saw the spirit in my church folks. That verse explains how God imputes the Holy Spirit into people." Olgilvie smiled. "And that's what you saw, and what you respected."

"One thing you can be sure of, Pastor, when I give my word, I keep it. The first night I stop, I will read that verse. After that, I'm going to light up a big cigar that Sheriff Olcott gave me."

Olgilvie's head rocked back, spontaneous laughter filling the office. Reaching out, he took Mckiever's hand. "Good luck to you, my friend, we will keep you in our prayers."

Leaving the church, McKiever glanced toward the restaurant. Two people were waiting outside. Mac spoke to Friend. "We have people waiting for us. Let's catch up."

CHAPTER 15

Under the Night Sky

The week passed quickly, McKiever riding every day. By the middle of the week, he let Friend trot, at the end of the week he let his horse run. With each day the slight pain in his chest lessened. It was after returning from an all day ride that he knew it was time to leave. That night at the dinner table, McKiever announced he would depart the following morning.

The morning broke without a cloud in the sky. Jeff and Sara stood at the bottom of the steps watching McKiever secure his canteens. Patting Friend's flank, Mac approached Jeff, stopping as he spoke, "I reckon I'm ready." Smiling, he held out his hand. "You know, Jeff, it would be easy to stay here with all the hospitality you've extended to me, but all good things do come to an end."

Jeff grasped the hand, no words coming from his mouth.

McKiever gestured at Sara. "Sara told me that there's a woman waiting for me in Silver Springs." He raised his voice slightly, "A Christian woman! What do you think about that, old partner?"

Jeff couldn't help himself, trying not to be too humorous. "I think you better practice up on what you're going to say when you meet her. It's not good for a man to be tongue tied."

"Good idea. While I'm on the trail I'll practice." Mac stole a glance at Sara. "You think this Christian woman will be as pretty as Sara?"

Jeff knew it was time to be careful. "Yep, not prettier, but as pretty."

"Jeff, I have to admit you're one quick thinker. Fact is, I always hoped you'd get married so that one day I'd have a chance. The only thing wrong was that you married Sara."

McKiever laughed, "And that wasn't part of my plan."

Mischief showed in Jeff's face. "Mac, didn't you always say that when a man makes his move, he should move boldly? I just followed your advice. Besides, she's still warning me that if I flirt around, there's always you."

Enjoying the banter, McKiever chuckled, "Anyway, when I meet this woman that Sara has told me that I'm going to meet, you will be best man. How's that sound?"

"Mac, I would have been offended if you picked someone else. I really would have. Truth is, I never rode with a better man than you. It was a privilege to ride with you, but even more important, to have you as a friend."

McKiever was moved. Releasing Jeff's hand, he stepped toward Sara.

"Sara, when am I going to meet this girl?"

"As soon as you go to church."

"What makes you think I'm going to church?"

"A promise."

"What promise?"

"The one you're going to make now."

McKiever looked at Jeff. "Has she always done this to you?"

Jeff rolled his eyes. "All the time."

Sara interrupted them. "Can I tell you why she's going to be a church girl?"

"Tell me, Sara."

"Because I've been praying that she will be, that's why."

"Oh." McKiever looked at Jeff, who was looking at the sky.

Stepping forward, Sara stared into McKiever's eyes. "When you get to Silver Springs, promise me you'll visit with the local pastor?"

McKiever winked at Jeff before answering, "At least once."

A touch of sternness entered Sara's voice. "Good, you just promised! Now, I want another promise."

"Tell me, Sara, how many more promises do I have to make?"

"Just two more, here's the first one. As soon as you arrive, send us a message so we know you arrived safely."

"Okay, what's the last promise?"

"I want you to send us a letter before Christmas. We want to hear about that Christian girl and when the wedding is. You know, the one I'm praying about." Sara's face radiated a sparkle.

Shaking his head in amazement, McKiever turned his attention to Jeff. "Tell me the truth, do you ask her, or does she tell you?"

It took a second for Jeff's answer, needling back, "How does it feel to be part of the Kincaid family?"

"Demanding, that's how it feels." McKiever's face changed from humor to affection. "Sara, come over here so I can give you my trail hug."

Sara melted into his arms, pressing tightly. McKiever, not wanting to let go, finally stepped back. Winking at Jeff, he turned, heading for Friend. Mounting, he swung the big male around. Looking down at Jeff and Sara's upturned faces, Mac measured his words, all banter gone from his voice. "When I get to the top of that hill, I'm going to turn and wave adios. I'd be obliged if you'd wait."

Sara snuggled into Jeff, her voice throaty. "We'll be watching and waiting."

McKiever hesitated, resting his forearms on Friend's shoulders. "You know, it's a lucky man who has at least two friends in his lifetime, and both of you have made me a very lucky man." Straightening, he turned to Friend. Crossing the yard, they passed underneath the ranch sign. Breaking into a trot, Friend climbed the hill. Reaching the top, Mac pulled back on the reins. Jeff and Sara were there, hands raised. McKiever lifted his hat, his arm slowly dropping. Taking a last look, he spoke to his horse. "Come on, old buddy, let's go to our new home."

Jeff and Sara looked at the suddenly empty hill, continuing to stare. Sara felt as though a part of her was gone. She wanted to get on her horse, ride to the top of the hill, and watch McKiever for as long as possible. Life could be so complicated, she thought. She was married to a marvelous man, a man she loved deeply, yet another man she loved was riding away. She snuggled close, wrapping her arms around Jeff.

Jeff's voice interrupted her thoughts. "Sara, are you glad you married me?"

Squeezing Jeff tighter, Sara's words were filled with emotion. "Jeffrey Kincaid, I would marry you again and again."

Her voice surprising him, Jeff nestled Sara's head under his chin, his voice a whisper, "Thank you, Sara."

Both remained still for the longest time. Finally, Sara spoke. "Do you think we'll ever see Mac again?"

"We'll see him again. Come on, honey, let's go inside and do something. Staying busy always seems to help a burdened mind." Starting up the steps, they paused, looking at the now empty hill.

McKiever and Friend made a good time. There was something exciting about uncovering new range. Funny he thought, the terrain was really the same, but a man always wondered what was over the next hill. He grinned, thinking how it was like going to a different place to eat. The food was the same, but the restaurant was different.

The miles passed, the valley giving way to foothills. McKiever checked the afternoon sun. Judging by the shadows he guessed it to be about three in the afternoon. If his calculations were correct, they should reach a water hole named Hidden Wells just before dark. Over the years while chasing hostiles, McKiever had found this hidden spot, a favorite resting place used by raiding Indians. Not only was water there, but also firewood. Once they got to the water, he would start a fire, eat, and then enjoy the cigar Sheriff Olcott had given him. It had been a long time since he'd camped under the night sky; McKiever was looking forward to it.

The terrain steepened before leveling off. Friend had settled down into a steady walk, McKiever's thoughts turning to the Indians. Remembering their ways, he talked to his horse. "You know what the Apaches say, old boy? They say white man build big fire and sit far away, but Indian build little fire and sit close." Friend jerked his head up and down as McKiever talked. "Which means they can't be seen. Some say they build a fire so small they sit under a blanket with those hot coals and stay warm for hours. I believe it too, 'cause whenever we tracked them, I never saw a big fire, just small piles of ashes." Friend snorted, the terrain steepening. McKiever looked back. Up here he could see for miles. It was a pretty sight. Soon they would level off onto a plateau which would bring them within two miles of the water hole. Mac prodded Friend into a trot. In the distance he could see the rocky outline where the rim gave way to the plateau. Swinging up onto the level ground, Friend lifted his head, his nostrils flared, smelling water.

McKiever decided they would swing wide, making sure he saw no fresh pony tracks leading toward the spring. The last thing he wanted was to be jumped by hostile Indians. Swinging west, they circled. The only fresh tracks he saw were those made by coyotes. Satisfied, he turned Friend north. They climbed higher before angling east. Approaching the spring, he pulled Friend to a halt. Two cactus wrens sprang into the air, disappearing into a small outcropping of bronze-colored rocks. McKiever eased himself from his saddle, his eyes scanning everywhere. Everything appeared normal. Approaching the pool, he bent over. The water was clear, indicating no recent disturbance. Dipping his hat, he watched the water rush in. The bubbling sound was pleasant to his ears, Rising, he kept both hands underneath the hat. Moving over to Friend, he watched his horse drink. Alert, he let his gaze sweep the boulder-strewn hillside. All the signs pointed to the fact they were the first visitors to the spring. Relaxing, he refilled his hat, his horse drinking. Mac led Friend away from the water. Moving up the bluff, he selected his campsite beside an overhanging boulder. Up here he would see any approaching danger. McKiever started crisscrossing small sticks, followed by larger branches. Striking a match, he watched the flames lick hungrily at the dry kindling, the wood snapping, then crackling. Piling on more wood, he watched the flames grow, leaping skyward. He was pleased that no dark smoke billowed into the late afternoon sky. It was time to let the fire die into hot cooking coals.

McKiever finished eating, eyeing the darkening hills. The sun was beginning its descent toward the horizon. With each minute the shadows lengthened, half the valley now cast in bluish shade, the other half in a golden hue. McKiever arranged his bedroll. Placing his saddlebags within the circle of light from the glowing coals, he propped his rifle within easy reach. Once the sun went down, he wanted to know where everything was placed. It wouldn't be much longer before the light would give way to the black of night.

McKiever figured he still had a half hour left. It was time to honor his promise to Pastor Olgilvie, and after he honored his promise, it would be time to enjoy the cigar. Opening his saddlebag, he removed the Bible, opening it to the marked page. Halfway down the page he saw the ink mark. He studied the words, they read, "Having been born again, not of the corruptible seed but incorruptible, through the word of God which lives and abides forever." McKiever lowered the Bible, letting it rest on his lap. Thinking back, he recalled their conversation. If he remembered correctly, he had complimented Pastor Olgilvie about his congregation. After that compliment, the Pastor had asked him to read a verse which explained how God's spirit gets into people. He also recalled Olgilvie saying that was why his church folks acted like they did. Thinking about the verse, Mac closed the Bible, mulling over the Pastor's explanation. If such a thing as a seed from God could be placed into a man, that would explain how people become spirit filled. If, of course, such a thing was possible?

Rising, McKiever placed the Bible back in his saddlebag. Feeling around, he pulled out the cigar. Removing the wrapping, he moved back to the fire, eyeing the hot coals. They glowed red, the blueish flames flickering in the darkening light. Placing a stick in the coals, he watched the tip flare into a yellow flame. Bringing the flame up to the cigar, he puffed, watching the thick white smoke billow out against the dark background. Feeling the heat from the fire, he leaned back against the boulder. Mac looked up at the dark sky. With each puff, the cigar tip glowed red. He shifted his gaze back to the fire, the glowing embers reflecting a tapestry of colors against the surrounding rocks. A coyote howl broke the quiet, another howl answering from a distant hill.

McKiever turned his head upward, staring at the night sky. It was quite a sight; stars were everywhere. Watching them twinkle, each separate from the other, he thought about Captain Frank. He could still remember the captain challenging him the day he left for Fredonia. The captain had asked him, where did the heavenly order come from? McKiever puffed his cigar. That was a fair question, he thought. For an hour he sat, puffing and thinking. Finally, he tossed the cigar into the dying coals. Picking up a stout leafy branch, he brushed the hot coals into a gap between the rocks. Making sure the ground was swept clean, he spread his bedroll over the heated ground. Placing his gun belt within easy reach, McKiever slipped between his blankets. Squirming into a comfortable position, he could hear the soft popping from the dying coals. The heat from the ground warmed him. His eyes gradually closed, sleep claiming him.

CHAPTER 16

Silver Springs

The man's hair was almost white, his face showing the effects from years of riding the range. The woman standing next to him was younger, her beauty stunning. Chestnut-colored hair hung down to her waist. Her face was deeply tanned, her figure shapely. She was a woman who turned men's heads, including jealous wives being escorted by their husbands. Both the man and the woman started down the steps leading away from the bank, their destination the general store. A large sign hung over the store entrance, it read: SILVER SPRINGS GENERAL STORE.

The white-haired man wore his gun low, his eyes missing nothing. Stopping, he touched his daughter, pointing toward a horse tied up in front of the store. "That's quite a horse. Looks like he could run all day. I'd say he's got a lot of stamina built into him."

The woman's voice was soft, well spoken. "That's a strange color, Dad. What would you call it?"

"Laura, that's what you call a roan color. That color ain't so pretty, so most folks wouldn't choose such a color." The man nodded, agreeing with his conclusion. "I'll tell you one thing, whoever picked that animal sure got himself one heck of an animal. I got a suspicion the man wanted a horse that could cover some ground with a purpose."

Two men watched the old timer with the beautiful woman, both reeking from whiskey. The older man rolled a cigarette. Lighting it, he inhaled, smoke curling from his nostrils. "Look at that, Nick, you'd be hard pressed to see a woman that pretty anywhere."

The younger man leaned against the porch post, agreeing, "She's sure a pretty one alright." He grinned, displaying yellow teeth. "Don't we need something from the store, Seth?"

Seth nodded, rubbing his pepper-colored gray and black beard. He took another drag before answering, "Yeah, we do. What we need is a closer look, that's what." He snickered, "How's that for needing something?"

"Sounds good to me. Let's mosey on over and get acquainted." Stepping out from under the porch overhang, they sauntered toward the store.

The store owner was pleased with his new customer. The man had just deposited fifty dollars in account, a rare thing in this town. Watching the man sign his name, the owner recognized the customer had some education. The man pushed the ledger back, asking, "You wouldn't know where I can find a man by the name of Manuel Santana, would you, Mr. Rathbone?"

Leonard Rathbone glanced at the man's signature. He looked up, respect showing in his voice. "I would be pleased, Mr. McKiever, if you call me Leonard. You can usually find Manuel at church on Sunday morning. During the week he often works for the hotel across the street. He does lots of odd jobs, but the hotel keeps him pretty busy."

The store door swung open, sunlight flooding in. An older man, escorting a beautiful woman, entered, Rathbone greeting them, "Howdy, Miss Laura and Mr. Ryan."

Sam Ryan acknowledged the greeting. "Morning, Leonard." Laura smiled at the store owner. Sam, sizing up the stranger, noted the way he wore his gun. Since no one else was present, Sam reckoned the man was the owner of the roan horse.

Leonard gestured in the direction of the stranger. "Let me introduce you to your new neighbor. This here gentleman is Mr. William McKiever. Mr. McKiever, meet Sam Ryan and his daughter, Miss Laura Ryan."

McKiever tipped his hat. "Ma'am." Reaching out, Mac extended his hand to the man. "My pleasure, Mr. Ryan."

Sam gripped the hand. The man's handshake was strong. There was something about this McKiever he liked. Maybe it was the way he looked you in the eye, or perhaps it was his well-spoken manner. Whatever it was, Sam's instincts liked what he was seeing and hearing.

Laura semi-curtseyed. "Welcome to Silver Springs, Mr. McKiever." She turned back to her father. "Dad, I'm going over to look at the dresses."

"Go ahead, honey, I'm going to catch up with my bill account, and then place some new orders. When I'm done, I'll get you."

Laura looked back at McKiever. "Please excuse me, Mr. McKiever. It is nice to meet you."

Again, McKiever touched his hat brim. As she moved away, he managed not to stare, shifting his focus to Sam Ryan.

Laura was halfway to the racks when she felt a curious urge. She stopped, her eyes studying the new neighbor. The man had a look in his eyes; she had seen it before. Her father had it. Her deceased husband had the same look. It was an observant, but fearless stare. For a moment Laura felt a strange feeling, one she hadn't felt in a long time. She pulled her eyes away, turning toward the dress racks. She gasped, delighted at the flowery prints and shiny fabrics.

Sam was more than curious. After all, Leonard had said new neighbor. Also, judging by the man's horse and how he carried himself, he suspected the man made a living with the gun. The question prodding his mind was, what type of living? The best way to find out was to ask questions. Sam got started. "That your horse tied up out front?"

"Yes, sir, he is."

"I spotted him when I came in. Actually, a better word would he admired. Looks like he can run all day."

Knowing he was being sized up, McKiever decided to cut through the questions. "Yes, Mr. Ryan, he can run all day. Texas Rangers need horses that can cover ground and over the years we were a pretty good team."

"Ah—" Sam's voice sounded surprised and pleased, but he saw no badge. McKiever's eyes focused on Ryan's gun holster. "I notice you wear your gun tied down."

Sam chuckled, understanding he was also being sized up. "That's because I used to be a Texas Ranger myself. Tell me, what barracks do you work out of?"

"None anymore, but I did work out of Los Quintos."

"You don't say." Ryan's eyes widened. "I used to work out of there myself. Fact is I know Captain O'Rourke quite well."

McKiever laughed, "I guess it's a small world. Fact is, the captain raised me like his son."

The store door opened, sunlight flooding the interior. Two men entered, moving toward the rear. McKiever saw Leonard's face tighten. Sam Ryan swung his head around, scowling. Eyeing the two men heading for Sam's daughter, Mac sensed trouble. He glanced at the store owner, his voice almost a command. "You know those two?"

Leonard's answer was quick. "I do. They're nothing but trouble. They don't buy anything, just come in and look the place over. You can smell them cause they're whiskey drinkers." He looked at McKiever, his face tightening. "Early morning whiskey drinkers!"

Sam's body stiffened, starting to move. McKiever's hand shot out, stopping him. "You paid your dues. I'll handle those two." Not waiting for a reply, he slid past Sam.

Smelling the whiskey, Laura saw the man. Ignoring him, she shifted farther down the aisle. Pretending to concentrate on the dresses, she almost bumped into the second man. He, too, reeked from alcohol. Recoiling, she backed into the dress rack.

The man smiled, displaying his yellow teeth, eyeing her body. "Howdy, Miss, that thar blue dress would sure look pretty on your body."

Trapped, Laura looked for her father. Seeing McKiever, her eyes widened. The new neighbor had a look of mayhem in his eyes.

McKiever felt out of control, and he didn't care. Always priding himself in his ability to control his emotions, now he didn't try. The two men were going to experience his stored-up anger. Maybe it was his near-death experience. Whatever it was, he was going to get it out. With a snarl on his face, he reached out grabbing a fistful of hair. With a wrench, he snapped the older man's head back, driving him to his knees.

Seeing his partner bent over, the other man reached for his gun. McKiever's gun swept upward. Pivoting, gun in hand, he drove his elbow into the face. The force of the blow lifted whiskey-breath off his feet, sprawling him onto the floor. The man's gun spilled out, sliding under the clothing racks. With a jerk, McKiever lifted the bearded one. Letting go, he shifted his weight, driving his left fist into the soft belly. The man doubled over, alcohol spewing out, the floor covered with chestnut-colored bourbon. McKiever drove his knee into the face, the crunching sound sickening. The man slumped, crashing into the garments, the racks toppling sideways, the floor a tangle of dresses, legs, and groans. McKiever kicked the clothes away. The younger fellow held his hands up, whining, "Now hold on, we wasn't doing anything wrong, just having a little talk."

McKiever's voice snapped, "Wrong, bothering a lady can get a man killed. Now, pick up your drunken partner and get out."

Slowly, the man rolled onto his stomach, rising to his knees. Blood trickling down his jaw, he spit, a piece of tooth flying out. Wiping his chin, he stared at the broken tooth. "You had no cause to do this."

"If," McKiever stood over the man, "I see you or your whiskey-drinking friend again, I'm going to kill you." Reaching down, he grabbed the man's shirt, hauling upward, he backhanded the foul-smelling face, his voice deadly. "If you and your lowlife friend are still in this town by tomorrow, you're dead men." McKiever shoved him. "Now, pick him up and get out of here."

The man staggered over his partner. Reaching down, he hauled up the limp body. Slipping his neck under his partner, the struggle for the door began. A belch escaped the man called Nick. Stepping into the brisk air, he began gagging. Taking several deep breaths, Nick stopped retching. He eyed McKiever, sweat droplets dotting his forehead. "How about my gun?"

"Buy a new one. You two have only two choices, ride or die."

"Now hold on, we got to get our belongings."

"You know," McKiever's hand dropped to his gun, "I don't think you understand the danger you're in." Eyes widening, Nick turned, dragging his partner toward the saloon. McKiever followed, alert. Reaching the hitching post, Nick half turned, eyeing McKiever. "I need some help."

"I reckon you do. You grab one end; I'll get the other. We're going to drape him over the saddle, and then you and him keep going, and don't look back!"

Watching the two move away, McKiever felt his rage dissipating. It felt good to be back in control. Keeping a wary eye on the two until they turned the corner, he crossed the street. A man with a handle-barred mustache stood next to the overhang. The man's voice had a raspy sound as he spoke. "Mister, I thought you was going to kill those men."

McKiever paused, thoughtful before answering, "Maybe in the store, I just might have done it then." He nodded, leaving the man. Somewhat disturbed at his loss of control, Mac climbed the steps, going inside.

Leonard Rathbone was stooped over, picking up the dresses from the floor. Sam Ryan held the rack, moving it as the store keeper gathered the garments. Seeing McKiever, Laura stared, a new look of interest on her face.

McKiever's voice interrupted the work. "Why don't you let me pick up the mess I made."

Leonard straightened. "Not a chance. You done my heart good, you sure did. Those two fellows was up to no good. The least I can do is pick up after you got rid of them two lowlifes!"

Sam pushed his hat back. "I'm also much obliged, Mr. McKiever. My daughter and myself surely appreciated you stepping in. You know, when men like those see a man my age, they're willing to take their chances."

"That," McKiever responded, "would have been a mistake on their part."

"Maybe so, but I also know I'm not as spry as I used to be. Again, thanks."

Laura's soft voice turned their heads. "Dad's right, Mr. McKiever. I was afraid for myself. I was afraid for my father. They were so vile, I didn't know what was going to happen. Please, accept our gratitude. We're so thankful you were here."

McKiever felt a twinge of excitement looking at Laura. "Thank you, it was my privilege." He looked at Sam. "I suppose I overreacted. I should have handled the situation more professionally. Maybe I have too much anger stored up in me."

Sam was quick, "Could be, but I was kind of glad you didn't act professionally. Kind of did my heart good watching you using those two drunks to wipe up the floor." Sam threw his head back, laughing, "Fact is, I'll bet my ranch against yours they won't be back!"

Rathbone bent over, picking up a revolver. He started toward McKiever, holding out the gun.

McKiever shook his head. "You keep it and sell it."

Leonard, hands on hips, eyed McKiever. "Young man, whatever I get for this gun, I'll add to your account balance."

"You don't have to do that."

Leonard gave a single emphatic shake of his head. "I know that, but I will because I want to, so that's that."

McKiever eyed Sam. "I have to admit, I'm liking some of the people in this town."

Everyone chuckled, the store becoming quiet.

McKiever hadn't forgotten he needed to find his handyman. "Leonard, you mentioned a good place to find Manuel was at the hotel?"

Leonard nodded. "That's right, I would start there."

"Please, call me Mac, that mister stuff is awful formal for me."

"Can't do that, too set in my ways. Tell you what, though, how's Mr. Mac sound?"

McKiever liked this Leonard Rathbone, agreeing, "That'll work." Shifting his attention to Laura, then back to Sam. "I hope you two aren't stuck in your ways. I really like being called Mac."

"Mac it is," Sam replied. "Tell me, is Manuel Santana the man you're looking for?"

"Yes, have you seen him?"

"Early this morning. He was on the trail heading out of town. Mind if I ask why you're looking for him?"

"Not at all. I've been paying him monthly to keep my ranch from falling down. I just need to catch up with him."

Sam glanced at the store owner. "Leonard mentioned you're our new neighbor. Are you the one who owns that small spread just west of my ranch, the one at the base of the mountain?"

"I don't know where your ranch is, but your description of my place sounds about right."

Sam glanced at his daughter, speaking to McKiever, "Well then, I guess you are our new neighbor. You picked a good man in Manuel, his work is good, and he's responsible. But you won't find him at the hotel. If I was you, I'd head for your ranch 'cause that was the direction he was riding."

Surprised, McKiever smiled. "My turn to say thank you. I can't think of a better place to catch up with my caretaker."

Sam interrupted, "Before you hit the trail, I'd consider it a privilege if you'd join Laura and myself for lunch at the town restaurant, no cost to you. Besides, you got to be hungry."

He was hungry, but McKiever's desire to see his ranch won out. "Thanks, Sam, but I'm real anxious to catch up with Manuel and see how my ranch looks. Maybe another time." He tipped his hat to Laura. "Miss Ryan, I hope the next time we meet violence isn't involved." Not waiting for her response, he wheeled around, leaving the store.

Rathbone eased between Laura and Sam. "That man can sure handle himself, can't he?"

Sam agreed, "I'd say so. For a minute I thought he might need some help, but then I wondered if he was going to kill those two." Sam rolled his eyes. "I never saw such a one-sided fight."

Laura had a question on her mind, asking it, "Dad, he said he had anger stored up in him. Why do you think he does? Another thing, he said he didn't act professionally. Why did he say that?"

Sam looked at his daughter, his mind digesting her questions. "Good questions. I don't know about the anger part, I do understand his feelings about not reacting professionally. We were trained under Captain O'Rourke to control our emotions. Whatever's bothering him, he sure got it out on them whiskey drinkers." Sam shook his head. "Those two are lucky they're alive."

Leonard rubbed his spectacles, nodding. "You're right, whatever was bothering him, he took it out on the right people. I never seen such a good sight. Yes, sir, that was something special. The best part was, he was on our side."

At first a chuckle came out of Sam, then a frown creased his brow. "Laura, I got something I want to do. Why don't you go back and take a look at those dresses you never got a chance to see. I should be back pretty quick."

"All right, Dad." Laura watched her father leave. Moving to the dress racks, she found it difficult to focus on the clothes. All she kept seeing was McKiever's face, that intense look as he was closing in on those two drunks. There was something about that look that made her feel safe. Separating some dresses, she stopped. It was no use; she couldn't concentrate on the clothes. Walking away, she passed the counter, calling out, "Bye, Mr. Rathbone!"

"Bye, Miss Laura!" Leonard watched her leave, the door swinging shut. Someday she was going to find a man to make her happy, he thought. He hoped it would happen soon. She had been mourning for a long time.

Standing on the porch, Laura looked at the hitch rack, remembering the roan-colored horse belonging to the new neighbor. Her eyes shifted, staring down the road. In the distance a horse and rider were getting smaller and smaller. It would be nice to see him again, she thought. Moving over to the bench, Laura sat down. She frowned, suddenly aware she hadn't asked her father where he was going. How did that happen, she wondered? But she did know. It was because she couldn't stop from being distracted by her memory recalling the sight of William McKiever rushing to her rescue. Even now, she could still see him slinging those two toughs around like rag dolls. Laura leaned back, her eyes closing against the noonday glare.

Sam saw his daughter's eyes were closed. Not wanting to startle her, he kept his voice soft. "You okay, honey?"

Smiling, Laura opened her eyes, looking lovingly at her father. "Yes, I'm fine. Where did you go?"

Sam looked at his daughter, thinking that someday a man would come along making her forget about her late husband, a man not fiddle footed, a man who would take care of his Laura. "You know me, I always need backup information. I sent a telegraph message to Captain O'Rourke at Ranger Headquarters."

"Why?"

"McKiever said he was a Texas Ranger under the captain's command, and I'm curious about him."

"You mean suspicious, don't you?"

"Not really, but you asked me two questions. One I knew, the other I didn't." Sam hesitated before speaking, making sure what he said to come out right. "When you rode for Frank O'Rourke, he trained you in his ways. One thing he always stressed was that a Ranger had to control his emotions, and we all knew why."

Laura was fascinated. "Go on, Dad."

Sam looked at Laura. "You see, the captain's philosophy rubbed off on all of us. It was about being a clear thinker in times of danger. That's why when McKiever said he didn't act professionally, I understood. But I did get curious why he has so much anger."

"But you said you were glad."

"I did say that, didn't I? That's because as he was whipping those two men. I was glad it was him and not me. Not that I'm proud of that, but I think you understand because of my age. But later he told us something concerning his anger. Do you remember what he said, Laura?"

"You mean about his anger needing to come out?"

"Yes, that's exactly right. Now, here's the thing, the good book warns us to be careful about what we say about someone, so I'm always careful about what I say." Sam's jaw tightened, his voice stern, "Honey, I ain't no gossiper."

Laura admired her father. Ever since she could remember, he always acted on his moral beliefs.

Sam reached out, holding his daughter's shoulders, "Laura, I sent that message so we might find out what's bothering him. You know, he helped us, maybe we can help him."

Laura jumped into her father's arms, hugging him. "That's what I like about you, Dad." She squeezed him tight. "You're such a good man, you make me proud."

Slipping his arms around his daughter, Sam felt moved. "Come on, precious, let's go home."

Crossing the street, both looked down at the now-empty road leading out of town.

CHAPTER 17

Manuel Santana

The road wound through sloping saddle ridges, evergreens dotting the hillsides. Patches of yellow aspens mingled with the evergreens. Most of the gold-colored leaves now littering the ground. Snow still lingered under the fir trees, compliments from a recent snowfall. The road suddenly forked, turning northwest, half overgrown from a lack of use. A single set of horse tracks wound through the stunted growth. McKiever studied the hoof prints. If Sam Ryan was right, those tracks belonged to Manuel Santana. Ahead the road leveled off, a finger ridge merged with another, a gap opening to the right. Riding through the opening, McKiever admired the gorge. Junipers mixed with pinyon pines clung to the canyon walls. The road began bending, the land leveling off. If his memory was serving him correctly, he was getting close to his ranch. Mac felt his anticipation building. Friend, sensing his master's excitement, snorted, shaking his head.

Cresting the rise, McKiever pulled Friend to a halt, enjoying the scene below. Nestled in the valley below them was his ranch. Darned if it wasn't pretty, he thought, small but pretty. Friend tugged at his bit, eager to go.

The small cabin, brown in color, was surrounded by meadow grass. Behind the house, a grove of aspens spread away from the cabin. In the near distance was the mountain, the peak snow covered. McKiever leaned over, talking to his horse, "That, old Friend, that's home. Tell you what, we chose well, we sure did. Let's go down and check things out." Straightening, he nudged Friend. Moving down, he eyed the large canyon oak growing in the corner of the yard. The tree was full of nuts. As they neared, Mac eyed the split rail fence enclosing the clearing. Nothing sagged; everything was in good repair. From where he sat atop his horse, he could see the cabin roof. The new cedar shingles were still brown, not yet aged by the weather.

A brown and white pinto was tied up at the front of the house. In the distance, a man was bent over, working on the north fence. Occupied with his work, the man still wasn't aware of their arrival. Dismounting, McKiever led Friend up to the mare. She greeted them with a whinny. Friend nuzzled her, snorting. Hitching the reins, he eyed the distant man. The man had heard the horses. Seeing the man start his way, McKiever began walking. Passing the porch, he noticed all the rotten boards had been replaced. A covered well, located between the house and barn, had a new roof. Mac was more impressed by the minute.

The man's voice greeted him, "Senor, may I be of help to you?"

The man was Mexican, almost six feet tall with shoulder-length black hair. The black hair made him look younger than his middle age. A thick, black mustache merged into his full sideburns. Ornate leather chaps covered his legs, a black-leather vest adorning his chest. A pearl-handled revolver was strapped to his left hip.

McKiever's response was a question, "Are you Manuel Santana?"

"Si, Senor."

McKiever stuck out his hand. "You already have helped me. I'm William McKiever."

Manuel's eyes widened, a grin spreading across his face. "Ah, finally we meet. You have finally come to Silver Springs, Mr. McKiever." Reaching out, he shook the hand.

"Yes, but before I came here, I stopped in town, looking for you."

"Ah, it is a pretty town, don't you think, Senor?"

"Yes, it is. But not as pleasant to my eyes as my ranch. Manuel, from what I see, you've done a great job."

"Thank you, Senor. May I show you what I've done, and what still needs doing?"

"Please do."

Manuel pointed at the well. "The water is plentiful, and clean to drink. It is filtered from the mountain." Turning, Manuel pointed up the mountain, his eyes twinkling, his voice infectious. "See that meadow, Senor McKiever? It is full of springs." He flashed an ear-splitting smile, displaying white teeth. "Also, you should know, often I see elk up there."

McKiever followed the pointing finger, seeing the meadow located halfway up the mountain's side. "Yes, I see it. I guess with some hunting luck, I won't need beef this winter."

Manuel's laugh was spontaneous, almost a cackle. His laugh faded as quickly as it happened, his face becoming serious. "But, Senor, on occasion, I also see Indians up there."

Startled, Mac looked at Manuel, his question spontaneous, "Are they friendly?"

"I just see them. They look down on me, then disappear. I think they hunt for elk." Manuel started for the barn. "Come, Mr. McKiever, let me show you what still needs to be done." Walking over to the barn, he looked up. "I have fixed the roof, but the sides need work. Let's go inside so you can see what must be done."

Entering, McKiever was pleasantly surprised. A wagon sat in the middle of the barn. Seeing McKiever's expression, Manuel's voice gushed enthusiasm, "Senor, I knew you would need such a wagon. There was an auction in town, so I thought it would be a good investment. Was I right?"

McKiever lightly touched Manuel's shoulder, pleased. "Are you kidding? It was on my mind to find one. You made a very good decision, my friend."

Manuel laughed, glad. "Senor, if you look you will see I fixed the north wall, and also the west side. I have more lumber behind the barn for the other sides, but I have not yet begun."

"Don't worry about that, Manuel, you've done more than I expected."

"Si, Senor, thank you. Come, let us go to the corral." Moving outside, they approached the circular enclosure. Manuel gestured toward the gate. "Mr. McKiever, I have replaced most of the posts along with the gate. Please, open it."

Lifting the latch, McKiever gave a slight push, marveling at how the pole gate swung without hesitation. Watching the gate swing back, he nodded at Manuel. It was obvious why Manuel was in demand. Latching the gate, Mac's voice reflecting admiration, "You have great skills with your hands. What's next, Manuel?"

Manuel turned. "We go to the house." Falling in step behind Manuel, McKiever followed. A double door slanted against the back wall of the cabin. Manuel touched the wooden door. "Senor, this is the root cellar," his voice becoming apologetic, "one can only enter from the outside. I was going to make an entrance from inside by cutting a hole in the cabin floor, but, Senor McKiever, I have been very busy. The hotel has kept me busy with many jobs. Please, accept my apology."

McKiever grinned, eyeing the logs stacked underneath the roof overhang. "Manuel, is there enough wood to get me through the winter?"

"Maybe, Senor. If you do not have a woman, I think so."

McKiever almost laughed, brushing against Manuel's ornate vest. The vest jingled, flashing in the sun. "You know, Manuel, they told me in town that I couldn't find a better man than you, and they were right."

"Many thanks, Senor McKiever. Come, it is time to go inside." Manuel grabbed the back door. It too swung open without hesitating. Walking inside, McKiever was astonished. The last time he walked on the floor it groaned everywhere, but not now. The boards were swept clean. Everything was spotless. Manuel walked over to a washbasin. Beaming, he pointed to a hand pump. "See, you have water inside, but later, during the winter cold, you may not."

Delighted, McKiever nodded, his eyes sweeping the cabin. Two cupboards were on each side of the washbasin. Shelves spanned the kitchen wall, reaching the ceiling. The window was bracketed with two racks containing hanging pots and pans. Located in the center of the floor was a large planked table, a chair at each end. The only thing fancy was the oil lamp hanging over the table. At the north end, a long-legged metal stove sat on loosely laid stones. The far wall was graced by a stone fireplace, complete with a brick baking oven. Near the fireplace was a wood bin. The bin was full, the split logs gray in color. McKiever could see the wood was well seasoned. He turned, aware that Manuel was watching him. At the other end of the room were two bunk beds. Both bunks contained mattresses made with overlaid evergreen boughs. It was apparent that Manuel was skilled at whatever he did, including using what nature provided. Above the bunks were wide shelves containing blankets. Each wall had a window, the one to the south the largest. Shifting his stare to the front door, Mac noted the worn broom propped up against the wall. To the left of the front door, an empty gun rack was nailed halfway up the wall.

McKiever faced Manuel. "I cannot tell you how pleased I am. Fact is, I was worried about not being ready for winter, but you have taken care of that."

Manuel's face was beaming, starting to comment, he stopped to listen as McKiever continued. "In the future I'm going to need a man like yourself. Right now, until I get some beef and make some money, I won't be able to afford you. But when I do, I hope you'll work for me."

Manuel had an eager look on his face. "I think I would like that, Senor McKiever. Come, I have one other thing you must see." Slipping out the front door, Manuel stepped off the porch, disappearing around the corner. Waiting for McKiever to catch up, he pointed. A shed was built against the outside wall of the cabin. Lifting a peg from the latch, Manuel swung open the double doors. Hanging against one of the walls was a hammer, a chisel, and a drawknife. A buck-saw adorned the far wall. Propped up near the saw was a double-bladed axe. Hanging over the tools was a two-man saw. The right corner contained a pitchfork, along with a pick and shovel.

Manuel closed the door. "Senor, one thing you will need is hay for your horse. Just a small amount is in the barn, but that is all. Also, mostly the wind sweeps out of the north and sometimes from the west. I think you must finish the barn siding on the west side before the winter comes."

"I will, Manuel, but I think I owe you some money. Tell me, how much am I behind?"

"Just a small balance for the boards behind the barn. Just yesterday I picked them up at the sawmill. I have not yet paid for them."

"How about work money?"

Manuel pointed toward the table. "There is a record with my hours in the center drawer of the kitchen table. You owe me a small amount." Reaching into his vest, he handed Mac a bill for boards. "This is what is not paid. If you want, you can pay the sawmill yourself, or I will gladly do it. As for me, there is no rush. Pay me when you can."

McKiever nodded. "Tomorrow I'll go to the bank. After that, where can I find you?"

Manuel thought for a moment before speaking, "In the morning and afternoon I work at the hotel."

"Good, I will find you. Let me walk you to your horse, you know, I have already met five people in Silver Springs, and Manuel, you are the one who has pleased me the most."

Manuel reached for the Pinto's reins. "Who were the others, Senor McKiever?"

"The bank president, a Mr. Morgan. The general store owner, Leonard Rathbone, and Sam Ryan and his daughter, Laura."

"Ah, you have met the most beautiful woman in the world." Manuel shook his head, sadness showing in his face. "She is broken hearted. Her husband was a handsome man, a captain in the U.S. Cavalry."

McKiever eyed Manuel, his curiosity aroused. "What happened to him, Manuel?"

"His patrol came under attack by Comanche; he was killed."

So, McKiever thought, that is why Laura Ryan was without a man. Manuel squinted at the far hill. "She has mourned for a long time. Often, she visits his grave. Always she brings flowers, always!"

"Tell me, Manuel, how long has her man been dead?"

Head bowed, Manuel thought for a minute, before raising his head. "Five years. Yes, it has been five years."

A strong breeze rattled the oak leaves. The pinto mare jerked her head up. Spooked, she stomped her feet, snorting. Manuel extended his hand. McKiever grabbed it, sincerity in his voice, "I will be in town tomorrow afternoon to pay my bill, and then settle with you." He smiled. "But first, first I must sit on my porch, have some coffee, and enjoy my new home. The home you have made ready for me."

"Si, Senor, that would be pleasing to any man." Manuel lifted his foot into the stirrup. Rising, he settled into the saddle, a sudden look of astonishment spread across his face, his voice almost scolding, "I have almost forgotten something, Senor McKiever. I hung a hindquarter of beef in the root cellar; it is well salted." Backing the mare away, he swung her around, looking down at McKiever. "Senor, you will not be hungry." With a wave at Mac, he booted the mare. Manuel Santana raced away, his sombrero bouncing against his shoulders.

McKiever was impressed with the man's infectious personality. Even better, his words had meaning. When a man says he will do something, and then does it, that shows character. It was obvious that Manuel Santana had character. Turning, he loosened Friend's reins. Leading Friend, they entered the barn. Lifting the saddle, he draped it over a wooden stand. Next was the blanket. The day was early, too early to leave his horse inside the barn. "Come on, partner, it's time for you to get acquainted with your new surroundings."

Moving outside, McKiever led Friend toward the corral. Stopping at the well, he cranked up the bucket. Pouring water into the trough, he watched his horse drink. Waiting until Friend finished, they headed for the corral. Swinging open the gate, he slipped off the bridle. Slapping Friend's flank, he watched his horse high-stepping around the enclosure. Closing the gate, McKiever wheeled around, heading for the cabin. For the first time he was about to be alone in his own place. He felt contentment.

CHAPTER 18

Invitation

The dinner table at the Ryan home was long. It was a beautiful table, made out of red oak. Sam sat at the head, his wife Martha at the other end. Laura was seated next to her younger brother. Todd had just turned twelve. He had his father's personality. He was curious about everything, and not afraid to express himself. Laura's inherited beauty could be seen in her mother. Most of Martha's hair was brown, but her temples were showing the beginning tinges of gray. Martha's face had a happy look, her age wrinkles curling upward. She was quick to laugh, and when she did, her blue eyes twinkled. Another characteristic of Martha was her gift of encouragement. Her wants were simple. She wanted young Todd to grow up and be like his father. She hoped her daughter would find a good man, one not in the military. She wanted grandchildren, lots of them. Martha was always threatening to get rid of the long table for a round one. She disliked how far the family sat from each other. A round table was her expressed solution, unless of course, the family grew. Her hope for family growth was in Laura, but her patience was wearing thin. Over the years Sam had made it a policy to invite one of the ranch hands to join them for the evening dinner. The invitation policy was followed at least three times a week, with Saturdays and Sundays strictly family days. Tonight, the honored guest was the ranch foreman, Bill Wade. Bill sat across from Laura and Todd, everyone waiting for Sam Ryan to sit down. Sam, never impatient, waited for Martha to join them before speaking, "Let's bow our heads and open our hearts to the almighty." Everyone bowed their heads, hands clasped, Sam's voice becoming reverent, "Lord we have much to be thankful for, family, good health, and lots of food. It is our desire to be mindful of you, and that we remember what you have already done for us. We truly need your blessings in our everyday life, and for that we are thankful. In your precious blood we pray, amen."

"Amen," echoed around the table.

Sam eyed the steaming platters, declaring, "Women first. Martha, you done the work, go ahead and fill your plate. Laura, you're next. Us men will get rid of our hunger last."

Conversation was encouraged at the dinner table, Sam always introducing the subject. He eyed his daughter before beginning. "In case any of you aren't aware, our new neighbor is a retired Texas Ranger." Sam took a bite, watching their faces, Bill's expression showing the most surprise. Sam went on, "I contacted Ranger Headquarters at Los Quintos and received a very interesting message from Captain O'Rourke."

Martha pushed her chair back, jumping from the table. "Oh my God, I forgot the biscuits!"

Sam laughed, watching her scurry into the kitchen. In seconds she was back, her voice a sigh, "Thank goodness they aren't burned." She placed the platter containing the rescued biscuits on the table. "Sam, I'm sorry, please continue telling us about our new neighbor."

Sam stole a look at Bill. "How many of you heard about the gunfight in Fredonia between a Texas Ranger and a gunfighter by the name of Sam Peckenpath?"

Bill responded, "I did. I heard this Peckenpath was deadly, unbelievably fast. I also heard he'd already killed a Texas Ranger."

Sam nodded. "Yep, you heard right. Now listen to this, our new neighbor, William McKiever, is the Ranger who killed Peckenpath."

Everyone stopped eating, silence capturing the table. Seeing the curiosity etched in their faces, Sam knew he had a captive audience. He spaced out his words, "But this McKiever almost didn't make it. He took two bullets in his chest, one ending up in his right shoulder."

Laura gasped, remembering how McKiever seemed so able. Stunned, Martha's face went white, her voice a whisper, "Dear me." Todd's eyes were wide.

Sam eyed everyone. "This McKiever was unconscious for several days, and bedridden for over a month. I understand it took him a long time to recover, losing lots of blood."

Wade interrupted, "Where was that gunfighter shot?"

"Through his heart."

Todd blurted out, "Wow, the gunman was killed by our new neighbor."

Sam nodded, agreeing, "Yep, the captain told me he raised McKiever like a son, said there isn't a faster Ranger anywhere. He told me that McKiever had no intention of meeting that killer alone, but the gunfighter waited in the alley for McKiever, forcing him to draw his gun."

A frown creased Wade's brow. "Why? Was he paid to kill McKiever?"

"Good question, O'Rourke didn't say. Maybe this Peckenpath heard about McKiever's reputation. You know, men like that live for their reputations." Sam looked at Laura. "We saw how good McKiever is with a gun, didn't we, Laura?"

Laura nodded.

Wade's voice registered curiosity, "How's that?"

"It happened in the general store. Laura and I were picking up some supplies. Two bums came in with whiskey on their breaths, going over to Laura, bothering her."

Martha's voice was sharp, "Sam, why didn't you tell me?"

"I guess," Sam peeked at Laura, his voice sheepish, "I didn't want you to worry. After that, I kind of forgot about saying anything."

"Sam," Martha shook her finger at him, "you should have told me!"

"I suppose I should have. Anyway, before I could move, this McKiever steps in and drops one of those fellows to the floor, and the other hombre goes for his gun."

"And—" Wade prompted.

"I never saw McKiever's gun clear leather; it was just there." Sam's voice reflected awe, "To think that hired gunfighter got off two shots to McKiever's one is tough to believe, especially after what we saw."

"Well," Wade rolled his eyes as he spoke, "it seems we got ourselves a good neighbor."

Sam agreed, "Yes, but there's more to the story. It appears that Captain O'Rourke didn't want McKiever to take that assignment for several reasons. First of all, he was returning from the field to turn in his badge to come here. In other words, he was going to retire. The other reason was that he knew McKiever wouldn't refuse the assignment" Sam, realizing his food was getting cold, excused himself, taking a bite of food.

Martha watched Sam, waiting for him to stop chewing, before asking, "Sam, why didn't he refuse the assignment?"

Sam ceased chewing, answering, "Because of a woman in that town by the name of Sara."

Laura stopped eating.

"The problem was McKiever had fallen in love with this Sara, so the captain knew he wouldn't refuse."

Laura couldn't contain herself, "Why didn't he marry this Sara?"

"Because he still hadn't finished paying off his ranch before coming here, and he needed several more years as a Ranger to finish those payments."

"But," Martha jumped in, "couldn't he have married her and still be a Ranger? I mean, isn't that allowed?"

Sam nodded. "Yeah, he could have done that, except she married another man, who just happens to be McKiever's former Texas Ranger partner and best friend!" Sam shrugged. "Both had been attracted to her, and she to them. So, his buddy proposes, leaves the Rangers, and ends up getting a big ranch as a wedding gift. As for McKiever, he finishes paying off his small place before coming here, and almost gets himself killed."

Wade broke in, "So, the end of a friendship."

"Not really, they still remained friends. But just think why the captain was so worried. I mean, look at the circumstances. First of all, he knew this rancher had hired the gunfighter, along with a bunch of hard cases. He knows McKiever's coming to turn in his badge, but he also knows he'll accept the assignment because of who's in Fredonia." Sam leaned forward, adding intensity to his voice, "Fact is, Captain Frank feels flat-out guilty. A man he raised as a son is supposed to be retiring, and now he offers him an assignment that he knows won't be refused, maybe the most dangerous ever!"

Wade agreed, "Talk about a guilt trip, I reckon Captain O'Rourke was mighty bothered."

"Not to mention," Sam emphasized, "how Captain Frank ends up receiving a report that a man he raised like a son is lying in bed fighting for his life!"

"I declare," Martha's voice was soft. "Talk about fate."

Sam shifted his look away from Martha to Laura. "But I'm not finished. The woman is a Christian and she nurses McKiever back to health."

Laura couldn't take her eyes off her father.

Sam leaned back. "So help me, what I'm about to repeat was told direct to me from the captain. The captain said it was the prayers from his friend's wife that kept McKiever from dying. After McKiever came out of the coma, he told the wife he was sliding toward this black abyss, and a powerful force kept pulling him back." Sam paused, aware that no one was eating. "He told her that this force kept coming from his right side, so he asks her where she was praying from when he was lying in the street. She told him she was at his right side and she never stopped praying."

Laura could hardly breath, chills raced through her body, she gasped, "Dad, does he believe in God?"

Sam didn't answer her question. "Later, McKiever told this girl that this force came from his left side." Sam's eyes swept the table. "And that's where she was praying while he was bedridden." Sam looked at Laura, answering her question, "The captain said McKiever has never believed, but after that experience he said maybe there is a God. Anyway, that's all I know. Anything else we'll have to learn from him. That's, of course, if he wants to talk about it."

"Sam," Martha's voice a soft command, "we have to extend our hospitality toward our new neighbor by inviting him to dinner. I think we should do that as soon as possible, don't you agree?"

"Yes, Martha, I reckon you're right."

"But," Martha's eyes bore into everyone, "let's not pry into the man's past. Let's just be his friends and neighbors."

"Goodness," Sam complained, "my foods getting cold."

Martha chided him, "That's what happens, Sam Ryan, when you talk and don't eat." Martha shifted her gaze to Laura. "While your father eats, why don't we clear the table."

"Okay, Mom."

Martha stood, hands on her hips. "When Sam finishes, I have a fresh pot of coffee along with a fresh baked, strawberry cake."

Laura stared at her plate, her food only half eaten. Probably cold like her father's, she thought. Laura shifted her eyes from the plate. "Mom, give me a minute."

Martha smiled. Turning, she left for the kitchen.

Laura looked at her father, a thought forming in her mind. "Dad."

"Yes, honey, what is it?"

"You know, I think you uncovered why McKiever had so much anger stored up in him."

For a second Sam was puzzled; then he got her point. "You know, Laura, you just might be right." He repeated himself, "Yep, you just might be right."

Laura stood, starting for the kitchen. She stopped, visualizing McKiever's face as he closed in on those two men. She felt a chill seep through her body. This man had almost died before coming here, and once again he had placed himself in harm's way. But this time it wasn't for a woman he loved; it was for a woman he didn't know, and she had been that woman. Laura felt her eyes misting.

Martha peered from the kitchen doorway, staring at her daughter. "Laura, you going to bring those dishes in?"

"Oh, sorry, Mom." Laura smiled, entering the kitchen.

Martha could see her daughter's mind was preoccupied. "Dear, what are you so thoughtful about?"

Laura took a second to answer. "I guess I was recalling what happened in the store, and the brief conversation I had with him."

"You mean, with Mr. McKiever?"

"Yes, Mom, he was so polite, but also very fierce."

Martha stopped washing the dishes, her focus on Laura's face. "Go on honey."

"To think that just a short time ago, this man almost died. It just keeps coming back at me."

Martha's voice became soothing, "That would be hard to get out of anyone's mind. I'm looking forward to meeting this man, especially knowing how he stood in for you and your father."

The sun hung suspended at the ten-o'clock-morning position. McKiever squinted upward at the yellow ball, no longer seeing his breath because of the sun's warming rays. Stepping back inside the cabin, he approached the stove listening to the sound of the percolating coffee. The coffee aroma filled the cabin, smelling special. Grabbing a white cup, he studied the color of the coffee as he poured. The color was golden brown. Just right, he thought. Moving back outside, he set the cup down. Settling onto the wooden bench, he sipped his coffee. Noise attracted his attention to the Canyon Oak. Two fox squirrels were chasing each other. First one would chase, then the other became the chaser.

McKiever was content. He had slept in his own house, he was sitting on his porch, drinking coffee that he made, and now he was enjoying a squirrel show. He looked at the corral. Friend was nosing around, checking each rail. Earlier this morning the air had been crisp, frost covering the grass, but not now. The frost had melted, the grass wet. The oak leaves, rust colored, rattled from a slight breeze. Last night's freezing cold, together with rising temperatures, had triggered a serenade of falling acorns. The nuts, a golden brown, littered the ground. Another breeze rattled the leaves. McKiever didn't feel the wind. Whoever had built this cabin knew wind direction. The breeze, coming out of the north, was brushing against the back of the house. Here on the porch, he was sheltered while being warmed by the morning sun. Mac heard Friend snort, his eyes jumping to the corral. Friend was alert, ears forward, staring down the road. McKiever saw the distant riders, two of them. He was about to have company.

The one rider rode a chestnut horse, with a white blaze running down the muzzle. The other rode a big black without any distinctive markings. They were still too far away for McKiever to see who rode the horses. Instinctively, his hand brushed his hip. His ever-present gun wasn't there. Remembering he had hung the holster inside the door, he shrugged. Whoever they were, he hoped they were neighborly.

As the riders neared, McKiever's heart jumped. It was Sam Ryan and his daughter, Laura. Rising, he stepped off the porch. He felt nervous, and it wasn't because of Sam. As they neared, he wanted to stare at Laura, but kept his eyes on Sam. Sam's voice bridged the rapidly closing distance, "Morning, Mac, I hope we're not interrupting your solitude."

"Not at all, please get down. Welcome, you're my first visitors. I'll have to record that in my ranch journal."

Laura's teasing voice gave McKiever a reason to stare. "You have a journal, Mr. McKiever?"

"Not really, but when I go to town, I'm going to get one." Smiling, Mac managed to tear his eyes away from her, focusing on Sam. "I made a fresh pot of coffee. Fact is, I just had my first cup, and I'd be pleased if you and Miss Laura would join me." He watched them dismount.

Sam Ryan understood hospitality. He really didn't want another cup of coffee, but it was still morning, so he'd make an exception, saying so, "I'd like that."

Laura moved close to McKiever. "Could I bother you for a glass of water?"

McKiever's eyes locked onto Laura's. She was looking at him with interest, something he hadn't seen before. He nodded, finding his voice, "I have water, good water." He shifted his stare to Sam. "We could go inside or enjoy the porch, your call."

"I like the porch. Today it feels awful pleasant outside."

"How would you like your coffee, Mr. Ryan?"

"Black, and call me Sam."

Laura was almost on top of him. "May I go in and help you?" She smiled. "Two extra hands always seems to help."

McKiever nodded, gesturing toward the door, following her.

Laura's eyes swept the interior, stopping at the table. She was surprised at seeing a Bible. Turning, she looked at McKiever, asking, "You read the Bible, Mr. McKiever?"

"It was given to me by a pastor in Fredonia. He asked me to read a verse the first night I camped while coming here." He changed the conversation, "I reckon you forgot our last talk. My name is Mac, not Mr. McKiever." Moving over to the sink, he washed his cup. Reaching up, he grabbed the lone remaining cup. Working the pump, he filled the cup, handing it to her, apologetic, "Sorry, this ranch doesn't have any glasses, at least not yet."

"Thank you. Tell me, Mac, did you read a verse when you camped?"

"Yes, I always keep my word." Moving to the stove, he poured Sam's coffee.

Laura liked his answer. "Do you mind telling me what you read?"

McKiever pushed his hat back. "Some writings that a fellow by the name of John wrote. Tell me, Miss Laura, are you a church-going person?"

"Every chance I get, and please, call me Laura."

McKiever hesitated, remembering Sara's prayer promise, how she had told him he would meet a Christian woman. He felt a strange sensation, and it showed.

Laura remembered to use his first name, questioning him, "Mac, you look surprised."

"I was just remembering something. Maybe sometime I'll tell you about it. Right now, I'd be too embarrassed. Besides, I think we better get this coffee out to your father."

Sam was also enjoying the entertainment provided by the squirrels. As McKiever approached, he reached for the steaming cup of coffee. "Smells good, much obliged."

Laura spoke, "I have a confession to make to you, Mr. McKiever, I mean Mac."

Half smiling, McKiever questioned her, "What confession is that?"

"I often rode out here. This is such a wonderful spot, very beautiful and quiet. It was very therapeutic for me."

McKiever studied Laura's face, guessing she needed a place to grieve after the loss of her husband. He encouraged her, "Please, feel free anytime you want. Matter of fact, just before you arrived, I was enjoying the surroundings. And you're right, it is very peaceful here."

Sam had a surprised look on his face, alarm etched in his voice, "Laura, I wish I'd known. I don't like you riding alone."

"I know, Dad, but I needed to be alone." A redness appeared in her eyes. Trying to hide her emotions, Laura lifted her gaze toward the mountain.

Seeing her emotions, Mac was tactful, "Well, I'm glad you visited here, and I'm glad for this visit. If you don't mind me asking, to what do I owe this unexpected surprise?"

Sam answered, "You wouldn't let me buy you lunch in town, and after my wife heard about the general store fracas, she insisted you join us for dinner. The only thing we want to know is when you can come?"

"I would consider that an honor, but you'll have to tell me when it's convenient for you."

Sam needed help. He looked at Laura, deciding to let her make the decision.

As if anticipating, Laura didn't hesitate, "How about this coming Friday?"

McKiever nodded. "Sounds like a plan. Say," he laughed, "what day is it? I've plum lost track."

Sam joked, "Seems like someone needs a calendar."

Laura answered Mac's question, "Today is Wednesday, which means in two days we will see you."

McKiever rolled his eyes. "Don't I feel stupid. I guess when I get to town, I'll need two things. A ranch journal and a calendar. What time should I be expected?"

Sam looked at his daughter. "Laura?"

"We would like you to come at least two hours before dinner. We could show you around before we eat. How does between three and four sound? We usually eat between five and six."

McKiever looked at Laura; it was easy to see who knew the social niceties. "Three o'clock it is. Anything I can bring?"

Laura's voice seemed enthusiastic, "Just yourself."

McKiever detected her tone as personal. He was tongue tied, a little uncomfortable, but liking it.

Sam saved him. "After we leave here, we're heading to town. While we're there we might as well get you a ranch journal and calendar. Save you a trip to town."

"Much appreciated, Sam, but I've got to order some hay for the winter, so I was planning on going to the mill anyway."

"You go ahead, but don't order no hay 'cause I got plenty. Monday, I'll send a wagon load up to your ranch. You just tell the men where you want the hay stored."

McKiever couldn't help but be pleased; finally, things were going his way. All the problems he had worried about were getting solved, and not by him. Gratitude showed in his voice, "I sure would appreciate that, Sam. Give me a bill, and as soon as I get to the bank, you'll get paid."

Sam held up his hand. "We'll worry about that later. Fact is, I don't sell the stuff anyway."

McKiever protested, "Sam, I couldn't take that hay without paying. Whatever it's worth, that's what I'll pay."

Sam gave in. "Fine, but for now, until you're up and running, don't pay me until later."

"How's this, Sam: I have to pay a bill up at the feed mill. While I'm there, I'll find out what they're charging for hay and that's how much I'll pay you."

Laura's voice stopped the negotiating. "Mac, let my father help you. He's been doing that all his life." Her voice softened, pleading, "Please?"

McKiever looked at her, then at Sam. Keep it simple, he thought. "Okay."

Sam interrupted them, "What else you need?" Making a point, he spread his hands. "What the heck, I got a wagon coming your way, so what else can you use?"

McKiever remembered Manuel telling him about the elk. "Salt, there's elk up on that mountain. I figure to shoot one and salt down the meat."

"Tell you what, when you come Friday, I'll give you enough salt to bring back. When the hay arrives, I'll include an extra supply of salt, how's that?"

"Right now, I'm feeling pretty fortunate. How about me paying for the salt? I'd like that."

Sam waved his hand. "No way. Listen, after we have dinner, I got another business proposition for you."

"You do?"

"I do. Now, this is a proposition you won't refuse and one you can pay for."

"Finally," McKiever chuckled. "You mind telling me about it?"

"It's about you getting a herd started. But I like to talk business after a nice lunch, or before dinner. That's how I operate, so you'll have to wait." Sam looked at his daughter. "Laura, mount up; we got to get going."

Laura handed McKiever her cup, her eyes twinkling, her voice teasing, "Please come early, I'd like some time alone with you."

McKiever almost gulped, without words.

Laura, seeing his discomfort, laughed, relaxing him. "That way I can find out all about you. Otherwise, my mother will scold me for being too nosey at the dinner table."

Mac's response held a touch of humor. "You know conversation can go both ways. After our chit-chat, I may know all about you."

Laura teased back, "Dad said I should have been a lawyer."

Remembering the captain's advice about letting a woman have the last word, McKiever looked at Sam, noticing the smile tugging at the corners of his mouth. Mac decided to be tactful by using her father. "Say, Sam, you think it might be better if I arrive late?"

Sam was enjoying their banter. He hadn't seen his daughter enjoying herself in such a long time. "Come on, Laura, get on your horse before you frighten our guest away."

Mounting her horse, Laura looked down at McKiever. "I'm not frightening you, am I?"

A look of mischief flickered in Mac's eyes. "Don't worry, I'll be there early, real early!"

Laura laughed softly.

Watching them ride away, McKiever waited until they were out of hearing range, talking to himself, "She's prettier than the last time." Walking over to the corral he struck up a conversation with Friend, "How about we double up? You get to meet that nice chestnut filly, and I spend some time with the owner. How's that, fair enough?"

Friend stuck his neck over the rail, eyeing the departing riders, as if understanding.

Mac continued, "You know, old buddy, a woman has a way of letting a man know if she's interested, and right now I'm kind of getting that feeling. Yes, sir, I do believe that's so."

Friend snorted, stomping his front hoof.

McKiever reached out, stroking his muzzle. "You think a woman that beautiful could stay interested in me?"

Friend didn't answer.

"You sure can be quiet when you want. Anyway, we have at least forty-eight hours before things get better or worse. Besides, tomorrow you and I are going to get an early start up to that meadow way up on the mountain. With some luck, we might get enough meat for the winter."

Sam shifted in his saddle, looking at his daughter. "I haven't seen you enjoying yourself with a man for a long time. Until now, that is."

Laura didn't answer, staring straight ahead.

Sam persisted, "You kind of like him, don't you?"

"You know why, Dad?"

"No, tell me why."

"It's because of the type of man he is. He reminds me—" her voice trailing off.

Unable to stop himself, Sam said what was on his mind, "He reminds you of Steven."

Laura looked at her father before answering, "Yes, he reminds me of Steve."

CHAPTER 19

Mountain Neighbors

A long white streak stretched across the black horizon. Horse and rider climbed upward, their breath hanging suspended in the predawn air. McKiever and Friend had been working their way up the mountain for over an hour. At times they lost the faint game trail, before finding it again. Mac was sure the trail led to the high meadow. The terrain began leveling off, the light strengthening, no longer just a white streak in the sky. Patches of white snow stood out against the black background. In the distance a night owl hooted, protesting against the coming dawn.

Slowly the black became gray. McKiever spotted the distant meadow, the field appearing like a luminous lake against the dark surroundings. Hauling back on the reins, he paused, hunting with his ears. Large game animals make noise when moving. He heard no sounds indicating elk on the move. With the coming daybreak, Mac was sure any elk remained bedded. Shifting his eyes, he saw a small clearing nestled below and to the right of the large meadow. Turning Friend, he let his horse pick his way around the numerous seedlings. Entering the opening, McKiever slid off the saddle, studying the ground. Numerous deer tracks covered the ground, but all were old. Perhaps, Mac thought, the elk's presence had driven the smaller cousins out? Whatever the reason, he was pleased. The last thing he wanted was deer warning his larger quarry.

Digging into his saddlebag, he quickly extracted what he needed. Bending down, he hobbled Friend's front legs. Reaching up, he slid the Sharps out of the scabbard. Groping in his right pocket, he pulled out a long brass cartridge. Slowly opening the action, he slipped the bullet into the chamber, easing the action closed. Pleased he'd made no loud alien sounds, he walked around Friend. Digging into the other saddlebag, Mac removed his telescope, slipping it into his wool mackinaw. Flipping a pair of moccasins to the ground, he removed his boots, wiggling into the soft leather. It was time to hunt.

Patting Friend, Mac tested the wind. Exhaling, he watched his breath whisk downhill, disappearing over his left shoulder. Again, he tested the wind, the results the same. Scanning the surroundings, he decided to work his way along the far corner of the meadow while searching for a place of concealment. Moving cautiously, he avoided the crusty snow patches, easing under a large evergreen. Here, hidden by the shadows cast by the tree, he stopped. Bringing the telescope up, he scanned the surrounding woods. No dark shapes loomed in the background. Studying the meadow, he focused on a large trampled area contrasting against the pale-yellow grass. Fresh mud was splattered everywhere, the mud still glistening from recent use. Excited, McKiever stared at the elk wallow. Now the question was, where would he set up his stand? He eyed a small tree halfway out into the field. The tree by on its side, surrounded by willow bushes. The blown down tree offered good concealment, but first he needed to find a branch to steady his rifle. Mac checked overhead. Finding a forked branch, he unsheathed his knife, cutting out his rifle rest.

Checking to make sure nothing moved, McKiever skirted along the edge, avoiding pockets of bright sunlight. Passing the downed tree, he turned, angling out into the tall grass. Reaching the tangle of willows, he searched for an opening. Circling, he found his entrance. Careful to avoid breaking any branches, he eased alongside the trunk. Mac was pleased; the uprooted tree offered good concealment. From this location, he could see everywhere, including the far corner of the meadow. Working quickly, he cleared the ground, removing any dead sticks. Satisfied, he made himself comfortable. Now it was up to the elk.

Filtered by the trees, flickering shafts of sunlight stretched across the meadow. Despite the sun, Mac felt the cold. Pulling up the wool collar, he huddled, shoving his hands deeper into the Mackinaw's roomy pockets. Trying to distract his mind from the cold, he thought about his quarry. Elk and deer had one thing in common: it was called caution. Hunted animals can't afford to be careless. They constantly check for danger, moving slow, standing still for long periods of time. Men are impatient, but not the hunted. McKiever reminded himself to be patient.

The hour passed, the meadow dormant from animal activity. Feeling the urge to inspect the wallow, McKiever scolded himself against his impatient boredom. Exhaling, he checked the wind, surprised that his breath was hardly visible. The morning was warming, but the cold still numbed his body. Two scrub jays began screaming on the lower hillside. Mac wished the birds would go away; their incessant noise drowning out his ability to detect any sounds from moving elk. Finally, the jays' scolding erupted farther down the hillside, their screaming muffled by the trees.

McKiever's eyes jumped. A large brown animal had materialized in the far-right corner of the field. The cow elk, head down, eased forward, a yearling following the mother. Grazing slowly, they angled out into the meadow. The cow raised her head, her nose testing the air. For a moment she looked at McKiever. Mac froze, the seconds ticking into minutes. Satisfied, the cow lowered her head. Another elk drifted into view, followed by a fourth cow. Detecting movement out of the corner of his eyes, McKiever shifted his stare. A young spike was easing from out of the cover of the trees, peering at the cows. The young bull appeared nervous, ready to flee.

Sure that a big bull was near, Mac shifted his eyes back to the cows, startled. At least fifteen cows now filled the meadow. Most of the females were of good size, but he didn't want to shoot a mother elk. Since it was the cows who carried the young, he saw no sense in shooting the future. He would wait for the herd bull. McKiever felt a sudden shift from the air, a slight breeze brushing the back of his neck. He grimaced. The warming temperature had triggered rising thermal currents. The air was now pushing up into the meadow. McKiever eyed the spike, relieved. As long as the young bull didn't cross above him, the breeze still remained favorable.

The lead cow, followed by her youngster, neared the young bull. The spike, his body becoming taut, stared past the cow. Suddenly, every cow's head was up, ears perked, peering in the direction of the far corner of the meadow. McKiever's eyes followed the turned heads. At first, he saw nothing. Then he saw the ivory-tipped horns moving over the tops of the bushes. The herd bull was arriving. The huge bull strode into the field, his muscles rippling the length of his body. The spike, his body quivering, intently watched the monarch assume command of his harem, Turning, the young male trotted into the trees.

McKiever forgot the spike, focusing on the herd bull, counting seven points. The big male strode into the cows, scattering them. Swinging his massive neck outward, the bull's eerie whistle captured the meadow. McKiever's thumb shifted to the hammer, easing it back, the double click disturbing the natural sounds of the meadow. The bull swung his head, staring into the brush. Mac froze, not moving. A minute passed, the bull staring intently at the strange form huddled next to the fallen tree. Finally, sure that no danger would come from within the tangle of brush, the bull turned his head, starting toward the wallow.

McKiever took a deep breath, letting half out, the barrel resting on the forked stick. Slowly, he raised the rifle butt to his shoulder, the sights settling just behind the bull's front shoulder. Squeezing the trigger, the Sharps slammed against his shoulder, the booming shot echoing across the valley. The bull buckled, straightening, he lunged forward, big chunks of dirt flying. Mac cleared the action, slamming another bullet into the chamber. Rising, he swung the sights ahead of the running bull. Starting to tighten his trigger finger, he stopped. The bull was down. Jumping to his feet, McKiever stared at the magnificent animal. Rifle up, he started towards the bull. From beyond the trees, he heard the crashing sounds from departing elk.

Reaching the bull, McKiever admired the enormous male. His antlers seemed like the branches from the trees of the forest, just like the land he inhabited. Now there was a job to be done, a chore that Mac liked to call a labor of love. None of the animal would be wasted. He glanced at the sky, estimating the time slightly after nine in the morning. Judging by the size of the huge male, it would surely take him most of the morning to quarter up the bull, and at least two trips down the mountain to get the meat stored. Pulling out his knife, he started his task. The sun climbed higher into the sky, warming the meadow. Finishing, McKiever rose, wiping his knife. Glancing upward, he eyed the sun, guessing it to be almost noon.

Pulling out his watch, he was pleased. He'd guessed right, finishing in good time. Turning, he headed for his horse. It was time to pack out the meat.

The trip down the mountain was slow, the return quicker. Approaching the bull's remains piled under the shade from a tall balsam tree, McKiever dismounted. Knowing the smell of meat often attracted bear, he kept his rifle in hand, scanning for danger. Everything appeared as he had left it. Bending down, Friend's explosive snort stopped him. Straightening, Mac eyed the roan. The stallion's nostrils were flared, his ears forward, staring north. McKiever turned his head, tensing. Two Indian braves sat astride their ponies, each had a rifle lying across their folded arms. From where he stood, McKiever guessed they were Shoshone. For several seconds time seemed suspended. Mac considered his situation. If the Shoshone had intended him harm, he reckoned they would have already jumped him!

Crouching, McKiever lay his Sharps on the ground. Standing up, he lifted his Colt, lying it next to the rifle. Straightening, he held his hand open, palm out. Turning his hand, he gestured for the braves to come. For several seconds neither Indian moved. Suddenly, both braves started towards him. Sitting atop their horses, both braves appeared regal. Leather leggings covered their legs, their long black hair framed their high cheek bones, their copper-colored skin glowing. Riding within twenty feet of him, the men halted their horses, staring down at him.

McKiever returned their stare, not rushing to speak. Being a nervous talker was a sign of weakness. Finally, he spoke, "Welcome keepers of the land." He pointed to the elk. "The creator has provided me with food for the winter. I am grateful for the spirit's blessing."

The older Indian stared at McKiever's feet, the moccasins capturing his attention. Shifting his look away from the feet, he asked, "From where do you come, hunter of the Wapiti?"

Mac knew that in the Indian world, the great spirit owned the land. Keeping his focus on both braves, he raised his hand, pointing toward the valley below. "I have purchased a house from the great white father in the land below, so that I might live amongst you in peace." Shifting his stare to the older man, he continued, "I have escaped death. I come here to heal, to walk amongst you as a friend, and take no more than is needed."

The elder Indian questioned him, "You know our ways. How is that?"

McKiever nodded, choosing his words carefully, "A man's years teach him many things. Some things are only taught by living through summers and winters. Understanding others can only be known by sharing like needs. Sharing those things please the great spirit."

The elder turned his head toward the younger man, nodding as he spoke, "He speaks as a man of wisdom; we will welcome him." The younger brave gave a single nod, the elder returning his look at McKiever. "Welcome, man from below. You have hunted well; you have spoken with understanding. I am the elder of my people. They turn to me for counsel. I will tell them we have a friend who is a recovering warrior who has laid down his weapons."

Suddenly, both braves turned their horses, without another word they rode into the trees, as quickly as they had appeared, they were gone. McKiever felt relief. He had spoken the right words. Reaching down, he retrieved his Colt, then his rifle. Straightening, he eyed the trampled grass. Just hours ago the meadow was full of elk, and a few minutes ago, Indians. Now, only he and his horse remained.

A gust of wind bent the tall grass, creating a wave of movement, followed by another gust. Seconds later, the grass bent again. Captivated by the wavelike movement sweeping the field, Mac marveled how the meadow almost seemed like the waves of the sea. It was almost as if he was standing on the bow of a ship bound for a distant land.

Friend's stomping hoof returned McKiever's mind to the present. Almost reluctant to break away from the spell cast by the undulating movement from the wind and grass, he thought about what had just happened. Today he had met new neighbors, not to mention a successful hunt. Tomorrow he would dine at the Ryan ranch while seeing Sam's daughter. Moving over to his horse, he stroked Friend's broad chest. "Thanks for the warning. Yes, I know, I'm using you as a pack horse. Sorry, I know it's not right, but soon you'll have company, and that's a promise."

CHAPTER 20

There Is a God

Laura Ryan was tired of watching the clock. Frustrated, she came up with a solution; it was a simple one. She would go outside and watch for the man instead of constantly checking the clock. Seeing McKiever coming down the road would be far more exciting than staring at that wall clock. Removing a white shawl from the closet, she walked out onto the porch. McKiever had said he would come early; she hoped he would. Sitting on the swinging sofa, she pulled the shawl up around her shoulders while eyeing the long winding road leading to the ranch. The door squeaked open behind her. Laura turned her head, watching her father approach.

Sam looked tenderly at his daughter, speaking warmly, "Kind of cold out here, isn't it?"

Smiling, Laura shrugged. "A little, but no wind. Besides, I brought a shawl."

"Yes, I see." Sam patted her head. "I suppose you don't want a meddling father hanging around when our new neighbor arrives, do you?" Sam didn't wait for her answer; he had a habit of not waiting for replies to his own questions. "No, I reckon you don't."

"Dad, do you think he'll come early?"

Casting his eyes down the road, Sam thought before speaking, "If I was a betting man, and I'm not, I'd bet he'll be right on time, maybe early. Tell you what, when he comes give me a yell and I'll come out." Sam looked down at his daughter, giving her a wink. "Don't worry, I'll say hello and suggest you show him around the ranch before dinner time. How's that for being an understanding father?"

"Perfect, Dad. Thank you."

Sam took another brief look down the road. "Honey, I only need one small favor. I'd like a few minutes with him before we sit down for dinner. I do have a business proposition for him. Now, I'm going back inside." Sam looked down. "You'll find me in the study. As soon as you catch sight of him, let me know." Swinging open the door, Sam slipped back inside.

Laura's eyes returned to the road, the wooden sofa creaking gently, her thoughts becoming questions. Would she still be excited when she saw McKiever? She hoped so; it had been a long time since a man had excited her. Over the years many men had shown interest in her, most of them falling all over her, but all of them boring. But this McKiever, despite his apparent lack of interest toward her, had caught her fascination. Adding to her curiosity was how he had been willing to risk his life for a woman he loved, despite knowing they could never be together. The more Laura recalled her father telling about what had happened, the more she became intrigued. Her mind shifted, remembering that moment in the store. She could still see the sight of McKiever closing in on the two drunken gunfighters. For a second, she shuddered, remembering his violence, seemingly without mercy. And yet, once the fight ended, he was different. Laura shook her head, thinking how McKiever seemed so much like her late husband, Steve. He was also quick to fight, seemingly unafraid of death.

Laura, deep in her musings, almost didn't see the distant rider. It took her several seconds before she remembered her father's request. Jumping off the swing, Laura stuck her head in the door, calling out, "Dad, rider coming in!"

Sam heard her, his voice drifting out of the study. "Okay, honey, be out in a minute."

McKiever was impressed; the ranch was huge. The multiple buildings were long, the main house two stories high. The land stretched endlessly, beef cattle dotting the landscape. The distant mountains towered over the range. What a difference, he thought, compared to his little spread. He couldn't help but think how Sam's place was a real ranch. Even the road appeared well kept. McKiever could see a lone figure moving on the porch. He checked his watch. He had said he would be early and he was.

Mac patted Friend's shoulders. "Some spread, don't you think, old partner? Sam sure has done well for himself, he most certainly has."

Passing under the gate entrance, McKiever could see the person on the porch was Laura Ryan. Feeling nervous, he whispered to himself, "Now don't get all tongue tied. Think of something smart to say." He grimaced, his mind going blank.

Laura descended the steps, waiting near the hitch rack. She opened the shawl slightly, showing a white blouse accented by a tan skirt. Her hair was braided, white ribbons gracing each braid. The only makeup she wore was a peach-colored lipstick.

McKiever was almost up to the porch when Sam stepped out. Feeling relief, he reined in his horse, tipping his hat toward Laura, his voice sounding confident, "Early . . . as promised."

Laura smiled, letting her father greet him. Sam didn't hesitate. "We like a man who keeps his word. How about getting off that horse and joining us on the porch?"

McKiever slipped from the saddle. Laura stepped forward. Reaching out, she pulled the reins out of his hands. "Please, let me." She was close, her eyes showing mischief.

McKiever watched her wrap the reins, listening to Sam. "Welcome, Mac. I told Laura we got plenty of daylight left, so I suggested she show you around before we eat. How's that plan?"

McKiever looked up. "Sounds like a good idea. Besides, I'm not much good at standing still." Looking at Laura, he asked, "Are we walking or riding?"

Laura's answer was quick. "Walking." She reached out, wrapping her small fingers around his hand. Mac felt his emotions soar, hoping they didn't show. She pulled at him, moving down the steps. He followed her like a young colt. Laura's voice was husky, "We're going to go around back and climb this little hill. We can see everything from up there."

Aware that Laura was keeping her eyes on him, he pretended not to notice, staring straight ahead, climbing a slight knoll, McKiever could see a wooden bench nestled in a grove of aspen trees. Most of the leaves were gone, the few remaining rustling in the slight breeze. As they neared the bench, Laura's question startled him. "Tell me about Sara."

Almost losing a step, he looked into her eyes. "How do you know about Sara?"

"Dad communicated with Captain O'Rourke. Dad believes in God, and I think the captain wanted to share those miraculous things that happened to you."

McKiever fidgeted for a second. "What would you like to know?"

"We heard about those prayers, and how without them you would have died." Laura squeezed his hand. "And I'm glad you didn't." She pointed to the bench. "My favorite place."

McKiever felt Laura's closeness, keeping his voice calm, he scanned the surroundings. "You're right, Laura: from here you can see everywhere."

Laura sat, McKiever following. Looking out over the landscape, she repeated her question. "Tell me about Sara Kincaid, and about those prayers."

Picking his words thoughtfully, McKiever shifted his eyes away from the leaves littering the ground. "I guess the best way to describe her is that she's a woman who takes a man's breath away." He watched Laura's face, looking for a reaction. Seeing none, he continued, "She's a Christian who believes in prayer, and I'm glad for her convictions. Truth is, when I was dying, I believe I actually felt and saw them."

Laura almost gasped, waiting for him to go on. She studied McKiever's face, her voice excited, almost a plea, "Please, tell me more."

"I was lying in the street, but it was like I was suspended in air. Above me was a white light, below me a black whirling tunnel. Every time I felt myself being sucked toward that tunnel, a powerful force enveloped me, pulling me back. First the force came from the right side, later it came from my left." McKiever paused, somewhat reflective, he continued. "And that was where Sara was praying. In the street she was at my right side, and later, when I was in the room, she was at my left. During that time, she never left me, and she never stopped praying."

This time Laura did gasp, her hands touching him.

McKiever felt her touch, adding, "I saw something else, at least I thought I did. I saw the man I killed disappear into that dark tunnel."

Chills ripped up and down Laura, her voice awed, "I've always known there's a God, but I've never heard such a testimony about prayers."

A question popped into McKiever's mind. "Tell me, Laura, did you still believe in God after your husband was killed?"

It was Laura's turn to be surprised, her reaction spontaneous, "You know about Steve?" Looking upward, she didn't wait for his response. "Steve knew God, and God redeems even the worst circumstances. One day I'll see my Steve again." She brought her gaze down, looking at McKiever. "How did you find out about Steve?"

McKiever felt a twinge of jealousy. Looking at Laura, he answered her, "I told Manuel Santana that I met you and your father in town. He told me." Mac's stare intensified. "Tell me, Laura, have you gotten over Steve's death yet?"

She looked away, choosing her words carefully. "I never will; he'll always be a precious memory. We cherished our time together, but I also know that I must live in the present." Laura fixed her eyes on McKiever. "Steve excited me, and I haven't felt that same excitement until I met you."

McKiever couldn't take his eyes off Laura's face.

Laura returned his stare. "How about you, have you gotten over Sara yet?"

McKiever shrugged, almost smiling before responding, "To answer your question, time has a way of helping. I'll get over Sara when I meet someone who compares." What McKiever blurted out next, he couldn't stop. "You're also a woman who takes a man's breath away." He cringed at his impulsive mouth.

Laura's eyes twinkling, she laughed, "I'm so glad you said that, I really am. I hoped you'd feel that way." She squeezed his arm. "Dad told me you were raised by godly parents, and by Captain O'Rourke. Tell me about them."

"Not much to say. My foster parents loved God, and along with the captain, they raised me. They all insisted I be educated, so I was tutored." Mac shrugged. "I guess I turned out okay."

"And the captain, what about him?"

"You couldn't be around Captain Frank and not develop your brain. Every man under his command had to maintain a certain standard, no exceptions. I guess you could say the captain's personality rubbed off on everyone."

"And what rubbed off on you?"

"To be a thinking man. He reminded us that we made our living with the gun, but a man survived by his wits. The gun was only a tool, but a man's conscience makes him responsible."

"What about God? Did the captain practice faith in God?"

"Yes, he was a prayerful man. He kept a Bible on his desk, always quoting from it."

Laura was intrigued. "I would like to meet this Captain O'Rourke. My father often talked about him with great fondness."

"If you ever do, you'll never forget him."

"What else rubbed off on you?"

"I guess the love of life. To stop and observe. Don't always be busy; spend time amongst nature. Become part of what's around you. Question things objectively. If they line up with truth, become subjective to that truth."

Laura loved his answers. "Do you do that?"

"Every chance I get. Besides, if a man doesn't do that, he can lose control of a situation."

"What is it about nature that attracts you?"

McKiever hesitated, hoping she would like his answer. "I guess it's a reprieve from people. Just spending time with yourself you get to hear the birds, listen to the wind, and forget. I think everyone needs some of that. I always felt time alone makes it possible to replenish yourself." He glanced at her, making a point. "And if you do that, then you can give more of yourself to others."

She nodded, remembering her lonely rides to McKiever's ranch, her mind recalling how the solitude gave her time to heal emotionally. It was that time alone that healed her. Not even her parents could comfort her. Spending hours watching the wildlife go about everyday survival brought her back to reality. As she watched the small critters scurry for everyday needs, she remembered her faith in God. Her anguish lessened during her prayers, and slowly Laura's life had returned to the everyday world. As she listened to McKiever, she understood, relating to what he was saying.

A long-billed thrasher flew by, whistling as it passed. Laura watched the spotted bird glide from sight. She looked at McKiever, attracted to him more and more. "You're right, Mac, some things can only be healed with time, and emotions need time. Time and solitude, they do help."

For several minutes all chatter ceased. A soft breeze rattled through the aspens. The thrasher began chattering, as if talking to them. Laura nudged McKiever, rising. "Come, the afternoon's getting on and I'm feeling the chill, unless of course you want to put your arms around me so I don't feel the cold."

Surprised, McKiever took a moment to stand, looking at Laura. "Do I dare?"

Leaning forward, she teased him, "Isn't life a dare?"

McKiever struggled for words, "I guess I'm not good at dares."

Her head cocked, Laura moved close, her eyes challenging McKiever, waiting. He placed both hands on her waist, pulling her to him. She snuggled close, her face lifted, feeling his lips brushing against hers. Laura didn't move away. Instead, he kissed her forehead, gently pushing her head to his chest. He wanted to kiss her more passionately but couldn't overcome his lack of boldness. He was never good at that.

Laura pressed her body to McKiever's. Finally stepping back, her voice husky, "Thank you, you're such a gentleman."

McKiever found his voice, teasing her, "Those dares, they're kind of nice."

Laura's eyes sparkled. "They are with the right man. Come on, William McKiever, Dad's waiting to talk with you." She laughed, "I think he's got a business proposition for you." She held her hand in his, tugging in the direction of the ranch house. "I guess I didn't show you much, did I? I mean, about the ranch."

Shrugging, McKiever gestured at the distant surroundings. "One picture is worth a thousand words. Besides, I liked what you said more than walking around the ranch."

Entering the ranch house, McKiever marveled. Everything was spacious, the main room was large, big enough to hold his little cabin. Several large leather sofas and two chairs faced a huge stone fireplace. Sam Ryan was sitting in one of the chairs. He rose, pointing toward the sofa and chairs. "Sit down, I trust you had a good tour."

McKiever chose the sofa, thinking that Laura might want to join him. "You can see an awful lot from that bench in the aspens."

"Ah, the grove, Laura's favorite place."

Laura's soft voice interrupted them, "Dad, I'm going to leave you two alone and see if Mom needs help."

Sam watched his daughter leave before settling back into his chair. "Mac, let's discuss my business proposition to you."

McKiever marveled at the plushness of the couch, thinking how all the furniture in this house made his furnishings seem like wooden boards. He looked at Sam. "Go on, Sam, I'm listening. What's your proposition?"

"The way I figure it, you need cattle. This spring I'll sell you cows carrying calves. You just tell me how many. That way you'll be getting two for the price of one. How's that, fair enough?"

"More than fair, you have a deal."

"Good. You know, Mac, we understand we got ourselves a good neighbor in you. Out here you never know, so we're pleased. Anything else I can do for you?"

Laura walked back into the room, sitting next to McKiever, declaring, "Mom chased me. I hope I'm not interrupting."

Sam nodded. "I think we're done."

McKiever remembered the Indian encounter. He glanced at Laura, directing his words at Sam. "Yesterday I met two neighbors up in the mountain meadow."

Sam's face scowled. His voice was a statement, "You don't have any neighbors but us."

"Apparently I do. I ran into two Shoshone while hunting elk above my place."

Alarmed, Sam leaned forward. "Were they hostile?"

"No, fact is I had just shot a bull elk. I was finishing up when my horse warned me we had company. They could have jumped me easy, so I knew they intended me no harm. At least not then."

Sam's curiosity was intense. He sat on the edge of his chair. "What happened next?"

"I laid down my guns, gave the peace sign, and we pow-wowed. I told them I was recovering from battle. I had come to live in peace and was thankful we could share what the creator provided."

Sliding back into his chair, Sam wrapped his hands around his right knee, listening.

"The older Indian did the talking. He liked what I said, telling the younger brave that I knew their ways, that I was a recovering warrior who came in peace. Right after that they left."

"Well, I'll be darned." Sam looked at his daughter. McKiever saw the fear in her face. Obviously, her thoughts about Steve's death were still a vivid memory.

McKiever touched her, his voice reassuring, "Your dad and I chased and fought Indians. We got to know them and respect them. They wouldn't compromise with us or the cavalry, but they did with individuals. That is, of course, if they respected you."

A tall elegant woman entered the room. Sam jumped to his feet, gesturing toward the woman. "William McKiever, this is my wife, Martha."

McKiever rose, hat in hand, bowing slightly. "I'm very pleased to meet you, Mrs. Ryan. It appears I'm a fortunate man to have such hospitable neighbors."

Martha was pleased; the man was well spoken, showing proper manners. "You honor our dinner table and I'm delighted to meet you, Mr. McKiever. I also want to thank you for standing up for my husband and daughter in town. I'm indebted to you."

"Glad I was there. It appears your husband and I have a common heritage in law enforcement work."

"Yes," Martha's voice was enthusiastic, "and I heard that both of you worked out of the same Ranger detachment." She smiled, adding, "Sometimes, even out here, it can be a small world. I trust my family hasn't been too intrusive about your personal life."

Mac teased, "To tell you the truth, for a little bit I thought I was under investigation."

"My goodness," Martha liked his humor, looking at Laura, "I can only guess who."

Laura blushed.

McKiever came to Laura's aid. "Actually, I kind of liked it."

Martha glanced fondly at her daughter. "Thank God. Out here new neighbors are rare, especially nice ones, and we are thankful that you are our new neighbor."

Sam spoke up, "Amen to that." He remembered something he'd forgotten. "Mac, can I offer you a drink? I plum forgot. Please, excuse my lack of proper manners."

"Thanks, but I'm fine."

"We have some nice wines?"

Tempted, McKiever thought for a second. "Maybe with dinner. I'm kind of partial to white wine."

Martha checked with Sam. "Sam, do we have white wine?"

"We do, but I'll also get a bottle of red, Martha, how long before we eat?"

"Dinner should be ready in ten minutes. Sam, is anyone else coming tonight?"

"Yes, I invited our foreman. I thought it would be good for Mac to meet him."

Martha scolded Sam, "It's a good thing I asked, wasn't it, Sam?" Turning she left.

Sam rolled his eyes upward. "It's tough to be perfect, Mac. Who knows, maybe one of these days I will. Right now, I better not forget the wine, or I'll be in real trouble. Be right back."

Alone, McKiever stole a look at Laura. The front door swung open, a tall man entering. The man was tall, well over six feet. Removing his hat, he hung it on a wall peg, displaying long, sandy-colored hair. The man glanced over, his weather-beaten face breaking into a toothy smile.

Laura stood, McKiever following, her greeting genuine, "Hi, Bill, I want you to meet William McKiever. Mac, this is our foreman, Bill Wade."

Bill stuck out his hand. The hand was big, reminding McKiever of Captain Frank's huge hands. Bill, like the captain, had a deep resonate voice. "Mighty glad to make your acquaintance, we've heard lots about you."

The foreman's grip was gentle, like the captain's. Mac smiled, acknowledging the foreman, "My pleasure, Bill. I hope all of what you heard was good."

Bill's voice had a slow drawl, "Fact is, you've achieved legendary status because of that shoot out in Fredonia."

McKiever grimaced. "That's not good."

Laura was surprised, questioning him, "Why isn't that good?"

"Gun fighters need reputations, and often they come looking for legends."

"Oh."

Wade understood McKiever's concerns, answering, "I think we can keep your reputation amongst us. But I got to admit, I am curious about what we've heard."

"Tell you what," McKiever answered, "why don't you save the questions until after dinner. That way I'll only have to answer anything about me once. Laura, you can help me."

"How?"

"Bring up the topic at the right time. I'll share everything, answer all questions, and then I'll be done with it."

Laura touched his arm. "How smart, thank you for trusting us."

The dinner chimes rang through the house.

McKiever stood before the table in awe. Fine china and long-stemmed crystal glasses sat atop white-laced linen. A beautiful gold chandelier hung over the dinner table. Mac felt like he was being entertained by royalty.

Bill Wade and Todd Ryan sat together, McKiever and Laura on the other side. Sam sat at one end, Martha settled into the far chair, facing her husband. Sam spoke, "Mac, at dinner we always say grace, so let's all bow our heads and be thankful." Grace was completed, and small conversation got started while the food was being passed. Young Todd kept staring at McKiever, finally blurting out that someday he was going to be a Texas Ranger, everyone laughing.

It was Martha who asked the first personal question. "Tell me, Mr. McKiever, why did you choose to come to Colorado and become a rancher?"

"Well, during my travels I noticed the landscape up here is a lot prettier than in Texas. Also, I got lucky. I ran into a man down on his luck, he sold to me real reasonable."

"Did you always want to be a rancher?"

"Kind of. The captain was always giving history lessons, which inspired me."

"Really," Martha showed sincere interest. "Tell me about that."

"Yes, Ma'am. Apparently in the old world you had to be royalty to own land. But here in this country, even a common man could own land. Captain Frank always said that owning land was the ultimate opportunity for free men."

Sam agreed, "I'd bet that any man who worked under the captain, if they turned in their badge it's because they bought a ranch. The man was always preaching that our responsibility was to protect those who were responsible citizens, which he considered to be landowners."

Young Todd couldn't contain himself anymore. "Tell us about the gunfighter you killed!"

Everyone stopped eating. Staring at Todd, Martha scolded him, "Hush, young man!"

McKiever held up his hand. "That's okay." He looked at Laura with a shrug. "I told Laura I'd tell everyone once, might as well do it now since it's been brought up." He kept his eyes on Todd. "Young man, I don't believe we've been introduced."

Sam and Laura each made a face, feeling guilty. Sam cleared his throat, "Todd, this is Mr. William McKiever."

McKiever kept his eyes on Todd, speaking slowly, "I'm glad to meet you, Todd. You know, Texas Ranger work is dangerous and at times lonely. Another thing, I always reminded myself that there is always somebody out there better than me, and I met him. The truth is, I'm lucky to be alive."

Todd's eyes were wide.

McKiever removed his stare from Todd, talking to everyone, "When I saw that gunfighter, I was sure I was about to die. At first, I was frightened, but I reckoned we're all going to die sometime, so I might as well die like a man."

Laura felt her body tighten.

Again, Mac took his time, spacing out his words, "Looking into that man's face, I saw death with no way out. When he spoke, his voice was like from another world. It sent shivers through me. His face and eyes really spooked me. He kind of looked like a walking ghost."

Wade couldn't help himself, "I'll be damned!"

McKiever looked at Bill. "That's exactly how I felt—I was damned!" Reaching for his wine glass, he sipped. Setting the glass down, he continued, "When I went for my gun, I dodged. I figured it was my only chance. They told me I shot him through the heart, which I don't remember. All I recall is his bullets hitting me, then blackness, followed by a floating feeling."

A chill seeped through McKiever's body as his mind flashed back, recalling that moment, he shuddered, startling everyone at the table. Seeing their reaction, he apologized, "Sorry, I didn't mean to do that. I often get flashbacks. There was this black funnel, and I kept being sucked towards it. But every time I was headed for that funnel, I got pulled back by a strange force. First it came from my right side, and later from my left side." Young Todd's eyes widened. Martha stared. Sam's face becoming intent. Laura half closed her eyes, trying to imagine herself there, squeezing her hands together.

"I was unconscious for three days with no water. My wounds didn't become infected, so I didn't run a fever. Doc said he's never seen anything like it, but what really intrigued him was how my heart and pulse didn't race despite my loss of blood." Mac stopped talking, taking another sip of wine.

Wade spoke up, "Where were you shot?"

McKiever touched his breast pocket, then his shoulder. "One bullet glanced off my badge, ending up here, the other passed through my chest." He looked up, a half-smile on his face. "Right close to my heart."

Martha and Laura glanced away, anguish in their faces. Young Todd was bold. "Why didn't you die?"

McKiever appreciated Todd's impulsive questions showing his youthful enthusiasm. "That's a fair question. I guess because of a woman named Sara. She's the wife of my good friend. She never left my side, not when I was in the street and not when I was bedridden. She prayed all the time." McKiever looked at each face. "I found out later that when I was in the street, she was praying at my right side. Later, when I was in a bed, she was always praying by my left side. And that's where that glowing force came from. First from the right, and later, from the left." His eyes swept the table. "You can draw your own conclusions."

Bill Wade finally broke the silence. "You said the doctor never saw nothing like it?"

"That's what he said. He told me when a man loses so much blood, the normal reaction is for a high pulse rate and a gasping for air. Doc said that blood brings oxygen to all the organs, so everything is affected. Plus, over time, I never became dehydrated from a lack of water. Doc said he couldn't understand it medically, much less scientifically."

"So," Laura leaned forward, "it was Sara's prayers to God that kept you alive?"

McKiever spread his hands, not answering.

"I declare," Martha's voice was a whisper, "an answer for prayers from the almighty—praise God!"

McKiever shrugged. "Seems like it. It took me a while to recover. I never felt so much pain. I did get to know the town pastor, along with his church congregation. It seemed like the whole town was praying for me." Mac smiled, addressing young Todd, "Any more questions, young man?" Todd stared, speechless, not answering.

Laura spoke, "Tell us about the force. What was it like?"

Placing the wine glass down, McKiever looked up. "I'll try. It felt like an energy tingling through my body, and a bright glow surrounding me. As I was heading toward that black hole, the glow grew stronger and stronger. I felt myself slow down to a stop, and then be pulled away from the darkness, back into the light. For long periods I was suspended between the light and the black, then the tug of war would begin. Truth is, I felt no pain, but I did sense back and forth movement."

Laura tried to picture what McKiever was explaining, asking, "What was the difference between the light and the dark?"

Reaching up McKiever scratched the back of his neck, thoughtful before answering, "The light was very peaceful, the black foreboding. The closer to that hole, the more you didn't want to go there. Of course, I couldn't do anything about where I went anyway."

For several moments no one talked. Finally, Wade broke the silence. "That gunfighter fellow, what was so disturbing about his appearance? What spooked you?"

"It was his eyes; they seemed to have no pupils. I once read a book about a seafaring man who described what a shark's eyes look like. He said that when you look into a shark's eyes, they're like black coals without life. And that how Peckenpath's eyes looked, like he had the eyes of a shark. You couldn't tell where he was looking, except you knew it was at you."

Wade couldn't stop himself, his voice reflecting astonishment at McKiever's eerie description. "If that doesn't beat all. For a lawman like you, that had to be difficult. I always figured it helps when a man can read the other fellow's eyes. Anything else bother you?"

"You're right, Bill, a man's eyes often give away his intentions. In answer to your question, his voice was like an echo, his face white. He had a narrow mouth, a cruel mouth." Mac scowled, adding, "When he smiled it was fixed, not real. The other thing was he was like a coiled rattlesnake, just waiting for me to move, and if I did, he would strike." Lifting his face up, he looked around the table. Every face was staring at him, as if hypnotized. "And I didn't want to move!"

The grandfather clock's ticking dominated the silence, everyone still. Sam broke the spell. "Did Peckenpath look the same after you shot him?"

McKiever shrugged, shaking his head. "I never saw him, but I heard his appearance was so spooky that everyone who looked at him was taken aback. One man told me it was like looking at someone who was never alive in the first place."

Martha's soft voice turned every head. "After what you just told us, I've never been more convinced that there is good and evil, and it took this Sara's prayers to God to spare you from that messenger from hell."

Sam broke his silence. "Martha's right. You had a direct encounter with overt evil, and but for the grace of God we wouldn't have the pleasure of knowing you. You know what else I think, Mac?"

"I'm listening."

"I think there was a divine purpose about everything that happened to you. Have you ever given that any thought?"

McKiever took a moment before responding, "I'm not sure what you mean."

"I mean chastisement from above, so that you'll turn to a belief in God."

"I see. I guess, Sam, I've come to a point of belief, but I'm still wrestling with that belief."

"Meaning?" Wade asked.

"Meaning that if I commit to God, I've got to give up my identity. I'm kind of comfortable with who I am."

Sam glanced at Martha before turning his attention back to McKiever. "I know what you're feeling. I wrestled with that same problem till I gave in. And you know what?"

Curious, McKiever eyed Sam. "What's that, Sam?"

"After I did, I wished I hadn't waited so long. All of a sudden my life had more meaning than ever before, and the things that had impressed me weren't so important anymore."

McKiever glanced at Laura. She was looking at her father, smiling.

Young Todd, impatient with the conversation, repeated his earlier statement. "I'm going to be a Texas Ranger and chase the bad guys."

Martha, listening to the laughter, addressed her son, "Todd, I think you should be a preacher!"

"No way, Mom, I'm going to be just like Dad and Mr. McKiever. I'm going to ride a big horse and be fast with a gun."

Sam glanced at Mac. "You think if we keep taking him to church, he'll change his mind?"

McKiever chuckled, "You better hope he was quicker than you."

Sam rolled his eyes, changing the subject, "You said you shot an elk?"

Mac nodded. "A big bull. I've got him hanging in my root cellar. Before I forget, when I leave, I'm going to need some salt."

"No problem, I'll give you a bag when you head out. When the wagon rolls on Monday, I'll send an extra supply."

"Much obliged, Sam."

Martha broke up the salt talk. "If you men clear the table, Laura and I will bring the coffee complete with dessert into the living room."

The men rose, Sam leading the way, talking as he walked, "Like I said, Mac, I'll send two men to help unload and stack the hay. Weather permitting that is, 'cause you don't want wet hay. I also got your calendar and ranch journal."

"I'll be waiting, Sam. I really appreciate this. Getting such a late start got me behind."

"Yeah, a lot later than you ever thought. You know, Mac, God works in mysterious ways. Maybe you better pay attention."

"What are you saying, Sam?"

"Stop being so stubborn."

McKiever changed the subject. "How long did it take you to build this ranch?"

Sam grinned, understanding, tactfully not pursuing his point. "Several years. What's that old saying? Rome wasn't built in a day. Yep, it took some time after I left the Rangers, but I had nothing but time. Besides, I started building big, so I wouldn't have to add on later."

Mac shifted his look to Wade. "Bill, Sam makes a lot of sense, doesn't he?"

Bill nodded, confirming McKiever's observation. "Yep, Sam always has. Also, he's a hard worker, and not afraid to get dirty with the rest of us."

Sam stopped them from sitting down. Winking at Bill, he pointed to the far door. "That there door leads to a room that I built special so I could enjoy a good cigar without my better half scolding me regarding a foul smell. I guess I should quit, but the good Lord hasn't cured me yet! You like a good cigar, Mac?"

"Fact is, I just puff on them. I suppose if I knew I was going to die tomorrow, my last act would be to strike a match to a big fat cigar as my last vice."

Sam liked Mac's answer, gesturing toward the door. "I built that room with what is called cross-ventilation. The air gets rid of the smoke. Martha and Laura stay out because of what they call, a foul odor, but I call it a pleasant stink. Let's us men talk without interruption. Anyway, the room's a little messy because it doesn't get cleaned up by the women folk. It gets a might chilly in there, but I guarantee it's downright comfortable. Furniture in there is as good as what's in the living room. During the summer I smoke outside, but when the weather turns sour, that's my smoking place. Come on, let's go inside and get comfortable."

McKiever's nose confirmed Sam's warning, the room reeking of stale cigar smell.

Watching Todd follow them surprised Mac; he looked at Sam.

Sam saw the look. "Martha scolds me but I don't pay her no mind. I'm raising a future man, not a sissy, so I let him in. Bill, tell Mac what those blankets are for."

McKiever followed Sam's pointing finger. Wade grinned, his slow drawl taking more time than usual. "When it gets cold in here you wrap yourself up in one of those blankets and keep on puffing. In the dead of winter, with those windows open, this room gets cold, colder than an Eskimo spinster!"

Sam picked up a long brass-box, opening it. He extended it to McKiever. The box was full of dark cigars. McKiever selected one, Wade was next, then Sam chose his cigar. Todd reached out, Sam chuckled, holding up his hand. "Not yet, my boy, not yet. Now, you men get comfortable and fire up them cigars. I'm going to open the windows. We got about ten minutes before Martha hounds us for dessert, so let's enjoy ourselves."

Mac's eyes swept the room. Everything was built out of stone except for the ceiling and windows.

Sam saw McKiever's examining look. "This room took the most time to build, but Martha insisted, afraid that someday I would accidently burn the house down."

Smoke began filling the room, as it neared the windows, the strong draft whisking the smoke outside. McKiever was impressed. He stole a look at Sam, two questions forming on his lips.

Sam saw his expression. "Go ahead, what's on your mind?"

McKiever hesitated, wanting to be tactful. "Tell me, Sam, how do you reconcile alcohol and cigars with God? Aren't Christians only supposed to do what is good for their bodies?"

Sam's head sagged. He rolled his eyes upward, stealing a look at his foreman before answering, "Bill, tell Mac I'm a work in progress." Sam chuckled, waving his hand. "Never mind, let me. I solved the alcohol problem by making my own wine. I did some research about the difference between Hebrew wine and pagan wine. There were three types of Hebrew wine back then. One type of wine is what was called new wine, which is like grape juice. Then there was a grape concentrate, which they mixed with water, no alcohol in it. Then there was old wine, with an alcohol content of under three percent, which was good for digestion, especially for older folks. Truth is, you could get bloated from it, and hardly get a buzz on. One thing the Hebrews refused to do, was to mix old wine with new wine. I guess it would ferment to a higher level and could bust the wineskins. As for the wine the pagans drank during ancient times, they mixed up some pretty potent stuff. It was part of their worship practice, getting into hallucinations and such, which was forbidden under Hebrew law." Sam sighed, "As for the smoking, I sure enough know it's not good for the body. One of these days I'll quit. Until I do, I thank God for grace and mercy." He looked at McKiever. "How 'd I do?"

Pursing his lips, McKiever stared at his cigar before responding, "Decent answer."

Sam looked at Bill, shifting the talk to the going price of beef and local politics. Wade's response was thorough, knowing every detail. Mac sat back, content to listen. From what he was hearing, he could understand why Bill was the foreman.

Sam shifted his stare, including McKiever in the conversation. "Mac, from what you just heard, any opinions about Silver Springs?"

Taking another puff, Mac watched the smoke curl outward as he spoke. "I've probably learned more about this town in the last few minutes by listening to you two than I would if I was here a month. Besides, I learned something a long time ago. You learn when you listen. You learn when you observe. You learn when you read. The only thing you learn when you talk is how people react to what you say."

Sam squinted, staring at Wade. "You know, Bill, that's about the wisest statement I think I ever heard. Mac, would you repeat that?"

McKiever smiled. "Sure, if I can remember what I just said. I think it went something like this. You learn when you listen. You learn when you observe. You learn when you read. The only thing you learn when you talk is how people react to what you say."

Bill shifted his gaze to the far wall, his voice a suggestion. "Boss, don't you think what Mac just said should be written down and stuck up on that empty space on the wall?"

Sam thought for a second, agreeing, "Sure do. As a matter of fact, I've got just the right person who has the artistic talent to write up such a nice thought and stick it in a frame."

Wade chuckled, "Let me take a guess, Laura?"

Sam winked at McKiever. "Besides, knowing who said it should give some extra motivation. I'm getting the impression that Laura kind of likes you, Mac."

McKiever almost blushed. The door creaked open, everyone shifting their focus. Laura's face appeared, her nose wrinkling in disgust. "Did I hear my name mentioned?"

Sam laughed, "The walls have ears. We were planning on using your artistic talent."

Laura's eyes found McKiever. "Dad likes to brag about me."

Sam agreed, "That I do, Laura, that I do. Do you have a message for us, my dear?"

"Yes, I have a message for everyone. Mom's artistic talent with baking is waiting." The door closed.

McKiever couldn't stop himself from having a second helping of cake. Smiling, he apologized, "My foster mom was great at baking, and I haven't had such cake since she passed away. Please, excuse my gluttony."

Martha's face beamed. "Thank you for the compliment. I declare, if you hadn't taken more, I would have been disappointed."

McKiever set his fork down. "Ma'am, I don't think I've ever eaten so well my entire life, much less sat at such a beautiful table."

Wade followed Mac's compliments, "Yes, Ma'am, me too." Bill looked over at McKiever. "Now you can see why I'm always pleased when it's my turn to dine here. Once you've eaten at this table, you get spoiled, you sure do."

Martha was delighted, and it showed, her eyes finding Sam. Nodding, Sam spoke, "Mac, I also got some sayings, marry them pretty, marry them talented, and let them know you know."

"Maybe," McKiever checked with Bill, "Sam should have Laura write that down to go up on the wall?"

Sam and Bill howled at their private understanding. Laura looked at her mother. "Mom, it appears they do need our talent no matter what they say, or how much they laugh."

"Yes, they do, but—" Martha held up a finger, "when they admit it openly, you've been complimented. However, don't ever ask them what they haven't told you, because it just gives them an opportunity based on your curiosity." Martha chuckled at her own advice. "Please, everyone have more cake. Otherwise, Sam will cheat on his diet and blame me."

Finished, McKiever pushed his plate back. "Mrs. Ryan, truth is I have no more room. Besides that, it's getting late, which means it's time for me to hit the trail. I can't thank all of you enough. I feel like I've found a place that makes me feel at home."

A hush captured the moment, Laura breaking the silence, "Why don't you stay here for the night? We have a nice guest room."

Tempted, McKiever thought for a moment. He decided enough was enough. He'd already been treated like royalty. "Many thanks, but I need to salt down that elk." Pushing back his chair, he rose. "Bill, good to know you. Mr. and Mrs. Ryan, thank you. Laura, this was special. Todd, I think being a preacher is safer. Sam, if you would get that salt along with them other things, I'd be obliged."

Sam stood up. "Meet you at the porch. Just give me a minute."

Moving out onto the porch, McKiever looked up at the night sky. The night was black, the stars everywhere. Laura joined him, following his gaze, her voice soft with wonder, "It's beautiful, isn't it?" She wrapped her arm through his. "Mac, I'm so glad you came. I was excited for days waiting to see you."

Turning his head from the night sky, he looked at her, feeling bolder. "How about now, you still excited?"

Laura lifted her head towards his. "Yes. I'm still excited, and I want to see you again. I also want you to see someone else."

McKiever could barely make out her smile in the reflected light from the house. "Who?"

"I would like you to meet my pastor."

A rush swept through his body. McKiever couldn't believe what he was hearing. He remembered Sara's last words about him meeting a Christian woman. Were her prayers being answered again? Could God be this real, he thought. He stared into Laura's upturned face. "Thank you for saying you want to see me again. Yes, I'll see your pastor, and Laura, there's something else."

"What is that something else, William McKiever?"

"I want to see you again."

Laura melted against him. This time he kissed her lips, gently but with passion. His body was soaring, his mind thrilled. He had found someone who made him forget Sara.

CHAPTER 21

A Letter from Silver Springs

Pastor McBride's face had a ruddy complexion, his square features highlighted by bushy eyebrows. The man had a pleasant voice, his demeanor so relaxed it seemed as if he didn't have a care in the world. McKiever was coming to the conclusion that such an attitude was a common trait amongst pastors. He remembered Pastor Olgilvie, who had the same personality. However, unlike Olgilvie, who was thin, McBride was fighting his weight.

"Please sit down, Mr. McKiever. I understand our community has acquired you as our new neighbor. It's my privilege to welcome you to our town."

McKiever sat, his eyes scanning the pastor's desk. An open Bible lay in the middle of the desk, a pen and white paper next to the Bible. Black ink writings covered the paper. "Thank you, Pastor. It's my privilege to meet with you."

"Laura has told me about your miraculous recovery before you arrived in our town. To be quite honest, hearing about it was very encouraging. Perhaps someday you'll share that event with my congregation."

"Perhaps, but right now I'd be scared to death to make such a speech."

McBride smiled with understanding. "I find that interesting. Here you are, a former Texas Ranger who has faced danger many times, and yet you would be uncomfortable giving a personal testimony. But I do understand. A number of years ago a prominent businessman joined our church. Because of his managerial skills, I along with others wanted to promote him into administrative responsibilities. He declined, and his reason couldn't be argued with. I never forgot his answer. He told us before he did anything, he just wanted to get to know God!"

McKiever was feeling very relaxed with Pastor McBride. The man had a way of making a person feel comfortable. "Thanks for telling me about him. I can relate to that man. Tell me, Pastor, what happened to him?"

McBride smiled. "Oh, he's an elder in our church and very active. If I recall correctly, it was almost five years before the Lord inspired him into service. May I offer you a cup of coffee, Mr. McKiever?"

"Thank you, but I can only drink so much of that stuff before it gets to my stomach."

"So that's what bothers my stomach. Oh well, it's the only vice I have, thank God! Tell me, how can I be of service to you?"

"Actually, it was Laura's request that I meet with you."

"Yes, she did mention that and for a good reason." McBride leaned forward, staring at the open Bible, before lifting his eyes. "You understand, Mr. McKiever, Laura knows that in my sermons, I stress that a man and a woman need to be equally yoked together with God."

Unsure, McKiever responded, "And by being equally yoked together— you mean?"

"I mean, two people committed to serving God. Those who don't believe in God tend to compromise, and for a believer that's very difficult." McBride eased back against his chair. "Let me try to explain it another way. You see it's really about truth. When God's spirit resides in a person, the spirit will prick the individual's conscience when they violate God's virtues through their actions. Although most people respect truth, in the reality of everyday life, truth is not very popular."

"That's an interesting statement, Pastor."

McBride nodded, encouraged by McKiever's interest. "Yes, and the reason I say that is because truth is a very respected, but not very desirable because of its uncompromising quality. People prefer to compromise; it's a way of getting around issues or having some fun. For a person under the influence of the Holy Spirit, to marry someone who may compromise creates a difficult situation for the one who won't."

"I can respect that reasoning."

McBride was pleased by McKiever's response, his voice remaining serious. "I also teach that marriage is like a community church."

McKiever was puzzled. "I'm not sure I understand."

"The best way I can describe marriage it is to picture a triangle. At the top is God, at the bottom right is the man, the woman at the bottom left. The husband's first priority is for God, then his wife, and himself last. The same is true for the woman. As children are born, both the husband and wife fall further back, because their love is sacrificial and that's how a church is. Remember, Mr. McKiever, only God offers salvation. Neither the man or the woman can offer each other eternal life. If God remains the most important influence in their marriage, then Satan cannot destroy what God has joined together. Also, the family has a Godly purpose in the neighborhood. They are a witness for God, just as a church is." McBride paused, hoping he wasn't confusing McKiever. "Okay so far, Mr. McKiever?"

"I think I'm getting the gist of what you're saying."

"Now, if the woman, or the man, have an affair with someone else, the physical relationship with God is broken. Why? Because a fourth person has entered into what we call the Temple of the Holy Spirit. That act breaks the trinity relationship with God. Instead of three persons, we now have a fourth person violating the sanctity of marriage. Because the purity is broken, catastrophe looms." McBride stopped, studying McKiever before continuing, "I think you understand what I'm saying."

McKiever understood. "I see what you're saying, Pastor. You see marriage as a trinity relationship. In other words, the husband and the wife are a threesome with God."

Pleased, McBride responded, "Yes, and again, that's how a church is. As long as Christ remains the first love, then the enemy cannot enter causing apostasy."

"Apostasy! Would you please explain that word, Pastor?"

"Apostasy is a spiritual condition of an individual, or a church, that is falling away from God. Now, as long as God is first then truth is served. But if worldly interests become more important than a relationship with God, then evil can slip in through the backdoor, neutralizing the church. The same is true regarding husbands and wives. And God will allow it because He allows for personal choices." McBride sighed, "In fact, the Bible reveals that Satan's very first attack was against the man and woman in the Garden of Eden."

McKiever couldn't help but admit what the pastor was saying was thought provoking, not leaving anything out.

McBride hesitated. Knowing McKiever was a retired lawman, he shifted his emphasis to the law. "You were a man of the law. I think you understand how important the law is. Without the law, it's every man for himself. I don't have to tell you what that can lead to. You see, Mr. McKiever, I used to be a doubter who didn't believe God. It was my study of Biblical law that changed my mind. As I uncovered how God's laws are prophetic concerning everyday life, I became a believer. When men and women in society obey God's laws, human culture behaves properly. But when humanity rejects God's virtues, I could see what that caused, and it wasn't good! I think you understand what I'm saying. It was then that I understood how God's words are true, and since he's the author, I became a believer. Let me close with this. As a former Texas Ranger, you certainly understand how important the law is, because without the law we would have a lawless society." McBride leaned forward making his point, his face glowing with conviction. "There are three reasons why God gave humanity the law. One reason was to reveal truth, the second reason was to restrain evil, and the third reason was that when evil happens, then the law serves the victims. You, as a lawman, must have seen how often men are lawbreakers. Without the law's restraint, there would be no safety for anyone." McBride leaned back, hoping what he said had registered with the former lawman.

McKiever had to concede he was impressed. His years of enforcing the law confirmed what McBride was saying, especially the three reasons for the law. "I'd say you're making a lot of sense, Pastor."

Pastor McBride coughed, clearing his throat before speaking, "Tell me, Mr. McKiever, how much do you love Laura Ryan?"

Surprised, McKiever stammered, "Very much."

McBride's eyebrows were arched. "Enough to commit your marriage to her and to God?"

McKiever felt a strange sensation, his nerves surging. Surprised at himself, he hesitated before answering, "Yes, but Pastor, I need to do it my way."

"And Mr. McKiever, what way is that?"

"To get alone by myself, asking God personally."

"And by asking God personally, you mean?"

"Pastor, I was raised by godly foster parents, my boss was a godly man, and a close friend has been constantly witnessing to me about God. I understand the drill; you have to ask Christ into your heart."

McBride nodded, pleased that he got the answer he wanted. "Yes, that's correct." He leaned backward. "When you make that commitment, let me know, because Laura wants me to perform the marriage ceremony, and I won't marry anyone unless they give their marriage over to God." McBride smiled. Reaching out, he patted McKiever's arm. "So, let me know."

Rising, McKiever shook the pastor's hand. Walking into the bright sunlight, he stared at Laura. He could see her face had a hopeful look, her beauty radiating towards him. Laura's voice was hopeful, "Well, William, how did it go? What did the pastor say?"

McKiever mounted Friend before speaking, "Let's ride for your ranch. I've got a few things on my mind that I want to discuss with you."

Watching Laura mount, McKiever collected his thoughts. For several minutes they rode in silence. The road turned, the stiff breeze thwarted by the tree-covered slope. For McKiever, the morning seemed brighter than usual, his voice finally breaking the silence, "You know that special place behind your ranch?"

"You mean, where my bench is?"

"Yes. Well, I have a special request. I want to spend some time there alone. I'm going to ask Christ into my heart, and when I get back, I'm going to propose to you. After that, and if you say yes, I would like you to give me some writing paper."

Laura's heart was singing, her voice choked with emotion, "I'm so glad. I knew if I waited on God that my faith would deliver me into a man's arms I could love." Reaching out, she touched Mac's arm, her voice soft, "Is the letter for Sara?"

McKiever stared into Laura's face. "It's for Sara." He could see tears gathering in Laura's eyes. Pulling back on the reins, he stopped Friend. "Do you remember that I mentioned there was something I wanted to tell you? Do you also remember that I said I would be too embarrassed?"

"Yes, I remember."

"Just before I came here, Sara told me that she was praying that I would meet a godly woman who would make me forget her. She asked me that when that happened, to write her how God answered her prayers. Well, Laura, God has answered her prayers. I have met a woman who's made me forget what I couldn't have, and given me what I thought was impossible. He's given me you!"

Laura slipped from her saddle, looking up. "Get down here and hold me while you're proposing. I want to say yes now."

McKiever eased from the saddle, keeping his eyes on her face. Laura slid into his arms, her face beaming, her heart filled with unbelievable joy. "Go on, propose to me."

"Will you marry me?"

"Yes, yes, yes."

The kiss was long, the embrace longer. Laura's voice was a whisper, "Mac, Sara's prayers have given me a man who's made me forget what I lost. One day, I'm looking forward to meeting her. Now, you must remember to ask my father."

Sara sat on the edge of the couch. Smiling, she placed both hands around her stomach. Carrying Jeff's child made her feel special. Staring out through the window, she watched Jeff dismount while removing the saddlebags.

Bringing in the saddlebags meant they must have more mail than usual. She wondered if there was a letter from Silver Springs.

The door swung open, Jeff entering. Laying the saddlebags on the floor, he straightened. A lone white envelope was clutched in his right hand, a strange smile on his face.

"So," Sara giggled, "somebody still loves us."

Jeff grinned, not saying anything.

Sara waited, Jeff remaining silent. "Okay, Jeffrey, who wrote us?"

Jeff looked down at the letter before speaking, "The letter is from Silver Springs!"

Sara's world stopped, her voice a whisper, "Is it from Mac?"

"Yes, it's from Mac."

"Have you read it?'

Jeff held the letter out. "Yes, Mac addressed it to both of us."

"What does it say?"

"There's something about prayer, and something else."

"Oh, Jeff, what?"

"Sara, I think you better read the letter for yourself."

Acknowledgments

Thinking back to my early school years, I have to give special thanks to the librarian at Locust Valley Public School on the north shore of Long Island, New York. Her name was Mrs. Switzer. I was one of those students who hid in the back of the classroom during those early years. With the intention of teaching me to read, the school sent me to Mrs. Switzer. Over time I came to realize that her patience and kindness was a special kind of beauty. I'll never forget Mrs. Switzer.

Years later, my high school teacher at Carl Place looked at the first two paragraphs of a short story I was writing. She asked me where I learned to write like that. I still remember her encouragement. During her class, there was a time when every student had to go up and read a poem they wrote. After I finished, class secretary Judy Grabel expressed how beautiful my poem was. She was also class editor for the high school yearbook. More encouragement.

A special thanks to Alice Mapes. Alice is a senior citizen, but no one would ever know it. She scolded me how my writing was exceptional, but there were too many errors, and errors distract. She asked me if she could edit for me. Of course I said yes!

I dare not forget my family, especially my wife Sharon. She was my first test case. Sharon devours fiction books, and one day she told me she can tell by the first two pages if a book is a good one. She then asked me to read my first chapter. After finishing, she mentioned the book had strong possibilities. Again, more encouragement!

My youngest son, Robb, offered suggestions and corrections, I followed his advice and it shows up in a big way.

Much thanks to my oldest son, Scott, for his help with the computer. He is my help desk in the time of trouble.

My second test case came from Dan Ho. Dan badgered me into letting him read the first two chapters. He then told me he was going to buy the book. Dan is currently composing a cookbook.

I also can't forget my professor friend, Doug Morris. Over the years we've had some lively debates, but his English admonishments have kept me on target grammatically. He and his wife, Gretchen, always welcome us when we travel south.

Special thanks to Pastor Jim Osborne, who is also an earth science teacher in public education. He refreshed my forgotten knowledge about science, and it appears in the pages of this book.

Another important contributor to my development is Gil Strausman. His astute knowledge of the English language is exceptional and educational.

Special thanks to my doctor, Jeff Carlberg. His medical expertise was included while writing this story.

Life is a journey, and over time the people I know made it special. Especially former airline employees and my neighbors, many who encouraged my writing.

In conclusion, the greatest friend I have is Jesus Christ. He has been my ultimate inspiration!

Bruce Aitchison
Last Assignment
P.O. Box 194
Marietta, NY 13110